SHADOWS IN DEATH

SHADOWS IN DEATH

J. D. ROBB

WHEELER PUBLISHING
A part of Gale, a Cengage Company

LIBRARY OF CONGRESS CIP DATA ON FILE.
CATALOGUING IN PUBLICATION FOR THIS BOOK
IS AVAILABLE FROM THE LIBRARY OF CONGRESS.

ISBN-13: 978-1-4328-8269-3 (hardcover alk. paper)

Published in 2020 by arrangement with St. Martin's Publishing Group.

Printed in Mexico
1 2 3 4 5 6 7 24 23 22 21 20

When the sun sets, shadows,
that showed at noon
But small, appear most long
and terrible.
— Nathaniel Lee

Not flesh and blood, but the heart
makes us fathers and sons.
— Friedrich Schiller

1

As it often did since he'd married a cop, murder interrupted more pleasant activities. Then again, Roarke supposed, the woman lying in a pool of her own blood a few steps inside the arch in Washington Square Park had a heftier complaint.

After all, he'd known what he, a former criminal (no convictions), was getting into when he fell for the cop. He doubted the woman in fashionable athletic wear had expected to end the pretty spring night with her belly sliced open.

He and his cop might have missed the last scene of an entertaining play, but the woman missed the rest of her life.

And here, on a balmy May night, in the blooming spring of 2061, he watched another kind of play.

His cop and the victim held center stage under the hard crime-scene lights. Together they made a sad silhouette against the thin curtain meant to shield the dead from the prying eyes of onlookers.

Uniforms had barriers up to separate the rest of the audience. The vendors, the lovers, the strollers and tourists, the buskers and dog walkers goggled at death.

He kept out of the way as the lead — Lieutenant Eve Dallas — performed her duties in this tale of morality and mortality.

She crouched beside the body, lean and tough in her leather jacket and boots, her field kit open beside her, her short brown hair shining under the lights.

"Victim is identified as Galla Modesto, age thirty-three, residence on Prince."

"Galla Modesto."

When Roarke spoke, Eve lifted her head, narrowed those whiskey-colored cop's eyes. "You know her?"

"No. Her brother a bit. Modesto Wine and Spirits. She'd be one of the heirs — third generation, I'd think. International, family-owned company, with their home base in Tuscany."

"Interesting. Married — Jorge Tween — six years. One offspring, a son, age four." She took out a gauge. "TOD, twenty-two-eighteen. COD, from on-site observation, would be the eight-inch vertical slice through her abdomen."

Now with microgoggles in place, she leaned closer to the gaping wound. "It looks like a deep stab into her lower abdomen, with an upward thrust to open her up. ME to confirm."

Still crouched, she shifted a little. "No visible defensive or other offensive wounds. No handbag recovered, but the vic's dressed for a run or the gym. She's wearing a good-size diamond and diamond-encrusted ring on her left hand, what look like diamond stud earrings — two in the left, one in the right. And a sport-style wrist unit.

"No evidence this was a mugging."

Eve opened the zippered pocket of the woman's warm-up jacket. " 'Link." She bagged it, then reached into the pocket in the running pants. "ID."

Rising, she moved around to the other side of the body, opened the other pocket. "Panic button. Obviously didn't panic in time."

"Here's our Peabody," Roarke told her, "with McNab."

Eve's partner hurried toward the barricades with her main man, EDD detective Ian McNab.

Since Peabody wore a dress — one covered with pink tulips under her pink coat — and McNab wore his version of party wear in pink baggies, airboots so violently green they glowed, and a shirt with jags and jigs of both colors, Roarke deduced they'd been out when the call came through.

They both badged the uniforms, moved into the cordoned-off area. Peabody, still sporting red streaks in the dark hair she'd styled in festive curls, went straight to Eve and the body.

"Sorry, Dallas, we were at a club on the East Side, got delayed getting here."

Eve gave Peabody's outfit — including the skinny-heeled party shoes — a flick of a glance. "Officers Frist and Nadir first on scene. Talk to them, start interviewing any potential wits." She glanced back. "McNab can see about any security feed since he's here."

"Got it."

"Seal up and help me turn her first. Vic's Galla Modesto," she began, and gave Peabody the main points as they worked.

With the body turned, Eve saw no more wounds or marks — and found another small pocket in the back of the running pants. "Key swipe," she said for the recording. "Body and Mind Fitness Center," she read, then bagged it into evidence.

She closed her field kit, took out her comm to contact the sweepers and the morgue.

When she turned, Roarke held out a go-cup of black coffee.

"Where'd you get this?"

"An enterprising vendor. I suspect it's somewhere between cop coffee and palatable."

She drank, shrugged. "Somewhere between. Thanks. You should head out. I need to talk to witnesses, talk to her husband, go by the gym she used."

"I'm having your car sent down — and arranged my own transportation."

She drank more — barely — palatable coffee, and looked at him.

That face, that face. One of life's serious miracles, and sure as hell one of hers. Eyes, boldly blue with lashes as silky as the black hair that fell nearly to his shoulders, looked into hers. He had a mouth creative angels sculpted on a particularly generous day. The planes, the angles combined in a result somewhere between the romance of a poet and the sexuality of one of those angels defiantly taking the fall.

Add the music of Ireland in his voice, and you had an exceptional package.

"Always handy."

And that perfect mouth curved. "We all do our part. I'll just stay handy until the transpo gets here." Absently, he scanned the crowd behind the barricades. "McNab should be back shortly with the security feed so . . ."

She saw his eyes narrow, saw something dark come into them.

"What?" She shifted instantly to look in the same direction. "What did you see?"

"Someone I used to know."

Before she could speak again, he walked away, quick and smooth.

"Well, shit." She gestured a uniform over to stay with the body, started to go after him when Peabody hurried back.

"We've got a few witnesses who saw her go down, and we have one who didn't but claims she was coming here to meet him. He's wrecked, so I'm thinking there might have been some hanky in the panky."

"Let's take him first."

What the hell was Roarke doing? she wondered.

He cut through the crowd. He knew how to move fast, sliding through. Once upon a time he'd have come out the other side with pockets full from pockets he'd picked.

But though he moved fast, eyes scanning, instincts alert, he didn't see the face again.

That bloody shadow from his past, Roarke thought as he looked beyond the lights, the crowds, the sparkle of the fountain, the empty benches, had shown himself deliberately.

A taunt. A kind of flipped middle finger, as he'd been — again deliberately — far enough away to easily melt out of sight and vanish again.

Well then, if the fecking bastard wanted to come out and play, he'd be more than willing for the game.

"We're a long way from the alleys of Dublin now, boyo," he muttered, and made his way back again.

Since the wit, Marlon Stowe, was shaking, with tears streaming, Eve took him to one of the benches.

Mid-thirties, she judged, about five-ten, a lot of thick, sandy hair, brown eyes, and a stubbly goatee.

"You were meeting Ms. Modesto here?"

"By the fountain. She said she'd try to be here about ten-fifteen, no later than ten-thirty."

Since he wore black pants, a thin black sweater, black boots, she understood they hadn't planned to take a run together.

"Why were you meeting?"

He swiped at his face. He had a smear of blue paint on the side of his thumb. "We were involved. We met last summer. Galla

13

bought one of my paintings. I had a sidewalk display, and she liked one I'd done in Tuscany. She — her family — they're from Tuscany, and she said it reminded her. And she came by a few times, and to this gallery, and . . . we fell in love."

"You had a romantic and intimate relationship with Ms. Modesto."

"We fell in love," he repeated. "Sometimes we'd meet here, and just sit and talk. Sometimes we'd go to my loft. I knew she was married, she told me. We never lied to each other. She has a little boy. She wanted to leave her husband, but she has a little boy. She wanted to leave him, even talked to her lawyer. But . . ."

Now he covered his face with his hands. "She told me, the last time we were together had to be the last time. We both knew . . . Right from the start we both knew it couldn't last. She had to think of her son first. She had to try to fix her marriage, fix her family."

"But she agreed to meet you here tonight."

"I asked if she would. Not to be together. Just to really say good-bye. I had something I wanted to give her."

"What's that?"

He opened the bag he carried, took out a package wrapped in thick brown paper. "It's a painting. Like a companion piece to the one she first bought. I thought, it's the first and it's the last."

"You must've been hurt and angry."

As he shook his head, his eyes welled again. "I loved her. I knew she was married, had a child. She never lied. She never promised. And . . ." He drew a long breath. "I knew she loved me. She couldn't be with me, but she loved me. If I hadn't asked her to come here tonight . . ."

He fell apart then, so Eve looked to Peabody, the soother.

"Marlon." Peabody sat beside him. "You can't blame yourself, but you may be able to help. Did anyone else know you and Galla were meeting here tonight?"

"No. We were careful — our relationship. It was private. It was . . ." He used the heels of his hands to scrub his face dry. "It was just for us. She said she'd tell her husband she was going to get some time at the gym. Just a quick solo workout. She did that, so it wouldn't be unusual. She wouldn't have told anyone she was coming here. I didn't tell anyone."

"How did you communicate?"

"Just texts."

"When were you last together, when she ended it?"

"Just last week. She came to the loft, and told me. We made love one last time. And today, the painting was ready, so I texted her and asked if she'd come here, so I could give her a gift. That it would help me say goodbye."

"When you met here, did you ever notice anyone paying particular attention to her, to the two of you?"

"No. It's such a good space. It always felt safe here."

"When she came to your loft?" Eve drew his attention back to her. "Did you ever notice anyone outside, anyone who made you feel uncomfortable?"

"No. I have a small loft right in the Village, over the gallery. I work there, show there, do some teaching. She could only come once a week, sometimes twice, but usually once a week when she could get away, when her son was out with his nanny or on a playdate. We'd only have an hour, maybe two. We loved a lifetime's worth. We knew we only had that little bit of time."

"Did she ever tell you she felt threatened or had been threatened?"

"No, no. God no."

"Did she fight with her husband?"

Almost absently now, he swiped his fingers over his eyes. "Not really, she never said so.

16

He was more interested in the business, and the show, you know? How they looked together, going to events. She wanted to go back to Tuscany, to take her boy. For us to live there. We dreamed about that, even knowing it was just a dream."

He thrust the painting to Eve. "Will you take this? I can't look at it. I don't want it. It's too painful."

"Peabody, give Mr. Stowe a receipt for the painting. We'll need to take it into evidence for now."

"I don't want it." He began to cry again. "I can't sell it. Just keep it."

"We're not allowed to do that. But we'll work something out. Detective Peabody will give you a receipt, and take your contact information."

Eve spotted Roarke, passed the painting to Peabody. "Then you're free to go. Do you need transportation?"

"No, no. I can walk. I'll walk."

"We're sorry for your loss, Mr. Stowe. Please contact me or Detective Peabody if you think of anything that may help our investigation."

She got up, moved quickly to Roarke. "What's going on?" she demanded. "You're pissed. Scary Roarke pissed."

He took her arm. "Let's walk."

"I can't just —"

"With me." He tightened his grip to lead her away from the crime scene. "Lorcan Cobbe," he began. "You'll want to do a run there. From Dublin, and he'd be three or four — maybe five — years older than me."

"One of your old friends?"

"Not remotely." He moved away from the lights so they stood in shadows. "He worked for my father, and as he had no talent for thievery and considerable for viciousness, he did enforcement, intimidation, helped with the protection racket. We can get into all of that at another time, but you'll want to run him. And you'll want to take care."

He put his hands on her shoulders. "A great deal of care, Eve."

"Why?"

"He'd do me in a heartbeat if he could manage it, but he'd kill what matters to me and enjoy it all the more. A killer is what he is, and always has been."

"And you saw him, at my crime scene."

"I saw him. He made sure I did. Aye, he made certain of that, bloody bastard."

He scanned the park again, but knew he wouldn't see that face again. Not tonight.

"I'm telling you, I didn't have to see him put the knife in that woman to know he did. He'll be your man on this."

18

"Why her? He couldn't know you'd be here."

"That's just a nice twist of fate for him. Killing's what he does, Eve, for pleasure and profit. He does his work primarily in Europe, but this wouldn't be his first job in the States, I'd think. I don't know of him coming, for business at least, to New York before, and I think I would. But he's here now."

She took it in. It was rare to see him agitated — more than angry — so she took it in, and took it seriously. "Describe him — as you saw him tonight."

"About six feet, a strong build, wide in the shoulders, light brown hair worn in what you'd call a topknot. Light complected, clean-shaven. Black pants and shirt, a red jacket. He stepped clear so I'd see him, looked right at me. Smiled."

He ran his hands down her arms, back again. "He'll know what you are to me. Or if he doesn't, he'll now make it his business to find out."

"Why does he hate you, particularly?"

"Particularly? He claimed to be Patrick Roarke's bastard, and as senior to me, his oldest son."

"Was he?"

"Unlikely, but not impossible, I suppose.

Unlikely, as the old man liked him considerably more than me, and if he'd been his blood, would have taken him in. That's not important at the moment. He bloody well didn't just happen to be in the park when a woman — a wealthy one — ends up gutted. And gutting, throat slitting, disemboweling are favorite pastimes of Lorcan Cobbe."

"All right, I'll run him. I'll put out a BOLO."

Now he framed her face with his hands before she could object. "And you'll take care. Take very good care."

"Yes," she said because he needed her to. "And same goes."

"He won't try for me right off — what's the fun in that? I have to contact some people."

"We're going to need to talk about this, in more detail."

"And we will. Your car's here." He gestured toward the arch. "I'll see you at home."

As she watched him stride away, she realized she was worried because he was worried.

Marriage, she thought. It could fuck you up.

"LT." McNab pranced over in his airboots, long tail of blond hair swinging. "Got

20

your security discs. I already looked at the footage of the kill."

"We have the kill on the feed?"

"Yes and no. I'm going to say the killer knew the cam angles, and kept his face clear. What we've got is the vic coming in, then what appears to be a male, about six feet, probably about one-ninety, black pants, black hoodie worn up, cutting across her path. We got him from the back, so no way to tell age or race or make a firm determination of gender."

McNab glanced back as the morgue team bagged the body. A line of colorful hoops glittered on his earlobe. "He had his hands in his jacket pockets, his head down, moving right along, then cuts in front of her. She stops. You can see his right arm jerk up, then pull back. He keeps right on walking, and she staggers a couple steps. A lot of blood even before she goes down. Then you've got a couple of people running over to her. One of them turns her over. And the screaming starts. He's already out of cam view by then."

"Take them in, run through them. I need copies. All feed, all angles."

"You got it. He had to be waiting for her, Dallas. The way he moved on her. It was purposeful, you know? Not random, it just

21

didn't feel random."

He might dress like a circus act, but she knew his cop instincts hit solid.

"No, I don't think random. Peabody," she said when her partner joined them.

"I talked to a handful of people, and to a couple of the uniforms who talked to people. Most didn't see or notice anything until she went down, but I have two who stated they saw a man in a black hoodie walking away as she fell. No solid description beyond the hoodie, worn up, and the assumption of male."

"That coordinates with the security feed. McNab, when you're going over the discs, look for a male — the height and build you described. Caucasian, late thirties to early forties, light brown hair — man bun deal — red jacket. Flag anything you find with a view of him."

"Okay. Is he a suspect?"

"Odds are. His name's Lorcan Cobbe, out of Dublin. Roarke saw him in the crowd, recognized him. He's a pro."

"I can start reviewing on my portable if I stick with you for now," McNab told her.

"Fine. Let's move. Peabody, start a run on the vic's husband, Jorge Tween, and let's go notify him."

"If this was a hired hit," Peabody began.

"The spouse is number one," Eve finished.

Her car waited at the curb, as advertised. She got in, sat a moment. "We'll run Cobbe, too, put out a BOLO, but let's see who we're about to talk to first."

Peabody got in the passenger seat, not so discreetly slipped her feet out of her party shoes as McNab climbed in the back. "Tween is forty-two, a VP in distribution at Modesto. He's worked for them for sixteen years. No criminal coming up. Married Galla Modesto six years ago — first and only marriage for both. Son, Angelo, age four."

Eve pulled out, started the short drive to the Modesto/Tween residence.

"They purchased their New York residence five years ago. Tween works out of the New York headquarters. Got his net worth here at just under nine million."

"Hers is more than ten times that," Eve remembered. "There's a fine motive added to her having an affair."

"She broke it off," Peabody pointed out, but Eve just shook her head.

"She had an affair, and more, if Stowe's not full of it, fell in love. It takes a little time to arrange a hit, so there's that. Then do you call it off because she called off the affair? Are you sure she did? Did she confess

23

all? Doubtful. Either way, what's to stop her from changing her mind, going back to her artist lover, taking her big mountain of money, and moving to Italy?"

Reluctantly, as Eve squeezed into a spot at the curb near the address, Peabody pushed her feet back into her shoes.

"I'll stick here with this," McNab said from the back. "Especially if I can get a fizzy from the AC."

"Do that."

He added a winsome smile. "Maybe you got some chips in here."

"I don't know what the hell's in the AutoChef." Leaving him to find out, Eve got out.

Peabody didn't quite hide the wince when they started the half-block walk, crosstown.

"Why are you wearing those idiot shoes?"

"They're pretty shoes! We went out dancing — date-night dancing. You need pretty shoes for date-night dancing. I didn't know they were going to be work-a-case shoes."

She moaned a little. "And they're killing me."

"Suck it up."

"This is sucking it up. So Roarke knew this Cobbe back in Ireland?"

"Dublin, when he was a kid. I'll get more details, but Cobbe let Roarke spot him.

Wanted him to. Roarke says he's a killer by nature and profession. I'll get more details," she said again, and stopped in front of the house to get a sense of it.

Three stories of whitewashed brick had an elegance, a quiet charm. The security light glowed pale green, but no glow came from the lights at either side of the front door.

The lights that would have welcomed someone home.

Windows stayed dark, so no one waited up for the woman who'd never come home again. Flowers spilled out of painted boxes on the windows flanking the door.

She caught the scent of something soft and sweet as she stepped up, pressed the buzzer.

The household has retired for the night. Please leave your name and contact information. If this is an emergency —

"NYPSD." Eve cut off the computer, held up her badge. "Inform Jorge Tween the police need to speak with him."

Please state the nature of your emergency.

"Your circuits are going to have an emer-

25

gency unless Mr. Tween is informed the NYPSD is at the door. Scan the damn badge, and get it done."

The scanner light swept her badge.

Your identity is verified, Dallas, Lieutenant Eve. Please wait.

"I hate those damn things."

"You actually have those damn things. You know, on the gates, and on —"

"Doesn't mean I can't hate them. Not a light on inside," Eve commented. "Your wife goes out to the gym, doesn't come back in, say, an hour. Do you just turn off the lights and go to bed?"

"Doesn't seem right," Peabody agreed. "Even if you're pissed at each other, it feels off. At least the lights here should be on if someone's out. Who doesn't do that?"

"Someone who's not expecting anyone. It's a little thing. It's a petty little thing."

Lights came on inside, flooding the windows with their cheerful flowers. Locks clicked.

The door opened for a woman of about fifty in a dark blue robe. Her dark hair tumbled around her face. Her eyes, gypsy brown, held fear and worry.

"You're the police."

26

"Yes, ma'am." Once again, Eve held up her badge. "We need to speak to Mr. Tween."

"Yes? The system alerted me. I'm the housekeeper. Please, excuse me, come in."

She had an Italian accent and bare feet with toenails painted bold red.

Narrow tables stood on either side of the entrance. They held slender purple flowers in long, thin vases, reflected back by tall mirrors. The tile floor spread in the color of gold sand.

"Please, here in the parlor you can sit." She gestured as she led the way. "You would like coffee? Tea?"

"We're good. Could we have your name?"

"Of course. I am Elena Rinaldi. I am the housekeeper. Please sit. I will alert Mr. Tween. He and Ms. Modesto are sleeping. It is very late."

"Ms. Rinaldi, when did you last see or speak with Mr. Tween or Ms. Modesto?"

"Ah . . . I think about nine this evening. Yes, about nine before I retired to my quarters for the night. Please sit," she repeated, and went out.

"Before Modesto went out," Peabody murmured.

"Yeah." Eve looked around what she imagined they called the front parlor.

More flowers — someone had a fondness for them. And a formal sort of feel with cream-colored sofas, peacock-blue chairs, tables with a slight sheen of gold. More gold in the ornate frame of the big oval mirror over a white marble fireplace filled with flowers and candles now for spring.

The art went for Italian scenes. Red tile roofs on stucco houses and great cathedral domes. Rolling hills and farmhouses. She recognized Tuscany — because she'd been there. As well as a painting of the Spanish Steps in Rome.

She walked to the one of Tuscany — those hills, those tall, slim trees, vineyards with purple grapes climbing, a winding path leading to a house of pale rose stucco with flowers rioting at its feet.

And in the corner, the artist's signature.

M. Stowe.

"It's good work," Peabody commented. "I sent the other one in, still wrapped. You've been there, right?"

"Yeah."

"Does it really look like that?"

"Yeah, it does. It's her room. This is her room."

"Why do you say that?"

"It's formal and elegant. The flowers, the paintings — especially that one. The couple of photographs?" Eve gestured. "The kid, her and the kid, but not the husband. Her family, most likely, but not with him. The dust catchers all feel female."

Frowning, Peabody looked around. "You're right about that. It all feels female. Not frilly, but female."

Eve gestured. "The tablet on the table by the chair that faces Stowe's painting? She could sit there, read or work or whatever, look up and see the painting. Think about her lover. Think about home.

"A company room," Eve added. "But otherwise hers."

She turned when she heard footsteps, and waited to meet Jorge Tween.

2

Average height and build, Eve noted. His pale blond hair swept back from a handsome face — golden tan, deep-set and sleepy blue eyes, soft rather than sharp features.

He wore black lounge pants with the faintest sheen, a white pull-over, and black house skids.

His expression read annoyed rather than concerned.

"As this is the first time I've been awakened in the middle of the night by the police, I'd like to see your identification."

A smooth, soft voice, like his features, Eve noted as both she and Peabody held out their badges.

"Lieutenant Dallas, Detective Peabody," she said. "We have difficult news, Mr. Tween. We regret to inform you your wife, Galla Modesto, is dead. We're sorry for your loss."

"Don't be ridiculous." He flicked that off, literally, with his fingers. "My wife is upstairs sleeping."

"You verified that before coming down?"

"I don't have to verify what I know. You've made a mistake."

"Did your wife go out this evening, Mr. Tween?"

"I don't know what business that is of yours, but yes, she went to her gym as she sometimes does in the evening before bed. She finds a workout helps her sleep."

"And what time did she come back?"

"I don't know. I had a headache, took a blocker, and went to bed. I occasionally suffer from migraines. Knowing that, Galla would use one of the guest rooms after she got back from the gym."

"So you haven't seen your wife since she left the house? At what time?"

"I don't know." Irritation, pure, without a hint of worry or alarm, sharpened his voice. "Somewhere around ten."

"At ten-eighteen, Galla Modesto died in Washington Square Park after being stabbed in the abdomen. Her body has been officially identified."

"That's not possible," he began as Eve took out her 'link.

She brought up a crime scene photo of

the victim, held it up. "Is this your wife, sir?"

He stared at the image, stared hard, before he turned, walked to a chair, sat. "How could this happen?" He put the flat of his hand to his forehead, shielding his face as he looked down. "Galla — Galla was attacked?"

Deciding not to wait for an invitation, Eve sat, gestured for Peabody to do the same. "Do you know anyone who'd want to hurt her?"

"Why would anyone want to hurt her? I don't understand, this is a very safe area. She was only going a few blocks. She carries a panic button. Who did this to her? Who did this?"

He dropped his hand. Though he hadn't managed to work up tears, he did well enough with distress.

"We haven't yet identified the attacker. We're analyzing the security discs. You weren't aware she intended to go to the park?"

"The park?" He looked away. "She said the gym. I don't know why she went to the park. I suppose she might have wanted the air. I don't know."

"You weren't aware she intended to go to the park to meet someone?"

"To meet someone? Who? Is that who killed her?"

"No, the person she intended to meet isn't a suspect. Were you aware your wife had an affair, Mr. Tween?"

"That's a disgusting thing to say!" Fury flooded his face, ate away even the pretense of distress. "You're insulting my wife, the mother of my child."

"We have substantial evidence of the affair. Are you stating you were unaware?"

"You dare to sit there, minutes after you tell me my wife's been murdered, and call her a whore?"

"That's an unfortunate choice of words, Mr. Tween, and not one I used." But, Eve thought, I bet it's how you thought of her. "How would you describe the state of your marriage?"

"I will not discuss my marriage with you." He pushed to his feet. "I want you to leave."

"This is a difficult time, but these are routine questions. Questions we ask to help us find the person who took your wife's life, who took the life of your child's mother."

"Could I get you some water?" Peabody used her sympathy voice, and the puppy dog eyes. "You've had a terrible shock, sir. Is there someone we can contact for you?"

"No. No. I need privacy. I need time to

cope. I need you to leave me alone."

"Of course." Sliding easily into the good, understanding cop, Peabody rose. "Before we do, it would be helpful if we had a copy of your security feed so that we can pinpoint exactly when Ms. Modesto left the house tonight. Every piece of information helps us find the person responsible."

"All right, all right." He yanked his 'link out of his pocket, keyed in a code. "I've alerted the maintenance droid. He'll show you the security station, take care of this. Then he'll show you out."

"We appreciate your cooperation," Eve told him. "And again, we're sorry for your loss. If you think of anything that might help in our investigation, please contact us."

As she spoke, Eve took a casual glance around the room. "You have a lovely home, Mr. Tween, and your wife's love of her homeland comes through. That's a wonderful painting."

She stepped toward Stowe's work, and saw not fury, not jealousy, but satisfaction flicker into Tween's eyes.

The first thing Roarke did when he walked into the house was check on Summerset. He went directly to the house comp.

"Where is Summerset?"

34

Good evening, Roarke. Summerset is in his quarters.

Satisfied, and having spent the trip home contacting those he felt he needed to contact, he went upstairs.

He bypassed his office and Eve's, continued up to his private office.

He used his palm print, the voice ID to open the secure doors.

"Lights on," he ordered, and in them, with the city spread outside the privacy-screened window, he poured himself a whiskey.

He gave himself a moment, just a moment to settle.

Eve could and would handle herself. Although . . .

He couldn't dwell on althoughs, not now.

Summerset remained safe in his quarters, and they'd have a discussion in the morning.

He'd ordered some of his best security people to keep watch on his family in Ireland.

If Cobbe didn't know about them before tonight, he'd make it his business to learn about them now.

He had other key people he'd inform and address in the morning, but for now, he had some digging to do.

He went to the command center of his unregistered equipment, equipment CompuGuard couldn't detect. He placed his palm on the plate.

"Roarke. Open operations."

The lights switched on, glowing like jewels against the black.

Operations open . . .

He sat with his whiskey.

"Open and display on wall screen all files on Cobbe, Lorcan."

Acknowledged. Accessing. Displaying . . .

He'd kept track. A careful man, and one with the means, kept track of enemies. Roarke might have believed Cobbe too careful to try for him at this point. If that was a mistake, it wasn't one he'd perpetuate.

He scrolled and scanned, refreshing himself on data gathered on his own, or picked out of the pockets of Interpol, the CIA, MI6, the NCA, Ireland's CSB, and others.

Cops around the world had data on Cobbe, knew him to be a killer for hire, or suspected him.

He'd done some time in his late teens for

being foolish enough to get caught in a sweep of an underground gambling den — and for having several illegal weapons in his possession at the time.

Roarke suspected Cobbe had put those eighteen months to good use, making contacts. Shortly after Cobbe's release, the police informant on the raid took a swim in the Seine with his throat cut ear to ear.

Pleasure, profit, payback, Roarke thought. Cobbe's Holy Trinity.

Sharps remained his go-to — though he did enjoy a bat or a boot on the smaller or defenseless to start. He'd use a garrote as a change of pace.

He liked the up-close kill, the personal kill. No one had data on him ever using explosives or any kind of long-range weaponry.

"He likes the blood," Roarke murmured. "The smell of it, the feel of it. The look in the eyes as life drains away. There's what feeds him.

"Computer, display last known ID, under any alias."

Acknowledged. Accessing. Displaying . . . Cobbe, Lorcan, DOB first September, 2020, Dublin, Ireland. Hair brown, eyes hazel, height six feet, weight 190. No fixed address. Consultant.

"Consultant, is it? That's a word for it. That ID's nearly a year old. He'll have others. Let's find them."

Roarke pushed up his sleeves, pulled a leather strip out of his pocket, and tied back his hair.

He got to work.

With Peabody, Eve walked out of Tween's house, started back to the car. "He's not very good at it."

"Man, I'll say he's not. He couldn't even work up a tear. Not even the pretense of fighting tears. Some people are stoic, right?" Peabody continued, "This wasn't stoic."

"Not stoic," Eve agreed. "And not the other end of the spectrum with jubilant. He's just satisfied the deal's complete. He never asked where she was, when he could see her, if she suffered. She basically doesn't exist anymore.

"We're going to want to talk to the housekeeper."

"I'll contact her first thing in the morning."

"And the vic's family — another thing he didn't mention." Eve checked the time, shook her head. "We should be able to keep her ID under wraps until morning, so we talk to them first thing."

"They keep an apartment here." Peabody read off her PPC. "But their main residence is Florence. The vic's brother's based in Rome."

"What the hell time is it in Italy?"

"Um."

"Never mind. I'll take care of it when I get home."

She opened the car door. McNab slurped on a fizzy in the back seat.

"I got you some views of the black hoodie, Dallas. Copied to your home unit. And of the red jacket — cued those up for you. He didn't worry about showing his face in the red jacket."

Shifting forward, he held the PPC between the front seats to show a still shot on his display.

Cobbe stood in the crowd, thumbs hooked in the front pockets of his pants. Smirking.

"He moves in and out of camera range. He sure as hell knows where the cams are and how to work the blind spots. Using his face or just the description of the jacket, the pants, I could track him when he moved into range. The last confirmed sighting's at double-zero-thirty."

"Good job. I'll drop you at home. Peabody, if the vic's family's in New York, plan to meet me at their residence at eight. I'll let you know. If they're in Italy, I'll handle it via 'link, and you'll meet me at the morgue. Contact the housekeeper in the morning, have her come in. McNab, get anything you can off the vic's 'link."

"Dallas, I did a quick run on this Cobbe while doing the search. He's all kinds of bad news."

"Brief Peabody on same."

"'Tween's bad news, too." Peabody shifted to look back at McNab. "A different kind, but bad."

"Brief McNab on same."

She swung to the corner near their apartment. "Out. Eight sharp, Peabody, one place or the other."

"On that."

"Oh, you've got six varieties of chips in the AC," McNab told Eve as he slid out.

"Great. Go."

The minute the door slammed, she swung away from the curb. She glanced in the rearview, saw them hold hands as they walked.

And now her car smelled like salt and sugar. She opened the windows to blow it out, decided she could actually use some sugar. After ordering a tube of Pepsi from the in-dash AC, she ordered up a run on Lorcan Cobbe.

That kept her busy on the drive uptown. The man had an impressive collection of aliases and suspected bad acts running for a solid three decades.

He'd started young, testing murky waters with assaults, B and Es, muggings, animal abuse — the reddest of red flags. He'd slipped in and out of kid cages there until he got better at it.

A shaky time, she knew, in post–Urban War Dublin, where corruption in the police ran like life's blood.

A couple of wrist slaps — eighteen months for possession of illegal weapons — a handful of forty-eight-hour detentions, but no court-appointed supervision she could find. No psych evals or mandatory counseling.

His mother, Morna Cobbe, did time of her own, primarily for unlicensed prostitution and illegals possession. No father on record. But high on the list of known associates sat one Patrick Roarke.

Cobbe found his groove in his twenties, and there the list lengthened, but with caveats. Suspected, insubstantial evidence, witnesses recanting. Or dying.

He'd either gotten considerably better at

thievery or had given it up to focus on killing.

It hadn't taken long, according to the opinion of numerous law enforcement agencies, for Cobbe to graduate to murder for profit.

Now he was on her turf. More, now he might very well attempt to settle a score — real or imagined — with her husband.

She turned through the gates, started up the drive of the elegant fortress built by a former Dublin street rat.

The towers and turrets, the parapets and grand expanse of stone made a fanciful silhouette in the night sky. Best of all, lights gleamed a welcome home in dozens of windows.

Love, the kind she firmly believed made a person stupid, had her wishing she could keep Roarke inside that fanciful fortress until she tracked down Cobbe and put him away.

And love — the kind she knew meant knowing, and, yeah, respecting, the person you'd joined your life with — understood Roarke not only would never hide but needed to be a part of putting Cobbe away.

Her go-to expert consultant, civilian, was about to get a serious workout.

After she parked, she grabbed the file bag.

Putting her board and book together before she got some sleep hit priority. But so did having a conversation with Roarke.

At least quiet reigned when she walked into the house. No lurking Summerset slid like fog into the foyer. She supposed a conversation had to happen there, too, but she expected to leave that one to Roarke.

She walked upstairs, knowing she had another couple hours ahead of her before she could catch any rack time. But when she turned into her office, the quiet held, and Roarke's adjoining office remained dark.

The idea of him crashing for the night hit high to absurd on the probability scale. In a moment of genuine, cold-sweat panic, she imagined Cobbe lying in wait, ambushing Roarke. She started to sprint to the house system, had reached for it when Roarke walked in.

"Fuck." It might not have been physically possible for a heart to turn upside down, but now she knew what it would feel like. "Jesus."

To compensate, she grabbed his face with both hands, kissed him hard.

"Hello to you as well." He skimmed a hand over her hair before lowering his forehead to hers. "I'm glad you're home."

"Same goes. I need coffee."

"I'd point out the lateness of the hour, but what would be the point? You spoke with the victim's husband?"

"Yeah." She walked to her command center, set down the file bag. Then hit the AutoChef for coffee. "It's not all that often you find someone your gut says is guilty who looks and acts guilty right off."

With the coffee, she paced. "Not a light on in the house, entrance door light's off, too. He claimed he had a headache, took a blocker, went to bed right after she left to work out. Then claims we're crazy because she's sleeping upstairs. In one of the guest rooms because she wouldn't have disturbed him due to convenient headache.

"Asshole can't even work up the pretense of shock and grief. I think he tried, but it's not in him. He's insulted we'd claim she had an affair, orders us out. He never asked how, specifically, she died, where she was, when he could see her. Never talked about having to tell their son, her family."

She leaned back against her console. "The guy she'd been banging's an artist. She's got one of his paintings in her parlor deal. The only real I saw was satisfaction — just an instant — when I said nice painting. I guarantee if I walk into that room now, that painting's gone.

"He paid Cobbe to kill her. Now I have to prove it." Watching him, she drank more coffee. "What you know should help me do that."

"I like to think so. Despite the hour, you'll want to set up your board and book. I'll do the board — I know by now how you like it — and I'll tell you what I can while we're about it."

"All right." She opened operations on her command center.

As he knew she preferred the physical to the virtual, he sat at the auxiliary to print out photos.

"If there's a law enforcement or intelligence agency on planet who isn't aware of Lorcan Cobbe, I've never heard of it. While his choice of profession keeps him largely in Europe, he's ventured afield a few times. He keeps no fixed address, not one they've found in any case. He'll have holes to crawl into between jobs, and they'll be on the lavish side. He always wanted the good life, and with his fees, he can afford it."

She stopped to look over. "You tracked down his fees?"

"Not specifically as yet. But I can tell you when you look at the hits he's suspected of in the last fifteen years or so, they'd all connect to the wealthy, the prominent. One doesn't slit the throat of the pregnant girlfriend of the vice president of Greece — a man of wealth and even higher ambitions — for loose change."

Her eyes narrowed. "I didn't see that in his file during my run. It should've stuck out."

"I used the unregistered. The politician had enough wealth and influence to bury it in Greece, but Interpol had a hard look. You may not be able to use some of what I've found, and will find yet, but you need to know it."

A thin line to walk, Eve thought, so she'd better keep her balance. "Can you find Cobbe's accounts?"

"I will."

"Do you think he took this job in New York because you're here?"

"I don't, no, or he'd have moved on me one way or the other without showing himself."

"But he did show himself."

Arranging her board, he glanced back. "That he did. And now I'm doing what he wants me to do. I'm thinking of him, and I worry about the people who matter to me. But he's the one who'll regret that in the end."

"I'll make sure of it."

He smiled at her, but it didn't reach his eyes. "I'll tell you how I see it then. I've no doubt you're right about Tween, which means Tween has contacts who could recommend him to Cobbe. When did the affair start?"

"Last summer."

"More than time enough. People who take lovers think they're being clever and careful, when they're rarely either. Tween learns of the affair — and you'll likely find he hired someone for evidence there. He can't risk her divorcing him, as it's her money, isn't it, and such a step could erode his standing in the family business. So, obviously, she has to be eliminated."

"For someone like Tween? Yeah, that's how I see it, too. Plus . . . she insulted him by cheating on him. He's not going to ask himself why she did it. It's not breaking his heart. But it's an insult — and with some artist? Insult to injury.

"Italy," she added. "You say Cobbe mainly works in Europe, so odds are the connection, the contact is in Italy."

"Odds are. For a job like this, while simple and straightforward for a professional killer, the client stands to inherit a great deal of wealth, and it's likely Cobbe factored that into the fee. I don't see him taking a job in New York of this nature for less than a million. That would be at least the half of it up front. That's his likely base, with additional for his expenses."

She didn't disagree, as she thought the same. But still . . .

"Then why didn't he take the money, do the job, walk away? Why was he still in the park when we got there?"

Idly, Roarke pulled the strap from his hair, slid it into his pocket. And with it, he felt the little button, Eve's gray button he carried for sentiment and luck.

"I knew him as a boy, though I've kept tabs on him since. But as a boy he considered cops idiots, especially any who weren't corrupt. Not that you found many in Dublin in those days who weren't. He'd often, back then, prove the cliché about returning to the scene of the crime. He liked to watch the cops and smirk at his superiority. Whenever he'd get pinched, it was always someone else's fault, you see."

"Yours?"

"More than once." Now the smile did reach his eyes. "And more than once he'd've been right about that. I knew a boy once, not a mate, just a boy I'd see, a young busker. He didn't have much, but he had a dog. A little thing, scruffy little thing who'd do some trick to help add coins to the boy's hat. Cobbe went after the boy for those coins once, and the little dog bit the bloody hell out of him, chased him off."

"Good dog."

"Well, he was until Cobbe went back for him, sliced him to pieces. Bragged on it, he did, on killing a dog that couldn't have weighed ten pounds after a soak in the rain. The old man? He thought it a fine joke."

"You ratted him out."

"I did. The boy and dog were fixtures, you see, and well liked even by the Garda. So a word passed on brought the cops — those who could bother to give a fuck — down on him. He'd taken one of the dog's ears as a trophy, so it didn't go well for him."

Now he shrugged. "Which is neither here nor there."

"No, it's here and it's there."

"In any case, he likes the sharps, always did, and it's likely held true he gets some jollies watching the cops go over his handiwork. You want what I think as much as what I know, so I'm thinking he waited for the murder cops for the fun of it. That turned out to be you, and me with you. He couldn't resist showing himself to me."

Again, she had to agree. "And you don't

think he'll take his fee and go?"

"He's started the game, you see." He came back, sat so they faced each other. "And it's more than a game for him, as seeing me dead is a lifelong ambition. He tried for me once before — not speaking of when I was a boy, for he tried more than once then. I was building this house, and my business here in New York. Doing considerable traveling to . . . we'll say enhance my business interests."

She met those beautiful eyes straight on. "We could say that."

"I was in the South of France on what we'll call an art deal. As it happens, on the same night I closed the deal — and as it turned out several hours after the patriarch of a prominent family had his throat slit while on his yacht — we saw each other."

Rising, he got a tube of water, sat, cracked it. "It was in a lively bar where I'd concluded some business and was having a drink. Now, I saw him come in, as it's wise to keep an eye on comings and goings even after the conclusion of a deal."

"Maybe especially."

He smiled again. "Maybe especially. And over he walks, and doesn't he sit right down as if we were the best of mates. He heard I was doing well for myself, so why not stand an old friend a pint."

"I'm going to guess you weren't in the mood to reminisce."

"I told him to bugger off, a suggestion he didn't take kindly. He had some unpleasant things to say, which ended with him saying while I'd been lucky, I'd always been weak, and he was Patrick Roarke's true son. But seeing as that made us half brothers, he wouldn't gut me with the knife he had under the table — and there he gave me a little jab with it to make his point — if I paid him five hundred thousand — pounds sterling he wanted — and admitted he was Patrick Roarke's true son and heir by letting go of the name."

"Is that all?" Eve said, dry as dust. "What did you do?"

"I said how that was an interesting offer, but I'd have to decline. And if he ever tried to come at me again, he'd be sorrier than he was about to be. I had a stunner under the table, and left him jittering on the floor of the bar. I can regret I didn't switch it on full and rid the world of him, but I had just completed that deal and had a strong desire to avoid the local police."

"Bet you did," Eve murmured.

"I didn't hear about the murder until I was back in my hotel. And putting two and two together, made an anonymous call, leaving a tip with his name and description. They couldn't pin him, but I'm told he spent considerable time in the French version of your box being questioned."

"Nothing since then?"

"I've kept tabs on him since that night — not careful enough, I suppose, but I rarely gave him a thought. But no, he's made no move. He kills for money, and if it's otherwise, he goes for the weak. He thought I was."

"You've never been weak." When he just looked at her, she shook her head. "I'm not your weakness, Roarke. I'm your goddamn weapon."

"Darling Eve, you're both and so much more." He took her hand. "I won't ask you to tuck yourself away any more than you'll ask me. We can want to, but we know each other too well for that. And we know we have to deal with this."

"I can't let you kill him."

"I missed my chance there in a lively bar on the Côte d'Azur. I will promise you this: If he dies by my hand, it won't be in cold blood, as it might have been before you. I'd rather prison for him, I'd rather think of him in a concrete cage far, far from what I love. I'd rather think of him spending what

I hope will be a long, long life knowing me and my cop put him there."

She turned her hand under his, gripped it hard. "That's fair. I'm not going to let him use me to hurt you. You have to trust me."

"He'll think I'm with you, using you as cover. He won't understand what you are to me, but that won't stop him from trying to end you."

"He's already made a mistake. He should never have let you see him. I'd have figured out, and damn quick, Tween hired the hit, but Cobbe could and would have been in the wind. He's on our turf now, Roarke. And he's going to pay for Galla Modesto because she's mine now. Ours now," she corrected.

"Ours." He gave her hand a squeeze. "How'd I do on the board?"

"You're a pretty solid aide. It's good."

"And will you call it now, get some sleep? I could use the quiet and the dark with my wife, and the cat who's likely already sprawled over our bed."

"What time is it in Italy?"

He glanced at his wrist unit. "About half eight in the morning."

"That'll work. I need to track down the victim's parents. If they're in Italy, I want to notify them now, and get a feel for things."

"They're in Florence. I checked while I was running other matters."

"Saves time. I'm going to do that now, then text Peabody on it, then I'll call it."

"All right then. I've a couple things I can deal with in my office. I'll wait for you."

She watched him go before turning to her 'link.

"No more coffee tonight," he called out.

And the hard knot in her stomach loosened. If he could still nag her about drinking too much coffee, he was smoothing out.

3

The scent of coffee stirred Eve awake so she opened one eye and spotted Roarke. He stood at the bedroom AutoChef in the dim morning light with a towel slung around his waist.

Not a bad image to wake up to, she thought. Not bad at all.

"Aren't you late for some 'link conference on buying the Southern Hemisphere?"

Without missing a beat, he programmed a second cup of coffee. "I put that off until later this morning."

He crossed to her with the coffee as the fat lump of cat curled into the small of her back rolled over lazily and stretched.

Having a mostly naked husband bring her coffee in bed equaled a pretty good perk of the whole marriage deal. She sat up, took it. "Did you sleep okay?"

"I did." After skimming a hand over her hair, he walked over and into his closet.

Eve exchanged a long look with Galahad. "I think okay's relative," she muttered, but rolled out of bed to shower.

The best — and only real thing — she could do was work the case, work it hard, and get this thorn out of Roarke's side.

Thorn, hell, she corrected as the hot jets pummeled her fully awake. More like a shiv right now.

She'd see what, if anything, the ME could tell her about Modesto's death she didn't already know, do a more comprehensive study of the security feeds — and check with McNab on that.

Modesto's family — parents, brother, brother's wife — all planned to arrive in New York this morning. So she'd have a conversation there and push for some straight talk regarding what they knew of her marriage to Tween.

Then she wanted to talk to the house-keeper.

Eve stepped out of the shower, opted — as always — for the fast, swirling heat of the drying tube.

Live-in staff, she understood from per-sonal experience (Summer-set!), knew a hell of a lot about what went on inside a house-hold.

She hopped out of the drying tube,

grabbed the robe on the back of the door.

She needed to dig into any intelligence on Cobbe, and might need her commander's assistance with that. And she wanted a consult with Mira, wanted the top profiler and shrink's take on both Cobbe and Tween.

Truth? she admitted. She'd take help wherever she could get it to shut Cobbe down, to lock him away.

When she walked back into the bedroom, Roarke, already in one of his king-of-the-business-world suits, stood tying one of his fancy ties in some fancy knot.

"We're in for fine weather today," he told her while Galahad inhaled his morning kibble.

She'd intended to keep things practical and pragmatic, but instead went with her heart instead of her head. Crossing to him, she took his face in her hands. "I'm going to get him."

"I have no doubt of it."

"Good."

She went to her own closet, grabbed a pair of trousers at random. She shimmied into them and a support tank, thought of good weather so grabbed a short-sleeved shirt and a jacket.

As she pulled on the shirt, Roarke stepped

to the opening of her closet. "Are you doing that deliberately to distract me?"

"What?" She reached for a belt.

"Pairing that jacket with those pants — and put that belt back."

"Why? The pants are black, the jacket's black, the belt's black."

He took the jacket, hung it up again. "The pants are indigo."

She rolled her eyes behind his back as he picked another jacket.

"And roll your eyes all you like," he said without turning around. "If you're going to wear indigo — which is a deep navy, not black — with the accent of gray-influenced celadon —"

"What the hell is celadon? It sounds contagious."

"It's green — in this case a gray-green. As is this jacket." He pulled one out. "With its indigo buttons. Take off that shirt."

"I don't have time for closet sex, pal."

He pulled it over her head himself, then pulled her in, just held her. "Wish we did."

She held him in turn. "Me, too."

"But since closet sex is off the agenda, let's use the closet for its more traditional purpose." Drawing away, he chose another shirt. "White to add crispness."

"I had on a white shirt."

With the demeanor of a patient teacher instructing a baffled student, he held up the first shirt. "This is cream. This?" He held up the second shirt. "Is white. And this belt?" He tossed her the white shirt, selected a belt. "Is indigo, as are your trousers. It's a pity you'd balk at celadon boots for a workday, as they'd complement that outfit perfectly. But . . ." He moved over to the wall of shelves that held the ridiculous, to her mind, number of boots she'd acquired.

"This will finish off the look and fall within your version of appropriate."

She took them. "Indigo?"

"There you have it."

He gave her a kiss that met the equivalent of a pat on the head, then left her to dress.

She hadn't done it on purpose, Eve thought as she put on the white shirt, the indigo belt. But fiddling with her clothes had lightened his mood a little.

She put on the boots — a new addition from the closet fairy — grabbed the jacket.

He stood at the AC again, ordering breakfast. She had to hope a fine day meant no oatmeal. Taking up her weapon harness, she shrugged into it. And thinking of international assassins, got out her clutch piece and ankle holster.

Since he'd already set the pot of coffee on

the table of the sitting area, she poured for both of them.

He brought two plates under warmers to the table — and the cat eyed them greedily while he washed.

No oatmeal, Eve thought with an inner cheer. Some nice fat berries, some sort of omelet, and best of all, bacon.

"You'd have thought out some of your strategy for the day in the shower. Tell me."

Eve cut into the omelet. Green stuff inside. She should've known. "Morgue first. I want to consult with both Whitney and Mira — Whitney can help with the alphabets, and Mira with a clear-sighted view of both Cobbe and Tween."

"Alphabets?"

"FBI, CIA, NCA, CSB, blah blah blah. Like I told you last night after I made the notification, her family's coming to New York. Unless they push for otherwise, I want to talk to them in my house."

The green stuff turned out to be asparagus and . . . "Peas?"

"It's spring," he said as if that explained it.

It didn't, but it worked somehow.

"You didn't tell me how her family took the notification."

"A lot worse than Tween." She could still

60

hear the pain, the shock, the grief. "I only spoke to the father. When he recovered enough, he said they would all come — including his son and his son's family. They all needed to come, to see her, to arrange for her, to talk to me."

"Did he say anything about Tween?"

"He asked if he should contact Tween, asked about his grandson. I suggested maybe they should wait until they got to New York before contacting Tween, and that I hoped they would agree to come in and speak with me, that I would tell them all I could at that time."

Roarke nodded. "I believe they're a close family. As I said, I know the brother a little — Stefano. He's a canny businessman, knowledgeable. Tennis, as I recall, is his sport, and he's fairly fierce about it. That's how he met his wife. She was a pro, and retired when she had their second child. She's a coach now."

Details, all details, helped.

"Anything I should know about the parents I can't find on a standard?"

"Nothing I can think of, but I can, and will, ask around."

"Meanwhile, I want to talk to the housekeeper — alone. She didn't come back down after going up to get Tween. That tells

61

me he sent her back to her quarters rather than letting me see her reaction to the notification."

She ate some bacon and waited while Roarke gave the covertly advancing Galahad a cool, warning stare.

Galahad decided he needed to wash again.

"What about you?"

"Besides what I couldn't reasonably postpone or reschedule, I have some sources of my own to mine. I want to talk to Brian as well."

Brian Kelly, Eve thought, Roarke's old friend and the proprietor of the Penny Pig, a Dublin pub.

"Brian must have known Cobbe."

"And sure he did. They didn't care for each other, but neither did they have any dealings to speak of. Still, having Brian's ear to the ground won't hurt. And I've put some men in Clare to keep an eye on the family."

"Your family?" She set down her fork with a clatter. "Jesus Christ, Roarke, you think he'd go after your family?"

"I won't risk it, so I've people looking out. Odds are he hasn't kept close tabs on me the last years. For what point? He likely doesn't know I have family, as I didn't myself for years. But I promise you he will know of them right quick, as he'll look into such matters or try."

"I can talk to the locals," Eve began.

"Not as yet. I'd rather the family not have this worry, or take the chance of one of the local cops letting out I've got a concern. That's all he'd need, trust me."

"I do." But she didn't like it. She added doing some quiet research into the locals to her agenda. She'd already consulted with them once, already had opinions.

"Then there's the school. We're about to open An Didean, and I want no trouble in that quarter."

"I'll have some cops keep an eye out there, and on Dochas," she added, thinking of the women's shelter. "I know who I can trust," she said before he could object.

"You do, of course. I'd appreciate it, as he might find it a lark to make trouble in those areas, or hurt someone just for the bloody hell of it."

"Then it's done. I don't care who your sources are, or however far they fall over my particular line, I need to know whatever you find out."

"And you will. There's no question of it. And I know who you are, Lieutenant, and how good you are at what you do." Looking at her, he trailed a finger down the shallow dent in her chin. "But I'm asking you to take more care, to watch out more closely for the woman I love. It would give him great joy to take you from me."

"He's not going to be happy when we're done with him. I promise you."

She rose to gather her 'link, her communicator, and all the rest. Then considered, dug into a drawer for a stiletto, a wrist sheath. After she put it on, she turned to Roarke, hit the switch that released the lethal blade.

He smiled at her. "Thanks for that."

"As an officer in the New York Police and Security Department, I can't advise you to arm yourself in a similar fashion. As the woman who loves you right back, I'm telling you to."

"You've no worry on that score."

She put on the jacket, walked back to kiss him goodbye. "Celadon and indigo?"

He pulled her back for a second kiss. "It looks well on you. You take care of my cop."

"All over that."

"I couldn't live without her," he murmured when she'd gone. He got up, hefted the considerable bulk of the cat, and walked to the elevator.

Before he did anything else, he needed to sit down and speak to Summerset.

He found the man who'd been his father most of his life sitting in the kitchen. He wore one of his severe black suits as he drank coffee and read the day's news on a tablet.

He glanced over as Roarke came in, as Roarke set the cat down, and the cat padded straight over to rub against Summerset's leg.

"Don't let him con you. He's had breakfast."

Summerset reached down, scratched the cat between the ears with his long, bony fingers. "As you have, I trust. Coffee?"

"Thanks, no, I've had enough." He walked over, sat across from Summerset, said simply, "Lorcan Cobbe."

"That's a name I'm sorry to hear again. What of him?"

"He's in New York. He killed a woman last night. It's Eve's case."

Summerset's keen, dark eyes stayed steady on Roarke's. "How do you know it was Cobbe?"

"Because I saw him. Because he made certain I did."

As Roarke added the details, Summerset accepted Galahad on his lap, stroked while he listened.

"The lieutenant's quite sure the husband

65

hired Cobbe." Considering all, Summerset nodded. "And intends to track Cobbe through that connection."

"In a nutshell, yes."

"As far as nuts go, it's doubtful Cobbe will be as easy to crack as the husband."

"No."

"You've accumulated data and shared it with her?"

"Of course."

"That's helpful. I still have some contacts with certain groups and agencies. It's a simple matter to contact old friends and compatriots, see if more can be found."

"Groups. Eve calls them the alphabets."

Summerset smiled. "Governments are fond of their acronyms."

"And not just official government groups."

The smile remained. "Not just. If you clear it, I could brief Ivanna. She also has contacts."

Roarke considered Summerset's old friend and current . . . *companion* seemed safest, he decided. A man didn't want to think too deeply about his father figure taking a lover. "Yes, I think reaching into any corner in this case is expedient."

"I'll speak with her, and others this morning."

"It would ease my mind if you stayed

inside the gates today, for a few days."

Summerset's eyebrows arched. "I have marketing to do, and other errands." He held up a hand before Roarke could insist. "Do you think I've missed so many steps, boy, I can't look out for myself or handle a ruffian like Cobbe?"

"He's a professional assassin, a successful one," Roarke pointed out. "It's not a matter of you missing steps, but of the steps I'd miss if anything happened to you."

Drawing air through his long, narrow nose, Summerset sat back. "That's a clever way you have, and I have to commend it. But I've no intention of hiding away, or of being murdered on the street. Nor do you, unless you're about to tell me you and the lieutenant intend to stay behind the gates. We'll all play gin rummy."

Despite a sudden weariness, Roarke smiled. "I always won."

"You cheated."

"So you always said, but never proved. You'll take precautions."

"Yes, as will you."

Now Summerset leaned forward, his dark eyes intense. "He doesn't know you, boy. He thinks he does, but he doesn't know you and never did. He'll look now, and hard, but still only see the surface. He'll envy your money and your reputation, the dark and the light there. And your freedom, because the life he chose doesn't allow him real freedom. But he'll never see who you are, he'll never understand what you're made of. And that's your advantage. Or one of them."

"I see him. I know what he's made of."

"Yes, you do. He's not a complicated man. I've no doubt by now the lieutenant knows him as well. She's a dangerous woman when she knows her quarry."

"She is that. I've things to see to." Roarke rose, then laid a hand over Summerset's. "Remember what you are to me, and take care."

"And you do the same."

Alone, Summerset sat another moment, stroking the cat. "Well, my friend, let's do what we can do to keep our children safe."

Eve spent the drive downtown listening to the audio of the files Roarke compiled on Cobbe.

Summerset was right. By the time she arrived at the morgue, she knew her quarry.

She walked down the long white tunnel with its air filters trying — and failing — to completely mask the scent of death. She was making her way down to the chief medical examiner's doors when she heard the clomping echo behind her.

Peabody had her dark hair with the strange red streaks in a short, bouncy tail. The clomping came from striped pink-and-white gel skids — likely chosen due to feet still aching from dancing shoes. She wore her pink magic coat over brown pants and a brown blazer with pink trim. And a shirt Eve suspected was cream.

She stifled a yawn.

"McNab went straight to Central to finish the security feeds, and to do a search on the vic's 'link."

"Good. I've already put in for a warrant for the electronics at her residence — Tween's included."

"He won't like that."

"Which only gives a lift to the start of my day."

Eve pushed open the doors.

Morris stood by the body just completing his Y-cut.

Peabody turned a little green — perhaps celadon — and turned her head to stare hard at the wall.

"Bright and early," Morris remarked, and ordered his music — Eve thought maybe Italian opera — to mute.

Under his protective cape he wore a sharp

69

suit of bold blue, a shirt of pale yellow with a tie that played both colors in slim stripes. His long braid fell down the back of his cape with yellow cord wound through the black.

When he efficiently opened Modesto's chest, Peabody made a soft gagging sound.

"A lovely young woman," Morris began as Eve stepped up to the slab. "Excellent muscle tone. No visible signs of body or face work. I've sent blood and tissue samples to the lab for tox, but see no signs of chronic use."

"What can you tell me about the wound?"

"Quick and vicious. The blade entered here, the hypogastric area, deep." He turned away to take a gauge from his tray.

Eve could see the gauge slide into the abdomen on-screen, but bent over as Morris did to judge it in the body.

"Six and a quarter inches in, and the width . . . point seventeen." Grabbing his microgoggles, he leaned in again. "It's a spear point, so I'd say a stiletto-style blade. After the entry, the blade was drawn up and into the umbilical region. Effectively gutting her."

He straightened again. "So many internal organs live in the belly, and others connect. The damage, the shock, the blood loss would have killed her within a minute or two, and she'd have been, blessedly, unconscious before that."

"She's got some slight bruising at the impact site. Hilt?"

"Yes, I agree. So the killing blade will measure those six and a quarter inches."

Though the screen showed the body, the wound magnified, Morris bent over Modesto with his goggles.

"He drove it in, up to the hilt. If you find it, it should be a button-release type. He shoved the hilt to her belly, flipped the switch to send the blade into her, then dragged it upward."

"Efficient," Eve commented.

"Yes, brutally efficient. Two seconds, and the job's done."

"The fucker she was married to knew where she'd be and when." Eve stepped back from the table, paced around it. "We're going to find communications between her and the man she went out to meet on her 'link. He knew about the affair. He knew she'd broken things off, but that didn't matter to him. He hired the hit, passed the information on."

She looked back at the body. "The killer gets there early, waits, sees her come in. He just walks over. If anybody happens to notice, it just looks like he's heading out through the arch, bumps into her, keeps walking. But in that two seconds, that bump, the knife's in her, ripped through her. He keeps going, she staggers a couple of steps. When she goes down, attention's on her, not him."

"He went out through the arch." Though mostly recovered, Peabody kept a discreet distance from the slab. "McNab caught him a couple times, still in the black hoodie. He walked back in before the first on scene arrived to secure the scene. Red jacket. He didn't go near the body, kept walking, circled around the fountain."

"You've already identified him?"

"Yeah." Eve turned back to Morris. "We know who he is — a pro. We just have to find him, and his six-and-a-quarter-inch stiletto. Something like this."

She flicked and twisted her right wrist to release the blade she wore.

Though his eyes widened a bit, Morris stepped to her to examine it. "Yes, something like. Is this new investigator wear?"

"For this one it is." She retracted the blade. "Her husband — Jorge Tween — may contact you, make some noises about coming in or making arrangements to cover his ass."

"So noted."

"Her family, parents, brother, will contact you. They should be in New York shortly."

"I'll have her presentable."

"Thanks." She started out, stopped. "If you get a tag from a Marlon Stowe, you could let him see her. Just keep it down low."

"The lover, which means you don't believe he's culpable."

"There're lovers and there's love. Cheating's still cheating, but you don't deserve to die for it. But don't tell Roarke I said that."

"In the vault."

As they walked back down the tunnel, Peabody gave Eve's wrist a wary look. "I don't have to wear one of those, right?"

"Up to you."

"I know how to use a knife — in combat — but I just don't like them. It's the sharp-thing-into-the-flesh thing. It's like Morris doing the cut on a body."

"A blade's personal. It's an extension of the person using it."

"I guess it is."

"Wear a clutch piece until this one's over."

"Okay."

When they got into the car, Eve leaned back a moment. "I'm going to tell you what I know about Cobbe. Some of what I know is from sources I shouldn't have at this time. I'm going to talk to Whitney and have him push to have some of the sources read me in, but I won't have my partner in the dark on an investigation."

Peabody simply nodded. "So you'll tell me what you know, but until we're able to access it officially, we keep it out of the book."

"That's right. If Whitney can't get us access to the information, we're going to use what we have anyway, and keep it out of the book. Are you all right with that?"

"You'd never ask me to do something that wasn't right. There's a difference between right and regs sometimes. That's why regs can change, but right doesn't."

And that, Eve realized, might be the long and short of why she'd made Peabody her partner.

"Okay. When we get to Central, contact the housekeeper. Ah, Rinaldi. We need her to come in. We should talk to the nanny, too, at some point. Set me up with Mira whenever she's got an opening. I'll make the meet with Whitney."

She started the car and told her partner what she needed to know.

4

When Eve pulled into the garage at Central, Peabody turned to her. "So, we're going after a professional killer a whole bunch of law enforcement agencies and intelligence agencies — worldwide — haven't been able to bag."

"Correct."

"Check that." They got out of the car, started toward the elevator. "The bad guy has a grudge against, maybe a kind of fixation, on Roarke."

"Also correct."

"No point in asking if Roarke would accept police protection while we go after the bad guy."

Eve barely spared a dour glance. "None."

"Check and check. But would he talk to Mira? I get he's giving you the overview, the details, and you're going to consult with Mira, but doesn't that end up filtered through you? If he talked to her directly, it's, you know, direct."

Eve started to give that the same response as police protection, then rethought. "That's a good point. That's a damn good point." For personal as well as professional reasons. "I'll see if I can work it."

"We're not going to let a bad guy screw with one of us," Peabody said as they got on the elevator. "And that's a fact."

"Stone-cold fact."

But she worried, worried enough she didn't automatically shove her way off and hit the glides when people crowded onto the elevator.

"I'll set up Whitney — I can get that, too — Mira, and the housekeeper," Peabody told her. "When you hear from the victim's family, let me know so I can work that in."

"Good. Fine." Eve let out a breath. "Appreciate it."

"One of us," Peabody repeated.

When she finally did muscle off the elevator, Eve went straight to her office. She hit the AutoChef for coffee, then buried worry in routine.

She set up her board, started her book. And glanced up when she heard Peabody's familiar clomp.

"The housekeeper's already on the way in."

"That was quick and easy."

"I mean she was already on her way in — I caught her in a cab en route. She sounded and looked upset."

"Okay, let's take her in the lounge."

"Whitney has a meeting, but he'll be available in about an hour. Mira can give you fifteen to twenty at eleven."

Eve sat back. "How did you get through her admin that easily?"

"Her admin likes me. Sort of. And I told her this profile is priority, as the subject is likely to target law enforcement and those connected thereto. Which Mira is."

"Cagey." Sitting back, Eve nodded approval. "Not completely untrue, and cagey."

"I learned from the cagiest. I'll check on McNab's progress and let you know when the housekeeper gets here. Oh, and FYI? Jenkinson and his tie are now at his desk. You should avert your eyes."

"They're drawn to it. They know better, they suffer for it, but they're drawn to it."

She finished her book, then started a dive into Tween's finances. She'd barely scratched the surface when she got an incoming from Roarke.

You'll find it interesting, no doubt, that Jorge Tween maintains a small, private account — poorly hidden and in a gray area. Two weeks ago he transferred five hundred thousand euros to a numbered, sheltered account in Andorra. Another five hundred and fifteen thousand euros was transferred last night at twenty-three hundred hours. I'll have the data on the Andorra account shortly.

"Bet you will," Eve mumbled.

She added the information to her board and book.

So he hired Cobbe two weeks ago, she decided as she got up for more coffee. Paid the first half of the fee. Cobbe sent proof of death — a 'link vid or shot when he came back into the park, after the cops — the first on scene — arrived. Tween pays up, with the additional fifteen likely covering expenses.

And for a million and change, he gets rid of an unfaithful wife, most probably inherits a really good chunk of her estate. And is the single parent and guardian of her only child, who most likely has a trust fund already in the works. Has loving and wealthy grandparents who would be very generous to the widower.

A fine investment from his point of view.

She walked to her board, studied Tween's

ID shot.

"We'll have you in a cage by the end of the day, hand to God, you fuck."

Her interoffice beeped. "Ms. Rinaldi's here. I'm escorting her to the lounge."

"Right behind you."

Eve took the coffee with her. As she passed through the bullpen, her eyes — and they did know better — scanned toward Jenkinson's desk.

And suffered, oh, they suffered from the blast of viral, virulent orange covered with whales. With grinning purple whales that spouted fountains of a blue that could only be a result of ingesting great amounts of plutonium.

"It doesn't even make sense," Eve managed.

When she finally averted her eyes, the afterimage haunted her while she strode to the lounge.

She saw Rinaldi at one of the tables, hands clenched together, and Peabody at Vending. Eve walked over, sat across from Rinaldi.

"You're the lieutenant," Rinaldi said before Eve could speak. "I remember from last night. Can it be a mistake?"

"No, it's not a mistake. Were you close to Ms. Modesto?"

She untwisted her fingers to press one

hand to her mouth, then dropped it to her heart. "I'm sick in my heart. I've known Galla — I was to call her that because I've known her since she was only fifteen and I went to work at the villa for her parents. She's lovely, do you understand? A lovely young woman. When she came to live in New York, she asked if I would come and work for her here. She wanted someone from home, you see?"

"Yes."

Peabody set water in front of Rinaldi, sat with a tube of Diet Pepsi.

"Thank you. I am not her mama nor her sister, but in a way a kind of aunt? And she has someone from home, which she misses. Someone to speak with in the language of her birth and heart."

"Mr. Tween doesn't speak Italian?"

"He speaks it" — Rinaldi lifted her hand, tilted it side to side — "but insists on English in the household. Angelo, he's a very sweet boy, smart and mischievous, but sweet. He can speak it better than his papa. Ah, it's not important."

She pulled out a little swatch of lace-trimmed white, dabbed her streaming eyes.

"Everything's important, Ms. Rinaldi. Were you aware she had a relationship outside of her marriage?"

The hand went straight back to her heart, and her eyes filled again. "No, not know it. Wondered if, but it wasn't my place to ask. I would have listened and kept her counsel if she had told me."

"Why did you wonder?"

"She was unhappy, then happy, then not. Small things, a look in her eyes. I think she's in love, but not with Signore Tween. That love began to fade when she carried the baby, and died, I think, after they moved here."

"You knew her. Do you know why her marriage began to fail?"

"He didn't want her to work, and that was not the way he said before they married, before the baby. She loved the work, and she was smart and knowledgeable and involved, but he complained, very much, until she — what is it — cut back? Until she worked less. He wanted her to be available to him, for society and for . . . is it image? This is how she felt, this she did tell me in confidence."

"Was he ever abusive?"

"With his hands? No, no, I think no. I believe she would not stand for such a thing. But with words, I think yes. Not shouted, not like this, but quiet and . . . like water against a rock, it eats away over time."

She lifted her water, sipped, sipped again before she set it down. "He is cold in his heart, you see? He didn't seem cold before they married, before she had the baby inside her. He brings flowers, he seems happy she is so good at the business, he shows pride and love. But it was false, I think, because he is cold by his nature.

"Today, this morning, before I even begin my duties, and I believe Galla is upstairs with Angelo, he calls me to his office. He tells me Galla is dead. When I'm shocked, when I'm upset, when I don't understand, he tells me she was murdered, a mugging when she was out in the evening. And as I weep he tells me my services are no longer required."

"He fired you?" Peabody demanded.

"He says he will see I have references, and he will pay me three weeks, but I must leave by tomorrow morning, only this day to pack and make arrangements. He wants only to be alone with his son, in his grief — but there is no grief in his eyes, you see? He will have a droid take my duties, and the duties of Angelo's nanny, who must also leave."

Isolate the boy, Eve thought.

"I beg him to let me stay, to help with the little boy, who's lost his mother, but he says I must go. And this isn't right, this isn't how a loving husband and father is at such a time. I think of you, how you came to the house, and I want to say all this to you."

"We appreciate that."

"You may think I'm angry and hopeful to make trouble for Mr. Tween, but this isn't true. I came to this country for Galla, and I would stay for her son. I would wish nothing more than Signore Tween be a good and loving father. But I fear, the way he spoke this morning, with no love, no grief, no shock, he . . . he maybe killed her. I fear it and fear for Angelo."

"Do you think he'd hurt his son?" Peabody asked.

"I never thought this, but I never thought he would hurt Galla. Now I think it. He's just a little boy. Can you protect him?"

"We'll do all we can," Eve assured her. "Ms. Modesto's family is on their way to New York."

Rinaldi closed her eyes, murmured something in Italian. "I thank the Blessed Mother. I thank her for hearing this prayer. I was to ask you if I could speak with them, but you will speak with them. Will you ask, if I can help them, they tell me?"

"Yes."

"Do you have a place to stay?"

Rinaldi looked at Peabody. "I will stay,

when I must leave, with a friend I have. I must decide what to do, to stay or go home, but I must know about Angelo first. I must know he is safe. Galla would want me to."

"We'd like your friend's contact information."

"Yes. Yes, however I can help. I will give you the same for Sofia, Angelo's nanny. She loves Angelo, and is broken in her heart as I am."

"That's helpful. I'll take that information and walk you out."

"Detective Peabody will also give you our contacts," Eve added. "If you remember anything, think of anything, let us know."

Eve went back to her office. Time, she thought, to pull in APA Reo. She wanted Tween in the box.

"Reo. I'm heading to court, Dallas."

"Last time I checked you could walk and talk."

Reo pushed back her blond cloud of hair. "I do have that skill. Modesto, stabbing in Washington Square Park. You caught it. So?"

"The husband hired a pro."

"And you know this because?"

"Because I have that skill. The pro's identified by an eyewit as Cobbe, Lorcan — look him up."

"I don't have that detail."

"Now you do."

"Name of wit?"

"Roarke."

That put a small hitch in Reo's purposeful stride. "That's complicating matters. How does Roarke know a paid killer?"

"He knew him when they were kids in Dublin."

"Friends? Associates?"

"Neither. You can say the opposite."

"Slightly less complicated."

"Quick version," Eve said, and gave the highlights as horns beeped, ad blimps blasted.

"He made sure Roarke saw him — interesting."

"I have information Tween shelled out over a million euros to the same account, two payments. One two weeks ago, one last night about forty minutes after TOD. I've just interviewed the housekeeper — whom Tween fired, along with the boy's nanny, this morning. I'll write that up and get it to you, but I'm telling you there's enough to bring him in."

"Bring him in then. If you want me in on it, I'm in court until two. Make it after two. Let's hold the warrant until you work him some, or at least until you talk to the family, and until you see what weight Whitney can lend to getting more data. I'll talk to my boss, you talk to yours."

"Done." Eve checked the time. "Right about now. I'll pull him in by fourteen-thirty. A man who can spend a million to kill his wife can spend a lot on lawyers."

With a smile, Reo fluffed her hair as she walked up the courthouse steps. "It's handy we're both so damn good. Gotta go."

Satisfied, Eve clicked off, swiveled to look at Tween on her board. "End of day, asshole." And rose when Peabody walked in.

"Write up the interview," Eve told her. "I've got Reo coming in this afternoon, and we'll time bringing Tween in so she'll be here."

"How stupid to fire the housekeeper and nanny like that?"

"Arrogant more than stupid, but it amounts to the same. Contact the nanny, see if you can get her to come in, make a statement."

"On it. McNab reports texts between Modesto and Stowe on her 'link. Two from each day before yesterday — asking for the meet, agreeing, confirming place and time."

"Excellent. He got his hands on her 'link, or he hacked into it back when she had the affair. Put it in the book. I'm with Whitney."

"Good luck there."

Eve took the glides up, took the time to think through her approach. She'd break Tween. Breaking the weak, greedy, arrogant didn't pose much of a real challenge. And she could — would — twist him into flipping on Cobbe.

But if Cobbe didn't prove to be a total idiot — and she had to believe he had some smarts to slip and slide through international investigations — whatever Tween knew wouldn't finish the job.

Taking down Cobbe was priority. She'd take all the help she could get to put him away.

Her 'link signaled, showing Galla Modesto's father on the display.

"Dallas. Thank you for getting back to me, Mr. Modesto."

By the time she'd arranged the meeting with the victim's family, she'd arrived at Whitney's outer office. His admin gave her the go-ahead. She knocked, opened the door, and went in.

Commander Whitney sat at his desk, a big-shouldered man, dark-complected, dark-eyed, with close-cropped hair threaded with gray.

Behind him the city he served and protected spread, its towers shining in the sun.

He ordered his wall screen off, then turned his attention to her.

"Lieutenant."

"Commander, thanks for making the time."

"I had back-to-back meetings so haven't read your initial report. Stabbing in Washington Square Park. What don't I know?"

"Galla Modesto, wine heiress."

"Modesto Wine and Spirits?"

"Yes, sir."

He nodded. "Continue."

"I have strong circumstantial Modesto's husband, Jorge Tween, hired a professional to kill his wife due to, at least in part, a previous affair. He lied during the notification interview, and not very well. He has a shadow account, and has withdrawn two payments. The first two weeks ago for half a million euros, the second forty minutes after the victim's TOD for that amount and change. Both were transferred to a numbered account in Andorra."

She paused. "I expect to have the details on the Andorra account shortly, and have engaged Roarke as expert consultant, civilian, to get those details."

"That's a considerable outlay for eliminating an unfaithful wife."

"A rich unfaithful wife. She's worth many times what he is, Commander. They had a child, age four, and he will now be sole parent and guardian. This morning he dismissed the live-in housekeeper and nanny. Peabody's writing up the statement by the housekeeper, who came in on her own this morning."

"And the lover?"

"Marlon Stowe, an artist. Though Modesto ended their affair, she agreed to meet him in the park last night. He'd done a painting for her, a kind of partner to one she bought when they first met. He came forward last night, told me about the affair. He rang true, Commander, and has no history of violence on record. Added to it, he doesn't have the means to hire a hit."

"And you're sure it was a hit?"

"A hundred percent. Lorcan Cobbe, identified by an eyewitness and through security footage —"

Whitney held up a finger. "I know that name. How do I know that name?"

"Most alphabet agencies on the planet know that name, sir. He's suspected of multiple hits in multiple countries. He works primarily in Europe, is an Irish citizen. Roarke —"

"Son of a bitch!"

The angry curse, the way Whitney shoved away from his desk, had Eve snapping to attention, and into silence. Whitney rarely lost his composure, and now, with his face thunderous, he paced in front of his glass wall and those shining towers.

"I know that goddamn name." He strode to his office door, flung it open. "Get Captain Feeney in here. Now." Slammed it shut.

"Home invasion, three dead. Adam and Ellen Solomen and their sixteen-year-old son, Thaddeus. The wife and son had their throats slit. Solomen was tortured, then gutted and left to bleed out. Feeney and I caught the case."

"You and Feeney? When you were partners?"

"No, after. It was about twenty years ago. Feeney had Homicide, I had Organized Crime, and I'd turned Solomen. He worked for Colin Boswell — human trafficking, illegals, protection racket — New York, London, Dublin. Solomen was his accountant, and my confidential informant. I'd started building a case on Boswell's racket in New York. Feeney and I worked it jointly."

Calmer, he walked to his office friggie, took out two tubes of water. He tossed Eve one. "One of the assassins also suffered a

wound. Left some blood behind. Come!"
he called at the knock.

Feeney stepped in, gave Eve a nod. "Dallas. Commander."

"Lorcan fucking Cobbe," Whitney said, and gulped down water.

Eve watched Feeney's droopy, bassethound eyes scrunch up in puzzlement. He scratched fingers through his explosion of silver-threaded ginger hair.

And she saw the memory flash back. "Stabbing in Washington Square last night? McNab's working the e's, but I didn't get the details yet. It was Cobbe?"

"Catch him up," Whitney ordered before he went to his desk, swiveled to his comp, and began to work.

"Galla Modesto, professional hit," Eve began, and ran through the details to the point she'd left off with Whitney.

She glanced at Whitney, who sat scanning the screen, scowling at it. He wound a finger through the air to signal her to continue.

"Roarke was with me on scene. We were at a play thing when I got the call. He ID'd Cobbe in the crowd. Cobbe made sure he did, then poofed. Roarke knew him in Dublin when they were boys. Cobbe's a few years older, and claimed he was Patrick Roarke's son. As far as Roarke knows,

Patrick Roarke never acknowledged this connection, but Cobbe worked for his . . . organization. Easiest to say Cobbe had it in for Roarke because he was the acknowledged son, and due to an incident where Roarke ratted him out for slicing up a dog."

"A dog?" Feeney repeated.

"Yeah, another kid's dog that objected when Cobbe tried to beat the crap out of the kid for the change in his pocket. They had one other confrontation Roarke mentioned, years later."

Feeney stuck his hands in the pockets of his rumpled brown jacket. "You figure he'll go after your man?"

"I think he'll try. He's not stupid, but it's a deep-seated grudge. He revered Patrick Roarke, and Roarke rejected him, or at least wouldn't acknowledge paternity. I think he'll also look toward getting even with the person who became Roarke's father."

"Summerset." Feeney nodded. "And you."

"Yeah, Roarke figures that. You want to pay back an enemy, kill what he loves. You end him after that, but he suffers first. I'm consulting with Mira shortly on the profile, but that fits what I know so far. What I didn't know is you and the commander had your round with him. I hadn't looked that far back yet."

"What's it, twenty goddamn years, Jack?"

"Yeah, it's twenty goddamn years. Where'd I stop?" Whitney pinched the bridge of his nose. "The partner on the hit. Thomas Ivan."

"Big Tom Ivan. Big as a freighter, dumb as a broken brick."

"And dead as Moses," Whitney finished. "We ID'd him from the blood he left on scene, tracked him. That wasn't hard, as he was holed up in his flop, dying from the wound that had gone septic."

He waved a hand for Feeney to take over.

"We got him to the hospital, and they did what they could, but the infection'd burned right through him. Asshole packed the wound with a sock, fixed it with duct tape. We got Cobbe's name out of him though. He claimed Cobbe did all the killing, including giving him that jab in the liver. Claimed he punched Cobbe good for it, but the kid — he couldn't've been more than twenty, twenty-couple — ran off laughing."

"The nine-one-one on it came in less than thirty minutes after Solomen's TOD," Whitney added. "Anonymous tip. We figured Cobbe got himself clear and hoped we'd catch Ivan still on scene. Ivan said Cobbe must have picked his pocket when he jabbed him, because his wallet was gone."

Feeney pointed toward the friggie. "Got anything sweet to drink in there?"

"Have you met my wife?"

"Ha. Right." Settling, Feeney took Eve's water tube, glugged some, passed it back. "Cobbe already had a sheet in Ireland, and we pushed on the Dublin cops. Sticking point? All we had was the word of a dead man with his own sheet. Ivan either didn't know who hired him for the hit or just wouldn't turn on Boswell. And we're talking a bad time in Dublin, corruption, and plenty of cops on Boswell's payroll or somebody like him. We couldn't get extradition. No record of Cobbe traveling outside Ireland, witnesses who swore he was with them at the time of the murders."

"We knew he'd killed three people, but we couldn't touch him." Whitney stared straight ahead. Looking back, Eve thought.

"I squeezed Solomen into weaseling for me. He paid for it. His wife and sixteen-year-old son paid for it. Big Tom Ivan paid for it. Cobbe never did."

"You did the job, Jack," Feeney reminded him. "Solomen knew what he was doing when he signed up with a shit like Boswell, and when he turned on him."

"The kid played basketball and wanted to be an astronomer. He had a telescope in his room, models of the solar system."

"You can't carry that," Feeney began.

"We always carry it, Ryan. We're not worth the badge if we don't. He's been busy the last twenty years." Whitney tapped his comp screen. "And now he's on our turf again. What do you need?" he asked Eve.

"Whatever the agencies keeping files on him have."

"I'll make it so."

"Permission to attach Roarke to this investigation, and to assign him a weapon."

When Whitney raised his eyebrows, Eve stepped carefully. "Officially, sir. He will be a target and should, legally, have the means to defend himself."

"I believe he already has plenty of means, but I'll put that through."

She turned to Feeney. "I could use all the time and assistance you can give me."

"No question of that."

"I'm bringing in Tween this afternoon, and will have a warrant and a search team at his home while he's here. I could use quick work on any e's, any communication between him and Cobbe, any leads as to how he found Cobbe and contacted him. Any —"

"You figure you have to tell me what to look for, kid?"

"No. I —" Her 'link signaled a text. "Give me a sec."

She pulled it out, read the communication. Shook her head. "Arrogant and greedy," she muttered. "Roarke's letting me know Tween just put the painting Modesto bought from Stowe up for sale. I gave Tween a flick on the painting last night, as it was on the wall in the room where I notified him. He knew about the artist, the painting. He couldn't leave it in his house, but didn't just burn the damn thing. Might as well make a profit, help offset the killing fee."

She put the 'link away. "I have the victim's family coming in at noon. Morris will have the body ready for them after we speak. As of this morning, Tween hasn't contacted the ME's office."

"He doesn't even pretend to give a shit," Feeney decided. "Send me what you've got. I'll have an e-team ready when you get your warrant."

"I will." She turned to Whitney. She thought about the weight, because he had it right. You always carried it. "We'll bring him down, sir."

"I depend on it."

5

Eve double-timed it back to Homicide. Swinging into the bullpen, she snapped, "Peabody!" and headed toward her office.

She almost made it.

Baxter rushed over. "Sorry, LT, I know you're tight for time, but my boy and I need to follow a lead."

"Then follow it."

"To some Bumfuck town out in nowhere rural Maryland. I need you to sign off for the shuttle trip, then a rental car because there's no shuttle service in Bumfuck nowhere."

She gestured for the tablet he held out, used her finger to scrawl her name. "Why?"

"Guy got himself beat to death and stuffed in a commercial recycler behind a hell of a good Italian restaurant over by Union Square. Wits saw a red rattletrap '52 Muscleman coupe go screaming off about ten minutes after official TOD of said beat-to-death guy, who was also known for transferring ill-gotten goods out of New York. One of his known associates in the trade, one Frankie Nalley, lives in Bumfuck and has a red rattletrap '52 Muscleman coupe registered in his name."

"Go get him," Eve advised, and continued to her office.

Peabody stood waiting, two mugs of coffee in hand. "I took a chance."

"In this case, good call." Eve took the coffee. "Take the crap chair because I don't have time to be nice." Eve dropped down at her desk while Peabody sat, gingerly, on the ass-biting visitor's chair.

"Twenty years ago Whitney and Feeney worked a joint investigation on a triple homicide home invasion. Solomen: Adam, Ellen, and Thaddeus. Look up the file, familiarize yourself. Cobbe's the one who got away."

"Cobbe? No shit?"

"None. I need to write all this up, update the board. Get the file, get the details. And send a copy to Mira now. Whitney's going to work the alphabets, and he's got a personal stake, so it'll get done soon. Additionally, Tween's put the Stowe painting hanging in his wife's room up for sale."

"He doesn't waste time."

"The Modestos are coming in at noon. Get a conference room."

"And neither do you."

No time to waste, she thought — and considering the vic's family, realized she needed to make them as comfortable as possible.

"Transfer some of my coffee in there."

"Yay!"

"And some tea that doesn't taste like piss. I have some of Mira's in my AC. While I'm with Mira, contact Reo — she's going to be in court — and let her know we have enough to arrest Tween and for the search warrant, which will include the seizure of all e's.

"Take your coffee, get on it."

As the chair bit both ways, Peabody stood up just as gingerly. "I'll text you which conference room in case you run over with Mira."

"Good. With this new data, I might."

Eve wrote up the notes on her meeting, sent a copy to Roarke. Then she dug up the old file, printed out the photos of the victims, of the crime scene, of Big Tom Ivan, and of Lorcan Cobbe, age twenty.

She studied the young Cobbe, and though she searched — objectively — found no familial resemblance between him and

Roarke. She'd have termed Cobbe handsome, somewhat smooth at twenty — if she didn't count his eyes.

Either he hadn't cared or hadn't been skilled enough to hide the killer in them.

She added them all to her board.

After a quick glance at the time, she did a run on Colin Boswell, then decided to save it for later when she noted he'd died — stabbed, bludgeoned, and tossed in the river in Dublin fifteen years before.

No doubt a man like Boswell had accumulated plenty of enemies; she wondered if Cobbe had decided eliminating the top guy was a way to move up.

She considered texting Roarke, then just tagged him. If it went to v-mail, she'd —

"Lieutenant."

His face came on-screen, and she could admit a measure of relief. Safe. Of course he was safe, but it didn't hurt to verify it.

"I sent you a report."

"I see, yes, but haven't had a chance to look it over as yet."

"Cobbe was in New York twenty years ago, likely working for a Colin Boswell."

"Boss Boswell. Now, there's a name I know."

"I thought you would. He and some enforcer from New York killed Boswell's accountant, wife, and teenage son. The accountant was doubling as Whitney's weasel."

"Is that so? Links and shadows everywhere."

"Whitney and Feeney worked the investigation. Read my notes. I may need more data on Boswell, what you can tell me about him, what I might not find in the file. You're to be assigned to this investigation and assigned a weapon."

He actually laughed. "I don't believe I'll comment on that particular aspect over the 'link."

"Your police issue will be for defense purposes," she said firmly. "I'll have Tween in the box this afternoon."

"What time?"

"Between fourteen and fifteen hundred hours. Reo's in court until fourteen hundred and I want her here for this. Keep an eye on that art sale."

"I don't have to. I bought the painting."

"You —"

"It's good work," he said easily, "and I felt it shouldn't go to someone who didn't understand its value."

"That's sentimental slosh."

"Perhaps. But as I said, I know Galla's brother a little. When this is done, he might want to have it, as it meant something to her."

Sometimes sentimental slosh was hard to argue with.

"Okay. I have a consult with Mira. I think it might help if you made time to consult with her, too."

He angled his head. She couldn't claim the man made for an easy read, but she knew suspicion when it blasted her in the face.

"For?"

"Insight into Cobbe. Your insight. Direct from you instead of passed through me. I've got three more faces on my board, Roarke, one of them a minor. They're twenty years gone, but they deserve justice. She may hear something you say in a way that opens something. It's what she does."

"All right then."

"I've got to go, or her scary admin will scold me. I'll keep you updated."

"I'll do the same."

Not a lie, she told herself. Her professional reasons for pushing him to talk to Mira arrowed straight to those four faces on her board.

If her personal reasons tagged along with that, it didn't negate the first.

If she felt a little guilty, she'd just have to

get over it.

She went straight to Mira's office, and though she was right on time, earned a scold anyway from Mira's admin.

"You could have told me you were consulting on one of the commander's old cases as well as a new one."

"I didn't know I would be when we asked for the time."

"The doctor has cleared her schedule. You'll have as much time as you need." The admin tapped her earpiece. "Lieutenant Dallas is here.

"Go right in," she told Eve.

Mira sat at her desk, her brows knitted as she scanned data on her screen. Her hair, rich and thick as mink, swept in loose waves around her face.

She wore lip dye in a popping pink. Maybe as a tribute to spring, Eve thought, or because it mirrored the color of the blouse under the white (not cream) suit.

Her eyes, a soft, pretty blue, lifted to Eve's.

"I'm refreshing myself on the Solomen case. Twenty years can blur the memory."

"Take your time," Eve said, though she hoped the blur faded fast.

"I assisted on the profile. Clinton Jones, since retired, had this office then. He was very good."

She rose, walked to the AutoChef on bright white shoes with the toes and high skinny heels in the exact shade as the shirt, as the lips.

It never failed to astound Eve anyone could think just that minutely about clothes.

She expected Mira to program her favored floral-smelling tea, so it surprised Eve to scent coffee. Good coffee.

"I stocked some of your blend," Mira explained. "I think we both can use it."

"I wouldn't say no."

"Sit. This will be difficult for the commander. I remember how much weight he took on over those three deaths."

"Solomen was his."

"Yes." Mira brought over the coffee in pretty cups, sat in the blue scoop chair facing Eve's. "And now the man responsible for those deaths is back, and has added another."

She sipped coffee, crossed her legs. "Let's start in the present. You seem confident — as I read your notes — you'll break the husband of this victim."

"I am confident. He's weak, arrogant, self-absorbed. And the circumstantial's already piled up past his ass."

"He's an egotist. His wife insulted him by having an affair. It was more about the

104

insult to his ego and manhood than a betrayal. And the person she chose wasn't in or of the same social and financial strata — another insult. His ego is his dominant trait, and therefore his dominant weakness."

"It won't be hard to poke his ego when I have him in the box."

Mira smiled. "No, you're good at it. Understand, too, that divorce was never an option for him. Her death protects his ego and his standing — even adds to his standing. Forgiveness or attempting to repair his marriage, simply impossible to consider. She insulted him, may even at some point would have ended the marriage if he attempted repair. She displayed, with the painting, a constant reminder of that insult, that unacceptable possibility. What choice did he have but to eliminate her?"

"At the same time, he's too weak to confront her."

"Yes, he is weak," Mira agreed. "Though he would see that as strategy, even cunning. Her ending the affair changes nothing," Mira added, sipping her coffee. "Hiring a professional killer? Efficient as he'd see it, and certainly worth the investment, as he would reap all the rewards."

"Her money, the kid, and the kid's money — or the authority over that. Her family's support."

"All of that, and he can rid himself of the housekeeper and nanny, giving him full emotional control of the child, choose replacements that suit his needs."

Mira lifted a hand, let it fall. "On the surface, it is cunning, simply poorly executed."

"He never asked how, specifically, she died, where she was, when he could see her, hasn't contacted the ME about her. He didn't even bother to leave the entrance light on as a pretense he expected her home."

"Poorly executed," Mira repeated. "He's done with her, and it's not in his nature to waste the time and effort. He'll cede arrangements for her to her family, make the necessary appearances, attempt to demonstrate grief, then move on. His marriage to her was a means to an end, as was the child. Her death is precisely the same."

"It's not jealousy or rage. I didn't get either of those from him last night."

"No, as they wouldn't have been there to get. Ego, advancement. His ego has been soothed, and the son is now his key to further advancement."

She paused for more coffee. "Do you have any idea how he made contact with Cobbe?"

"Not yet. Working on it."

"Cobbe," Mira murmured. "Lorcan Cobbe. You can read the initial profile in the Solomen file, so I'll just touch on it. Evidence indicates Ivan told the truth about the killings, as all were due to knife wounds. Ivan didn't use sharps. He used his fists or the occasional blunt instrument in his role of enforcer. Though both the wife and son were killed in their beds, each showed defensive wounds — cuts on their hands. The wife and Solomen shared a bed, and she may have awakened when Cobbe and Ivan entered. The ME report indicates bruising around her mouth — a hand clamped over it. Her death came first."

"Contain the biggest threat — the adult male — with a blow to the head — Ivan. Efficient would have been Cobbe killing the wife simultaneously, before she woke, or fully woke. He opted to let her wake up enough to try to scream before he killed her.

"He wanted her to know."

"Killing a sleeping woman would be unsatisfying for someone who enjoys killing. We did consider his age, potentially his inexperience, but given what Whitney and Feeney were able to learn of his background, Clinton believed it was the former. I agree.

"The son's room was on the opposite side of the house, and it's unlikely he heard anything," Mira continued. "Yet he was also awake when his throat was slit. Unlike his mother, his death came in degrees. Rather than one slice, several. He suffered, and that suffering was deliberate."

Eve had seen their faces now, reviewed the crime scene record.

And could see it all, as clearly as she saw Mira sipping coffee in her perfect white suit.

"Ivan had the target under control, the woman was dead, so Cobbe had more time to enjoy killing the boy."

"Yes. Solomen was brutally beaten over a period of nearly an hour, and also suffered multiple stab wounds. None of the wounds were fatal until the final gut wound — one similar to your current victim's. Solomen was bound and gagged during the torture, indicating the orders weren't to get any information, but to punish him, and kill him along with his family. As Ivan was a long-term and loyal employee of Colin Boswell's, there's no indication, no evidence Boswell ordered his elimination."

Eve brought the photo on her board — the young Cobbe — into her mind.

And she could see it, see just how it had gone down.

"Cobbe stabbed him because he wanted to. All that blood, the entertainment, the high of it all. Why stop? Ivan's a moron, a brute, you're so much smarter. Take his wallet because he was probably stupid enough to put at least part of the payment in there. Then run," Eve considered. "Because even with a hole in him Ivan's strong. Run, get back to Ireland with a solid professional kill under your belt."

Considering, Eve looked at Mira. "Does that jibe for you?"

"Right down the line. He's not driven by ego like Tween, but ego is a factor. He found, at an early age, a profession he enjoys and has a terrible talent for. He grew up in a time and place where law and authority were largely corrupt, and violence a tool. In your report you say he believes he's Patrick Roarke's son."

"Yes, and true son. Oldest son and true heir, I guess you could say. It doesn't wash for me."

Mira arched an eyebrow. "Because?"

"Physically, there's no resemblance — he's got light brown hair, hazel eyes, a heftier build, deeper coloring. The shape of his face, his features — just nothing connects."

"I agree, but genetics can be tricky. And there's no DNA on file for Cobbe."

"If Patrick Roarke believed he had another son, one who admired him, who wanted to be him, he'd have acknowledged him. Ego," Eve repeated. "But the point is Cobbe believes it, and considered Roarke an obstacle, an object he could despise. I'm guessing the fact that his father knocked the hell out of Roarke routinely was not only satisfying to Cobbe but a kind of proof Roarke wasn't the true son. Even when Summerset took Roarke in, Patrick Roarke didn't acknowledge Cobbe as his son, or take him under his roof.

"He had the perfect replacement," Eve said. "And he didn't take him."

"Only more reason for Cobbe to focus his hate on Roarke."

"Roarke gave him a couple more."

She told Mira about the boy and the dog.

"I skimmed over some details in the report on a second incident. I'm keeping them out of my report."

Not unsurprised, Mira simply nodded. "All right. We'll consider this privileged, and I'll keep it out of mine."

"Years later, Roarke ran into Cobbe in a bar in France. Cobbe sat down, confronted him. Poked a knife in his ribs. He wanted money — a lot of it — but more he wanted Roarke to admit Cobbe was Patrick Roarke's true son, and to ditch the name so Cobbe could take it."

"Ah. The money, as I assume when this happened Roarke had begun to accumulate some wealth. But the heart of it? The acknowledgment, the name. This is a fixation." Frowning, Mira leaned forward. "And a dangerous one."

"Yeah. We've all got that."

"How did Roarke respond?"

"He had a stunner — illegal. He already had it under the table, as he knew Cobbe. Basically, he told Cobbe to shove it, then he deployed the stunner, left Cobbe convulsing on the floor, and walked out. It's the last time Cobbe came at him directly."

"I see." Digesting the information, Mira drank more coffee.

"So two instances — and I suspect there were more throughout childhood — when Roarke bested him, humiliated him. Let me add to the original profile. He's accumulated the skill and the contacts to reach a high level of success in his profession. He kills for enjoyment and profit. He lives well, travels well and frequently. He has no friends, but contacts. No loyalty, no center but his work. In spite of his skill, his success, he has never, and will never reach the success Roarke has built. Cobbe must stay in the shadows to work and survive. Roarke lives in the light, has a family, has friendships. And is still the only son Patrick Roarke acknowledged."

And the clear profile, one she'd already built in her own head, still caused ice to ball in her belly.

"It's a bigger word than *jealousy*. It's jealousy mixed with obsession mixed with hate and resentment. When you add in the fear, because it has to be there, it's lethal."

Mira nodded. "I would conclude eliminating or at least displacing Roarke has been Cobbe's goal throughout his life. Why come back to New York? He works, successfully, throughout Europe, is suspected of murders in Australia, Tokyo, India. Yet he takes a job, one that certainly doesn't require his level of skill, here, in New York. Where Roarke lives, where he has his headquarters."

She hadn't gone there, Eve admitted. Maybe she hadn't wanted to.

"You think he took the Modesto job because it brought him to New York, to Roarke?"

"It's possible. What's changed for Roarke over the last three years? He married, something Cobbe may have initially seen as a clever cover, marrying a cop, and one of your level. But if he scratched even a little at the surface, he knows better. Roarke doesn't just have a wife, a cop, but a woman he loves. Something else Cobbe will never have. He's not only built a real family here — and I count Dennis and myself as part of that — but he found his family in Ireland."

"Roarke put security on them."

"I'd say that's wise. No need for Cobbe to go in that direction, for now, but it's a risk. Roarke's not only built a staggeringly successful business organization, on- and off-planet, but he's done good works. The shelter — and though by its nature you've kept the shelter low-key, Cobbe would know. Just as he knows Roarke is about to open a school for children in need."

Eve set the coffee aside, pushed up to pace. "I thought of this, but I've tried to keep a lid on it. Just keep the lid closed and work it. Learning he'd been here twenty years ago and not since, as far as we can find, has shaken the lid off some."

"He couldn't have known or expected Roarke would be on the crime scene last night."

"No, but when he saw Roarke, he couldn't resist."

" 'Here I am,' " Mira said, lifting a hand.

" 'I did that, and was paid handsomely. And I'll do that to you and everyone who matters to you for free.' He's killed most of his life with impunity, and for profit. Roarke's eluded him, but he believes he's ready to change that, to reach that goal. He'll stay in New York until you stop him."

"I will stop him."

"How is Roarke?"

"He's handling it, taking steps. He's —" She broke off, stopped pacing, pressed her fingers to her eyes. "He's worried. Not for himself, because ego. But for me, for the rest."

"And you're worried about him, not for yourself. Ego."

Mira rose, took Eve lightly by the arms. "In both cases the ego's well-founded. You both know there are risks, and you're both equipped to deal with them. You have your considerable skills, Eve, and the entire NYPSD behind you. Roarke has his considerable skills and vast resources. Separately, you're formidable. Together? I would never bet against you."

"It shook him, seeing Cobbe last night. He's almost never thrown off."

"A ghost from the past. It would shake anyone."

"It shook Whitney, too." She breathed out,

and breathed easier for saying it out loud. "Hell, it shook me to see two of the toughest men I know shaken. So that's that end of it."

Eve dropped down in the chair again, scrubbed her hands over her face, raked them back through her hair. "I played him a little — Roarke — over something. Not all the way, because there's a core of truth in it, but I played him to get him to agree to talk to you."

Mira sat again, crossed her legs again. "Well played then."

"It was actually Peabody's idea, but it's a good one. Having him talk to you directly instead of me passing what he knows about Cobbe."

"That's a very solid core of truth. It would be helpful."

"But around that's the squishy part, because I want him — I want you to . . ."

"I understand. Why don't I contact him? I could talk to him early this evening, at your house, where he's comfortable, if he likes. Or at my home. Either is less official than here."

"Yes. Thanks. Thanks. I have to get back. I have the victim's family coming in."

"I'll write the profile, copy it to all parties."

"Okay." Eve rose. "I appreciate the extended time." She started out, stopped. "I don't want you or Mr. Mira to take any chances, I want you to stay aware, but I don't see Cobbe looking at either of you. He wouldn't understand you're family. He wouldn't get that."

"His lack of understanding, of being capable of understanding Roarke or you, is how you'll stop him."

Eve counted on it, worked it all over in her head as she took the glides back to Homicide.

Only Detectives Carmichael and Santiago manned desks — Santiago working his comp, Carmichael her 'link. Baxter and Trueheart were in Maryland, she remembered, Jenkinson and Reineke — according to the bullpen board — in the field.

Peabody prepping the conference room.

"Santiago, Carmichael — both Carmichaels — Shelby, coordinate with EDD on a search and seize. Plan on moving on it at fourteen hundred hours. Take your fine-tooth combs."

"What the hell is a fine-tooth comb?"

"It's a comb with really skinny teeth close together so you don't miss anything," Santiago told her.

"Okay, take those and don't miss any

fucking thing. Modesto homicide. Husband's going to be in the box around fourteen-thirty hours unsuccessfully weaseling his way out of confessing to hiring a hit on his wife.

"Read the file."

The rest she had to say to her squad would wait until all were present and accounted for.

She went to her office, put together the file she wanted for her interview with Tween. Since McNab had come through, she added the text messages. Added the art sale, the shadow account and transfers.

Her comm signaled.

"The Modesto family just arrived. I'm escorting them to conference room two."

"On my way."

She took the time to text Reo.

Search team assigned. Will be ready to roll out by fourteen hundred. Will send officers to bring Tween in for questioning at that time. He's going to lawyer up, so you'll have plenty of time to get to Central for the interview. Put through the warrants.

She made her way down to the conference room, stepped in as Peabody offered the family coffee or tea.

Two men, two women. The older woman — an older version of the victim — wept openly. The younger man — dark hair, green eyes, soft voice murmuring in Italian — comforted her.

The older man — silver hair, long nose, carved-in-stone face — sat stoically, but gripped the hand of the younger woman. Son's wife, Eve thought, blond, blue eyes, what anyone with eyes of their own would call a stunner.

At the moment, she did the talking.

"You're so kind. Please, tea for my mother, and for me. My husband would have coffee, with just a little cream. My father will have black coffee. Thank you."

Eve walked to the table, stood as all eyes shifted to her. "I'm Lieutenant Dallas. We're sorry for your loss. We know this is a very difficult time for all of you, and appreciate you coming in to speak with us."

"Will you find him?" Anna Maria Modesto demanded through her sobs. "Will you find the monster who did this to my baby?"

"My partner and I, and the New York City Police and Security Department, will do everything we can to find the person who took your daughter's life. Coming in to speak with us will help us in our investigation."

"Angelo, our little Angelo, he has no mother now."

"He has you." Stefano pressed his lips to his mother's temple. "He has Tereza. No one can replace Galla, but we'll all look out for Angelo."

"You have a reputation." Antonio arrowed his dark eyes on Eve. He had a commanding voice. His precise and perfect English carried only a trace of accent. "This reputation says to me you will do all necessary to find the one who took Galla from us, from her child, from her husband. From the world. But how? He kills her in a moment, then is gone."

"We're following every lead, Mr. Modesto. Do you know of anyone who'd wish to hurt your daughter?"

"No, no!" He slapped his free hand on the table forcefully enough to make the cups of tea and coffee jump. "This was a moment, do you understand? He doesn't know her, he simply lashes out because she was there. She does no harm to any. My daughter was loving and kind. She was a good wife, a good mother. This one, he kills her without thought."

Eve considered. If she wanted their help, she needed to give them a reason. "We believe there was thought. We believe your daughter, your sister, was specifically targeted."

"Why?" Stefano's incredulous question rang out. "My father is right. Galla was kind. She was a good person, and I can think of no one who would wish her harm. We would tell you, without hesitation, if we did."

"I believe you. Did you know your sister had an affair?"

Again, Antonio slapped a hand on the table, and his face went furiously red. "You would say such a thing?"

"Mr. Modesto, this is a fact that has come to light in the course of our investigation." Even as she spoke, Eve's gaze remained on Tereza's face. "You knew."

"I . . ."

"The truth. You want justice for your sister-in-law? You cared for her? The truth is the weapon needed to defend her now."

Tereza closed her eyes, then pressed her hands to her face. "I'm sorry. I'm sorry." She looked at her husband, tears spilling as she spoke in Italian.

That opened the floodgates to the entire family speaking at once, again in Italian.

"English, please!" Eve held up a hand. "We need to hear what she has to say. You knew," Eve repeated. "Galla told you."

"Yes. I'm sorry. Yes. She was unhappy. Please, you have to understand."

"I'm not here to judge her, but to stand for her. Tell me."

6

"I came to New York, some business, some shopping, a visit for my children and Angelo. We were close, Galla and I. We were sisters. Our children enjoy each other."

"When was the visit?" Eve asked.

"This was late last spring. She was so unhappy, and though she tried to hide it, we were sisters. I could see, and I pressed her to tell me."

She paused, closed her eyes a moment, this woman with strong shoulders and the athletic build of her former profession.

Though tears glimmered in her eyes, she didn't let them spill.

"She told me she felt no love from her husband. She wished to work, but he would not have it."

"She said . . ." Antonio gathered himself. "She told us she wished to step away from the business for a time, to be only a mother to Angelo."

"I know. I think . . ." Tereza rubbed his fisted hand. "I think she said it so we wouldn't think less of Jorge, but she missed the work, missed the family, missed home. And Jorge, she told me, became more distant, more — it would be restrictive. She said he only wished her to present herself as his wife, to attend the social events with him, the business dinners."

She managed a smile at Eve. "She was so beautiful, you see, so charming and knowledgeable about the business. This made her an asset to him, and I think she felt that's what she had become. Only that to him. An asset.

"She wished to take Angelo to Tuscany, to show him his mama's home, but Jorge wouldn't allow it. He worked very much, and gave her little time. She was lonely, and she missed her family, her home. She had no real friends, as he wished her only to socialize with the wives of clients, to take them to lunch or host parties."

"Why didn't she tell me? I'm her mama."

Tereza turned to Anna Maria. "She didn't want to disappoint you. You didn't want her to marry so soon, to marry Jorge without more time. And still when she wanted him, you gave your blessing. You were right, Mama. Galla said to me you were right. But

123

she had married him, and they had a son. She asked for my promise not to tell you or Papa, not even to tell you, *mi amore.* I'm sorry."

"Do you think I'd be angry with you for keeping your word to my sister? For giving her comfort when she was unhappy?"

"I told her, come back with me. I would help her bring the baby home, but she wouldn't. She said she couldn't take her husband's son from him. And then . . ."

She rubbed a hand over her heart. "Is there water, please?"

"I'll get you some." Peabody rose, walked to where she'd stacked tubes of water. "She was lucky to have you. To have someone to talk to."

"Thank you. Thank you. It was weeks later. We kept in closer contact after the visit. I tried to speak to her or write with her every day if I could. She told me she'd met someone, an artist. She bought one of his paintings — one of home. She would go for walks, or for runs — this was an outlet. And she met him when she was walking. They became friendly. They became more. And she was happy. She found love. She knew it was wrong to break her vows."

Her family said nothing as she stopped to drink some water.

"She thought of divorce, of going back home to see if her heart stayed with the artist. Then she thought, again, of her vows, and the child she had made with her husband. Though she was happy, she knew she couldn't simply end her marriage, break her family. She had to try to mend it. She tells me all this. Tells me, a week or two ago — two, I think — she ended her love affair. She said her lover wept with her, and so I wept with her."

Tereza closed her eyes. "I wept with her because I think she makes a mistake, and should have gone with her heart. I don't say this to her. I think I wish I had."

She fought back tears, drank water before turning to her father-in-law. She spoke softly in Italian. He shook his head, drew her toward him, kissed her temple.

Then he straightened in his chair, those dark eyes burning into Eve's. "You think this artist killed her because she ended it?"

"No, sir, I don't. She went to the park that night to meet him, at his request. But —" she said as the rage came back into his face. "He asked her to meet him to say goodbye with a gift. A painting to be a companion to the one she'd bought when they'd met. He came forward to me, and told me what your daughter-in-law has just confirmed. He had the painting. I believe his grief was as real as yours. More, the evidence we have doesn't support his involvement in her death."

"Jorge." Unlike Antonio's wife, Anna Maria's face had gone stark white. "There is coldness in him. Galla couldn't see it. She was blind to it, but there is coldness in him."

"We have no evidence that places him in the park at the time of her death. All evidence indicates he was at home, never left the residence that evening. However, we'll interview him extensively.

"Mr. Modesto?"

"*Sì?*"

"Your daughter-in-law keeps her word. Do you?"

"If I give my word, I do not break it."

"I need the word of everyone at this table. Everyone here who loved Galla, who wants justice for her, that what we discuss now won't leave this room. That no one in this room takes any action that will interfere with this investigation."

"You'll have it." Antonio looked down the table. "She has the word of the Modesto family. It won't be broken."

"Peabody, put Cobbe on-screen. Lorcan Cobbe," Eve said as Peabody got up to do so. "Is that name familiar to anyone?"

"I know of no one by that name," Antonio told her as the others shook their heads. "Is this who killed my daughter?"

"Yes."

"Why? Why would this man kill Galla?"

"Because it's his job. Lorcan Cobbe." Eve gestured to the screen, and his ID shot. "A professional killer. We have evidence he was in the park. We have evidence he was hired to kill Galla. Do any of you recognize this man?"

"I've never seen that face," Stefano said. "He kills for money? Who would — ?"

He broke off, and, like his mother, went very pale.

"What did you remember?" Eve demanded.

"It must be nothing, nothing. It was a joke."

"What was?"

"Jorge was in Rome for meetings, a presentation. After many meetings, the long presentation, I took him for drinks. He says, poor joke, where is the Mafia when we need it? We have a competitor who is undercutting our prices, and he jokes we need — how does he put it? — we need the men in the black limousine to take them out, for good.

"In this spirit — we had a very long, difficult day — I joke back. We only contact Bellacore — Salvadore Bellacore."

At his father's hiss of breath, Stefano lifted his hands. "I know, Papa, a very poor joke."

"Who's Bellacore?"

"From the old mafioso," Stefano told her. "He is very old, retired — and no longer in prison, where he spent many years. It's said he has a fine villa in Sardinia. It's also said — and this I tell Jorge — he knows the cutthroats, and where to find them, as he was one himself. There are rumors that he brokers such matters in his retirement. I said all this. Did I give him this idea?"

"I have no doubt he already had the idea. Can you pinpoint the date of this conversation?"

"In March, in the third week of March. I can check for exact."

"That's exact enough. Excuse me a minute. Peabody, continue."

Eve stepped out of the room, tagged Roarke.

"Check Tween's account for March, the third week and forward. I'm looking for a payment, a kind of consultant fee. It's probably covered, but it would be to a Salvadore Bellacore."

"Bellacore the broker. I should've thought of him myself, but he's a hundred and ten if he's a day. Hold a moment."

Since he cut her to waiting blue, she paced. But he was back in seconds.

"March twenty-fourth, ten thousand euros transferred to Bellacore."

"Jesus, he didn't try to cover it?"

"It's to Bellacore's farm — oranges, olives, lemons. Which, with a bit of time, I could break down as a front for the brokerage. Is this helpful?"

"Bet your fine Irish ass. Send me the file. Talk later.

"Got you, fucker," she said after she clicked off.

She stepped back in while Peabody asked about Galla's will.

"She spoke to me about this after Angelo was born." Stefano rubbed his eyes. "Her portion of the business, she wanted to go to her son, in trust. She asked me to be in charge of the trust. Her estate, the money, stocks, properties, were to be divided between her husband and her son, with some specific bequests to family, to charities, to Elena Rinaldi, who was her housekeeper, to Sofia Grinaldi, who is Angelo's nanny."

"Did she name guardians for her son in the event something happened to both her and his father?" Peabody asked.

"Tereza and I, yes. We have two children,

Angelo's cousins. She wanted him with family, of course."

"He will not have the child." Anna Maria spoke in a voice of cold, quiet steel. "If he is responsible for this, he will not have her child."

"Here's what I need you to do," Eve began. "Go see your daughter, your sister. Do not contact Tween. If he attempts to contact you, don't respond at this time. It would help if after you've seen Galla, you went to your apartment. I need that information. I'll come to you there when I have anything more to tell you."

"Roarke arranged a suite for us at the Regent, as the apartment isn't large enough for the family all together."

"Did he?"

"We're acquainted," Stefano told her. "He contacted me to express his condolences, and to tell me I could trust you, your partner, your people to get justice for Galla."

"And you can. Do you need transportation?"

"We have our own."

Eve rose. "Detective Peabody will escort you out."

Antonio got to his feet. "I can thank you for your kindness, and I do. But I don't care about kindness from you now. I want your fierceness."

"You'll have it." When they left, Eve studied Cobbe on-screen. "And so will you."

When she walked into Homicide, she gestured for Peabody to follow her into her office.

"They're a good family," Peabody commented. "The kid's going to be okay with them."

"Unless we really fuck this up, he'll be with them by dinnertime. Tween paid Salvadore Bellacore ten thousand on March twenty-fourth."

"Well, kick my ass! I don't want to jinx it but this is almost too easy."

"Cobbe's a different fish in the kettle."

"It's a different kettle of fish."

"Neither one makes any sense." Eve sat at her desk, pressed the heel of her hand to her temple.

"You okay?"

"Half a headache. Any one of them does something different, she's still alive. But you can't say that, and anyway, any one of them does something different, she could still be dead because she fell in the shower or something."

Peabody turned to the AutoChef, hit menu, programmed what wouldn't be ignored by her lieutenant.

"We're having pepperoni pizza because we're both hungry, and we need to be sharp and focused to take this asshole down."

"I need to write this up."

"I can do it."

"No, I need you to contact Child Services, get somebody who's not a dick, and make sure any paperwork will be expedited when we lock the asshole up so we can get the kid to his family."

"I can do that." She put a slice and a tube of Pepsi on Eve's desk. She eyed the visitor's chair, then decided to have her own slice standing up.

"We can throw Italians, or Interpol or whoever works best, at Bellacore. It's a nice exchange." Eve checked her incomings for anything from Whitney.

Not yet.

Even as she finished the slice, thought maybe she could go for another, she got an incoming from Reo.

"Defense asked for and was granted a recess until ten tomorrow. I'm putting the warrants through, and on my way to Central."

"Copy that," Eve answered. "Arrest warrant: conspiracy to commit murder, murder in the first."

"Solid on that?"

"Solid. Briefing in my office on arrival. We got him cold."

Headache gone, or almost, Eve swiveled in the chair. "Get a couple of female officers to execute the warrant and bring him in."

"Females specifically?"

"Fucker used a woman to advance his career, social status, and line his pockets. Then he had her gutted. Female cops? He'll consider it more of an insult. It's petty, but I feel petty."

"I'll get on it, but I have to finish this. If I go out there with even a piece of pizza crust, it might start a riot. We're going for the gold with Tween?"

"That's right, because we'll plead it down."

On a cough, Peabody thumped a fist to her chest. "I almost choked on my last bite of pizza. You want to plead it down?"

"We start with two consecutive life sentences, off-planet. We give them room to take it down to concurrent, possible parole in thirty, if he not only flips on Cobbe but gives information that leads to Cobbe's arrest. He's an asshole, and deserves to spend his life in a cage. He's also weak, and the possibility of getting out in thirty, still having some kind of life? He'll take it. We get Cobbe out of it, or he does it all."

Eve downed some Pepsi. "And that doesn't address additional charges, after the thirty, which the alphabets may hit him with. I can live with it."

She swiveled back. "Go."

Eve hammered out a report, adding the payment to the broker as well as the timing of it, the known details of the will, the corroboration of the affair, its ending.

Reo walked in as she sent it.

"I smell pizza. Why did I scarf down a street dog on my way here? I still have room for decent coffee."

"Get it. Sit. Take the desk." Eve rose to vacate it. She remembered her tube of Pepsi, retrieved it.

She briefed Reo as she added Bellacore's ID shot to her board.

"Well, well, well, when you said solid, you meant it. He's not going to be able to explain those payments away. You don't have ID on the numbered account in Andorra?"

"If it can be got, Roarke'll get it. The timing of all three payments is going to choke the bastard. And I can guarantee the search team's going to find more. He's an arrogant son of a bitch. He honestly doesn't think anybody's going to look. After all, he was in bed with a headache. Here's where I won't be surprised: if we find payments to a PI somewhere along the line. He could've buried that in a business account, charged it to Modesto. Roarke's got enough going, but if it's there, the team's going to find it.

"I'll break him. Then you deal."

Reo flicked imaginary lint off her pinstriped skirt. "You want me to deal?"

"I want Cobbe."

"So do half the law enforcement agencies on-planet — I did some research."

"And won't it be sweet if the APA of New York City has a part in bringing down an international assassin?"

Reo sipped coffee, smiled. "It wouldn't hurt my feelings. Concurrent sentences, possibility of parole in fifty."

"Thirty. He needs incentive, needs to believe he can have a life outside."

"It's sure interesting being on the other side of this argument. "Thirty-five. Dallas, he had his wife, the mother of his young son, gutted in a public park. I can't go lower."

"Thirty-five," Eve agreed. "He won't get out in thirty-five. He's an asshole. He'll screw up. And I can promise in thirty-five when and if he's up, Galla's family will speak at his parole hearing. He'll do forty

135

— and then he'll do more on other charges. He used international banking to buy the hit."

"Aren't you the clever one?"

"That's why I make the crappy bucks. If he ever gets out, he'll get out broke and broken. Galla's son will be raised by family, by good people in the home she loved. We get Cobbe, we'll have gotten her justice, and that's the job."

"That's the job. Let me do some work here, and we'll take him after he's booked and lawyered up."

"Take the room. I need to brief the search team."

It didn't surprise her to find the captain of EDD in her bullpen along with McNab.

"Whitney's working his way through red tape," Feeney told her. "Better him than me. He said he'd have some data for you by end of shift."

"Good. I need you and McNab to do as much as you can on the e's in the residence. Financial data — hoping for a payment to a PI or an investigative firm. He'll have his own safe — that's his type. Get it open. If he didn't contact Cobbe with his personal 'links, he'll have a clone in a safe. Who's handling his office e's?"

"I got two on that. Callendar and Rosco."

"Make sure they check financials, and any clones. Santiago, both Carmichaels, Shelby, front and center."

While she briefed her team, her 'link signaled. "Hold on," she ordered when she read the display. "Dallas."

"Lieutenant Dallas! They have arrested Signore Tween! The police, they come to the door. They —"

"I know, Ms. Rinaldi. I sent them."

"Oh! What should I do? He shouts at me, he orders me to contact his lawyer, Mr. Milton Barkley."

"Go ahead and do that. You can tell the lawyer Mr. Tween is being booked at Cop Central. Where's the boy, ah, Angelo?"

"He has a nap. He is upstairs with his nanny. He doesn't understand where his mother has gone, why his nanny and I must leave."

"Do you have Stefano Modesto's contact number?"

"Yes. Yes, of course, but —"

"Contact him, tell him the situation. He can take Angelo with him to his hotel in New York."

"Oh! *Grazie a Dio!*"

"The police are coming with a search warrant. Let them in when they get there. After the minor child is with his guardian, you and the nanny are free to leave."

"I will tell Sofia, the nanny. We will pack for Angelo. So many thanks to you, Lieutenant Dallas."

"It's my job. I'll get back to you." She clicked off. "Peabody, let Child Services know Tween's in custody and the minor child will be with his legal guardian. Any questions?" she asked the team.

"We've got it," Santiago told her.

"Move out."

She walked back to her office, barked at Reo, "He got a lawyer on tap. Milton Barkley."

"Give me a minute." Reo toggled over to search on her PPC. "Hmm. Prestigious, but corporate. Not criminal. Which says Tween doesn't have or know a criminal attorney. Barkley will bring one with him."

"I need my desk."

"I'm about done anyway. I'm cleared to deal to the thirty-five. I know how to work it," Reo added. "And I know how to play it with you and Peabody. I expect you'll fling some impressive insults my way for my bullshit lawyering."

"It's so easy to insult lawyers."

Reo tapped a finger in the air at her, rose. "I'll find a desk in the bullpen."

At her desk, Eve added to the file she'd

take into Interview. As she reviewed its contents, Roarke came in.

"Hey. Didn't expect to see you."

"I have some business nearby, but have a window right now." He moved to her Auto-Chef. "Coffee?"

"Is that an actual question?"

He programmed two. "Galla Modesto owned a farmhouse in the Chianti region of Tuscany. A few acres, working gardens, a small vineyard, a custodian's cottage, a lovely view. He has it listed for sale."

"He really is an asshole."

"He's also given the custodians three weeks to vacate."

He wandered to her skinny window, looked out while he drank his coffee. "He's also listed her flat in Florence. She has a young cousin, an art student, currently living there. She was given a month to vacate."

"We can and will block all that."

"You will," he murmured, still looking out the window. "Aye, you will. Money and property, they were desperate needs of mine. Now it's business, and it's pleasure, and the game of it. But at one time it was survival, and that desperate need. But there's a difference between need and greed, isn't there?"

"Yeah." Because he needed it, she rose,

went to him, wrapped her arms around him from the back. "I've got him, Roarke. Trust me."

"Oh, I do." He closed a hand over hers.

"And I'll get Cobbe. We'll get Cobbe," she corrected.

"For him, it's business and it's pleasure and the game of it as well."

She could feel it in him, that tension, that anger, that grief all swollen together.

"That doesn't make him anything like you."

"We sprang from the same alleys and slums, had our lives dominated as children by the same man. And for a time, we ran on parallel paths."

"Bollocks to that. Did you ever kill for money?"

"No. That I can say, that at least, was never in me."

He turned, pressed his lips to her brow, then moved away. "I can confirm Cobbe in Amsterdam three weeks ago. A businessman with interest in an upscale bordello, a popular sex club, and other enterprises of that nature died in what police are calling a bungled break-in. Under that public stance, Cobbe is the prime suspect."

"Under that."

"The unfortunate businessman suffered a

severe facial beating and multiple stab wounds. All incurred after his throat was slit. The investigators believe the bungled aspect of the break-in was staged after the murder. An hour after time of death, Cobbe visited the bordello using one of the VIP passes the victim often presented to friends or clients, enjoyed the services of two of the ladies employed there and a bottle of Cristal."

"Bold fucker."

"And always was. They've yet to find how he entered or left the city."

"It's still another brick in the wall. I need the name of the primary on it."

"You'll have it."

"Meanwhile Tween's being booked for conspiracy to murder and murder. Once he's consulted with his lawyer or lawyers, I'll have him in the box."

"Fast work, Lieutenant."

"You contacted Stefano Modesto."

"I did. It seemed . . . appropriate."

"It was more than appropriate. He and his family appreciated your offer of accommodations while they deal with this loss. His wife knew about the affair, and held her sister-in-law's confidence. I got it out of her, and it confirms Stowe's account down the line. Anything, anything at all Tween knows about Cobbe, I'll have."

"You're worrying about me." After setting his coffee aside, he gripped her shoulders, gave them a light shake. "Stop. You have a job to do."

"The Marriage Rules clearly require me to worry about you when applicable."

It made him laugh. So he released her shoulders to take her face in his hands and kiss her. Long, hard, deep.

"Expert consultant, civilian, fraternizing with the primary investigator while said investigator's on duty is a violation." Now she took his face in turn. "Might as well do it again."

And when she had, he held on another moment. "You're the heart of me." He drew back. "I wish I could stay and watch you take on this particular asshole, but I've already shifted and juggled quite a bit today."

"I'll give you the highlights at home."

"I count on it. I may be a bit late. If more than a bit, I'll let you know."

"Same."

"One day," he said as he started out, "you might send me a copy of those Marriage Rules."

As Roarke had, she wandered to the window. An airtram dipped by close enough she could spot the bored faces of locals, the thrilled ones of tourists.

Below, pedestrians and vehicles swarmed the streets and sidewalks. Somewhere out there Cobbe walked or rode or hid while he plotted the death of the man she loved.

She'd find him. There was nothing more important in her work, her life, her world than finding Lorcan Cobbe and locking the cage door behind him.

She'd take down Tween. That was the job, that was duty, that was justice. And she'd use him to help her reach the bigger goal.

She heard Peabody coming, didn't turn.

"Tween's booked, and consulting with his lawyers. That's Milton Barkley and Denise Gotte. Gotte's criminal defense. She joined Patterson and Franks — now Patterson, Franks, and Gotte — as full partner six months ago. She relocated from Atlanta."

"Okay. We're ready when they are."

7

Just over an hour later, Eve walked into Interview A.

"Record on. Dallas, Lieutenant Eve, and Peabody, Detective Delia, entering Interview with Tween, Jorge, and his legal representatives on the matter of case number H-32108."

She sat at the scarred table across from Tween. His lawyers flanked him. "Mr. Tween, you've been arrested on charges of the conspiracy to murder and the murder, in the first degree, of your wife, Galla Modesto. Have you been read your rights, and do you understand your rights and obligations in this matter?"

Gotte answered. She was a sturdily built woman of fifty-three with a short, sleek cap of blond hair and marble-hard blue eyes.

Her voice, as hard as her eyes, held no hint of Atlanta.

"My client has been informed of his rights

and understands them perfectly. He denies, absolutely and clearly, any involvement in the tragic and violent death of his wife, and is appalled — as is his counsel — that you would levy these ridiculous charges and add to his grief."

"Right. Well, his denial is bullshit."

"We won't tolerate that sort of abusive language or behavior."

"You're going to tolerate a lot more before we're finished."

"Lieutenant." Barkley, a dark-skinned man of sixty with a handsome head of curling hair dashed with silver, held up a hand. "I've been Mr. Tween's attorney for nearly ten years. I knew Galla, and am shocked and saddened by her death, by the violence of it. I ask you to respect the tragedy of this situation."

"I will always respect the victim, Mr. Barkley. Mr. Tween, when my partner and I notified you last night about your wife's murder, you stated you had no knowledge of the affair she'd engaged in and subsequently broken off."

"My client maintains he had no knowledge. Your attempt to use the victim's transgression as my client's motive is ludicrous." Gotte tapped an imperious finger on the table. "My client's home security discs show he did not leave the house after his arrival home at six-thirty that evening. He —"

"Nobody said he left the house." Eve opened the file, took out — thank you, Feeney — a copy of a report — with photos — from a private investigator.

"However, on November sixteenth of last year, you hired Oscar Gill Investigations with instructions to shadow your wife. Why did you do that, Mr. Tween?"

"That's none of your business."

"It's exactly my business." She spread the contents out. "This report is a copy of the report sent to you by Oscar Gill, for which you paid him — through your Modesto Wine and Spirits expense account — eight thousand, three hundred and twenty-five dollars. Do you consider hiring a private investigator to follow and photograph your wife a business expense?"

"That's my property. That's my personal and private business."

"Accessed through a duly issued and executed warrant." Eve took out a copy of that, slid it toward Gotte. "You didn't answer the question, Mr. Tween."

Gotte held up a finger to keep him silent as she read the warrant, then glanced at the report, at the photos of Galla strolling hand in hand with Stowe, of a shared kiss, an embrace, obviously taken with a long lens through an apartment window.

Gotte leaned toward Tween, spoke in his ear. Face furious, he muttered in hers.

The lawyer's not happy, Eve observed. She didn't have a cheery face to begin with, but Eve knew pissed off when she saw it.

Nobody liked being lied to.

"My client denied knowledge of the affair in an attempt to protect his wife's reputation, to spare her family."

"So he lied."

"He had just learned of his wife's murder. He —"

"Actually, he learned about it approximately twenty minutes after the murder. The warrant also authorizes the police to open any and all locks or safes in the residence. We found your clone 'link, Mr. Tween, which still held a number of messages to and from another clone. The final message to you on this clone also contained a photo. Do you have a copy of that message and photo, Detective Peabody?"

"I do." Peabody opened her own file. "The message reads: 'Proof of completion. Wire final payment as agreed.' And offers this as proof."

She laid the copy in the middle of the

table. "As you can see, the first responders were on scene, working to secure and preserve it, but it's a clear shot of Galla Modesto with her gut ripped open. You got what you paid for, Tween."

"They planted it. They planted it all."

"Right, several members of the NYPSD decided to plant evidence. Such as the two payments you made to a numbered account in Andorra. The first two weeks ago, the second on the night of Galla's murder. Like this additional piece of evidence here: your payment to Salvadore Bellacore, a criminal broker — a man who, for a fee, matches clients with the enforcer of their needs. That one's from March of this year. The local police in Sardinia are having a conversation with Sal as we speak. He'll roll on you and back again."

Gotte snatched the copy. "This is to a farm in Sardinia."

"Bellacore's farm, and his cover. I happen to have a copy of his sheet. It's a long one. You might also want to take a look at the earlier communications on the clone, where your client gets his first message from someone using the name Blade — funny, as that's his weapon of choice. That message logs in on April nineteenth, sets the terms of one million euros plus expenses. Half to be transferred immediately to the aforementioned account, the other half, with expenses, to be wired immediately following proof of completion."

She shoved more copies across the table, and just kept hammering.

"You're welcome to read the transcripts of their communications wherein the hired killer asks for information on the target, and is provided with same. Wherein the hired killer asks if the client wishes the wife's lover dispatched for an additional fee, and the client declines. Wherein the professional killer sought by, hired by, and paid by Jorge Tween — as is evidenced by a shadow account under that name — confirms his arrival in New York two days before the killing. And wherein your fucking client informs the professional killer of his wife's plans to meet Marlon Stowe in Washington Square Park, at what time, and at what place in the park, with the order to complete the job at that time."

Eve shoved the entire file across the table. "It didn't matter that she'd broken off the affair, was meeting Stowe to say a last goodbye. She'd insulted you, and you couldn't tolerate it. You couldn't opt for divorce, because she had buckets of money compared to you, and the only way to get it was as her widower."

"This is all lies! All fabricated. The Modestos put her up to this! Clearly, they're paying her off. They —"

"Be quiet," Gotte snapped. "Not another word. We need to consult with our client."

"I bet you do." Eve rose. "Just FYI, Tween, putting your wife's property in Tuscany, in Florence up for sale while she's in a drawer at the morgue? Cold and obvious. Also blocked."

"You didn't even bother to go see her," Peabody said as she rose. "You couldn't even pretend to give a damn."

"Dallas and Peabody exiting Interview. Record off."

Outside, Eve leaned back against the wall.

"I didn't expect you to hit him with all of that in the first round," Peabody commented.

"Did you watch Gotte? She's pissed. He lied to her, right down the line lied, and she doesn't like it. She'd have repped him knowing the truth, it's her job, but he lied. And now she knows he's guilty, she knows we have a big pile of evidence, and she has to figure out how to get him the best deal. And the other — the corporate lawyer? He's stunned, shocked, sick. He'll remove himself as counsel before the next round."

"I guess I was too busy watching Tween. He was shocked, too. He was genuinely shocked we found all of it, that we went into his house, his e's, and found all of it.

"He never mentioned his son, Dallas."

"He will. He isn't thinking about the kid now. The kid's just a means to an end. He'll try to use that means eventually."

She glanced over as Reo and Mira walked down from Observation.

"I wasn't sure you'd make it," Eve said to Mira.

"I heard enough. I wouldn't term him a true sociopath. It's situational. He has no conscience regarding his wife, as he doesn't believe she deserves any regret, remorse, guilt. She's done, as she deserves to be. He's entitled to what belonged to her. He's angry he's caught, as he never considered he would be. After all, he didn't actually kill her. There's no fear in him yet, but there will be. He's still processing how you could have learned so much, and so quickly."

"Because he's an arrogant fuck."

"That doesn't hurt," Reo said cheerfully. "Gotte's going to want to deal. She's mad she got blindsided. The PI, the broker, the pro? She might have had room for him playing some part in the thing, but not all that. She's going at him now. If he doesn't fire

151

her, we'll make a deal. And I may not have to go down to the thirty-five. I've got twenty that says I can get her to bite at fifty."

"If we get whatever he knows about Cobbe and you deal at fifty, I'll give you the twenty and a case of Roarke's fancy-ass wine."

"That could be construed as attempted bribery of a public official." Reo fluffed her hair. "I'll take it. In that spirit, does anybody want a fizzy? I'm suddenly craving a cherry fizzy. I'm buying."

"I'm in," Peabody said.

"I can't think of the last time I had one." Mira considered. "Lemon."

"No — thanks." Eve took out her signaling 'link, paced away.

After several minutes she paced back, grabbed Peabody's fizzy, took a slurp. "Ugh. It tastes like —"

"Bubbly cherry goodness?"

"No. And remind me not to do that again. Roarke got the data on the numbered account. Lorcan Cobbe."

"How did he get the data?"

Eve studied Reo as she rocked on her heels. "My official statement on that is Roarke used his influence with an official of the financial institution whose name he can't reveal."

Reo slurped at her own fizzy. "I'll accept

that. I need to update my boss there."

"I already passed it to Whitney, who said he'd inform the PA, among others."

She went silent as the interview door opened. Barkley stepped out. "Lieutenant. I — It's APA Reo, isn't it?"

"Yes."

He nodded, looked from one woman to the next, the next. Nodded again. "It seems appropriate that I find women who are working to find justice for Galla Modesto. I liked her very much. I'm no longer Jorge Tween's legal counsel, on this or any matter."

He lifted his hands, let them fall. "I'm unable to say more on that. I would like to ask, as you said, Detective, my former client has not contacted the ME or apparently made arrangements for Galla, if I could assist in those arrangements in any way."

"Her family is in New York now," Peabody told him. "They'll take care of her."

"Good. That's good. I . . . I liked her," he said again, and walked away.

Mira looked after him. "Death, especially murder, casts long shadows. I need to get back to my office. If you need me, I'll come back."

"We've got this, but thanks for your help."

Moments later, the door opened again.

"In order for my client to make a statement, we require a representative of the prosecutor's office."

"That's handy. I've got one right here."

Reo stepped forward, held out a hand. "APA Cher Reo. I'll be sitting in on the interview."

"We need to have a discussion."

"No problem. Let's have it in Interview, on the record, just so all parties, including your client, are fully apprised and aware of the details of that discussion."

"Record on," Eve said as she walked by Gotte and into the room. "Dallas and Peabody reentering Interview. Reo, APA Cher, now in attendance. Looks like you're down a lawyer, Tween."

It also looked like some of that fear had begun to cut through the arrogance.

"Mr. Barkley has removed himself as counsel," Gotte said briskly. "Before my client agrees to answer any questions or give any statement, we need to be assured of considerations."

"You want a deal?" On a dismissive snort, Eve rocked back in her chair. "We've got you nailed, Tween, up, down, sideways. You're going down, and hard. Two consecutive life sentences, no parole, in a concrete cage off-planet. There's your goddamn deal."

Gotte merely folded her hands on the table. "You don't make the deals, Lieutenant, the prosecutor does. I'm sure APA Reo understands the expense, the risks, the difficulties in a long, complex, public trial."

"I understand this." Reo slid Eve's file over, opened it. And took out the copy of Galla's body with the message from the killer. "I understand how a jury's going to react when I put this on the screen in the courtroom."

Casually now, Reo flipped through the file. "I understand your client hired a PI to spy on his wife — and paid for it in a fraudulent manner. Just a little thing considering all, but something a jury's going to tsk over. I understand he contacted a convicted felon with known ties to the old Italian Mafia who acted as a broker — for a fee your client paid fraudulently — to put him in contact with a professional hit man."

She hammered, just as Eve had, only with the hint of a Southern drawl.

"I understand your client communicated with this hit man, and paid him a million euros plus expenses to rip a knife through his wife, the mother of a four-year-old boy, from crotch to sternum. And aided said

155

individual by giving him the details of where she would be at the time and place of her murder."

Reo closed the file, folded her hands on it. "There's more, but golly, that should do it."

"There are avenues I can take to convince a jury to sympathize with my client, the betrayed husband, and reduce his sentence, if indeed they convict. The victim's family and her young son would be spared the pain and scandal of a trial if we come to terms here."

"I met the victim's family," Eve put in. "I think they'd revel in a trial."

"One that paints their daughter as a faithless wife, that brings her lover into court to answer questions on their sexual relationship?"

Those hard eyes bored into Eve's.

"One that brings in experts to discuss my client's emotional break, his temporary loss of reason?"

"That lasted six weeks?" Eve shot back. "You want to try to convince twelve people and a judge that this selfish, greedy excuse for a human being just, what, lost his mind for, oh, a month and a half? That's some temporary loss of reason."

"Reasonable doubt can be established,

and it only takes one juror to hang a jury. A second trial, more expense, more time, more emotional pain for the victim's family. When what you want is the person who used the knife, who took her life."

"He might as well have."

"But he didn't," Gotte snapped, "which we can prove. Which you know to be true. If my client has information on this person, it has value. Conspiracy to murder, drop the second charge, twenty-five years on-planet with possibility of parole in twenty."

"No! Jesus Christ, Reo."

Reo waved Eve back, rolled her eyes. "No. Your client solicited and paid for his wife's death. He worked at it, and he's actually tried to cash in — to cover those fees, I imagine — the day after. Both charges stand."

"Concurrent."

"No. If your client knows something that leads to the killer he conspired with, let's hear it."

"I told you I want immunity."

Reo snapped her head toward Tween so quickly, Eve wondered it didn't fly off. "And I want a mansion in Connecticut with a pool boy named Steve. I will put you away." She leaned forward, all the fragile magnolia she could put on burned away. "I will put you away for two lifetimes so far from the world you know it's not even a vague memory."

"Consecutive," Gotte broke in. "Fifteen each."

"No. Give me a nibble or I walk and see you both in court."

"Lorcan Cobbe. He —"

"Not another word," Gotte ordered. "You got your nibble. Seventeen and a half each, twenty-five total, before my client agrees to give you more."

"No. Peabody, do me a favor and run that name."

"Sure. Peabody exiting Interview." She rose, walked out.

Reo leaned back. "Here's how I see it. First, we establish whether or not your client's a liar, as he's proven to be. If, in this case, Lorcan Cobbe proves to be the sort of individual a man like Bellacore would broker, and if your client further provides information that aids the authorities in apprehending this individual, in arresting and charging this individual in this matter, we will offer thirty years on each charge, to be served consecutively."

Both Eve and Tween erupted.

"That's sixty years! That's my life!"

"That's only sixty years! Goddamn it,

Reo, this isn't the time for cheap, lazy lawyer bullshit. We've got the son of a bitch."

Ignoring both of them, Reo kept her eyes on Gotte. "Two people are responsible for Galla Modesto's murder. I want them both."

"My client will be over a hundred at the end of that sentence. He'll have less than twenty years of life expectancy at that time — and that's not factoring in those years in prison. Twenty-five for each charge, with the possibility of reduction to twenty on each for good behavior."

Eve shoved up, cursing. "Fucking lawyers. I gave him to you on a platter."

"Twenty-five on each charge," Reo agreed, "with the possibility of reduction to twenty as stated. If, and only if, the information is valid and assists in apprehension. If it's discovered your client has withheld any information or lied about any information, the deal is voided."

"On-planet."

"Not a chance. Ms. Gotte, you and I both know if we go to court, your client's never getting out. You may, on an outside chance, convince a judge and jury to lessen the sentence, but not by much more than I'm offering. And he'll spend most of that potential reduction in prison awaiting trial, standing trial, and so on. You're not going to get a better deal."

"I can't go to prison for fifty years."

Tween began to shake now. Not from fear so much, Eve thought, but the hard cold reality.

"Give me a moment with my client."

"Dallas and Reo exiting Interview. Record off. Goddamn it, Reo," Eve began as she went out.

When the door shut, Eve turned. "If I went for girls, and if polygamy was legal in this state, I would fucking marry you."

"Oh, that's so sweet. Give me the twenty. I'll trust you for the wine."

Eve dug out twenty, slapped it into Reo's hand. "You're one hell of a cheap, lazy lawyer."

"Hey!" Peabody hustled back up the hall. "I was just heading back in. All prepped with a shocked face and data on Cobbe."

"She got the fifty."

"Yes!" Peabody offered a fist bump.

"Now we see if he has anything we don't already know."

"He had his name," Peabody pointed out. "It's a good start."

"There's a lot of road between start and finish." Eve jammed her hands into her pockets. "Cobbe's the finish. How much

Tween actually knows about him? That's only part of the road."

"It's sinking in," Reo pointed out. "What he's facing. Fifty years is terrifying, but the alternative's worse. And he's got that dangle of knocking it to forty if he's a good boy inside. Gotte's making it clear he spills everything he knows or gets the alternative. How sure are you Cobbe will stay in New York?"

"He wants Roarke. It's not a job, it's personal."

"Still, he had to know Roarke had his base in New York, so why now?"

Eve blew out a breath. "He's Irish. Cobbe's Irish."

Reo angled her head. "And?"

"They're — from my observation, they can be . . ." Pulling her hands out of her pockets, Eve waggled them in the air. "It's not just superstitious, it's —" She broke off again, frustrated. "I don't have the word for it. But Cobbe takes, as far as we can track, his first job in New York in twenty years — and maybe he took it figuring he'd get a line on Roarke. But when he does, who walks on scene? Roarke. It's like a sign to him, that's how I see it. He's Irish, it's a sign. Roarke, Roarke's cop, the successful job. The fucking universe is telling him this is the time and place."

"That makes an odd sort of sense."

"Perfect sense, really," Peabody decided.

Eve pointed at her. "Free-Ager. Sort of the same deal in that area."

She paused when Gotte opened the Interview door. "My client is ready to continue. He'd like some chilled spring water, flat."

"Slice of lime with that?"

Gotte merely gave Eve a dour stare.

"I'll get it. Can I get you something, Ms. Gotte?"

"Thank you, Detective. Green tea, no sweetener."

While Peabody headed off, Eve and Reo stepped back into Interview.

"Record on. Dallas and Reo reentering Interview with Tween and Gotte."

As she folded her hands on the table, Gotte's face stayed dour. "My client appeals to you on behalf of his young child. My client's son is only four years old. Serving his sentence on-planet will allow this young, innocent boy regular contact with his father."

"I'm all he has." Tween's voice shook. His eyes glimmered as he tried for tears.

"Seems like you should've thought of that before you hired Lorcan Cobbe to gut your wife in a public park."

"Regardless," Gotte snapped at Eve.

"No regardless. The minor child's mother's dead because your client paid to make her dead. I think that disqualifies him for the Father of the Year Award."

"He remains the child's father and legal guardian."

"Wrong. He sticks on the biology, but he is no longer the minor child's legal guardian. Stefano and Tereza Modesto have legal custody, as is clearly stated in Galla Modesto's will."

"We can bring this before family court, of course," Reo added. "But you know as well as I, that guardianship will stick. The deal stands. Take it or leave it."

"I'm his father!"

"And she was his mother," Eve shot back. "You made him a motherless child. Do you really think you'll get daddy points?"

"She cheated, she lied."

"And you killed her for it." Pushing up, Eve braced her hands on the table, leaned forward. "Toss the deal. Please toss it so I can put your greedy, arrogant, murdering ass away for fucking ever. How many times have you poked into the kid's trust fund, looked at ways to take it over once you eliminated his mother? Do you think we won't find that, too? Do you think we won't show he's just another moneymaker to you?"

She saw the quick flash in his eyes before they cut away. And knew she'd hit the mark.

Gotte saw it, too, and gripped Tween's arm. "We accept the deal, as outlined on record."

Peabody announced herself for that record when she came in with water and tea. Tween's hands shook as he lifted his to drink.

"Lorcan Cobbe," Eve said and turned to Peabody. "Detective?"

"Lorcan Cobbe, age forty-two, Irish citizen, originally from Dublin. Mother, Morna Cobbe, age sixty-three. Father unknown."

Peabody glanced up from the scroll on her PPC. "Cobbe has a history of juvenile bad acts that has continued and escalated in adulthood. He is on the lists of multiple international law enforcement agencies. Under his name and a series of aliases, he is a known contract killer operating primarily in Europe. At this time we are compiling data from those agencies. Commander Whitney and Captain Feeney of EDD investigated him for the murder of two adults and their teenage son in a home-invasion case in New York twenty-one years ago but were unable to apprehend him and close the case."

Eve leaned back. "How'd you find him?"

"She had sex with another man."

"Established. Known. Move on. How did you find and contact Lorcan Cobbe?"

"Bellacore. It's Stefano's fault! He said the name. I wouldn't have known about Bellacore otherwise."

"Are you naming Stefano Modesto as a coconspirator?" Eve demanded. "Did he give you the name to aid you in the murder for hire? Lie, and you do the full weight. Remember that."

"He made a joke. He put it in my head. She was fucking that artist, and whining about going back to Tuscany. We came to New York because it was time for me to be in charge. She whines about missing her home, about wanting another kid, about going back to work part-time. Always what she wanted, and then she wants some third-rate street artist? My career, my life was on the line. I had to defend myself."

"She ended the affair."

"Always mooning at that damn painting, and whining, whining. She'd have gone back to him, and then where would I be? Her family would take her side. They always take her side."

"But they'd support the grieving husband."

Anger flashed through the fear. "She whored herself! I was the injured party, but they'd have pushed me out, all the years I worked, catering to them, to her, I'd have been out."

"So you went to Bellacore."

"To explore possibilities. He understood my issues. He said he could put me in touch with someone. Or rather put someone in touch with me. He told me what to do. He named a price."

Eve nodded. "What did he tell you to do?"

"I was to acquire a clone 'link and secure it. I was to pay him, Bellacore, either in cash or through his farm. I didn't have that kind of cash. I said I needed more information before I paid that kind of money. And he told me about Lorcan Cobbe."

8

"He gave you Cobbe's name, even before you paid the broker's fee?"

"I brought him a bottle of wine, and he drank most of it. He's old, and he likes to talk about his glory days. I listened. He told me Lorcan Cobbe was one of the best he'd ever brokered. That he had over twenty years' experience in his profession. How he got early training from some Irish gangster in Dublin. It would be costly, a million euros plus expenses, but it would be money well spent. And there would be no trace back to me.

"Liar." Tween tapped his fist on the table, over and over. "Liar."

"How did Cobbe contact you?"

"I sent Bellacore the contact number on the clone. He told me to check it every day. Cobbe would contact me. If, for any reason, he turned down the job, Bellacore would provide another name. He also told me never to let Cobbe know I had his name. His actual name. Bellacore laughed and said if Cobbe knew I knew, we could both end up with our throats slit."

Tween drank more water. "I tried to push for an actual meeting, but Bellacore said to trust him, the last thing I wanted was to come face-to-face with Lorcan Cobbe. He'd still kill my wife, but very likely come back for me. So I pushed to have a conversation, like an interview. Bellacore thought that was funny, but I made it a deal breaker. He said to acquire two clones. He would arrange for Cobbe to contact me, to talk, on the first. Then I'd destroy that one, and all other contacts would be via text on the second 'link."

"And?"

"First I got a text from Bellacore. Just a time and a day. I used my office at home, locked the door, and Cobbe contacted me. He blocked video, but we had a conversation. He wanted to know specifics about my wife, about the artist. I wanted more specifics on his experience and success rate before I made the down payment."

Tween picked up his water again. His face had gone very pale and shiny with sweat. "He — he seemed to find that amusing. He gave me some names, places, dates. Told me to use the clone to do a search. He'd wait. I did, and found each of them, all in Europe, all within the last year, had been murdered. Person or persons unknown.

"We talked a bit more, and he told me he'd let me know how and where to wire the down payment if he took the job. And he told me to destroy the clone. That he'd know if I didn't, and he'd do me for free. If I thought of making a copy of our conversation, he'd know and kill me."

"Did you destroy the clone?"

"Yes. I put it in the office recycler, and ran it. But . . ."

Eve felt a quick pump in the blood. "You made a copy."

"I made one while we talked. I almost destroyed that, too. He scared me, I admit it. But I wanted documentation. I wanted a record."

"Where's the copy?"

"You have it."

"I have it?"

"I mean, the police. They took everything from me when they did the booking. I have a micro disc under the false bottom of my business card case."

Peabody was on her feet even as Eve turned to her.

"Peabody exiting Interview. Keep going,"

Eve ordered.

"We only communicated by texts after that. He sent me instructions, I sent the down payment. When he contacted me saying he'd arrived in New York, I told him I wanted it done when I was — with the security showing I was home, and that she often left to go to her fitness center late in the evening. I would let him know. But then I monitored her communications — she got a text from the artist, made arrangements to meet him in the park. I sent Cobbe the time. He offered to kill the artist as well, at a discount, but I wasn't going to spend any more. Last night, she went out, and before long . . . I should've destroyed the clone, like the other, but —"

"You wanted documentation," Eve finished.

"She would've ruined me, do you understand that?" Anger, and genuine outrage, darkened his face. "Ruined me. And all for some man she met on the street because he painted her goddamn hills. She had obligations to me."

"Right. Cobbe sent you the documentation of her dead body, and instructions on where to send the final payment, with expenses."

"I should've asked for a list and verification of the expenses, but I thought if I challenged him or quibbled, he might . . ."

Tween drained his water. "He's a dangerous man. He's a killer. You won't find him. You won't catch him. He'll get away, and I'll lose everything. It's not right. It's not fair."

Laying his head on the Interview table, he cried like a baby.

Eve got to her feet. "I'll put a man on the door to take him back to his cell when you're done finalizing the deal." For the hell of it, she sent Reo a hard look. "A deal we clearly didn't have to make. Dallas, exiting Interview."

Eve heard Reo's, clear and deliberate, "Cops. What can you do?"

As Eve started back to the bullpen, Peabody jogged up the hall with an evidence bag. "Just where he said. I signed it out."

"Let's go have a listen."

She scanned the bullpen, noted all her detectives were in place.

"Unless there's an invasion of killer ninjas from space, everybody hold here," she announced. "I need ten first."

In her office, she took the bag, removed the disc. "Coffee," she ordered, and plugged the micro disc into her unit. "Full audio."

It started with a *click* — the recorder engaging.

Yes. Jorge Tween.
You'll call me Blade. A mutual acquaintance tells me you're in need of a contractor.

Now she knew his voice, Eve thought. His accent was thicker than Roarke's, the tone of it rougher.

I might be. I need to know more about your qualifications.
Oh, I've more than plenty of those, and I may be inclined to tell you a bit about myself, but first, you'll be telling me about your wife. I like knowing the ins and outs before I say aye or nay. She's a woman of wealth and means and fine looks, that I can find myself. But tell me, Mr. Tween, what makes her tick? What makes her tock? Draw me a picture.

When he attempted to, Eve realized Tween didn't really know or care to understand the woman he'd married, had a child with, had murdered. He spoke of her background, her family business, her — as he termed it — obsession with Italy and Tuscany in particular.

172

Obviously Cobbe recognized the same, and managed to pry out a few details. Her interests — art, fitness, the family business. Her attachment to the housekeeper, her devotion to her son.

Interspersed with those details came the repeated accusations of cheating, ruining him, whining, nagging, sulking.

Well now, that's all very interesting for certain. But I'm after asking you one more thing. Why is it, Mr. Tween, you don't just kill the whoring bitch yourself?

I'm not a killer!

Remember this, Mr. Tween, if you don't do all I say, if you're not smart and careful, the cops'll see you the same if I take this job for you.

I haven't hired you yet, have I? I need those qualifications.

So you said. All right then, have this. Ulga Rominov, Budapest, June last. Nigel Harris, London, November last. Julietta LeFarge, Cannes, February. There are more, of course — I'm a busy man — but if three won't do you, we'll end the potential business. Use the clone, do a search. I'll wait.

"Stream through the hold. Resume on

voice," Eve ordered.

She listened to the rest as she drank her coffee, verified the basic truth of Tween's statement.

"Peabody —"

"Already done. Rominov, Ulga, age thirty-eight. Multiple stab wounds — throat slit as coup de grâce. Signs of torture over estimated six-hour period. She was a high-level, high-clearance employee of Vandam Pharmaceutical. A scientist. Married six years. Her wife, a surgeon, reported her missing, and is not a suspect."

"Torture. Somebody wanted information, maybe work related."

"Harris, Nigel, age sixty-one. Throat slit. Jeweler. Attacked in his shop, after hours. Police believe trying to thwart a robbery. Several pieces of jewelry missing — cases smashed. Divorced twelve years, wife remarried and residing in Bath. While his son — and heir — was in Paris at the time, they had a history of disagreements. He was questioned. His alibi held."

"Bet it did."

"LeFarge, Julietta, age forty-nine. A human rights attorney. Married fourteen years, three children. Gutted, like Modesto, feet from her own doorstep after a late-night meeting. Her husband and associates claim

174

she was working on information that would expose a sex-trafficking ring operating in Eastern Europe."

"All right, we'll pass this information on — and we need the files on each. He gave his fucking bona fides, so we use them."

She set the coffee aside, rebagged the disc, put it in a file bag to take with her. "With me," she said, and went back to the bullpen.

"Put the Cobbe file on-screen," she told Peabody. "Listen up! Whatever you're working on, you'll shuffle this in. Lorcan Cobbe. Put him up, Peabody, and everybody take a good look. Our subject is a contract killer with a fondness for sharps. Born in Dublin, working primarily in Europe, he's made his second-known trip to New York. He made a million euros and change to take out this woman. Galla Modesto, killed last night in Washington Square Park. Her husband, Jorge Tween, ordered the hit, paid the fee, and will shortly be on his way to Omega to serve two consecutive terms of twenty-five years."

"You bagged him?"

She nodded at Santiago. "Squeezed, twisted, flipped, and bagged what was left. If —" She broke off as Whitney walked in. "Commander."

"Continue."

"If the information squeezed and twisted out of the greedy fuck holds up, he serves the fifty. If not, he does two lifetimes. Either way, Tween's only half. Cobbe's spent the last twenty years, again known, making a living off murder. We're going to make sure Galla Modesto's his last."

"Are we going to Europe?" Baxter wondered.

"Don't grab your go-bag yet. There's every indication Cobbe is still in New York, and plans to be here for a while."

"He's got another target?" Reineke asked.

"Yes, a personal one. Roarke."

Reineke's eyes narrowed even as he shook his head. "Not going to happen."

"We'll make sure of it. Roarke knew Cobbe when they were kids in Dublin, and Cobbe became a protégé of Patrick Roarke — whom Cobbe claims is his biological father."

"I don't see any family resemblance," Carmichael commented.

"No. And there's no evidence to confirm this claim, as yet. Doesn't matter," she added, "as Cobbe believes it and has, most of his life, considered Roarke a rival, an obstacle, a threat. He made sure Roarke saw him in the crowd of lookie-loos at the Modesto crime scene."

"Chew him up, spit him out. Sorry." Baxter waved a hand. "Just imagining what Roarke'll do to this asshole."

She felt the same, just the same, but . . .

"We're not going to underestimate Lorcan Cobbe. He's successfully eluded worldwide law enforcement, including every damn alphabet you can think of."

"Not the NYPSD," Jenkinson said.

"But he did." Whitney nodded as Feeney came in. "Twenty years ago. More accurately, twenty-one years ago last month. Captain Feeney and I carry that one. You'll have the report. Study it. You'll have Dr. Mira's profile. Study it. The same for the Modesto case. Good work, Lieutenant, Detective, on Tween."

"Thank you, sir. But he was an idiot," Eve added. "I don't see Cobbe as a mastermind, but he has solid instincts."

"I'd put this department, including the expert consultant, civilian, up against those instincts every day of the week. He doesn't walk away from another body on our turf."

"No, sir, he doesn't."

"He won't threaten our civilian consultant or our lieutenant with impunity."

"He threatened you, LT?" Jenkinson pushed up in his chair, shoulders suddenly steel-beam straight.

"He will," Whitney said before Eve could speak. "It's pattern."

"Fucker's going down." The outrage on Jenkinson's face shined brighter than his tie. "Fucking fuck's going the fuck down! Pardon my fucking French, Commander."

"I depend on you taking the fucker down," Whitney returned. "Lieutenant, I came down to brief you on my discussions with law enforcement and intelligence agencies, foreign and domestic. With your permission, I'll brief the room."

"The room's yours, sir."

"You'll all have a written report," Whitney began, "but I'll summarize here. I've been in contact with the FBI, Homeland, the CIA, as well as their counterparts, and ours, throughout Europe, in Australia, South Africa, Asia. Chief Tibble has already been briefed, and had part in several of those conversations. He's available to you, Dallas, at any time on this matter."

"That's appreciated, Commander."

"Lorcan Cobbe." Whitney studied the screen. "His various known aliases are listed in the report. He is a person of interest or suspect in four hundred and forty-three murders."

"Sir." Trueheart, young face earnest, shot up a hand. "Did you say four hundred and forty-three?"

"That's correct. In a twenty-four-year span, which is the consensus of his length as a pro, that's an average of eighteen bodies a year. Several agents and LEOs believe he tops that, but these are his known or strongly suspected numbers worldwide."

Detective Carmichael made notes on her PPC. "Nothing off-planet, sir?"

"No, which results — according to intel — from his fear of off-planet travel. His fee, currently, ranges from one to two million euros — plus expenses. He uses brokers or trusted contacts to acquire work. He prefers the close-up kill, prefers knives. Is said to have an impressive collection of them. He also prefers the quick kill — as illustrated with Modesto — but will, for an additional fee, spend additional time or torture. Sometimes because the client wants the target to suffer, sometimes because the client wants information from the target.

"His mother," Whitney continued, "who still lives in Dublin — though in a far more comfortable situation than she provided through prostitution, before legalization, and street LC work after legalization — claims she's had no direct contact with him in twenty years. Authorities have not succeeded in tracing the income she receives semiannually to any specific account."

"Takes care of his ma, does he?" Baxter put in.

"Apparently."

"She's been questioned over the years," Feeney added. "Her electronics confiscated, stripped down. Nothing, so far, has led back to Cobbe. Best guess? They communicate rarely, and through a code of some kind. Doubtful she knows where he is." Feeney glanced at Eve. "She still claims she and Patrick Roarke made the kid. Mostly she keeps her mouth shut, keeps to herself. Travels most winters to sunnier climes. Nobody's spotted Cobbe visiting her, in Dublin, or on her travels.

"What we got on her's in the report, but that's the gist. Commander?"

"He has been spotted, usually after the fact, around Europe. He will on occasion dye his hair, wear a wig or a minimal disguise that wouldn't stand up to solid face recognition. He has many passports and credentials — top-of-the-line. Our expert consultant managed what the alphabets haven't thus far, and identified two num-bered accounts. He very likely has others, and safe boxes. Those accounts will now be watched for activity. Intel states he lives and travels well, but is unlikely to remain in one place for any length of time. He has no known companions or friends, just associates."

"He wouldn't use a hotel in New York, not after Modesto," Eve began. "Not while he's working out how to kill Roarke. Sorry, Commander."

"You're right, as far as we're advised, he would rarely use a hotel for anything longer than one or two nights. He's more likely to rent a furnished apartment or house for longer periods."

"House," Eve said. "He'd want room. He may have taken an apartment or a hotel room for Modesto, but he needs room and more privacy now. He won't want to kill Roarke quick."

"Or you, kid," Feeney added.

"Or me. He'd want some time. Life's goal and all that. How about transportation, Commander? How does he handle it?"

"He likes to drive, and it's believed he often drives to jobs in Europe, even considerable distances."

"More control," Eve assumed. "More privacy, more flexibility."

"He can also pilot a shuttle. He once eluded authorities by killing a shuttle pilot, replacing him, and flying a group of twenty businesspeople from London to a resort in

Provence for a conference. By the time the authorities discovered the body, traced the switch, he'd stolen a car, which was later found in a parking area outside of Venice."

"Slick," Eve added. "He's slick."

"Be slicker. There's considerable more in the report. You'll be working with Inspector Abernathy, Interpol. He's due here tomorrow."

Eve felt the itch between her shoulder blades, ignored it. "A joint investigation?"

"Modesto was murdered in our city. Cobbe's next targets are our family, in our city. We've invited Interpol in, but you're in charge. Abernathy has been working Cobbe for nearly eight years, and will assist in any and all ways. This is your case, Lieutenant. These are your cops. I'll end by saying that any and all overtime incurred through this investigation has been cleared. And you have Feeney for the duration. And myself if I can assist."

"Thank you, Commander." She turned to Feeney. "Can you hit the Italians for any of Bellacore's e-data, records, communications, financials?"

"Can and will. You want McNab?"

"He's handy. Detective Carmichael, Santiago, start looking at private shuttles into New York from Europe with single passengers, arriving within the last week. Cross-check with any cancellations on a departure from New York and vehicle rentals. Baxter, Trueheart, solo, male check-ins, high-end hotels, same time period. Jenkinson, Reineke, recent rentals, houses or multiunits with private entrance. He would've booked his transpo and accommodations when he took the Modesto job."

Her entire squad, she thought. And even with it, so much ground to cover.

"Feeney, can you spare somebody to check on vehicle rentals, along with Carmichael and Santiago? He likes to drive, and if he hopes to have me or Roarke to play with awhile, he'd need a way to transport us. I'd go for a van or an all-terrain with a good-sized cargo area."

"You got it."

She turned back to the screen, and Cobbe's picture. "He won't want to waste time, so he might just seize an opportunity. Steal a vehicle, take over a suitable house, eliminate whoever's inside. Stolen vehicles, missing persons."

"I'll take those," Whitney told her.

"Thank you, sir. Peabody, we start with Cobbe's known associates from the commander's report. We dig down, find their known associates. We look at any with connections to New York, who have recent travel to New York, who have a third cousin with an ex-boyfriend whose pet schnauzer's mother lives in New York.

"He's slithered around law enforcement since he was a street rat pissing in a Dublin alley. You don't do that unless you know who to use and when to use them."

She shifted, scanned her cops. "Talk to your CIs. Weasels hear plenty. Your current cases are priority. Work this in. Work it here, work it at home, but work it. If you need any assistance on your caseload, you'll get it.

"Officer Carmichael, uniform support will be key. I need you to work out a rotation. If you need any help with that, ask. Lastly, whatever you learn, I learn. Whatever you know, I know.

"Get hunting," she said.

She stepped to Peabody's desk. "Start on the associates. I'm going to write up the Tween interview and deal, then I'll go by, inform the Modestos, see if I get anything else there. I'll work from home."

"I can work the Tween report in."

"I've got it."

Feeney tapped Eve's shoulder. "Need a minute in your office."

"Sure. Commander, thank you again."

He merely gestured toward her office. She led the way, and got an uneasy feeling when Whitney closed the door.

Feeney scratched the back of his neck. "I'm putting a tracker on you."

"Like hell."

"Consider it an order," Whitney told her.

"Sir —"

"An order," he repeated.

Feeney let out a barely audible sigh. His baggy eyes offered sympathy. "I got a second one here for you to put on Roarke."

"Is that before or after I stun him unconscious?"

Now he shrugged. "However it works, Dallas. You're both targets."

"Cops are always targets."

"They're not always targets of a contract killer with over four hundred kills under his belt. He gets lucky, manages to snatch one of you, we'll know where you are."

She resisted, barely, stepping back when Feeney took the trackers out of the pocket of his rumpled suit jacket.

"Sir, you can order me to wear one, and I'll follow orders. I can't order Roarke to do the same."

"Convince him." With that advice, Whitney walked out, left her with Feeney.

"This is just bullshit."

"No bullshit. A little insulting, I get that, but it ain't bullshit, Dallas." He eased a hip onto the corner of her desk. "I spent a lot of time working with the commander on this today, getting intel and data, supposition, speculation. This son of a bitch knows how to slink into holes. He knows how to blend into the shadows, sink the blade in, and slide into a hole."

"I know that, just like I know this is different."

"Because it's you?"

"Because it's personal. When it's personal, you make mistakes."

He gave her a long look. "Damn right."

Smacked right back at her, she realized. She'd served it up for him.

"Lose the jacket. You got anything on under the shirt?"

"What do you mean, do I have anything on under the shirt? Where are you putting that damn thing?"

He poked her under her right arm about an inch out from the armpit.

She took off the jacket, but just shoved up the short sleeve of the T-shirt.

A tremendous relief for both of them.

"It's thin, and it's pliable, and it'll blend right in with the flesh patch."

Eve stared up at the ceiling when he

picked his spot, got to work.

"It'll hold up to fluids — sweat, swimming, shower. Heat, cold. Try to peel it off, it'll take some skin with it. So don't do that. I've got a solution that removes it. Best we got, 'cause it's the best there is. Guess who makes them?"

She didn't have to. But knowing she wore a Roarke Industries product didn't make it easier to swallow.

Lips pursed, he checked the seal, then pulled out his 'link.

"See, there you are."

She frowned at the blinking red blip on his screen. When he tapped it, the screen showed Cop Central and the location of her office.

"You drive uptown, it'll read you. You hop a shuttle, it'll read you. End up in fricking China? It'll fricking read you. The boy's a fricking genius."

"I'll be sure to tell him that when he kicks my ass for trying to stick one of these on him."

"Jesus, Dallas, just pull out some wife shit."

"What wife shit?"

"How you know he's smarter and stronger, and whatever other crap you need to toss in, but how you're worried, how worrying messes you up. Shit like that, so he does it because he's worried, and guilty, because you're worried. Just wife shit."

It fascinated. "How do you know wife shit?"

"Because I've had one more'n half my life, for Christ's sake. Sheila doesn't pull out the wife shit regular, and that's why it works. Every goddamn time."

Wife shit, Eve considered. It seemed like, maybe, it could run parallel with the Marriage Rules if she stretched it just enough.

"If it doesn't work, I'm calling you in. You're probably better at it."

"Might be." He handed her the box with the second tracker. "Instructions're with it, but he'll know how it works. Hell, he made it. Get it on him." Feeney headed for the door.

"Hold on. If there's wife shit, there's husband shit. What is it?"

Feeney merely smiled. "Figure it out."

A puzzle for later, she decided, and, lifting her arm, looked at the tracker, felt the tracker with her finger. Even eyeballing it, rubbing her finger over it, she couldn't really see it, barely felt it.

Okay, a fricking genius.

Deciding to ignore what she couldn't change, she sat down to write up her report.

9

While Eve finished her work at Central, Summerset did his marketing. He'd completed his other errands in good time, but still ran behind.

He'd spent most of his morning — previously earmarked for errands — at home, speaking with some contacts regarding Cobbe. Between errands, he'd had lunch with Ivanna at her apartment to ensure privacy for the information exchanged.

He used a car and driver, because Roarke had insisted — but still walked to and from some of his preferred shops. He had his routine, after all.

Though he realized his appreciation for routine largely stemmed from the carnage and chaos he'd lived with, and through, during the Urbans, it didn't make routine less gratifying.

He could admit the lieutenant often upended routine, but he'd learned to compensate. He considering maintaining order and calm, particularly in times of chaos, not only his duty but his gift.

He bought strawberries — on the small side, but ruby red and perfectly sweet. Though it wasn't his usual baking day, he decided he'd make a shortcake when he got home. As the day was as perfect as the berries, he enjoyed strolling along the outdoor stalls of the market, visiting the merchants and growers, having easy conversations.

He bought flowers that appealed to his eye, sampled some cheese — sharp as a blade — and bought a small round, though the cost hurt his practical heart.

He stopped by the fishmonger, eyed the salmon.

"And how are you today, Mr. Summerset?"

"Very well, and you, Mr. Tilly?"

"Fine as this day in May." Tilly, round in his big white apron, gestured at the salmon. "For your people or your cat?"

"The head of the house, of course."

"That'd be the cat." Tilly winked. "How's your Sir Galahad?"

"Well, too. And your ladies?"

Since Tilly's ladies were a pair of Persian cats, he and Summerset shared cat stories in the spring breeze before Summerset bought Galahad's salmon, and moved on.

He'd known since the berries that he'd picked up a shadow. He had to give Cobbe credit, as he'd yet to spot him. But he felt him — or whoever Cobbe had sent for the task.

Intrigued, he spent more time at the open-air market than intended, wandering, weaving, backtracking.

He never spotted the shadow. When the feeling passed, he called for the car.

On the drive home, he contacted Roarke.

"I gathered some information that may be helpful," he began. "And I picked up a tail in the marketplace."

"Where are you?"

"In the car, on the way home. You've no worries here. He never got close enough for me to make him, but he was there. Unless, of course, you put a shadow on me and I mistook."

"I didn't, no, and don't tempt me."

"And where are you?"

"An Didean. I have another stop to make when I'm done here. I'm likely to be a bit late. Stay at home once you're there, will you?"

"I've no plans for otherwise. Have a care, boy. He's better than I assumed."

"I'll see you at home."

Clicking off, Roarke continued his walk-through. Workers loaded in more furniture. Several instructors busily set up their class areas to their liking.

The air smelled fresh, clean. Did it smell hopeful, or was that just his need for it? In a matter of days, it would be filled with youth, noise, movement.

He had a meeting with key staff in short order, but found himself going up the stairs, wandering the dorms, and up all the way to the rooftop garden with its beds ready for students to plant.

He sat on a bench with the city all around, the sky as blue as a man could wish. And the memorial for the girls lost long, long before the school had been a glimmer in his mind and heart shining in the sun.

He might've been lost like them if Cobbe had had his way. No doubt he'd be dead and done if he hadn't been quick enough to get clear or had mates around him. No doubt at all, Roarke thought now, Cobbe would have put him in the ground all those years ago if he'd have managed it.

The old man would've done the same, Roarke considered, unless he'd been of some use to him. But he'd had nimble fingers for picking pockets, and that had spared him. Not that it had spared him from

the boot or the fist, but that early skill had kept him breathing.

Why in hell had Cobbe wanted such a man as Patrick Roarke for a father? Simple enough, Roarke decided. Whether or not they shared blood, they were much the same under the skin.

Ah well, he mused, it would come down to it after all these years, and this time, he'd neither run nor walk away. He had more, much more, to lose now than he had when he'd left Cobbe stunned — but breathing — on the floor of that bar in France.

It had to end here. And so it would.

He pulled out his 'link when it signaled, read the name of one of those old mates on the display.

"Brian," he answered. "Have you anything for me then?"

After the conversation, he filed away what his friend passed on. He took the meeting, and afterward watched with real pleasure as instruments were delivered and unpacked in the music room.

When he stepped outside, he scanned the street as his own car and driver pulled up.

He saw no sign of Cobbe, and continued on to his last stop before home.

He got out in front of Mira's pretty house on its quiet street. They'd potted flowers

beside the door, he noted. Deep purples and sharp reds in bold statements with something like foaming lace and some tender green vine just beginning to spill over the edge.

As much as he liked and admired the Miras, he saw this visit as duty — something to get through.

Once done, he wanted home.

He watched the street as he rang the bell. He'd have known if he'd been followed. And if he'd missed it, his driver — one of his best — wouldn't have.

But still, he watched until the door opened.

Dennis Mira, with his hair carelessly mussed, his eyes kind and green, opened the door. He wore house skids and a red cardigan with a missing button.

"Come in, come in. So good to see you! Charlie said you were coming by."

"It's always good to see you, Dennis."

Just as the house always felt like welcome with its pretty colors and quiet, casual dignity.

"How about a beer?" Dennis gave Roarke a friendly slap on the back as he led the way into the living area. "She won't make a fuss if you have one with me."

"I'd love one, thanks."

"Have a seat, and I'll get them. Charlie's . . ." He looked around vaguely, as if expecting to see her. "I think she went upstairs to change. She hasn't been home long. I'll find her."

When Dennis wandered off, Roarke moved to the window, scanned the street yet again.

Quiet, he mused, and the traffic that went by moved smooth.

He turned as Mira came in wearing pale gray pants and a light pullover as softly blue as her eyes.

"I thought I heard the door." She walked straight to him, took his hands, kissed his cheeks. "Where's Dennis?"

"He went off to get us a beer."

"Hmm." She gestured Roarke to a chair, took the sofa, curled up her legs. "I spoke with Rochelle today. She says you're loading in the last of the furniture at An Didean."

"We are. I've just come from there." He looked over as Dennis came in with a tray holding two pilsners, a glass of white wine, and a tray of crackers, cheese, nuts, olives.

"There you are, Charlie. I thought you'd earned a glass of wine. She had a long day," he told Roarke.

"And I'm adding to it."

"Not at all. We would've happily come to you."

"I was out and about, and you're nearly on my way home in any case."

With a nod, Mira picked up her wine. "Are you comfortable with Dennis here?"

"Of course." Roarke ordered himself to relax, took up his beer. "Always."

"You may not be aware that Eve, Peabody, Reo have Tween's confession, and made a deal with his attorney. He'll do fifty years, and gave them what he knows about Cobbe."

"Not all the details, but Nadine broke the story shortly before I got here."

"Eve must have tipped her." Mira nodded again. "Which means Eve must be with the family, or she wouldn't have let it break. Tell me your first memory of Lorcan Cobbe."

He hadn't expected the question, or one like it. It took him a moment, then he realized his instinctive answer wasn't accurate. "On Grafton Street in Dublin, watching me. I'd forgotten that. I was with Brian and Mick and Jenny, working the tourists as we did. I recall not liking it, but then he moved off. It would've been the next day, I'm thinking, he came knocking on the door."

"How old were you?"

"Seven or eight, I suppose. I remember it was time for supper, such as it was, and I'd just earned a backhand, as I didn't want to go out again until I'd had something to eat. The old man had likely had a pint or two by then, and he'd decided I hadn't brought home enough that day to earn whatever Meg put on the table.

"Then Cobbe was at the door, and pushed by Meg when she opened it. Not an easy task, as she wasn't a delicate sort. He walked straight to the old man. Strutted," Roarke recalled now, as looking back, he saw it clearly. " 'I'm Lorcan,' he said. 'I'm your son, first born. I'll be living here now and working for you.' The old man laughed, picked him up by the scruff of the neck, the back of the trousers, and tossed him out of the house."

"Tossed him?" Mira repeated.

"Oh aye, heaved him out. I heard him tumble down the stairs. And the old man said to me if I didn't want the same, I'd get my lazy arse out and earn my keep. So out I went. Cobbe was lying at the bottom of the stairs. I made to give him a hand up, as I'd taken that tumble myself a time or two. He pulled a knife, took a jab at me, but there was blood in his eyes, and I was quick. He was camped on the doorstep when I came back, so I went around the back, climbed in the window. He was still there in the morning."

Roarke took a drink. "You could say our relationship never improved from that initial meeting."

"Did he try to hurt you again?"

"He tried, succeeded a time or two, but never got the blade in me." Roarke shrugged, a slow lift and fall of shoulders. "The old man warned him off that when he saw how it was. As I did earn my keep."

"Patrick Roarke never took him in, so to speak, or acknowledged him as his son?"

"Gave him work, but as for the rest, no. And I think the old man had the right of that."

"Why?"

"Ah, genetics, I suppose. He looked nothing like the old man. Had light hair rather than dark, eyes of what you call hazel, not blue. Shorter and stockier of build."

"His mother?"

"Brown hair, though she often dyed it red, blue eyes that leaned toward gray. We'll say voluptuous. I made a point back then to travel to their neighborhood, get a look at her. They had rooms over the pub where she worked. I grew up in a hovel," he added, "but their circumstances made mine near to a palace. And still . . ."

"Still?"

"I think the woman loved him. He had that. Knowing your enemies is a vital part of surviving, so I made it a point to know him. She never raised a hand to him, it was said, and praised him to the skies. He was a young prince in her eyes."

Mira nodded as the picture formed. "But he wanted what you had."

Because that wasn't the whole of it, Roarke shook his head. "He wanted me not to exist, and to have what I had. The first I can see if I look through his eyes. I was in his way. But why he wanted a life with the old man and Meg — who had a hand like a brick, I'll add, and used it liberally — I can't see. He had a mother's love in his hands, but coveted a place at the table of a man who'd beat him for sport."

"A child —" Dennis blinked. "Sorry, interrupting. Thinking out loud."

"Think out loud," his wife invited.

"I'd say it's a natural, an innate need for a child to long for a father, a mother if he lacks one. He might look for substitutes, surrogates, replacements. In this case, the boy Cobbe was told by his mother, this is your father. It may be he was born with his own cruelty, a bent toward violence. And what I know of that time and place, it could be cruel and violent, so nature, nurture, environment combined. He would have, it occurs to me, not just striven to emulate the man he believed was his father, but to outdo him, and so earn his respect and pride."

He paused, so obviously thinking through the rest Roarke said nothing.

"A mother's love, to such a personality, is weak, isn't it? It's soft, and has no real power. But the pride and respect of a father, one who lives outside the law, who takes what he wants, this would be strength. It's a power, and one that can be inherited. Especially to a coward who believes himself brave."

Mira smiled, squeezed a hand on Dennis's leg. "Yes. You blocked that power from him," Mira told Roarke. "You still are."

"The old man's dead."

"That makes him more powerful. Sorry, Charlie."

"No, Dennis, you're absolutely right. Dead — and dead by violence — he's an icon, a goal unattained, a right stolen from him before he could earn that pride and respect. And you're living proof of what he never had."

Watching Roarke, Mira sipped her wine.

200

"What sort of work did he do for your father?"

"Well, he never had a talent for straight thievery, and had he four hands couldn't have picked a pocket. Enforcement's what he did to earn his place."

"Of what sort?"

Odd, so odd, Roarke realized, to sit in this pretty, welcoming room and think of those hard and miserable days.

"If someone balked at the protection fee, Cobbe might be sent along to persuade them. Or if someone didn't pay the old man what he deemed as his fair share of a take on a job, he might send Cobbe to collect. One way or the other."

"How old was he when he started?"

"Ah, about twelve or thirteen, I'd wager. It sounds young, but it was a different time and place."

"Still young," Mira said. "And his father figure selected him to cause physical harm to others. Did he kill, even then, at your father's behest?"

"Possibly. Probably, yes," Roarke corrected.

"Did he ever send you with Cobbe?"

"Christ no. I was too useful to end up gutted, and the old man had sense enough to know Cobbe would at least try to do me.

My talents lay elsewhere. I was born a thief." He shrugged again. "And the need to survive honed that natural talent. I worked the tourists and the shops, and then the homes and flats of the rich. I won't insult two people I care for by denying I enjoyed it."

"We tend to enjoy what we excel at," Dennis commented, and earned a flashing grin.

"True enough."

"And how did your father treat him when Cobbe worked for him?"

"Well enough, I suppose, if Cobbe did the job in what the old man considered good time and brought back the approved amount."

"And if he didn't?"

"The fist, the boot — but you'd get that as well if the old man had a mood for it, and he often did. It was rarely more than that, as Cobbe did his work — and enjoyed it. I got worse, as I squirreled some of my take away. It was worth a beating to know one day I'd have enough to get out and gone."

Roarke paused as he lifted his beer.

"You remembered something else."

"I did, yes. A time Cobbe got the worst of it. This would be a year or more after he first knocked on the door. In he came with his day's take, and it must've been enough to please, as the old man had Meg pour Cobbe a half pint. Cobbe sat, as if at home, and told the old man some tale on me. I don't recall what it was now, or if it was truth or lie. Hardly matters. He beat Cobbe bloody for it. He didn't tolerate whiners or rats, you see. I got bashed as well, but Cobbe took the brunt that time."

"That would be your fault, in his mind. And still, the beating was attention. Focused on him. A kind of proof he mattered. All of this helped foster what he became."

"Did — I can't call him Roarke's father, Charlie. Biology doesn't make a father."

At that Roarke looked down at his beer, said nothing. Could say nothing through the sheer flood of simple gratitude.

"Did he ever show Cobbe any of the pride or respect?"

To give himself a moment, Roarke sipped his beer. "Some respect, I suppose, but pride, no. And more than once I heard him tell Cobbe he had no drop of Roarke in him, and he'd crack his skull if ever he used his name as his own. He called Cobbe's mother a whore. And sure he'd had his share of whores, but he'd know if any of them grew a brat of his in their belly. And the like of that."

"And Cobbe took it?"

"He did, yes."

"What did he call him?" Dennis wondered. "The boy Cobbe was?"

"Cobbe. Or sometimes Jabber if his mood was fine. As Cobbe liked jabbing with his knives."

"And you? Is that too personal?"

"It's not. He called me boy, or young Roarke, but most often he and Meg called me *dailtín* or *diabhal.* They didn't have more than a handful of Irish — curses and insults. Those would be brat or devil, respectively."

"Was Cobbe there? Did he witness the last time Patrick Roarke beat you?"

"I don't know," Roarke realized. "I think no, but can't tell you for certain. There are some blanks there, as I can't tell you for certain, either, why he went at me as he did. It was the worst of the worst, and felt like dying. I likely would have died if Summerset hadn't found me, taken me in, tended to me. I . . . It was the book. Odd to remember that now."

"What book?"

"Yeats. I found an old book in an alley. Yeats, poetry. I taught myself to read, after a fashion, with it. Jenny and Brian helped, as they could both read and write better than the rest of us. It was the world inside the book, the words so strong and lovely. I kept it with me most of the time. No, no, Cobbe wasn't there. No one was there. He caught me on my own, not working but practicing with the book.

" 'Come away, O human child! To the waters and the wild.' "

" 'With a faery, hand in hand,' " Dennis continued. " 'For the world's more full of weeping than you can understand.' "

"Aye, it was magic, those words. I knew about the weeping world right enough, and wondered how it would be to come away. And he found me. He took the book, and cursed at me for loafing, not working."

Roarke closed his eyes a moment, searching, searching through the shadows and gaps. "I tried to get it back from him. It was mine, you see. I hadn't even stolen it, but found it. He knocked me down, tore a page out of it. And that tore something in me."

He opened his eyes. It came back, clear as the day it happened. Part of him — the most of him, he admitted — wanted to draw the shade down again, right and tight.

Looking the past clear in the eye was looking at pain.

He'd spent so much of his life believing

the point of living was looking ahead, not behind.

But now, what had been stood ahead of him.

"I went at him. Blind rage and stupidity, as he was twice my size, and strong. He was a strong man, I had reason to know. But I went at him. It's likely the shock of me wading in's the reason I managed to hit him — once. I landed one, I did, and busted his lip open."

He nearly laughed. "Now, that moment of intense satisfaction was very short-lived. He tossed the book aside, and, well, I didn't land another. So." He shrugged.

"So," Mira said after a long breath. "Did you see Cobbe again after you lived with Summerset in Dublin?"

"A few times once I was out and about again, but I kept clear of him. I know after the old man got a knife in his throat Cobbe tried to take over the operation."

"Could Cobbe have killed him?" Dennis asked.

"He didn't — nor did I. The old man's gang fell apart, scattered to others, as Cobbe couldn't hold them. So he went to work for others and moved to Belfast for a time. I didn't have what you'd call a conversation with him again until years later, in a bar in

France."

"He pulled a knife on you," Mira said. "Eve told me during our consult this morning. Is that accurate?"

"It is. I saw him come in, and saw clearly what he had in mind in his eyes. Down he sat, put the knife in my ribs — not deep, as he needed to have his say before he jammed it in me. So as he's talking, telling me how he'll gut me with the knife under the table if I didn't give him money and the name rightfully his, I took him down with the stunner *I* had under the table. I walked away, leaving him breathing, which I hope you understand I regret now."

"He thinks you're weak, because you left him breathing. At the same time, you bested him, just as you did when you were children. You have the name he covets," Mira continued. "You have wealth and position he can't compete with. While he's surely accumulated wealth, the only respect he has is from fear. That feeds him. I don't believe he came to New York to confront you. Maybe to test the waters, to gauge the ground. But seeing you, after he killed, after he'd earned his fee, riding on that, then there you are, he had to gloat.

" 'Here I am,' " Mira said. " 'That could've been you. I can do that to you, and claim my birthright.' He'd have kept track of you through the years, like worrying a sore, and that angry pain, that feeds him."

"It's not hard to keep track of what I let people see."

"He will try to kill you, and because it's so personal, so deeply dug in him, he'll make mistakes. But because it's so personal, so might you."

"I won't." And there, Roarke was certain. "Because it's not only my life he'd try to take. It's Summerset's, and it's Eve's — because they're with me."

Studying Roarke, seeing that absolute certainty, Mira sipped her wine. "He'd understand Summerset being with you as a job, and your marriage to Eve as a convenience and cover for you. He isn't capable of understanding love."

"Summerset saved my life, and has been an integral part of my life since. Killing him would be a by-product, even a distraction, but a pleasurable one. Eve is mine. Whether he understands what she is to me or not, she's mine."

He leaned forward. "I was born a thief. The foundation of everything I own came from that. I continued to steal when it was no more than a pleasant hobby. I have no regrets. I gave that up for Eve because she could never have belonged to me or me to her otherwise. I have no regrets.

"He's only to dig down deep enough, to ask the right questions of the right people, to learn that. Understand it, no, but know it, he could. If he did know it, what would he do?"

"Try to kill her, or at least take her, first. And I know of no one more capable than Eve of stopping him."

"Agreeing with that is what will keep me from making a mistake. I trust her to see he lives his life in a cage. But if he gets past her considerable skill and harms her in any way, he won't be breathing when I walk away."

"He won't get past her, or you," Dennis commented. "I believe that absolutely. Separately, you're strong, clever people. Together you're a force. There are parallels in your childhoods. You were meant to be together."

"Two lost souls," Roarke murmured, but Dennis shook his head.

"No, not lost. Only waiting. Can I get you another beer?"

"Thanks, no. I've taken enough of your evening. Unless you need more."

"Tell Eve I'll adjust the profile. She was

right to ask you to speak to me — to us — directly. We know more, and the more we know, the quicker we'll stop him."

Before Roarke took his leave, Eve headed home. She'd done all she could — or wanted to do — at Central, had gone by the hotel to update the Modestos.

And that, she thought, was about all the emotion she could take for one day.

She had work, and plenty of it, but she needed a break. A quick swim, maybe, a glass of wine, and a meal with Roarke so they could update each other.

She really wanted him inside those gates. Hoped she'd find him there already.

But when she turned toward them, she saw the bag — some sort of sack, tossed in front of them. Even as the gates started to open, she backed up.

While they closed again, she drew her weapon. Another scan of the street before she slid out of the car.

A sack — and she knew bloodstains when she saw them — with a note dangling from the tie that secured it.

She took out her comm with her free hand. "Dallas, Lieutenant Eve. Send a couple of beat cops to my residence. Now."

She slid the comm away, crossed to the bag.

She smelled blood. She smelled death.

Tipped the note up with a fingertip.

Curiosite killed the cat.
Your next!

"Can't spell worth a — Oh Christ, no, no, no."

She didn't seal — didn't think of it, but ripped at the tie.

The cat, the cat. Her cat.

The cat — but not her cat — had been gutted, its throat slit.

Pity and relief churned through her as she straightened up, turned on her recorder, turned to get her kit out of the car.

And then she saw him. As with Roarke, he made sure of it.

He stood a block away so she saw him throw his head back as he laughed.

She ran, full-out. And so did he.

10

As she ran, Eve yanked out her comm.

He whipped east, as she'd have done, pumped into the great park.

"Officer needs assistance in pursuit of suspect. Male, Caucasian, brown hair, man bun, age forty-two. Six feet, a hundred and ninety. Black pants, black hoodie. Pursuing on foot, into Central Park at West Eighty-third. Son of a bitch!"

She made up ground, she knew she made up ground. He wouldn't win any sprints, but he'd positioned himself well for the chase. He wanted the chase, no question.

"Suspect is Lorcan Cobbe," she barked out as she charged into the park. "Consider him armed and dangerous. Get me some fucking backup! Alert park security to locate him on cam."

Her comm beeped in her hand.

"Get me backup!"

"Why are you running?" Feeney demanded. "Why are you in Central Park?"

"In pursuit of Cobbe. Get me fucking backup."

"Done."

She had to stop, not to catch her breath, but to gauge that ground. A perfect spring evening welcomed tourists, natives, families, and kids — lots of kids. People strolled, lounged on benches, walked dogs, licked ice cream from cones, embraced in the green shade of leafy trees.

And one, with a puzzled expression, held a black hoodie.

Eve ran toward her, watched the woman's eyes widen in alarm — and remembered she held her weapon.

She yanked out her badge. "Police officer, where did he go, the man who dropped the hoodie?"

"He — he just sort of flung it off when he was running."

"Which way?" Eve snatched the hoodie for evidence. "Which direction?"

"I'm not sure. I think . . ." She pointed vaguely north.

Eve clipped on her badge, ran north.

"He ditched the hoodie," she told Feeney, "pursuing north."

Somebody played a guitar. Somebody sang. Some kid laughed like he'd bust a gut.

Another carted an airboard, limping along on scraped knees that dribbled blood.

She spotted two park security officers jogging her way.

She stopped because the son of a bitch was gone. Just gone.

"I need the security feed for this sector," she snapped. "And I need security to comb in for the suspect."

Frustrated, she jammed her weapon away. "Send me a copy of the feed. And any feed that shows the suspect. Dallas, Lieutenant Eve, Cop Central. Homicide. Get me the feed and start a video and foot search. Now, goddamn it."

"We'll need to get clearance from —"

Eve resisted — very narrowly — grabbing the park cop by the throat. "You want somebody gutted in here on your watch like the woman in Washington Square Park? Because this is that guy. This is that fucking guy."

"Yes, ma'am. We'll get right on it."

"And don't fucking ma'am me," she bit off as she stalked away.

"Lost him," she told Feeney. "I'm heading home."

"Backup'll meet you. What the hell happened?"

"Fill you in later," she said, disgusted. "I

need to get the manhunt started."

Went north, she thought, and then cut west and walked right back out of the park again. That's what she'd have done anyway. Have a vehicle nearby, or just walk over to Columbus, catch a cab, a bus, hit the subway.

He'd wanted to see what she'd do. And she'd shown him.

A couple more cops — NYPSD uniforms — ran in as she strode back. She unclipped her badge, held it up. "Come with me."

As she walked, she used her comm to order a search from West Eighty-eighth south to Roosevelt Park — since he seemed to like damn parks — and from Central Park West to Columbus Avenue.

Maybe, just maybe, since he got his jollies off, he'd be even more careless. And they'd get lucky.

When she started to cross to the gates, she saw they were wide open, and Summerset stood between her car and the dead-cat bag.

"What are you doing out here! Don't touch that bag! Goddamn it!" She sprinted across. "Get in the car. Get in the damn car."

"It's not Galahad. He's in the house."

"You touched the bag."

"Of course I touched the bag," he snapped right back. "The gates opened, then shut again, and the monitor showed your vehicle out here and that thing. I —"

"Get in the car." Frustrated, furious, she grabbed his elbow — sharp point. "Do you understand you're a target?"

"Do you understand you are?"

"In the car before I cuff you. I swear to God."

With considerable dignity, Summerset got in the car.

Struggling for calm, she ordered sweepers, snapped out those instructions as she stormed to the trunk. She sealed up, got evidence bags and boxes.

She tossed the boxes at the uniforms. "Put those together."

She put the reversible jacket in an evidence bag, and, crouching, she took the dead cat out of the bloodied burlap.

"Sick fuck does that," one of the uniforms commented.

Saying nothing, she used tweezers from her field kit to remove several hairs from the body, bagged those, took swabs of blood, bagged those, bagged the cat, labeled the bags. She put the sack and note in another.

Taking the boxes, she boxed, sealed, and labeled.

"You're going to take the body to the morgue, tagged for Morris."

"You want the ME to autopsy a cat?"

"Isn't that what I said?"

"Yes, sir."

"The jacket, the hair, the blood, and the bag and note go to the lab. The hair is tagged for Harvo, the rest for Berenski. They're priority. All the fuck of them are priority. Is that clear?"

"Yes, sir."

"You're on foot?"

"Yes, sir."

She pulled out her comm again, ordered a cruiser to pick up the beat cops.

"Do you want someone to stand by the gates, keep the scene secured?"

"No." No point, she thought. No real point in the sweepers, either, but she'd cover all the bases.

She stowed her field kit, got behind the wheel.

Summerset offered her a spotless white handkerchief.

"You have blood on your hands."

She wanted to snarl, but took it. No point, either, in smearing dead cat blood all over the steering wheel.

Later, she'd think just how upset Summerset had to be not to object when she balled up the bloody cloth, stuffed it in her jacket pocket.

Instead, he folded his own hands as she drove through the gates.

"As you know," he began, "the gate security reads your vehicle ID. I became concerned when the gates opened and closed, but your vehicle didn't appear on the monitor in a timely fashion so I could remote it to the garage. I then checked the gate monitor, and became only more concerned at seeing your empty vehicle, the bag."

"So you open the damn gates and stand there like some scarecrow waiting for the crows to shit on your shoulders and peck your eyes out."

"I was hardly —"

"What if he'd doubled back? He had a damn crosstown block on me when he ran into the park. He could've doubled back and gutted you."

His stiff neck managed to swivel enough for him to glare at her. "I'm not without my own resources."

"I don't give a rat's ass about your resources. What the hell would I say to Roarke if I'd come back and found you bleeding out beside that dead cat?"

218

"I'm armed," Summerset said as she slammed to a stop in front of the house. "And I'll remind you I survived worse than this thug during the Urban Wars. And beyond."

"The Urbans weren't on my watch." She shoved out of the car.

He shoved out of the other side. "And what the hell would I say to Roarke if I hadn't bothered to check, and he came home to find *you* dead beside that poor cat?"

"I'm a cop."

"That makes you invincible?"

"It makes me trained."

"As I am, as I have been longer than you've been alive."

"And you figure being old means you can outrun and outmaneuver a professional killer?"

Summerset took a mini blaster out of his pocket. "I believe this would compensate for age."

"Jesus, that's illegal!"

"Arrest me," he suggested. "But at this moment, I need a drink. We both need a drink."

When he walked to the door, she pulled viciously at her own hair. Then went in after him, because she damn well did want a drink.

Galahad trotted to Summerset, did his wind and rub, then went to Eve. For a moment, the three of them stood in the grand foyer.

Summerset cleared his throat. "I saw the note on the bag. Despite the poor spelling, the message was clear. I knew our boy here was safe, but you didn't."

She stripped off her jacket, tossed it on the newel post. "I want a really big drink."

With a nod, Summerset walked into the parlor. He poured her a generous glass of wine, and himself three fingers of whiskey.

"When did you start carrying a blaster in your damn pocket?"

"Since Liam Calhoun got past my guard and into the house, and you stepped in front of a stream meant for me. Lorcan Cobbe will not get into the house."

Because he found the entire incident upsetting, Summerset sat.

"How the hell did he know we have a cat?"

And because he'd had time to think of that, Summerset sighed over his whiskey. "He may have used an amplifier when he shadowed me today."

"He — What? When?" She didn't want to tear her hair out now. She wanted to tear

Summerset's out. "Why am I just hearing this? Where?"

"Oh, sit down, girl, instead of pacing about." Summerset drank some whiskey, rubbed his temple. "I told Roarke, and he will — or would have — of course, told you. During my marketing — the open-air market."

"You saw him?"

"No. I felt him. I know when I'm being followed. He never approached, and I'd have known, so he must have used an amplifier and overheard me talking to Mr. Tilly, the fishmonger. We chatted about our cats, as he has two Persian females. I bought salmon for Galahad. The shadow faded away not long after that. I felt it.

"He butchered that poor animal, one that might have been someone's pet, because I bought salmon and chatted about cats."

"He butchered that animal because he's a sick fuck, and wanted to see what I — or Roarke, depending on who got here first — would do. He stepped into plain sight — just like he did at the murder scene — so I'd see him.

"He laughed," she added. "I could see by his body language. It was all a big joke."

When Galahad leaped into her lap, stretched his considerable weight across it,

Eve gave him a long, slow stroke. "If the body or the hair have anything to say, Morris and Harvo will find it."

Summerset took a small device out of his pocket. "Roarke's at the gate. And so are your crime scene people."

"Crap. Crap. I should've alerted him." She took another drink. "Oh well."

"So should have I. I'd say we were both a bit distracted. Sit," Summerset added before Eve got up. "I'll bring him in."

She had to get to work, Eve thought. But this had to come first. Stroking the cat into delirium purrs, she laid her head back, closed her eyes for one precious minute.

She heard the door open.

"And why are sweepers at the gate?" Roarke demanded. "Refusing to tell me more than 'Ask the lieutenant.' "

"She's in the parlor having some wine. Go join her. I'll take those."

She sat straight, eyes open when he came in. Delirious or not, the cat deserted her to greet the next member of the family.

"What the bloody hell, Eve?"

"Cobbe left a dead cat — in a sack with a note — at the gates."

"A cat? Why would he . . ." Roarke looked down at the pudgy gray ribbon winding between his legs. "Ah. He tailed Summerset

222

at the market. He must've somehow figured we had a cat."

"Salmon from a fishmonger — a word I don't understand — and another cat person," Eve said.

"Amplifier," Roarke surmised.

"He was a block away — made sure I spotted him. I pursued him into the park, but he had a big lead, and I lost him. I have security sending me the feed, but I'm figuring he zipped back out again, kept going."

Struggling with fury, Roarke tugged his tie loose as he dropped into the chair beside Eve's. "He may have tried to get in."

"Summerset didn't say anything about the alarms. He would have."

"Doesn't mean Cobbe didn't try a jam. I'll check. A note, you said."

"Curiosity killed the cat. You're next. With bad spelling."

"You found it when you got home. You must've thought . . ."

He stroked the cat, who'd now chosen his lap.

"My head knew better, but yeah, for a second."

Summerset came back in. "Wine or whiskey?"

"I'll have the whiskey."

"I understand you'll need to go up, work

on this matter, have a meal, but I should tell you both about my discussion with Ivanna."

"You told your . . . lady person," was the only term Eve could come up with.

Arching his brows while he poured, Summerset continued. "Ivanna was, as you should remember, a covert operative for many years. She has many contacts."

"Whitney took care of that."

"And does your commander have personal relationships with agents and others who've investigated Cobbe?"

Eve frowned at him as Summerset gave Roarke his whiskey. "A guy named Abernathy, Interpol, coming in tomorrow to consult."

"She mentioned him." Taking out his PPC, Summerset scrolled. "George Abernathy, initially with Scotland Yard — and, you'll appreciate, a murder cop. Transferred to Interpol seven years ago."

"You wrote that down?"

Summerset angled his head. "Would you like to try to decipher my code, Lieutenant? I've used variations of it since —"

"Before I was born. Yeah, yeah, fucking yeah."

"In any case, Ivanna knows of him, knows those who've worked with him, just as she knew — as she knows such things — he's been dogged if unsuccessful in his pursuit of Lorcan Cobbe. He's forty-eight, married — fourteen years — has two sons. His wife, forty-five, is a botanist of some renown. His sons enjoy cricket and football. Not American football," he qualified. "Actual football."

Summerset picked up his whiskey. "If you choose, you can mention her name to him, as an acquaintance. She told me what she knew of various investigations regarding Cobbe. I wrote them into a report. Both of you have copies on your units."

"Thanks for that," Roarke told him. "Have you eaten?"

"Not as yet."

Eve knew what that hanging silence said. She might have mentally rolled her eyes, but she understood. "So we'll eat in the dining room. All of us."

"I'll see to it." Rising, Summerset left the room.

"He's carrying a mini blaster in his damn undertaker jacket."

"Yes. And?"

"Christ." She decided to let it go — at least for now. "How'd it go with Mira?"

"I'll tell you both over dinner. You should both hear. She did say she'd be adjusting the profile, and she'd send that to you."

"Okay, that's okay. Are you?"

"I'm not altogether sure."

Reaching over, she closed a hand over his. "I'm going to get him."

"I trust you will."

"He wanted to see what I'd do. I'm betting he expected I'd get back in the car, close the distance fast."

"Why didn't you?"

"Because the park's right there. I'm in the car, I have to stop, get out again. He's going to go into the park because it's right there."

Roarke turned to her. "You knew what he'd do."

"That's what I'm telling you. He takes the easy way when he can, and the park was easy. Tossed off his hoodie so I don't have a full description — but now I have the hoodie, and maybe we find something. Better if he'd tied it around his waist when he ran. But tossing it was the easy way. And I'm saying the surveillance is going to show him going north in the park, then heading out, fast. In and out, and either to a vehicle he stashed, or catching transpo a few blocks away.

"I've got the dead cat for Morris, some of its hair for Harvo, blood for Dickhead, and possible DNA on the jacket. No label in it, but they could find something. We could find out where he got the cat, how he got it. It's not going to be a stray," she added, thinking it through.

"If he got the idea from listening to Summerset, he's not going to be lucky enough to just find a stray cat in a few hours. He doesn't know New York well enough to know where to look. So a vet, a shelter maybe. Or he spots one in somebody's window — too much luck on that," she decided. "He breaks into a vet or a shelter. We track that, we'll know where he went."

She rose to pace. "If he followed Summerset, he had to see him go out in the first place, which means he watched the house. Getting the lay of the land. And he had to have transportation."

"I can't imagine Summerset or the driver I assigned wouldn't have spotted a tail."

"I can assure you," Summerset said from the doorway. "I've set the meal out on the back patio, as it's a lovely evening."

"Amplifier?"

"No," Roarke said as he removed the cat and rose. "Not anywhere on the grounds or in the house, as we have virtual walls to block them."

"Okay then." She started to follow Summerset, stopped. "In the car? Would one, a good one, pick up anything said in the car?"

"It would have to be a damn good one. Bloody hell, it's possible. I'll be fixing that."

"Did the driver have your route, or did you tell him as you went?"

"I'll add my own bloody hell," Summerset said as they walked to the back of the house. "I told him as we went."

"I need everywhere you stopped, who you talked to, dealt with. I want the time on every stop."

"You'll have it."

They went outside, and yeah, she supposed *lovely* hit the mark. Dusk spread, sending the lights along the patio, the paths, sprinkled through some trees glowing. Flowers scented the air, and shimmered in those glowing lights.

He had little white candles in clear cups on the table, three domed plates, the wine she'd already started on, a covered glass basket — and since she could smell the warm yeast, that said bread.

"A meal well presented can be a comfort. I thought we all could use some."

"If there's spinach under here, I'm not going to feel the comfort."

Instead, she found asparagus, her least disliked of the green things, some sort of medallions drizzled with sauce, tiny potatoes still in their thin, golden skins coated with butter and herbs.

She started to refuse the wine, then thought: comfort. Decided she could handle another glass.

"Jorge Tween will be transported to Omega within forty-eight hours. More like thirty-six now," Eve began. "Galla Modesto's minor son is with her family, and will remain that way. They're taking her remains back to Italy — to Tuscany. The housekeeper and nanny will go with them, remain with them."

Roarke took her hand, squeezed. "Good work."

"Not done yet, but you helped that outcome. He — Tween — well, he wasn't much of a challenge. He'd have been more of one without the data you dug up."

She cut into the medallions. Lamb.

"Cobbe's not as much of a challenge as he thinks."

"Far be it from me to insult you, Lieutenant."

Eve ate some lamb, gave Summerset a sardonic stare. "Really?"

"In this case," he amended. "But he's challenged global law enforcement for two decades."

"I'd say he had some luck early on. But by and large, he's good at what he does —

the work. This isn't work, it's personal, and he's already screwing it up. Showing himself to Roarke at the crime scene? Impulse, ego. Staying in New York? Pride, anger. The cat? Arrogance and just plain stupid.

"This isn't just slit a throat, collect a fee, move on. It's hate, it's ego, and it's a need to taunt an old rival. More, a — what do you call that thing? — usurper."

Out of habit, Roarke buttered a roll, broke it, handed her half. "All that, yes, more than I realized until speaking with Mira and Dennis."

He looked around, the lights, the flowers, the roll of lawn. At the world he'd built for himself. For Summerset. For Eve, he thought, though he hadn't known it at the time.

For family, which included a fat cat.

"I remembered things I hadn't, either because they'd blurred with time or I'd shoved them aside, or simply hadn't considered them before. She has a way of listening, and of asking somehow the right question, the right way to open things."

He looked at Eve. "As you know."

"Yeah, she has a way."

"As does Dennis. And so what I thought of, really, as a duty to you, Lieutenant, became little revelations. The first time I saw Cobbe," he began, and told them.

"He tried to kill you pretty much off the bat," Eve observed. "He won't have forgotten that, or that he failed."

"He won't, no. What was, to me, just another bastard, was more to him. And I didn't care if he was the old man's — in fact, I likely hoped he was, until I saw his mother, and even then knew how implausible."

"Because?" Eve asked.

"Other than hair color, and build, I have to assume he took after — physically — his bio father. The darker complexion, the features, eye color. There's no resemblance to the old man, at all.

"But it mattered to him," Roarke added.

"More than mattered," Summerset commented.

"True enough. Looking back, it's as Dennis said. When the old man cuffed him or booted him, it was attention. He craved that. Even the night the old man beat him bloody."

Listening, Eve juggled the profile herself.

"And that would be a reason he didn't go after you directly, not for years," she concluded. "If he did, he wouldn't take your place, he'd lose his. He hated you more after that."

"No question, though at the time, I saw no difference. He was one of the old man's enforcers, and nothing more to me. I stayed clear, as he had a viciousness, and I had enough of that to deal with already. I remembered more, but can't say it applies to Cobbe."

"What did Mira think?"

"I couldn't say. It was when he beat me near to death, when Summerset found me. I never remembered exactly, still don't, but there's more."

Lifting his wine, he frowned into it. "I thought more on it on the way home, and I wonder now just how the old man found me in the alley with the book."

"The book?" Summerset repeated.

"I always assumed I'd left it back, hidden in my room. But I remembered I'd tucked myself up to read the Yeats, to practice, instead of working. I'm thinking it might be Cobbe spotted me, and somehow told the old man. Even if ratting on me earned him a fist, it would be worth it, wouldn't it?

"I fought for the book. He could've had anything else I'd squirreled away, but not that. I hit him, and he beat me into the ground. I never remembered precisely why until today."

He looked over at Summerset. "And you

found me. Do you know, when I finally woke — what did you tell me? — after a full day — and I saw you and Marlena. I thought you were the two faeries come to take me hand in hand. I only remembered that today.

"I said terrible things to you, to her, those first days."

"Stop." Summerset reached over to grip Roarke's hand. "Stop. You were a child, brutalized, terrified. Put that part of it away, or you'll disappoint me."

"Your disappointment came to cower me more than the bastard's fists ever did. That's a power."

Despite having Summerset as witness, Eve shifted, took Roarke's face in her hands, pressed her lips to his, held them there.

Summerset rose. "I bought fresh strawberries today, and made a shortcake. We'll have dessert."

He went inside.

Roarke pressed Eve's palms to his lips. Then, laying his head on her shoulder, found more comfort.

11

They talked of other things over shortcake and coffee, let the past rest a bit. Roarke said nothing more about it until he went upstairs with Eve to her office.

"I want to thank you for that."

"What that?"

"Dinner with Summerset when I know you wanted to get up here, push into the work."

"You needed it, he needed it. And I got plenty out of it, including cake." But Roarke took her hands, just held them. "He saved your life. That counts with me. We all know it counts with Cobbe, too. He needs to be more careful."

"Agreed. And he will. So will we all."

"Glad to hear you say so." She opened her file bag, took out the tracker case. "Because you're going to wear this."

"How do I put this?" He seemed to consider as she opened the case. "Oh, I have it. No."

"Cobbe has over four hundred and forty kills — and I'm going to say well over — and wants you dead. So you wear the tracker. I'm requisitioning another for Summerset."

"Who'll give you the same response. I'm not being tagged like a family pet."

She remembered Feeney's advice — play the emotional card. Thought, fuck it.

She stripped off her jacket, yanked up the sleeve of her shirt, jabbed a finger on her arm. "You think I like it? You think I like having Feeney slap one of these on me like I'm some rook who doesn't know her ass from her ear? The weight of the entire NYPSD is behind this because some fuckhead wants to kill us so your dead father can give him a high five from hell. I wear it, you wear it. That's it."

Enough heat pumped off her to fry him where he stood. He pumped it right back for a moment, then turned on his heel.

"Bloody fucking hell." He stripped off his suit jacket, his tie, tossed them at the sofa. "I'd peel Cobbe's skin from his bones for this alone."

Turning back, he pulled off his shirt. "All these years, living by wits and guile, and here I am, tagged by a cop in my own bleeding house. Do it then, and finish the insult."

"The bleeding cop got the insult first from her former partner, so don't whine to me."

When she started to refer to the instructions, he just snatched the case out of her hand. "Give me the fecking thing before you bollocks it."

"In about three seconds," she muttered, "I'm going to bollocks you. My entire division," she continued as he attached it, activated it, secured it, "the commander, Tibble, EDD, Reo and her office, Mira — and as of this afternoon Nadine's considerable resources — are working this. We might get that kind of unilateral support and screw the budget if Cobbe was just your average international contract killer, but we sure as hell have it because he wants to add you to his four hundred and forty-three kills. So don't bitch to me about bleeding cops. Because they would. Every goddamn one of them would bleed for you."

She stormed away, dumped the contents of her file bag on her workstation. And while the cat watched them both warily from the sleep chair, began to update her board.

"I want no one bleeding for me."

"It's not about what you want."

"Clearly." With a precision that would

have met Feeney's approval, Roarke smoothed the patch over the tracker. "What was has been dredged up inside me, and some of it stings more than I'd like. Add to it, I've spent my life avoiding what I've just done to myself. A man's entitled to complain after a solid kick in the balls."

"I don't like it, either, and I don't have balls."

"Metaphorically, you've the biggest, toughest I know." He crossed to her. "Everyone you just threw at my head, with some justification, matters to me a great deal."

"I know that."

"If he finds a way to harm any of them —"

She spun around. "Will he get to you?"

"Not in this life or any."

"Then trust me and mine to do our jobs."

"I do. I am, or I wouldn't be wearing this bloody thing, would I? Neither of us would. And you needn't requisition one for Summerset."

He took her shoulders before she could explode at him. "It's my own make you're using, so I'll see to it. He'll have one on him in the morning. My word on it."

"Fine."

He tightened his grip before she could turn away again. "Understand this. I swear to you, a man could hold a blaster to my head and not have me agree to wear this damn thing. Only you."

She tapped her arm again. "Back at you."

He smoothed his hands down her arms. "And it's elbow."

"Whose elbow?"

Despite it all, his temper just drained. "It's your ass from your elbow, not your ear."

"What's the difference? They're both body parts that start with *e*. At least your ear has a hole in it."

He dropped his forehead to hers. "Christ Jesus, I love you."

Resentment, and he'd sparked plenty of it, slipped away. She put her arms around him.

A crap day, she thought, for both of them. Just a crap day all around.

"You're already half-undressed," she said, and sighed. "I'm never going to get to work."

She lifted her head, found his mouth, took it.

Need, she thought as the kiss went quickly hot, quickly deep.

For and from both of them.

So she gave what he needed, took what she needed as they stood in front of murder and loss.

She rolled her shoulders when he released her weapon harness so it fell to the floor with a *thud.*

They followed it, a tangle of limbs.

Heat pumped again, the sort that churned need to urgency. His hands, quick and skilled, dragged the T-shirt up and away, peeled the support tank off so they could claim her breasts.

When he rolled her, his mouth staked that claim as his hands grazed down her torso to unhook her belt. She arched under him, thinking: Hurry, hurry, hurry. She wanted him inside her, trapped in her, lost in her.

She tugged his pants down as he tugged hers. The fingers of one hand dug into his hip as she gripped his hair with the other, pulled him back up so her mouth could feast, just feast, on his.

"Don't wait," she told him as she bowed up again. "Don't wait."

He couldn't have.

All that had been, that was, that might be swirled inside him. She was the answer, the only true thing, the reason.

Inside her, with her body a hot whip of demand under his, nothing else existed. In the wild beat of her heart, he found his own. Nothing and no one could match what she brought to him, what she gave to him, what she took from him.

When she cried out, he felt an almost savage thrill that he had ripped that release out of her. He made her shudder, he made her go limp.

So he slowed, pressed his lips, gently now, to the bird-wing beat of the pulse in her throat to take her up again. Now with love outpacing need the pleasure spun, spun, spun out for both of them until he let himself spill into the open heart of it.

She lay quiet, stroking his back. She knew they had to surface, deal with the reality of what they faced. She could wish it otherwise, but the world refused to be locked out for long.

"Just another moment," he murmured. "This — not the sex, but this — is why we go through all the rest, isn't it?"

"It wasn't always. I guess it is now. This one's too close to home, Roarke. Neither of us are going to sleep easy until it's done."

"We won't, no. And still." He sat up, drawing her with him so they sat, still tangled. "I would put either of us up against him. Together? He has no real concept of what he's facing. Not only because we're smarter, and we are, or because we have all those resources. But because of this."

He took her hand, gripped it. "Because of this."

"Then let's use it."

"I'm wearing the shagging thing, aren't I?"

"And not much else." She started to smile, then had a horrible thought. "It doesn't track, like, what we just did. I mean, that kind of movement."

He made a noncommittal noise as he rose, and again drew her up with him.

"Oh, fuck me."

"I believe I did, and quite well. It's doubtful they're monitoring that . . . minutely, we'll say."

"God, God, God! I'm not going to think about it." Reaching down, she grabbed clothes, started to dress. "It's messing with my head, and I have work."

"We have work," he corrected, and began to dress. "Tell me what you want me to focus on."

"Coffee," she muttered and strode to her command center. "I need coffee."

"We."

"Right, we need coffee." She programmed a pot. "As soon as Summerset sends me his stops today, I'll have uniforms tracking that, talking to merchants, clerks."

She huffed out a breath. "Unlikely we get

anything, because he used an amplifier, but we check. I have files, more inclusive and extensive now. Probably not that much in them you don't already know from your own monitor and more recent dips into the alphabet soup, but you could take a hard look at his known associates. Anything you can add there is good. New York associates in particular."

"All right." He poured two large mugs.

"I figure if he intended to come to New York, do the hit, leave, he'd book a hotel or an apartment. Downtown, in the area of Modesto's residence. Upscale because that's what he goes for. But probably not one of yours because he wouldn't want to put money in your pocket."

"Good point, and we'll agree on that. So you're looking for a single male booking. And for a quick job like this, it would be a hotel."

"Right. I've got a team on it, but you can give that a skim if you want. But he's changed his mind, right? Not booking out right after the hit. More extended stay, and, as in his dreams he wants to take at least one of us to play with, more privacy."

"He'd want a house, single residence, or a duplex that's well soundproofed. But he'd try for that single residence first. And furnished. He doesn't have time to get a decent bed and so on."

As he thought it through, Roarke sat on the edge of her command center. "He might look for one near here, to help him keep track of our comings and goings. Or closer to Central, to mind you. And still possibly near my headquarters."

"I hadn't thought of that one."

"He'd need a vehicle. He could rent, even buy. He might boost one, but that's risky unless he's so confident he thinks he can meet his goal before a stolen vehicle's reported."

"We're looking at all of that. And missing persons — Whitney took that. It's a long shot, but he could just take over a house, kill whoever's inside."

Roarke stared into his coffee. "Not a long shot at all. There's a good possibility. But you won't have a missing person's report to check, not right off in any case. With the right contacts he could target someone. You force them to contact work, if work they have, or friends, family, whatever it is. Need to go out of town, family emergency, work, whatever suits. A curious neighbor? How do you do, I'm Joe's cousin, friend, associate, what have you. Doing some house-sitting for him while he's on a business trip."

"That could hold, for a while."

"Awhile's all he thinks he needs. But he'd need the contact. He couldn't just pluck a house that suits his needs and has a convenient sort of tenant or owner inside also suiting them."

Eyes narrowed, Eve followed that path. "The tenant or owner would have to be someone who's a bad guy himself, or involved on the fringes, or a victim. Goddamn it, why pay when you can just take? And if that's how he's working it, it closes off an angle of investigation."

"I have contacts of my own," Roarke reminded her. "I'll do what I can. One more possibility. He has a previous employer who has a property. He agrees to do the next job at a discount for use of the house for a week or two. There'd have to be trust there, of a sort, but it simplifies. It's cleaner. I'll, ah, reach out, as you say."

"Careful with your reach."

"Always, darling."

"We're checking on private shuttles — that's his usual. And he can pilot, so he might have come over on his own. Either way, if he booked a shuttle, he'd have canceled or postponed the return."

"Well then, we have quite a bit to keep us busy." He rose. "I'll start with that reaching out. You'll copy those files to my unit."

"Did it on the way home. Roarke, if you use the unregistered, I need to know."

"Not for this in any case." He topped off his coffee from the pot. "I'll use my office for now, but at some point, I'll likely just use your auxiliary."

"You don't especially want me to hear the conversations with these contacts."

"I don't think you especially want to hear the conversations. I'll give you the gist of them, and whatever bears fruit."

Good enough, she thought as he went into his office.

She opened operations, and got down to work.

It shouldn't have surprised her Summer-set had already sent his day's itinerary. What did surprise her was how many stops he made.

Greengrocer, cheesemonger, fishmonger — what the hell was a monger? — flower stall, dry goods (were there wet goods?), and on and on.

She sent the list to Uniform Carmichael with orders to assign officers to track and question.

She read Whitney's report, making her own notes along the way. She did the same with Mira's updated profile, and there had

to fight for objectivity when reading conclusions in stark terms.

Cobbe's need to eliminate Roarke is
more than a goal. It is his mission, central
to his identity. Only cowardice and lack of
clear opportunity, in addition to a desire to
build up his own status and wealth, has
stopped him from acting on this since their
last altercation.

As long as Roarke exists, Cobbe remains unable to claim his most essential
desire. He cannot be Patrick Roarke's true
son, as he perceives Roarke stands in his
way.

Moreover, the fact Roarke rejected this
father, replaced him with another, de-
mands retribution. Roarke built his life,
successfully, lives openly with the fruits of
that success — businesses, home, wife,
family, friendships — and commands
respect, all while carrying the name
Roarke — the name Cobbe desires above
all; this seeds envy.

Unable to acknowledge envy, as this is
an admission Roarke is better than he,
possesses — beyond the paternity —
what he himself lacks, Cobbe knows only
his hatred.

His fear of Roarke, the boy and the man

who consistently bested or outwitted him, thereby denying him the love and respect from the "father," feeds his hatred.

By his nature, and by this need, Cobbe concluded that seeing the object of his lifelong hate, and fear, this obstacle to his greatest wish, on scene after a fresh kill was a sign that this was the time and place to fulfill his destiny.

All true, Eve thought, and if she let herself feel too much, all terrifying.

The solution: Think like a cop.

Cobbe's mission: Eliminate Roarke.

But the mission itself was his weakness.

He'd taken a risk, and made a mistake, with the dead-cat ploy. Hell, he'd made a mistake from the jump by showing himself to Roarke. That was ego — another weakness. If he'd kept to the shadows, he'd have had a better shot at taking Roarke out. But he'd wanted that moment.

Here I am, you fuck, and I'm coming for you.

Sure, he'd been cagey enough to use an amplifier on Summerset — but Summerset still knew he'd been tailed.

Why hadn't he tried to take out Summerset, who he'd have seen as a skinny old man? Biding his time? Unlikely. Hoping for information, for routine to establish, that she'd buy.

He'd gotten a cat out of it, then rashly used that information to taunt.

Pattern?

Frowning, she went back over the file, trying to find other known instances that might fit.

"Nothing, nothing, nothing," she muttered. "So . . ." She looked back at her board. "New pattern. Not new, not really. Roarke pattern."

Rising, she put a secondary board together. She poured more coffee, started a secondary book.

While she let that cook in her brain, she took a portion of the searches for real estate.

She snatched up her 'link when it signaled, saw Baxter on the readout.

"Give me something."

"How about the Parkview Hotel? Penthouse suite, under the name Reginald J. Patrick. He used a Brit passport and a One Universe credit account."

"Where's the hotel?" She pulled up a map even as she asked. "Never mind, I've got it. Just a couple blocks from Modesto's residence."

"Small, pricey, quiet hotel. No doorman, but good security. We're getting the security feeds, talking to staff. They remember him. He checked in two days before the hit, checked out the morning after."

"Good, get all you can. Get the sweepers to process his room."

"It's been cleaned."

"Get them in there. Find out when and how he booked — how long he booked. When he ate, what he ate, what he wore, when he went out, when he came back. What he said, who he said it to."

"I got it, Dallas. We're on it."

"Stay on it," Dallas ordered as Roarke entered the room. "Copy me the feed as soon as you get it. Good work."

Rising again, she put the hotel on her board. Close to the target's residence, her fitness center, the park, her general comfort zone. A good choice.

"Baxter and Trueheart found his hotel. Parkview, right in the vic's neighborhood."

"He's checked out, I take it, or you'd be heading out the door."

"Yeah, but we'll get the feed, statements, his bill, sweep his room. He goes for a small, upscale hotel. Because of location, because he likes the higher level of service? Both."

"I'd agree with that." He started toward the coffeepot, stopped when he saw the secondary board.

It featured Cobbe, himself, Patrick Roarke, Cobbe's mother, Summerset, maps — Dublin, New York — the Parkview. The mutilated body of a tabby cat, a burlap sack, bloodied. Time lines stretching back to his childhood.

"Thorough," he murmured.

"It has to be. I'm sorry."

"Don't be sorry." He touched a hand to her shoulder, then continued to the coffeepot. "It's . . . disconcerting, but don't be sorry."

"There's a pattern," she began.

"Is there?"

"Yeah, there is, one exclusive to you. He takes risks. His profession's a risk, but he minimalizes them in his paid work from what I can see. Sure, I can spot some of the mistakes he made when I read his file, but I can't say he's sloppy. In the beginning, more sloppy, but he learned. He'd be dead or in a cage otherwise."

"All right."

"But with you, all along with you, he's let his ego, his — Mira calls it his mission in her amended profile — push him to take more risks, to make more mistakes.

"Patrick Roarke literally tosses him out of the house the first time Cobbe tries to stake his claim, and when you offer him a hand up, he tried to knife you. That's stupid, sloppy. Now you're forewarned, right? If he'd taken the hand, tried making friends, let's say, you'd have been more vulnerable to an attack later. It had to be then for him."

"We were children," Roarke began.

"He was a killer. He was born one. I'm telling you he was made that way."

Roarke lifted his coffee, again said, "All right."

"I don't say that because he wants you dead and I don't. I don't even say it because of how he makes his living. I say it as a murder cop who's looked at his file, who's looked at four hundred and forty-three — forty-four with Modesto — victims. Killing's in his bones, in his blood, in his gut. Killing is what he is, and that gives him pride."

Roarke watched her face while she spoke — the cop's eyes, flat and dispassionate because they had to be.

"All right." This time he nodded. "All right, yes."

"We can get into philosophies later, but right now, pattern. The first time wasn't the only time he tried for you when you were kids."

"No. I was faster, and smarter. And had mates."

"And when he couldn't get to you, what

251

did he do?"

Roarke looked back at the board. "The dog," he realized. "The little dog. And here, a cat."

"There you go. You protected the kid and the dog, he kills the dog. You have a cat. He kills a cat. Can't get to you yet, or isn't ready to try, but he can stick a thumb in your eye."

She pointed back to the board. "He rats you out to Patrick Roarke. You get a beating, but he gets worse. But then what happens?"

Frowning, Roarke shook his head. "He let me be awhile, steered clear."

"Did he? Or did he watch your pattern? Maybe pay or threaten others to tell him where you went, what you did?"

"He could've done, I suppose."

"You wondered tonight if he told Patrick Roarke you were in that alley with your book. I say that's just exactly right. Why did you choose that time and place?"

"Ah . . . I can't say to the timing, it's vague. But that little hideaway in that alley was a safe spot. So I thought. Had been. The old man . . . he didn't venture there, not in daylight. He had . . . He had business elsewhere. Fuck it, it's blurry, but he was off, wasn't he, meeting — someone. The

252

Drowned Rat, was it? Might be, that was his usual pub, and it was blocks from that alley."

"What would he have done if Cobbe came and told him he'd seen you loafing with a book instead of working?"

"Given Cobbe the back of his hand, maybe the boot for good measure." No doubt of that, Roarke thought, no doubt, but . . . "And aye, he'd have come to see if Cobbe told him true."

"And you got worse that time. A lot worse. He got rid of you. It didn't work out the way he wanted, but he got rid of you. You just wouldn't stay down."

She came back for her own coffee. "I'm going to say there were other times he tried to get to you, or as you went about making your living after Patrick Roarke was dead, tried to screw your plans. He couldn't get to you, but —"

"Marlena."

Eve set her coffee down, took Roarke's face in her hands. She felt the anguish. "Don't go there. You can't know, you'd never know for sure. Don't take Summerset there. Don't."

He met her eyes. "I'll say nothing to him. Be sure of it."

"Stay with me here. It's his pattern, with

253

you. Only with you. It was pattern when he saw you in that bar in France. Just like the first night, he couldn't stop himself from making a move. And you put him down. And humiliated him. Whatever he might have tried between then and now, he failed. But this is now, and the pattern holds. Showing himself to you in the park. He's skilled enough to have stayed out of sight, to have watched, waited. He couldn't, because it's you. With you, he's sloppy."

"Clearly, you and your board have the right of it. You'd never have looked for the hotel and found it. If Interpol made the connection, and they likely would have, he'd have been gone, not right here as he is."

"He doesn't care if they make the connection. Doesn't care about anything but this time, this place, and finally taking you out. I'm going to bet he already has credentials — has had for years — in the name of Lorcan Roarke."

"Why in flaming hell he'd want such a father I'll never understand."

"I do. He is Patrick Roarke's true son. Not his bio son, but you and I know it's not blood that makes a father."

"Dennis said that tonight," Roarke murmured. "He said just that."

"We know that, we're proof. Summerset's

yours. How else could I tolerate having that bony corpse under the same roof?"

Because that made him smile a little, she picked up her coffee again. "He doesn't get — Cobbe doesn't get that he already has what he wants. The rest is just a name, and even then —"

"Summerset told me to make it mine. To make it worth something, and make it mine."

"So you did. But you could've changed it to Hickenlooperstein, and Cobbe would still want you dead."

"Hickenlooperstein?"

She shrugged. "It's probably somebody's name."

"You're right on all of this — maybe not Hickenlooperstein — but the rest. It's been harder for me to get through the fog of it, but you've managed to clear it away, and I can see you're right on all of it."

Her comm signaled an incoming.

"That's the feed."

"Let's have a look."

Roarke ordered it on the wall screen, cued it up to where Baxter noted on the attachment.

The door cam picked up Cobbe exiting a black limo. The driver — female, about forty, mixed race, gray uniform — opened the passenger door. Assisted Cobbe — black pants, black leather jacket, light blue T-shirt, black sunshades — with his luggage.

A black midsize rolly, a black messenger-style briefcase, and a second case, metal. His sharps, she thought.

"Those, in the metal case, tools of his trade. He had to fly private to get them through. That's good to know.

"Not getting the plates on the limo, but we can track it. Find where he came in. Yeah, sloppy."

He walked into a lobby that could've been some historic mansion's elegant and generous foyer.

The marble floors, white streaked with gray, shined under the light dripping from a trio of chandeliers. Flowers speared out of clear tubes from pale gray walls. High-backed chairs in velvety fabric offered splashes of red.

A woman — blond hair sleeked back — wore pale pink as she sat at a long, polished table with curved legs. She rose, smiled a greeting, offered a hand.

After gesturing him to one of the facing chairs, she took her seat to check him in.

"He used a Brit passport," Eve told Roarke. "A One Universe credit account. Name Reginald J. Patrick. I bet the J's for

Jabber. The nickname Patrick Roarke gave him. It's in Mira's report."

"Just can't let the old man go," Roarke murmured.

A man came out — dark skin, black suit — exchanged handshakes before taking the suitcase, the messenger bag, while Cobbe refused help with the metal case.

"Definitely his sharps in there," Eve said as the man in the suit gestured to the elevators.

Chatting, Eve noticed, as they walked. The usual blah blah, she imagined as the elevator cam followed them up to the penthouse floor.

Steel-gray carpet here, cream walls, more flowers, some art, doors to match the carpet. Full security on every one.

Double door, corner suite.

The man unlocked the door before offering Cobbe the swipe, then they both went inside.

"The room's been cleaned, but I'm having it swept. You never know. We'll track the limo, and Baxter and Trueheart are interviewing the staff. Lots of mistakes here — and all because he couldn't resist you seeing him."

She watched the man exit, walk to the elevator. Checking the attachment, she ordered the new cue point.

"Two hours and ten later, he goes out. Jeans now, different shirt, no jacket. Going to stroll around the neighborhood, that's what he's going to do. Walk past the target's house, check out what the husband's told him are her usual haunts. Grab a meal maybe."

Using Baxter's cues, they watched him come in, go out, come in. Watched the evening desk clerk — brunette — greet him.

Then they followed him from his room to the door cam forty-four minutes before Modesto's murder.

He strolled out casually, lifting a hand to the brunette on the desk as he left the hotel. In black pants, a black hoodie — hood down — black high-tops.

"Look at his face." Eve paused the feed. "Nothing there. Empty. He's going out to kill someone. He might as well be heading to the office to deal with some paperwork."

"It's the same for him. I've known others, not so different."

"Yeah, so have I." She continued the feed. "He's giving himself plenty of time for an easy walk to the park. Then, hood up, around it to get a feel, to blend in. Next cue's one hour, twenty-four minutes. Wants to wait for the cops to come, take his proof of death. Has to leave the park first, reverse the jacket, come back in, blend again."

She cued up the return.

"Not empty now. He's revved up, and a little pissed, but mostly excited. Red jacket — smarter to have reversed it again in case the brunette noticed the switch. Too revved to think of it. Moving fast for the elevator. Fists bunched.

"Look at her," Eve said. "She noticed — she's puzzled because he's been moderately friendly, but now he storms right by her. She'll remember, and that's another little mistake."

Glancing down, she scanned the attachment. "He's got two more cues on here. Cobbe hired an LC. Baxter and Trueheart have her name, will interview. Let's have a look."

Fifty-six minutes after Cobbe stormed in, another brunette — late twenties, blue dress on a curvy frame — got out of a cab, entered the lobby. After a brief conversation at the desk, the desk clerk tapped her earpiece, had another brief conversation, then clearly gave the licensed companion a room number and the go-ahead.

They tracked her through the elevator cam — where she checked a thin, glittering wrist unit, shook back long, wavy hair. She made her way down the hall, pressed the buzzer on Cobbe's door.

He opened it, unsmiling, wearing one of the hotel's robes.

She came out again in twenty-six minutes, looking mildly amused and a little baffled.

"Not much staying power," Eve commented.

They watched her take out a 'link in the elevator, speak with someone, laugh, shrug. Another check of her wrist unit, and she glided out, across the lobby, and away.

12

Eve watched Cobbe check out, noted he seemed in a better mood. He strolled out of the lobby, turned right, and went off the feed.

"Thinking of the cams now," she said. "Making sure he gets his ride away from them. He's got his place already set. He's got the smirking confidence back on. We'll track the limo he arrived in, and that'll give us a little more. We'll try cab pickups within a few blocks, but I don't think he'd go there. Maybe, maybe, he'd use the same car service as arrival, but low odds on it."

She glanced at Roarke, who nodded.

"In his place, I'd have already booked another service, under another name, take that to another drop-off, walk again, then catch a cab to my hole. It's just basic precautions."

"Agreed, but he may not take that extra step. And if it's the same service, even if he did take that step, we can hit the cabs for pickups in that area."

She paced away to the board, added the name of the LC and the ID photos she'd printed out. "We'll get more from the LC. It's in their interest to pay attention, notice details on a job. Baxter and Trueheart will get those out of her."

She paced back. "Unlikely, highly, he'd have been able to rent or buy that hole so fast, wouldn't be able to zero in and take somebody out to use their place. So it's a contact, someone he knows. Bad guy safe house, that's what it is."

"I've some lines out there," Roarke told her. "It may take a bit of persuading to get a bite on those lines, but I can be persuasive."

"Yeah, you can. I'm going to review the feed again, and push on the other angles. He booked a shuttle, a limo, an LC, he got the cat from somewhere. The bad-guy safe house, that's going to be a single-family residence. Upscale, good neighborhood, high-end security."

"I have to point out there's no lack of those in New York."

"It's a jump point, and if it's what I think it is, it has rotating tenants. Upscale, good neighborhood, people notice that. It's got a cover."

She started pacing again. "Owner travels extensively for business, uses it as a New York base, renting it out short term to execs, blah blah. Wealthy individual or couple — no kids — friendly enough, but no socialization. Too busy."

"Alternatively, it may be owned by a dummy corporation, and there's your cover. It's a space available to execs again, or clients."

"Could be even better." She stewed on it. "Yeah, even better that way. You'd want staff, but you could — and likely would — stick with droids. So we'll look for single-family residences, and so on, owned by a business."

"Why don't I take that while you push your other angles?"

"That'll work."

Roarke took her auxiliary while she went back to the security feed. Details, she thought.

Check in — wearing black. Friendly enough, but with a bored look in his eyes. Just another job.

Heading out, the casual wave. Showered off the travel, she thought, casually dressed.

Same boots, she noted, he'd come in wearing.

She froze, enhanced, got a closer look at them. Since Roarke insisted on buying her boots every five minutes, she recognized custom. Another angle, and she added it to her notes.

Going to check out the area, maybe get a good meal.

Murder night. Black hoodie — and black running shoes. Freeze, enhance.

"He's wearing one of your brand of running shoes."

"Sorry, what?"

"I bet he doesn't know you own the company that makes the running shoes he's wearing. Top-of-the-line's what he knows. Running shoes because he's going to have to move fast, he may have to run. And they work better with the hoodie. Just some guy out for a jog or a stroll through the park."

She noted down the brand of the shoes, did a probability on size.

Red jacket. Had to be custom, too. Reversible to black hoodie. Private tailor? No telltale emblem, brand name, no label, she remembered. Long shot didn't begin to cover it, but she put it in her notes.

Back to checkout. Urban black — not the

hoodie, but the same jacket worn at check-in.

"He's going to want more clothes," she murmured. "He packed for a couple of days, but he's extending that now. He's going to shop. High-end menswear."

Another ridiculous long shot, but it went into her notes.

She paused her searches to read the preliminary sweeper report on the hotel room.

Nothing.

But within an hour, the next incoming gave her a boost.

"We've got the transpo service, the car and driver. And that takes us to his shuttle." She glanced over at Roarke. "A team's heading over to interview the driver, another's heading to the transpo center."

She rose to update her board. "We'll get feed again, plus we'll know where he came in from. The ground service was booked under Patrick R. Blade. He used Blade with Tween. Switched the name for the hotel, but he likely used one of those two names to book the shuttle."

Roarke sat back. "You can follow him, and I understand every detail matters. But it's harder to understand how those details help you find him."

"Track his movements, follow his pattern. He came in for a quick job, packed for a quick job. Private shuttle because that's how he rolls, and he needed his knives. Now we'll know where he came in from, we'll interview the pilot. Did he have a meal on the shuttle, a drink? What did he eat, what did he drink? Private's going to have an attendant. We interview. Did he work, did he chat, did he sleep?"

She stuck her hands in her pockets, studied the board.

"He adjusted his plans. Now he has to buy some clothes. No time for private tailoring, so high-end but — what do you call it?"

"Off-the-rack. Ready-to-wear."

"Right. How long's he had that reversible hoodie? There's nothing in his file about that one — reverse to red jacket. Maybe it's a detail missed or left out, but maybe he had it made by a tailor where he flew in from. We track that. Maybe there's something there that tells us where he's most likely to shop here. Maybe. We nail that, we have a better idea of the area where he may be staying now."

"And still."

She walked back, sat facing him. "We find the tailor. Has he used that tailor before? You're more likely to stick with one, or go to one on a recommendation. We interview the tailor, pull out more. Does the tailor work for any of Cobbe's known associates? If so, we use that. It's a process."

"It is. I know it."

"Then there's the LC. She's going to have observations. Fast bang or BJ, she'd wash up. What did she see? What was on the bathroom counter?"

"Seriously?"

"Yeah, seriously. What was in the bed-room, or whatever room they used? What did he say? What didn't he say? Did any communications come through while she was there? Did he drink anything — and what? Men like Cobbe? Licensed compan-ions equal a means to an end — there to serve. They might as well be droids. Plus he was revved up, angry. If there's any time he'd be careless, that would be it."

"You've a point with that," he agreed.

"Same with the limo driver. But he was on his way to a job, he'd have been polite, most likely. A little dumb-ass small talk on the way to the ride. Privacy screen engaged there, I expect, but up until. What did he say? Did he have an accent? Did he ask her for a good place for dinner near his hotel? Her impression of him."

Eve shrugged. "Things can add up." She

grabbed her signaling 'link. "It's Baxter," she said. "Dallas. What've you got? I'm putting you on speaker."

"My boy and I just had a nice chat with a very interesting woman. Yvette Conroy, who serves a superior cup of coffee, works through Discretion. You interviewed the owner on the Pettigrew case."

"Yeah. She was cooperative."

"Still is. Yvette contacted her, just to clear things, and was — in turn — cooperative. She took the last-minute job as the hotel's close to her also superior digs, and she didn't have a booking. The company's standard security run on Cobbe — or Reginald J. Patrick — produced a single male, age forty-two, no criminal, with an income that could afford the fee — which includes an additional ten percent charge for a booking in under two hours. Dublin-based businessman who owns several art galleries."

"Fancy," Eve said. "Important."

"Yeah, so our girl's expecting the fancy, likely with a side of charm. He doesn't live up to the hype. He points to the bedroom the minute he closes the door. She adjusts expectations, but tries some get-to-know-you. You know, lovely suite, lovely view, are you enjoying New York.

"He tells her to strip and get on the bed, he's not interested in fucking conversation, just fucking."

"And she didn't see the charm?"

Baxter laughed. "Nope. She said she considered canceling because he looked mean, but she could handle mean. So she walked into the bedroom behind him. He watched her strip, but didn't seem interested in any flourishes. He took off his robe — was already wearing a condom. Basically, she said, it was a two-step. He got on, got off. About ten minutes on the outside. No eye contact, no kissing. Rough with his hands, but straight missionary wham-bam, with no thank you, ma'am.

"She said he didn't seem to enjoy it, because he snarled and swore the whole time. And I quote, 'I'll do the fucker this time. Fucking bastard, lucky prick bastard gobshite. I'll drink his fucking blood before it's done.' "

"Descriptive."

"He worked up a sweat with it. She assumed he needed to get some business problem — competitor — worked out, then they'd connect. Instead, when he finished, he told her to get dressed and get out, but he seemed deflated — in more ways than one. Sulky, in her term. She said she needed

269

to clean up, and he waved a hand at the bathroom. So she did, and said she considered she'd made nine K — she gets the full grand for the late booking, and eighty percent of the ten K fee — in under a half hour.

"He was back in the robe when she came out, sitting in a chair and brooding into a glass of whiskey. She said goodnight, he grunted, she left. She called it in on the way down to the lobby, got another late booking offer, decided why the hell not.

"Kind of makes you wonder why everybody's not an LC."

"Right. What did she notice?"

"A lot. Well built, gym fit, and muscular. No visible scars, tats, or piercings. Manicured hands, groomed pubes. No devices sitting around, no personal items in the bedroom or the living area of the suite. He'd showered not long before she got there, because there was a damp towel on the floor. He had his kit out on the counter. High-end products — travel size. When we pressed, she remembered a couple of brands. He uses That Man skin products — and I can tell you they're steep. Underworld hair products — including the daily treatment to address hair loss."

"Hair loss. Interesting."

"You have to get that line direct from a licensed salon, and it's generally used to supplement salon treatments, recommended every three months. Trueheart looked it up. And since we're smart cops, we've done a search for salons so licensed in Dublin. Thirty-two of them."

"That's good. That's very good."

"So say we all. We'll go ahead and run the search in New York."

"I'll take that."

"It's all yours, Loo. He'd had at least one drink before she got there. She smelled the whiskey. He wasn't drunk or impaired, but he'd had a drink, and was having one when she left."

"Got it. That's good work."

"Yvette's on alert to notify us if he books again, and agreed to do the same if she happened to see him in her jaunts around town."

"Good enough. Call it a night."

"You need more, just give a tag and we're on it."

"Appreciated."

"I stand corrected," Roarke said when she clicked off. "Out of a twenty-minute session he had with an LC, you have those details, those lines. You may not be happy to hear there are eighty-eight salons in Manhattan

271

licensed for Underworld hair products and treatments, but you'll cull that down."

"Yeah, we will. First way, how many of those — and the ones in Dublin — also carry the skin stuff he uses."

"Ha. Well, of course."

"People tend to stick with the same person and place with stuff like that. Even if it's Trina," she added in a mutter.

"They do, yes — and our Trina's salon is so licensed."

"When we nail down the salon in Dublin and his Trina-type person, we'll get more. And we'll get the last time he had the in-salon deal, see when he'd want another. If his usual recommends other places when he's traveling."

With more coffee, she studied the board again.

"Sloppy to leave the kit out, but the LC's just a vehicle for release as he sees it. Sloppy to hire out for sex anyway when for what he used it for, he could've whacked off and saved eleven large."

"Whacking off provides release, but it doesn't feed the ego like a beautiful woman who's there to do whatever you want."

Eve sat again, pointed a finger at him. "That's absolutely right. He needed the vehicle, needed to know he could pay top dollar for ten minutes. And now we have more details."

She gestured toward the auxiliary. "How about you?"

"I've a number of possibilities. It'll take longer to cull through them."

"Can it cull on auto?"

"For a first pass."

"Let's do that. I'm tired. I need some sleep."

When he simply looked at her, she hissed out a breath. "Okay, let's say we both need some sleep. And most of what I need to do has to wait until morning anyway. So do me a favor."

"On auto then."

"Good, and I'll do the same with the salon angle."

Once she had, in twice the time it took him to set his up, she rose. "I'm going to dump all these angles and results on Abernathy's lap tomorrow."

He took her hand. "Would that be ego?"

"Damn right. How come the alphabets never figured out Cobbe worried about losing his hair?" As they walked out, Galahad streaked by in his quest to beat them to the bed. "That's some gold to mine."

"And you know Cobbe likely didn't get quite so sloppy — as you put it — before.

But still, it gives you a one-up on the inspector, which you'll enjoy."

"Some. But I can set that back for getting Interpol's resources on the angle."

When they reached the bedroom, the cat had stretched himself over as much of the bed as possible. Eve sat to pull off her boots — gave them a study.

"Then there's the boots. Custom boots. Who's his bootmaker? Does he have one in Dublin? Same with suits, because he'd want some of those. He'd need a tailor for that reversible jacket. He needed to find a cat to kill, a hole to hide in. Private shuttle and ground service.

"Lots of gold to mine."

When she got into bed, he drew her against him. The cat shifted to curl into the small of her back.

"Who decided gold was worth digging out of caves or whatever?" she wondered. "And why? Because it's shiny?"

Roarke brought her hand to his lips to kiss. "The world's full of puzzles."

Yeah, it was, she thought. But only one interested her now. Where was Lorcan Cobbe?

He rarely dreamed of Dublin. The city represented the canvas for the worst of his childhood memories, and the best of them as well. He had begun to build his fortune there — by both thievery and by fair means. And though he still had business interests there, he'd left Dublin, the bright and the dark of it, behind.

When he traveled there now, he didn't travel home, not emotionally. Memories would come, of course, and some would bite with keen teeth.

But he'd overcome, hadn't he? He'd done what he'd set out to do, and more.

But dreams had the canny skill of blending the bright and dark together into shifting shadows, and hiding those keen teeth until they tore into the throat.

So he traveled back in dreams, a man who watched the boy he'd been. Skinny and quick, grubby, Christ knew, running the streets on a damp, gray day with his hair falling into his eyes and a hole worn into the knee of his trousers.

He ran with his mates — all but one gone now. Pretty Jenny with her tumbling hair, and Mick with his sly grin and big plans. Shawn up for anything on a dare.

Gone, all three, taken in vengeance and gone to dust.

And there Brian, the one he had left, crafty as he was steady, with his cap cocked

— jaunty-like — over his left eye.

Gloomy day or not, remnants of the Urbans lingering still, the tourists continued to flock to Grafton Street. They frequented the pubs and the shops and stalls, took their vids of buskers playing tunes.

The man he was couldn't help but admire the boy's nimble fingers lifting a wallet here, slipping it to a mate — or using the quick bump and begging your pardon, sir! to snag a wrist unit, and pass that to another mate.

He might cop a 'link, smooth as you please. Even a handbag or two.

He'd share the spoils — a testament to teamwork — and if he judged it enough, might squirrel away a bit for his personal nest egg.

He heard the boy with the angel's voice and the little dog. A crowd would gather there, so he wandered that way, judged his marks.

The boy — had he ever known his name? — sang an old one. One designed to bring a tear to the eye and put money in the cap.

He found his mark in a man with a gold wrist unit and a camera — a real one, a beauty. As the man focused the camera on the boy and dog, the boy he'd been edged closer.

He pined for the camera. Oh, that would

bring a good price! And the wrist unit as well. But from the angles — and he'd known the angles — settling for the wallet was his best bet.

As he moved into position, as the boy sang of young, dead Willie McBride, he spotted Cobbe — boy and man — across Grafton Street.

For a moment, in the odd way of dreams, they stared at each other — the vague past, the possible tomorrow.

The boy he'd been looked up at the man he was. "Well now, he's after killing me dead, isn't he then? But he won't be having what he wants today. You'll have to make for certain he doesn't get it tomorrow. We could've used that bloody camera," he added with pure regret.

And ran.

The boy Cobbe had been pulled out a knife and ran after him.

And Cobbe, the man, grinned across Grafton Street before sprinting in the opposite direction.

He pursued, through the crowds, the music, the yeasty smell of beer from the pubs.

He was faster, had always been faster. But he kept losing him. He'd catch a glimpse, then lose him, catch another.

277

Away from the crowds and music now, through alleyways he'd known too well as a boy where the air smelled of wet garbage and babies wailed in cries pinched with hunger.

All at once he stood in the alley over the broken, bloodied boy he'd been. The girl Eve had been sat on the filthy ground beside him. Hollow-eyed, cradling her broken arm, she looked up.

"They like to hurt us, the fathers."

He crouched down, heartsick, as he could do nothing for either of them. "I know it. We'll be all right. We'll get through."

"He broke my arm. I think yours, too."

Even in dreams he couldn't help himself, and reached out to stroke her tangled hair. "But they didn't break us, did they, darling?"

"I won't break you." Cobbe, both boy and man, stood just two feet away. "I'll just cut you to pieces. Her first."

With knife in hand, the man grabbed Eve by the hair. When the boy charged, Roarke lunged.

Into a void, and out of sleep.

"That was a bad one." Warm, strong, Eve's arms wrapped around him. "I should know. I'm the expert. Lights on, ten percent. Bad dream, okay? Just a bad dream."

She held on to him while the cat rubbed his head against Roarke's side.

"I'm all right."

"A bad one," she repeated. "Bad enough for a soother."

"I don't need —"

"We'll split one." She stroked his cheek, shifted to get out of bed. "I'm not used to being on the other side of a nightmare, so I could use half."

He figured that was likely bullshit, but he let it go.

"Do you want to tell me?"

"Dublin," he began, and told her while she got the soother for both of them.

"So a mix of then and what's going on now." She drank her half, making sure — he knew — he did the same. "You're worried about me on top of it. You should've dreamed me as a cop. We'd've kicked his asses together."

"I'll try to work that in next time."

She set the empty glasses aside, then took his face in her hands. "We're going to get him. We're going to put him away. I swear it to you."

"I trust you will."

"Then trust this." Now her whiskey-colored eyes held him as her hands did his face. "I know who he is. I know he'd love to kill me — just to hurt you, to break you. I won't let it happen. I won't let him hurt you that way. I swear that, too."

He rested his brow on hers. "All right then. I know it, Eve, I can swear that back to you. And still, I fear it."

"Don't. I can't — and don't — promise you to come home safe every day I go out to work. But I'm promising you this. I'm giving you my word on it."

She drew him back, curled against him, laid a hand over his heart. "In the dream, you said you told me they didn't break us, and you were right. I'm telling you, Cobbe won't, either."

So he was soothed, a little at least, and willed himself to sleep in the quiet, in the now, while the love of his life held his heart.

13

Routinely, when Roarke woke at some ungodly hour to take a meeting in some weird place where the time insisted on being different, Eve didn't stir.

But routine fell off the charts the minute Cobbe showed himself in the park.

So when Roarke started to slide out of bed in the dark, she shifted, grunted, blinked. "What the hell continent are you buying in the middle of the damn night?"

"Europe, but only a small portion. Go back to sleep."

She rolled over with every intention of doing just that.

But lay awake.

She called for the time. Four-fifty-five.

How was that even possible?

She lay quiet while he showered, while he dressed, and considered he did this virtually every morning, quiet as a cat while she slept on.

She rolled back again when she heard — actually sensed more than heard — him leave the room. Called for lights, then studied the dark sky through the sky window over the bed.

She might not have a continent, or any portion thereof, to buy, but she had plenty of work.

So while the cat slept, she got up, inhaled coffee. Not enough, she decided, and threw on workout gear. Still half-asleep, she took the elevator down to the gym, programmed a run on the beach to get her blood moving.

She did a solid three miles, put in fifteen with weights, and worked up a nice sweat while her brain started to engage.

Back upstairs, she hit the shower, let the heat, the pummeling jets cap it off while she mentally organized her day.

Check the auto searches, and angle off from the results. Check any incoming reports and do the same.

Hit the morgue about the dead cat, Harvo at the lab about the same.

Prep for Inspector Abernathy.

Custom boots, she thought as she stepped into the drying tube. Custom suits. Reversible hoodies. Fancy salons.

Bits and pieces, she thought as she headed

for her closet. She had lots of bits and pieces. Now she had to fit them together, expand the picture.

Since she had to consider wardrobe — it surrounded her, after all — she assessed her top priority. Moving fast when and if necessary.

Instead of grabbing pants at random, she searched through and found a pair that sort of melded workout gear with office wear. She hunted up a tee, a jacket, boots.

Since Roarke hadn't returned by the time she'd put herself together, and the cat now sat, awake and staring, she handled breakfast.

While Galahad devoured his salmon, she programmed more coffee.

She thought of pancakes, deemed them too heavy, opted for omelets. And since she held the controls, no weird-ass vegetables in hers.

Then, on a flash of inspiration, she ordered the choices sent to her office kitchen.

As the sun broke the dark, she headed to her office, opened the terrace doors. Cool, yeah, but not cold, she decided.

She put the meal, under their warming lids, on the table, poured herself more coffee, and moved to the adjoining door, where Roarke held a holo-conference with six people in business suits.

Staying out of range, she gestured to her office, then left him to it.

At her command center, she pulled up the results from her auto-search. She now had sixteen salons in Dublin that fit her criteria, and an even fifty in New York.

Including, she noted, Trina's.

Manicured hands, according to the LC. And the upscale skin junk. He'd need one of those all-purpose type places. Where people, for reasons she'd never understand, could choose to spend an entire day of their life.

She adjusted the criteria, ordered another search.

While it ran, she checked updates. The numbers on rentals or purchases of vans, trucks, A-Ts looked daunting, but they'd cut that down by end of day.

Missing persons. Not much likelihood there. So far, anyway.

The limo driver, however, there was the gold.

She glanced up as Roarke came in.

"We've got his shuttle. He came in from Brussels, private, and we've got the name of the pilot, the shuttle company, the works. We'll hit those this morning."

"That's good work."

"Too late for more interviews after the limo driver, but she had the data. I've adjusted criteria for the salons to the full torture opportunities. It's coming in now. Yes! Down to eleven in Dublin, forty-two in New York."

"An early start for you."

"Yeah, yeah, but I didn't buy a continent. Did you?"

"A deal's been struck on the small piece." He glanced at the table, the open doors, the rise of the sun. "It's a lovely idea, this."

"I thought so. Let's go for it."

When she rose, he waited for her, then just wrapped his arms around her. "You didn't go back to sleep."

"I got in a workout instead. Revved me up."

"So I see." When he ran his hands down her arms to her wrists, he cocked his head, narrowed his eyes.

She stepped back, flicked her wrists. The blades shot out from under her sleeves.

"And." She flipped back her jacket, revealing not just her usual weapon and harness, but the mini blaster on her hip.

He smiled, but it wasn't humor she saw. She saw relief.

"He won't hurt you through me."

"I believe you."

"Good." She retracted the blades. "Let's eat."

He poured more coffee for both of them, brushed a hand down her hair, then sat.

"Thanks," he said as he removed the warming lids. "For arming yourself for war, and for breakfast."

"No problem. As you're officially consulting on this case, I'm going to go ahead and copy you on the reports and updates."

"Appreciated. Why don't I take your Dublin salons? I still have contacts there."

"Plenty of cops in Dublin to make those rounds."

"True enough." He sampled his omelet. "But sometimes a less official question provides an easier opening. Give me an hour or two on it, then you can pass it off to the Garda, or this Abernathy."

She considered. "It would be sweet, wouldn't it, to hand Abernathy Cobbe's Dublin salon. Oh, look here, I think you guys might've missed this angle. And how fucking easy it might've been to plant somebody there, have a whole buncha badges ready to swoop in when Cobbe strolled in for his goddamn hair boost."

Roarke smiled as he ate. "Feeling competitive, are you?"

"I haven't decided yet. But I'm not

wrong." She crunched into bacon, waved the rest of the strip. "Why didn't they have this intel?"

"Apparently they never managed to find an LC fresh off the job who spotted his open travel kit."

"I'm not saying we didn't get lucky, because we did. But they've had years to get lucky."

"Bureaucracy." He shrugged. "And I assume territorial issues and battles. Add this is personal for Cobbe, so his emotions — such as they are — are clouding things. But overall? They're not you. You're not just good, not merely exceptional. You're an extraordinary investigator."

"That's not —"

He held up a finger to stop her. "I've watched you over the years, Lieutenant, pick up a detail others might miss as a spot of lint. It might mean little on its own, but you dig at it, pull at it, intuit from it, and fit it into the rest."

He smiled at her as he ate. "I'd've given you a run back in the day, and I believe I'd have evaded you well enough. But you'd have worried me, and I'd have done quite a bit to stay out of your way."

"I'd've done more than worry you."

Now he grinned. "And aren't we happy

we'll never know?"

She ate, nodded. "I'd really miss the coffee." So she drank more. "Anyway, you've got the two hours on the salon."

"I'll take it, and anything else you want to hand off to me. I'm keeping my schedule light — that was already in the plans. The first students are moving into the school today, and I want to be there on and off."

"Today?"

"The first of them, yes. Rochelle suggested we do it in groups rather than all together. So we'll have three days of easing in, light classes, orientations, and so on. Nadine assigned Quilla to do a vlog on the staggered opening. I saw her yesterday, in fact. The girl's going to be a force."

"Should I be there?"

That she'd ask meant, well, everything.

"You're welcome, of course, to come in whenever you like or can. We're not having a media opening. We decided that some time back. Nothing formal, no speeches, no media and so on, as that would end up about good works and all of that when it's about the children. As it happens, with Cobbe in New York, I'm more than glad we decided that way. I'm adding to the security until, but I don't see him focusing there."

"No point," she agreed, "if the media's

not hyping you. Push the rest away a minute," she told him. "How do you feel about it? Kids are moving in. Kids will eat there, sleep there starting today. Some of them will never have had a place they could feel that safe."

He looked at the view out the terrace windows — the green of the grass, the flowers blooming.

"I think of the dream I had last night. My mates and I, working Grafton Street. I don't regret it, not a bit. But I know full well I might not have survived without Summerset. He gave me that safe place. Not a place or a way you'd find . . . we'll say correct, but safe, and clean, when I'd known neither. Books, all I could read. Food, so I never went hungry. He had his standards and his rules, but never once did I feel the back of his hand."

He took hers now. "Even after Richard Troy, you didn't have that, not altogether, not day in and out. It was the Academy that gave you that."

"Yeah, it was."

"I like to think we're giving those who come to An Didean a mix of both what Summerset gave me and what the Academy gave you. And so I feel more than fine about it."

"I'd say it's a good mix, as long as there aren't classes on how to bypass security systems."

"Nothing formal in any case." He gave her hand a squeeze. "I'll see to the dishes."

"I've got it. I'd rather you check the housing search."

"All right then."

While she cleared, he sat at the auxiliary, called up the results. "Ah well, that's a bit better, but we can do better yet."

"How many?"

"More than two hundred, but I can narrow it. I'll refine it when a contact or two gets back to me. And I can slim that number before that with a bit of adjusting."

He got up. "A little time's what I need on this, and the salon. I should have something you can work with on both this morning."

"Okay. I'm going in, putting a report together before I meet Peabody at the morgue. I'll keep in touch."

"I'll do the same." He laid his hands on her shoulders, his lips lightly on hers. "He's never known the likes of you. I'm sure of it, as neither had I."

He kissed her again. "Take care of my cop."

"Your cop's locked and loaded."

She found the pale gray topper on the

newel post, and had to assume Roarke deemed it worked best with what she had on. With a shake of her head, she shrugged into it, went outside to where her vehicle waited.

The earlier start meant less traffic and no ad blimps. Always an advantage. Halfway — smoothly for a change — downtown, her 'link signaled. She saw Harvo's name on the display and took it on the in-dash.

"Dallas."

Harvo, her spring-green hair spiked up, said, "Yo. Got the goods for you."

"You're in early."

"Yeah, I couldn't get to the sample yesterday, so I came in early because, you know, poor kitty. And fuck the fucker who killed it and wants to do the same to Roarke."

"I appreciate it. What can you tell me?"

"Got details, solid, as Berenski already did the blood work."

"He did."

Harvo lifted her shoulders. "Dickhead's a dickhead, but he comes through when it's, you know, family time. So. Young female tabby with a history of mange, still on meds."

"Mange."

"Yeah, which was being treated — along with flea treatments. I'm betting she was looking and feeling a lot better before the bastard cut her up, because the hair sample's healthy. I'm going to send you the medical name for the topical — the dry shampoo. Blood work confirms the oral meds and supplements. Somebody was taking good care of her, Dallas. You can only get the mange med from a licensed vet."

"This is good, Harvo."

"Well, natch." She fluffed at her hair, then her eyes turned sober. "You get anything more, I'm all over it."

"Thanks."

"Report on its way in five — just wanted to give you the heads-up. Cha."

"Yeah, uh, cha." Whatever the hell that actually meant.

So, a cat who'd had fleas, mange. A stray? Maybe taken to a shelter, or just taken in by a cat lover. And importantly, taken to a vet who'd have records.

She didn't want to think, yet, of how many vets New York boasted. She could work with the data, drill down into it.

She checked the time, considered, and headed for the morgue. She could work there until Morris came on, save a little time.

And where are you, Cobbe? Still sleeping, she thought, on nice smooth sheets paid for in blood.

Enjoy it while you can, you bastard, because your time's coming.

As she walked the white tunnel, bootsteps echoing, Eve texted Peabody.

At the morgue now. Go straight to Central. Review Harvo's incoming report. Start search for applicable vets.

More time saved, potentially, she thought.

She prepared to find a seat, start her morning report, but, through the porthole windows of his doors, spotted Morris already at work.

She swung through. "Early morning or long night?"

He glanced up. "A little of both. I had a floater last night, accidental death as it turned out. Demonstrating one shouldn't drink to excess, chasing vodka tonics with Erotica, while going on a moonlight sail."

"Bad choices will get you every time."

"Won't they just? Your kitty didn't have a choice."

Eve studied the cat on the slab. "No, she didn't. I didn't expect you to come in early to work on her."

Morris bent back to his work, examining stomach contents.

"The one who did this would like to do the same to Roarke?"

"Yeah, he would."

"Then it's the least you should expect." He straightened a moment.

He wore a clear protective cape over one of his excellent suits, a steely gray with pale, delicate pinstripes, offset by the bold blue of his shirt. His dark hair coiled in a braid with a thin cord of that same bold blue woven through.

Microgoggles hung around his neck as his eyes met hers.

"When I lost Amaryllis, you were there for me, not just professionally, but as a friend, as family. So was Roarke."

"That's just . . ."

"The way it is, and should be. Threaten one of ours, deal with us all. I can tell you while this poor creature had no choice, she did, before her death, have someone who cared for her."

"Harvo said she'd been treated for mange and fleas."

"I agree. You can see the remnants of both, but you'll need the goggles. She'd been well tended. I can tell you she was fed the morning she died, and enjoyed a few treats about two hours before TOD. I can run the analysis of the contents here.

"She's been spayed, about three weeks ago, no more than four. A healthy female, common tabby, of approximately one year, with signs of early malnutrition, the previous mange, fleabites. Equate her to a sidewalk sleeper who'd been taken into a shelter, cleaned, treated, fed, and given that shelter and care for a month. She rebounded because someone took the care."

"Okay. I can work with that."

"She suffered," he added. "Her killer tortured her. I wish I could say he paid for it, the sadistic fuck, but I found traces of leather under her claws and in her teeth. No skin or blood."

"He wore protective gloves so she couldn't scratch or bite him."

"Yes. I'll send the trace to Harvo, though I imagine the leather will turn out to be fairly common. The multiple stab wounds, slashes, punctures were likely inflicted with the same weapon that killed Modesto."

"Stiletto."

"Yes. Causing pain, blood loss until she was too weak to fight."

"Then he shoved her in the sack. A lot of blood on the sack. That's who he is," Eve murmured. "Roarke said he did the same to a little dog when they were kids in Dublin. He's killed four hundred and forty-four human beings, that we know of. I wonder how many like this."

Morris started to lay a hand on hers, remembered the blood.

He moved over to a sink to wash. "We deal with the humans, all the time. And we feel. But something like this outrages on a different level."

He came back. "I attempt to have some objectivity, some intellectual understanding of the sickness that drives some to take lives. But in this case, I find none."

"He did it to make a point. He enjoyed it, but he wanted to make a point. His mistake. She's going to help us find him."

"It would be unprofessional of me to suggest you kick him in the balls when you do."

"Yeah. Just like it's unprofessional of me to hope I get the chance to."

"I hope you find who cared for her."

"I will, and when I do, I'll let them know she's in good hands now."

Eve drove straight to Central. She could update Peabody on the cat — knowing it had been fixed three to four weeks prior gave them a timeline for the vet.

She'd write her report, with that included, then . . .

Roarke would be running out of time on the salon deal. They'd get on that.

But when she walked into Homicide, every eye turned to her — like she had a box of damn doughnuts.

Might as well brief everybody then and there.

"As you know by now, Cobbe slaughtered a cat, left it at my gates."

"Sick fucking fuck," Jenkinson muttered.

"While I pursued Cobbe into the park, he eluded me. It's probable he had a vehicle nearby, as he also eluded the grid search. However, Harvo identified a medical treatment used on the cat to treat her for mange. The blood work confirms oral meds and supplements."

"I've got her report." Though Peabody's eyes were a little damp, her voice didn't quaver. "I'm working on the list of vets now."

"We can add to that with Morris's conclusions. The cat, a young female, had been spayed three to four weeks ago. He concludes she was most likely a stray, taken in and cared for in that period of time. So we'll look for a vet who treated a cat of her description for mange, malnutrition, fleas, and who spayed her."

"The timeline helps," Carmichael put in. "But there's a crapload of vets in New York. I can give Peabody a hand."

"Do that. We find the vet, we find the caretaker or owner, and we figure out how Cobbe got his hands on the cat."

"Sir." Trueheart signaled from his desk. "It could just be somebody who picked up a stray, but it sounds like a rescue. There are groups and individuals who rescue and foster cats and dogs. They put them up for adoption, or keep them. But you can find them online, on websites, with pictures of the cat or dog."

"That's right." Reineke pointed at Trueheart. "My sister got her hound that way. Nice dog."

"There's a lot of them," Trueheart added, "but you can filter the search, cat, female, an age span. And add the timeline when the treatments started."

"That's good. It's good. Do that," she told him. "Peabody, stick with the vets for now. Carmichael, try the pounds.

"Another angle. Baxter and Trueheart interviewed the LC Cobbe hired on the night of the Modesto murder. She observed hair and skin products in his bathroom kit. The hair products can only be purchased through a licensed salon. The asshole's worried about losing his hair, so he's given us another lead. Roarke's checking on Dublin salons at this time. I've culled down those in New York in case he needs a boost or a refill.

"Additionally, we're taking another angle on his hole. Given the timing, how fast he moved out of the hotel, we're looking for safe houses. Private residences available for a fee to high-level criminals. He has the contacts, and this feels more solid to me than him snapping up a rental. I'll have a list within the hour.

"He'll need more clothes," she added. "And he likes the good stuff. Reineke, Jenkinson, start with high-end men's stores that offer quick alterations, top-of-the-line sportswear."

"Going to need underwear," Jenkinson added. "Private residence, no laundry service."

"Might have a droid on-site for that, but yeah."

Despite the throb it put behind her eyes, she studied Jenkinson's tie — an explosion of multicolored stars on a neon-blue sky. "Maybe you can find a tie that doesn't cause temporary blindness."

He just gave her a toothy grin.

"He made a mistake with the cat. He made a mistake with the LC. He made a mistake letting Roarke see him. He's going to keep making mistakes. We won't. Lock it in."

Before she could turn to her office, write it all up, Trueheart signaled again.

"Ah, Lieutenant. I think I found the cat."

"Are you fucking with me, Detective?"

He flushed to his ears. "No, sir! I've got a year-old female, orange tabby, adopted yesterday. They do that, leave their pictures and stories up for a while."

"Up on-screen," she snapped.

When he did she studied the photos — a kind of progression from a scabby, and yeah, mangy skin-and-bones cat dated four and a half weeks prior, to the gradual and substantial improvements, to the image of a healthy, fluffy-coated cat with clear amber eyes.

Each picture had a short description.

"See, it says she was found five weeks ago," Trueheart said. "Taken into foster care, taken to the vet for exam, treatment, shots, topical meds, antibiotics, then a couple weeks later when she was well enough, taken in to be spayed."

"It fits. It fits. And adopted, with love god-damn it, yesterday. Caring Hearts Pet Rescue, in Soho. Pin it down, Trueheart, shoot me the name and address of the foster. Peabody, let's roll."

Eve was already at the glides, heading down, when Peabody caught up.

"That could be a big break."

"It's going to be."

"I'm sick about that poor cat. I shouldn't have looked at the crime scene shots. It's just so cruel."

"He'll pay for it. He's going to pay for all of it."

"He wanted you to think it was Galahad."

"For half a second, I did. He'll pay for that, too." She yanked out her comm. "Who and where?"

"Tara Undall, 21 Worth."

"Good work."

"That's close," Peabody said as she tried to keep up with Eve on the glides.

"His safe house is going to be close, too. Why haul a cat uptown or across town? Plenty of those rescue places, Trueheart said. So you find one convenient."

"The hair thing. Do you really think he'd go to a salon in New York?"

"You need the pro treatment every three months. It's going to depend on how long ago he had one. We need to add Brussels to the list there. He came in from Brussels."

"It's hard to keep up with the data coming in."

"We're going to have more. We don't need

the vet, so tell Carmichael and Santiago to interview the shuttle pilots, the transpo station. Anything hot comes in, Baxter and Trueheart catch it."

Peabody relayed the orders as they crossed the garage.

"We're supposed to meet with Inspector Abernathy at ten," Peabody reminded her.

"We're going to give him a lot to chew on."

Tara Undall lived in a white duplex with a blue door. The door opened even as Eve and Peabody approached.

She stepped out, a woman of about forty-five with a bouncy tail of red hair, glittery sunshades, and a fit body in running tights and a flowy T-shirt.

She had two dogs on leashes, one small and spotted, one big and yellow.

"Ms. Undall?"

"Yes? Oh, I'm sorry, I'm just going out to walk the dogs."

Eve pulled out her badge. "We need to speak to you."

Undall lifted her sunshades, blinked at the badge. "I have all my inspection certificates and licenses. Can this wait?"

"It's important."

As she sighed, a woman came out of the adjoining house — green door — with another dog.

"Dory, can you take Baby and Max? I'll catch up."

"Sure." Dory, short hair under a cap, pink sneakers, walked over. "Problem?"

"I'll let you know. I hope this can be quick," Undall added as she walked back to the door.

"Sweet dogs," Peabody commented. "Are you fostering them?"

Undall thawed a little. "Baby's mine. Max is a foster. He needs room to run, and he just loves kids. He wants a big family and a big yard."

She let them into a sun-washed foyer that opened into a sun-washed living area where a trio of cats lounged on different levels of a kind of upholstered tree.

"Are you looking to adopt?"

"One of these days."

"Well, what can I do for you? I really need to catch up with Dory. Max is a handful."

Eve drew out her 'link, brought up Cobbe's photo. "Do you know this man?"

Now she shoved her sunshades to the top of her head, looked at the screen. "Oh, yes, that's Mr. Patrick. He adopted Sweetie just yesterday. I was tempted to keep her myself because that's what she is, a sweetie. But you have to resist temptation when you foster."

"His name isn't Patrick, Ms. Undall. It's Cobbe, Lorcan Cobbe, and he's wanted by the authorities."

"For what?"

"Are you aware a woman was killed in Washington Square Park recently?"

"Of course. I heard her husband was arrested."

"He was, for hiring Cobbe to kill his wife."

Her mouth opened and closed; she took a stumbling step back.

"Oh my God. I don't see how that can be. I did the standard background check. You must have him mixed up. Mr. Patrick's a widower with a young daughter. He adopted Sweetie for her."

"The man who took the cat is Lorcan Cobbe. He's a contract killer. We need any and all information you can give us regarding him."

"Officer —"

"Lieutenant."

"Fine, Lieutenant. Why in the world would a contract killer adopt a cat?"

Eve decided to treat it like a notification. "I regret to inform you, Sweetie is dead. Cobbe killed her. We're sorry for your loss."

"That's not true." Her milk-white skin

went even paler. "Don't say that."

When she took another stumbling step back, Peabody gently took her arm. "Why don't we sit down, Ms. Undall?"

14

"I don't understand." Tears slid down her cheeks as Peabody guided her to a chair. "I don't understand how anyone could do that."

"How did he get in touch with you?"

"Through the website. Oh, that poor, sweet thing. She'd had such a hard life. He contacted our headquarters through the website. Dory and I cofounded Caring Hearts six years ago. My husband's a vet, and he examines and treats our rescues. Dory's husband is a lawyer, and he helped us set up the nonprofit."

In a signal to give her a moment, she waved her hands, then pressed them to her eyes.

One of the cats, sleek and Halloween black, leaped off the tree, then straight into Eve's lap. She gave Eve a long stare out of eyes so green they glowed, sniffed at her, kneaded her way in a circle three times, then curled up.

That produced a watery smile as Undall brushed her fingers at tears. "That's Regal, because she is. She's usually considerably more aloof with strangers. I hope you don't mind cats."

"No, she's fine. I've got a cat."

Who would make her pay, Eve thought.

"Oh, that explains it. She knows you're simpatico. And she's missing Sweetie. Regal really took to Sweetie."

"She's beautiful," Peabody said. "Ms. Undall, did Cobbe come here, to your home?"

"No, not here. He came to our office. We have a little office a few blocks from here. And twelve certified foster homes now. He called our office, asked about Sweetie, gave all the necessary information, filled out the online form."

"When?"

"Yesterday afternoon, about three, I think. Michael took the information — he manages our office — and I agreed to bring Sweetie in so they could meet. He was so polite, so gentle with Sweetie. He had a charming accent. He said he was from Wexford, in Ireland, and he and his daughter moved here a year ago — his parents live here — after his wife died."

Undall swiped at her eyes. "He said his

little girl — she's nine — came across our website, and saw Sweetie. She said Sweetie was all she wanted for her birthday. Her birthday's today, and her first without her mom, so . . . He promised to send me a picture of Sweetie with his little girl.

"I let him take her. What have I done?"

"You took a sick, starving cat into your home," Peabody said. "You took care of her. And you gave her to someone you believed, had every reason to believe, would give her a good, loving home."

"He gave me five hundred, in cash. The adoption fee's only four to cover the medical expenses, the food, the paperwork. But he said he wanted to make a donation. He told me how happy this would make his motherless child."

To draw Undall's attention to her, Eve leaned forward. "He's a liar, and he's good at it. You saw what he wanted you to see. You aren't to blame for what he did. What was he wearing?"

"Wearing? Ah, jeans, I think."

"Close your eyes," Eve advised. "Picture him. You spent time with him, you wanted to evaluate."

Undall closed her eyes. "Jeans, good ones. I accepted the donation — we can use it — because I could see he could afford it. Carbelli jeans, good boots, both black. A silk T-shirt, an amber color, and a black leather jacket. Real leather. He had a wrist unit — sport style."

"Was he driving or walking?"

"I . . . I'm not sure. He bought a cat carrier — I'd forgotten that. He didn't have one, and we have them at the offices. He didn't want a collar, because he said he wanted his girl to pick one out. He took the congratulations basket we give you. So he had that and the carrier."

"Okay." Absently, Eve stroked the cat purring in her lap. "You made small talk. He said he was from Ireland. Did you talk about that?"

"Yes. I said I'd always wanted to go, and he said he hoped I would. It was beautiful, and he missed it. I asked what he did for a living — even though I'd run the background — and he said he and his wife had owned and run a small hotel, which jibed, but he'd sold it because after she died his heart wasn't in it. Now he helped manage his parents' rentals — businessman rentals."

"Businessman rentals?"

"Yes, where people traveling who don't want a hotel can stay in an apartment or townhouse and that sort of thing. His check said hotels and hospitality for employment, and that seemed to match. I went through my litany of how to introduce a new pet to a household, to the people in it, about diet, and how she still needed the topical, just to be sure, for another few days. He listened so attentively. He took her meds — she's off the antibiotics now, but still needs the special vitamins.

"She took to him, you could see it. She liked him, curled up in his lap like Regal is with you when he sat to fill out the rest of the paperwork. He took all his copies, and the adoption certificate we make. He put it in his little girl's name, Colleen. Sweetie was to have a follow-up exam in two weeks, and he took all my husband's information."

"You have the paperwork he signed?"

"Yes."

"I'm going to need that."

"I'll get it off my computer here." She rose, then looked at Eve with grieving eyes. "Did she suffer?"

"No," Eve lied. "It was very quick. And she's in good hands with the doctor who's in charge. He's kind."

"Thank you."

When she walked out, Peabody looked at Eve. "He worked it perfectly. The dead wife, the little girl's birthday wish. Played the heartstrings."

"Yeah, he did." Eve looked down at the cat in her lap, wondered if she took a spin in the fume tube Galahad wouldn't smell the invader.

Screw that.

"He's not stupid," she continued. "And he knows how to read people. He read me," she added. "Read the way I panicked for a second, tore open that damn bag at the gates."

"Galahad's family."

True enough, Eve thought. And her family was going to be pretty pissed off when he smelled another cat on her.

After she turned over the paperwork, Undall walked out with them. "I have to tell Dory. And Michael and the rest. I —"

She broke off, breathed through. "I hope you catch him. I hope you lock him away forever. Because he's a monster."

"Got that right," Eve mumbled as she got back in the car. "And he left with a cat in a carrier, the goodie basket, meds, paperwork. Not on foot unless it was a couple of blocks."

She considered knocking on some doors herself, but she needed that prep time for Abernathy. "Get some uniforms to canvass with Cobbe's photo," she told Peabody. "Have them check parking lots and garages.

We could get lucky."

Back at Central she told Peabody to update the squad. She had to get the new data, the new angles organized and on paper before meeting with Interpol.

She assumed Whitney would hold the meeting in his office, then wound that back, and sent her commander a memo.

Sir, with your approval I'd like to meet with Inspector Abernathy in the bullpen to demonstrate our manpower and commitment to this investigation. I believe my officers should be involved and included.

She sent it, then began to organize her notes and data into a report. She'd barely started before Whitney's response came through.

Agreed. Ten o'clock.

Great. Excellent. Fuck.

"Peabody!" she shouted it, kept working.

The clump of pink boots came on the run. "Sir!"

"Change of venue. Whitney's bringing Abernathy into the bullpen. Let everyone know. Get the board on-screen — I'll make updates there."

"I got it."

Eve finished the report, shot it off. She got up to get coffee, noting that Roarke's time wasn't quite up on nailing down the Dublin salon. Still, she needed to move on that.

She took the coffee back to her desk. Before she could start the search her 'link signaled. And her comp signaled an incoming.

She saw Roarke's name on the display. "Gimme," she said.

"Style and Substance Salon and Spa. His hair tech is Milo Cummings. Skin, Genita O'Brian. Nails, Breen Casey. I have the rest, in the memo I just sent you. His last visit, for a full round, was five weeks ago."

She did an internal happy dance. "I didn't think you could pull it off this fast."

"I'm wounded."

"Seriously, Roarke, more gold. How much did it cost you?"

He simply smiled. "Some things are beyond price. Will you call in the locals to interview?"

"Me first. I might not have time before Abernathy to hit them all, but I'll grill the hair guy first. Real quick, we found the cat — I mean where he got the cat."

"Someone else works fast."

"I just sent an updated report. It's all in there. I've gotta go, but we're building the box. And we're going to nail the lid on him."

"I trust we will. I'll send you the list of potential safe houses shortly. Good hunting, Lieutenant."

"Back at you."

She clicked off, brought up his incoming. All there. The man was thorough. She made the first contact.

With five minutes to spare, she strode out to the bullpen, handed Peabody a disc. "More updates. I'll write it up later, but get this up. And listen up!" she said to the room at large. "Whatever you're eating, put it away. If you need coffee, get it now. Be prepared to speak on your specific part of the investigation, the progress or lack of same. If somebody gets killed during this meeting, Reineke teams up with Santiago to take it. I want one member of each team in the room at all times."

"Holy shit, Dallas." Peabody stopped her updates. "This is fricking mag data."

"That's right. That's damn right. We're going to show Interpol how the NYPSD catches bad guys."

"Bet your ass," Baxter said. "Hey, Dr. Mira."

Eve turned as Mira came in. "Somebody

314

get Dr. Mira a chair."

"I'm fine." Mira waved it away as she moved to study the board. "Fascinating," she murmured.

Since Eve sincerely couldn't believe anyone could stand for long on skinny needles topped by sassy bows, she gestured for a chair.

Feeney, McNab, Callendar came in next. Feeney shoved his hands in the saggy pockets of his shit-brown suit and joined Mira at the board.

Eve considered logistics, admitted a conference room would suit better. But the hell with that. Her house, her turf, and she'd use it.

Peabody, board complete, walked over to give Eve a laser pointer. "You might want it."

"Right." She slid it into her jacket pocket.

Whitney came in, a contrast with a slim, almost slight man in his late forties. He'd hit about five-nine, Eve thought, maybe carried about a hundred and forty. Mixed race with deep brown skin, sharp cheekbones, and enormous eyes. Amber, like the dead cat's.

He wore a buff-colored suit, perfectly pressed, with a crisp shirt of minute checks that crossed quiet blue and a rose nearly the same color as Mira's sassy bows. The carefully knotted tie went for the rose. His pocket square matched it.

He carried a black briefcase.

"Lieutenant Dallas," Whitney began. "Inspector Abernathy of Interpol."

"Very pleased to meet you, Lieutenant."

He had one of those rich, somehow fruity voices of the British upper class.

"Welcome to New York, Inspector," Eve said as they shook hands. "My partner, Detective Peabody." Very deliberately she named every detective in the room. "Our uniform support, with Officer Carmichael as senior."

She continued, introducing Mira, then the EDD team.

"I'm very much looking forward to working with you. I hope to expand on the hard and the speculative data in the files we've amassed on Lorcan Cobbe. I will say it would break his long-term pattern to remain in New York more than another twenty-four hours. Our window is quite small."

"He's not going anywhere," Eve said flatly. "He has a longer-term goal. Eliminating Roarke."

"I understand he appears to hold a grudge against Roarke, and eliminating him would be satisfying for someone of Cobbe's predilections and nature, but Cobbe knows accomplishing that goal would take careful planning, considerable research. Our analysis is, he'll take the next day, or a portion of it, to continue on-site research, then continue same at another location."

"Your analysis is wrong. It's not a grudge. It's a mission. Dr. Mira."

"Yes." Crossing the room, Mira gave a thumbnail sketch of her profile.

Abernathy listened, full attention, until the end.

"I'm aware of your skill and reputation, Doctor, and don't disagree. But I've been studying Cobbe for several years. He's a skilled, pragmatic, professional killer, and one with considerable resources. He can wait."

"He could," Mira said. "He should. He won't. His obsession with Roarke, with Patrick Roarke, is neither pragmatic nor professional. The pattern you speak of no longer applies. He's forming a new one, one intensely personal, emotional. I've studied the file, Inspector, and clearly Cobbe has made more mistakes in forty-eight hours than he has in twenty years. For him, this is birthright. This is identity."

"There's no evidence, whatsoever, that Patrick Roarke was Lorcan Cobbe's biological father."

"No, but Cobbe believes he was. And that's what's driving him. He's tried, and failed, to eliminate Roarke before. Ego, identity, rage — and the fact he saw Roarke on the scene of his last successful murder — all cloud his professional judgment now."

Frowning, Abernathy held up a hand. "We don't have any data on any attempt to eliminate Roarke."

"You do now. We have a comprehensive report for you, but to sum up," Eve began, and started with the night Cobbe presented himself to Patrick Roarke.

"More extensive details are in the file. As to resources, you now have one of his contacts in custody, and the location of his financial accounts."

"Yes, and both are very helpful. We're watching for any activity on those accounts, and will freeze them when we substantiate he's left New York, and the window closes. That will put a hitch in his stride. The man enjoys living well."

"Which included a brief stay in a penthouse suite at the Parkview Hotel, and a top-level licensed companion hired the night of the Modesto hit and his sighting of Roarke. Baxter?"

"Loo." Baxter kicked back in his chair.

"On the lieutenant's orders, my partner and I searched for and located the hotel Cobbe used. We interviewed the staff, and viewed the security feed. A copy of which is now in the file."

As Baxter ran through it, Abernathy glanced around, sat in an empty chair. And taking out a notebook, began to write down key points.

"He frequents LCs, we know. But any we've been able to identify and interview in the past stated they meet him in a hotel room — usually nondescript, a business hotel where he, routinely again, checks in for that purpose only. He doesn't bring them where he stays, or lives."

"He was pissed," Eve said. "Charged up. He didn't take the usual precautions. Go on, Baxter."

Once again, Abernathy took notes. Then he stopped, stared. "Hair loss products? He left them out, let the LC use the loo where he left them out?"

"Pissed," Eve said again. "And already making arrangements to leave the hotel. The Modesto job's done. He's not thinking about that anymore. He's thinking about his Holy Grail."

"That's very careless," Abernathy murmured. "Extremely careless. We should be able to track the products."

"Done," Eve said, and pulled out her laser pointer. "On the board. Style and Substance, the salon he uses — regularly — in Dublin is managed by Carleen Digby and Aidan Pierce. I spoke with Digby, who identified Cobbe's photo. He uses the name Niall Patrickson for his spa and salon deals."

"We don't have that alias."

"You do now." And yeah, she had to admit the satisfaction of dumping accumulated data in Interpol's lap. "I spoke with three of his techs — hair, skin, nails — and have their statements. To sum up, he's polite, fussy, exacting, tips well, doesn't like to chat. He's been having the hair loss treatments by a licensed tech every three months — for nearly a year."

"Bugger me sideways," Abernathy mumbled as he pushed to his feet to move closer to the board. "A bloody day spa? Regular appointments?"

"Vanity," Mira supplied. "Ego, arrogance. He sees himself as invincible."

"We're tracking locations here that carry the same products, the same service," Eve added. "He has weeks before he needs another onsite treatment, but he may want or need more supplies for his kit, as he's extending his stay."

"I don't know about the last part, but this is prime. This is bloody brilliant police work. Have the Dublin police been informed?"

"Not yet."

"If you'd let me report this to my superiors, take this part of the investigation from here?"

"All yours."

"I'm grateful. I'm impressed." He turned to Eve with a wide grin that convinced her he wouldn't try to bogart the investigation. "I'm bloody gobsmacked."

He beamed back at the board, then frowned. "A cat?"

"That's right." As Eve told him, Abernathy ran a hand over his close-cropped hair.

"This isn't like him." Pacing now, Abernathy shook his head. "Not the killing of animals, that is like him. But to do so when it's not related to another kill. To simply do it to taunt, to take those steps, that time, risk that exposure.

"I need to . . ." He circled a hand in the air. "To think. If I could . . . think, walk. I noticed Vending. I'll get some coffee, think."

"Don't get that coffee. Peabody."

"How do you take it?" Peabody asked.

"With what passes for cream, and a lump of what passes for sugar. Thank you. I'm just going to . . ."

He wandered into the hallway.

Baxter held up his comm. "Caught one, Dallas."

"You're finished here, so you take it. Santiago."

"I'm with you, Baxter."

"This is good work, Dallas," Whitney told her. "I didn't see your last report."

"Trueheart gets credit for the fast turn-around on the cat — as do Morris and Harvo and Berenski. The civilian pinned the salon."

"It's good work."

"Thank you, sir. Feeney, if you'd brief the inspector on EDD's area in this. Jenkinson will take his, Carmichael hers. If Abernathy has questions after, we can address them."

Abernathy came back in, intercepted Peabody and the coffee. "Thank you, Detective. I apologize, I wanted to clear my head, let this all filter in. I've worked on Cobbe for nearly six years. I've gotten close once or twice. But I've never seen so many solid breaks, so many missteps to exploit."

"It's personal for him this time," Mira repeated. "It's not a job."

"You've convinced me. He's so off his game, so off his pattern. It's as if he's had a psychic break."

"He has," Mira confirmed.

Abernathy nodded, sipped his coffee. Paused. "This isn't my first time in the States, or in New York. I have to say, the coffee's improved by leaps and bounds."

He sat again. "While we've gathered considerable intel on Cobbe's background, going back to his early days in Dublin, we didn't have this specific data on his relationship with Roarke. Not to this extent, not in this detail."

He glanced over at Eve. "Details on your husband's background are hen's teeth."

"They're what?"

"Rare. Rare as hen's teeth. I wonder if he'd agree to speak with me."

"That would be up to him. Either way, what applies to Cobbe from him is in the file." Shifting, she turned to Feeney. "Captain, if you'd brief the inspector on your area."

Abernathy listened, took more notes, asked more questions. Eve decided he wasn't an idiot. More, he didn't seem territorial in a way that would hamper her investigation.

At the end, Abernathy rose again. "I want to thank all of you for bringing me fully up-to-date. Commander Whitney, I'll reiterate that you'll have my cooperation and any and all of my resources in this investigation."

"As you'll have ours," Whitney assured him. "I've had an office prepared for you on this level. Lieutenant Dallas will assign a uniformed officer to serve as your aide."

"That's very considerate, but I wonder — if it's not intrusive — if I could have a desk in here, in your bullpen. It would help me immerse myself in the rhythm, so to speak."

"If you prefer."

"If Lieutenant Dallas agrees, I would."

"No problem."

"I'll take care of it," Whitney told him. "If you need anything else, you have my contact. Fine work, everyone." Whitney turned to the room. "Fine, solid work. Keep it up."

"An imposing man," Abernathy commented as Whitney left. "Captain Feeney, I wonder, after I settle in a bit, get my bearings, if I could visit your EDD. I'd like to get a sense of it."

"Door's always open."

"Brilliant. Lieutenant, if I could impose on a little more of your time, have a word?"

"Sure. Feeney, as soon as I get more data on potential safe houses, I'll pass it to you. We'll start scanning them for heat imagery."

"We'll be ready when you are."

"My office," she said to Abernathy and led the way.

When he stepped inside, he looked around. "How . . . cozy."

"No, it's not, but it suits me. What can I do for you, Inspector?"

"I hope there's considerable we can and will do for each other. I'm in your house, Lieutenant, and want to make it clear I understand you're in charge. This will and must be a joint investigation, but this is your house."

She gestured to her board. "There isn't enough room for all his victims up there. I have the four he's killed in New York, five with the cat he slaughtered because I have a better chance of using the hows and whys there, but the NYPSD, my house, stands for all four hundred and forty-five."

"I know the faces of the others, particularly those he killed after I began the hunt. I nearly had him two years ago in Berlin. I believe we missed him by less than an hour. Eluding us there, he drove out of the city with the body of a thirty-six-year-old mother of two in the trunk of her own car."

Eve said nothing as Abernathy wandered over to glance out her single skinny window.

"We had a leak, and the media reported the authorities were closing in on a suspect in the murder of a prominent industrialist. Instead of taking the private shuttle he'd booked, he killed Ingrid Frederick, who'd stopped to pick up a cake for her youngest daughter's fourth birthday.

"She haunts me."

"My department doesn't leak unless I authorize it."

"I would have thought the same. I'm not contradicting you," he added, "merely explaining this is not just a job for me, not simply an assignment. Perhaps it should be, but it's long past that point. I don't care about being in charge, I don't care about credit. I want him stopped. I want him to pay."

"Then we're on the same page."

"I did some research on you on the flight over, so I believe we are. I wanted you to know my position. In addition, I wanted to ask if you'd approach Roarke with my request to speak to him. Over the last few hours, I've learned fresh information about Cobbe's childhood due to this connection, this interaction. We knew, of course, about Cobbe's — I don't think *obsession* is overstated — with Patrick Roarke. We knew pieces, confirmed some, speculated on more. But we never knew about these personal encounters between Cobbe and Patrick Roarke's son."

"Those encounters are well documented

in the file. I don't know what Roarke can add to them. But I'll pass along your request."

"Thank you. If you have any questions for me, I'll be close by. And if we learn more from the salon, you'll be, well, the second to know after myself. I hope I'll be high on your list if and when you locate credible safe houses."

"You will be."

"I'll let you get back to work."

"Inspector," she said as he started out. "I believe you want justice for Ingrid Frederick, and all the others. If you attempt to interrogate Roarke, it would be a mistake."

He nodded. "So noted."

Considering the guest in her bullpen, Eve closed her door before she took out her 'link.

When Roarke answered, she heard a lot of voices, a few squeals, what sounded like running feet before he found his own door to close.

"Where are you?" she demanded.

"An Didean. It's going very well."

"It sounded like a riot."

"Children. They're very loud as a group, it seems. And enthusiastic at the moment, even the ones pretending to be bored by the whole thing."

"You look happy."

"It's hard not to be. I hope you'll make it by. It's a different matter to see it, feel it, when the first dozen or so students begin to fill it. Entirely different."

"Louder."

He smiled. "Absolutely. So. You met Abernathy?"

"Yes. He's solid. Right now he's taking a desk in the bullpen."

Roarke's eyebrows winged up. "Your bullpen?"

"That's how he wanted it. We'll see how that goes, but for now, like I said, he's solid. He wants to talk to you."

"An inspector of Interpol wants to talk to me. Why, I'm stunned and surprised."

"Yeah, right. The thing is, it's the Cobbe connection. I can see him trying to fit the new pieces in, see what kind of different picture he can make. If you're not interested, I'll nix it. I'm just saying trying to jam you up isn't his priority. I can't guarantee it, but that's my take."

"I tend to trust your take on such matters. Give me another. Do you think my talking to him will add anything, will help lead you to Cobbe?"

"I don't know." But the more data the better, she thought. "Maybe's the best I can do."

"All right then. I'll see what I can do."

"Good enough. Meanwhile, why don't you go ahead and send me — and Feeney — the list you have of the safe houses. Feeney and EDD can hit them with imaging, maybe eliminate more that way."

"I'd hoped to have more eliminated by now."

She knew all about being pulled in too many directions at once. And God, she wanted to give him a break.

"You're needed where you are, too. We can get started."

"All right."

"And I'll get by the school." Life had to matter, she thought, or what was the damn point? "Even if it's not until I'm on my way home, I'll get by there."

"Let me know when. I'll try to meet you. I love you, Eve."

"Well, yeah. I love you, too, and all that."

He smiled, sighed. "I needed to say it. I find I'm standing at some sort of bisection of my life here. With Cobbe and the old man and the hard memories of Dublin on one side, and all these children, this place, the potential of it all on the other. And you, my darling Eve, right here with me. So I love you."

God yes, he needed a break.

"I am with you. Go back to the happy."

When she clicked off, she sat back a minute, and hoped to Christ she wasn't making a mistake with Abernathy.

Then she got up, opened her door. She got another hit of coffee before sitting down.

And continuing the hunt.

15

Roarke spent another moment behind the closed (and quiet) door of a storage closet. The only convenient place, at the moment, he'd been sure to find unoccupied.

Though he'd wanted — and intended to — spend another solid hour on refining the potential safe houses, time had drained away with this essential day at An Didean.

So he'd leave it to the cops, at least until he could find more time. And sent what he had to Eve.

When he stepped out, the time-crunch annoyance simply fell away. He could watch students exploring classrooms under the eye of staff, asking questions, talking over each other.

They'd brought in the upperclassmen first, so teenagers swarmed the building. Most had come in solo — from shelters, other schools, troubled homes, foster homes, through Child Services. But he could see some had formed little groups already.

A trio of giggling girls, a pair of boys slouching by ignoring the giggling girls.

He imagined most were here because they'd been given little to no choice. And he hoped — had to hope — that most would find something here that sparked their interest, imaginations, talents, that gave them a sense of self and purpose.

Time would tell.

He heard music from the music room, and wandered that way, expecting to find one of the music instructors entertaining kids.

Instead he found a boy of about fourteen playing as if he'd been born holding a guitar.

He stood spread-legged, black-streaked blond hair flopping into his eyes. And his fingers blurry miracles as he finessed a complex riff.

The smile dropped away, and the fingers stilled when the boy spotted Roarke.

"I wasn't hurting it."

"On the contrary," Roarke said, and continued into the room. "You illuminated it. Played brilliantly," he amended when he saw confusion. "Where did you learn to play?"

The boy shrugged, and tossed back his mop of streaked hair. "Just picked it up. You can make some decent money playing in the subway if you get the right station. And I was doing fine before they scooped me up."

"I imagine so." When the boy put the guitar back on the stand, Roarke shifted — subtly — to block his exit. "What do you think of Avenue A?"

This got a sniff, another shrug. But interest showed in his eyes. "They can scream it, even for old guys."

"Jake Kincade will be guest instructing here from time to time."

"Yeah, right. Like a rock star gives a shit about any of this, any of us."

"It happens he does. He'll instruct occasionally for the music department, and speak to those interested about songwriting, composing. His bandmates will give time as well."

"That's chilly, I guess."

"What do you think of Mavis Freestone?"

The kid had green eyes, sharp as a shard of glass. "She can rock it, for a girl."

"You'll be seeing some of her as well, as no doubt you'll sign up for the music courses."

The corner of the boy's lip curled. "I don't need no frigging courses."

"Perhaps they need you. Is your own

guitar in your room?"

"I don't have one anymore." And here Roarke heard grief under the defiance. "Asshole busted it up in the shithole foster home they dumped me in before they dumped me here."

"I see. Well then, you're not in a shithole foster home now, though I imagine you'll run into a few assholes here as well. The world's full of them."

That got a reluctant snicker.

"Roarke," Roarke said, holding out a hand.

Clearly the boy didn't want to take it, but did. "Gee. Just Gee."

"Well, just Gee." Roarke lifted the guitar off the stand, held it out. "Have this one then. It's yours if you sign up for the music program. It's a fair trade," Roarke added when Gee hesitated.

"They'll say I stole it and boot me."

"Unless you're a complete git, you know who I am. Give me your word on the program, and it's yours. No one will say you stole it."

"Why?" Suspicion darkened those sharp eyes as the boy stuck his hands in his pockets. "You looking for a BJ or something?"

"Ah Christ, do I look like I solicit underage boys for sex?"

Gee's gaze held Roarke's. "Plenty do who don't look like it."

"That's true enough, isn't it? Sign up for the program, take the guitar, and the only strings are the six on it. Take the deal, Gee. It's a fine one."

When the boy still hesitated, Roarke pushed. "There was a time in my life no one gave me a bloody thing either but a hard hand. Then someone did, and it changed my life. Take it, give the program, give the school a chance. See where it takes you."

"I can just keep it?"

"That's right. I'll make sure Ms. Pickering and the rest of the staff know it's yours."

"I . . . Okay." Gee pulled his hands out of his pockets, took the guitar, smoothed his fingers down the neck. "Can I keep it if I get booted?"

"It's yours," Roarke repeated. "Don't get booted," he added as he started out.

He barely made it through the door before the music rocked out again.

He hunted up Rochelle to tell her about the guitar, and the student.

"Gee." Rochelle, in jeans and a peach-colored sweater chosen to give the day a more informal feel, consulted her PPC.

"That would be Gregg Harding — I have thumbnails on here."

Roarke smiled at her. "Of course you do."

"Age fourteen. Father unknown, mother . . . Multiple citations for neglect, abuse, signed away her parental rights when he was eleven. Foster homes — runaway. Child Services picked him up again about five months ago. His social worker did some serious work with him, and pushed to get him enrolled. I can check the files for more details."

"Not necessary for me. Just make sure he keeps his end of the deal. I'll replace the guitar."

"That's our job — out of your budget. I'll take care of it." She put the PPC away. "It's a good day, Roarke."

"Is it that."

"It's going to be a good week, a good start. Middle grades coming in tomorrow, then the early grades follow that. I'm so proud to be a part of this. We're changing lives here, and, I believe, saving some."

So did he.

Before he left, he decided to walk up to the roof, to the gardens, the memorial for the lost girls, the air, and the open.

And there he found Quilla with her vid cam.

A sharp one, was Quilla, Roarke thought. She'd know where the boy Gee came from, how he'd gotten there, as she'd come from similar. Music wasn't her skill, as far as Roarke knew. But observation was — and she wanted to use that skill to become a reporter.

Interning with Nadine Furst had, he supposed the term would be, polished her up a bit. She wore snug flowered pants and high-top sneaks with a loose purple T-shirt that matched the streaks in her hair.

Confidence — never a problem for Quilla — radiated as she panned the city for her vlog.

"And from here," she said, "we can look out on where we came from, where one day we'll go back. We'll be smarter, we'll be stronger, and we'll make the city, maybe the world beyond it, a better place. This is Quilla, reporting for An Didean."

She turned, jolted a little, then grinned at Roarke. "Hey. Didn't hear you come up."

"Hey yourself. I didn't want to interrupt your report."

"I have to edit the crap out of it. I got so much stuff! I figured to end the first part up here, you know, like the big visual."

"You're a clever one, Quilla."

"Oh yeah. Anyway, probably Ms. Pickering's going to want me to cut out the swear words and all — but that's really censor-ship, right? Still, I want Nadine to see the raw footage. She has opinions." She rolled her eyes, then laughed. "Really good ones mostly.

"I got some of you on here. Nothing, like, embarrassing or anything."

"That's good to know."

"I kinda wanted to get some of Dallas."

"She's going to try to get by today."

"Okay, frosty. Anyway . . . Nadine said she would maybe use some on her show — the *Now*! That would be beyond mag. If it's good enough."

"Show me some."

Her eyes widened. "Really?"

"Pick ten minutes," he said, and sat on the bench by the memorial.

Clutching the vid cam, the ever-confident Quilla showed nerves.

"Will you be, like, totally honest? Even brutal? Nadine says if you pretend some-thing's good when it's not, you're not doing anybody any favors."

"Who'd argue with Nadine? Sit, show me. I'll be brutally honest."

After she had, and went back inside pleased and satisfied, he sat in the quiet alone.

When his 'link signaled — one of his contacts on Cobbe — he accepted the optimistic part of his day ended.

"This is Roarke," he answered.

Once he'd passed what spotty information he had on to Eve, Roarke went to his headquarters determined to do at least some work. He couldn't and wouldn't let Cobbe dominate every damn minute of the day.

From the garage, he took his private elevator up to his office level, and found his admin, Caro, manning her desk.

"I wasn't sure you'd make it in today."

"Neither was I, but things are running smooth at the school, so I've time enough to see to a few things."

"Speaking of that." In her ever-efficient way, Caro swiveled, called up a log. "Fitzwalter sent his report on the Monrovia meeting, and Dolliger sent the specs you've been waiting for. Your morning was clear for An Didean, but you may want to look over those two items and the latest counter from the lawyers on the Kovax merger."

He eased a hip on her desk. "More bullshit there, is it?"

She smiled at him. She wore a dove-gray suit with a bold red shirt that set off her wedge of snow-white hair.

"For the most part, yes. I imagine you'll cut through it easily enough. It's posturing, and obvious posturing at that. I suspect they're hoping you'll tire of the back-and-forth and just give them some of the less far-fetched perks they're pushing for."

"They'll be disappointed."

"Yes, I suspected that, too. One other thing?" She lifted a hand, rubbed at the little pearl stud in her ear. "You've had three calls come in over the main contact in the last hour. All from different 'link numbers, but clearly from the same person. Blocked video each time."

Cobbe, he thought, and felt a heat spread inside him. One he recognized as anticipation.

"Is that so?"

"It is, and knowing what's going on, I initiated a trace on the last."

He expected no less from her. "And?"

"The last contact, at thirteen-oh-six, originated from Hudson Street, moving uptown from Christopher to West Tenth. The caller, who identified himself as Grafton, was either walking or driving — very slowly if driving — on Hudson."

"All right. If another comes through, start the trace, then pass him on to me. Well done, Caro."

"Roarke." With the affection of long standing, she laid a hand over his. "You will be very careful."

"Depend on it." He squeezed her hand before he rose, then went into his office.

And contacted Eve.

"Cobbe was walking on Hudson Street fifteen minutes ago."

"What? You saw him?"

"He's been trying to contact me here at my office, which proves him a rare git. Caro started a trace."

"Stay put, let me know if he contacts you again. I'm on this."

She clicked off without another word.

He turned in his desk chair, stared at the wall of glass to the towers of New York. Downtown then, and so — high probability — would his safe house be.

That would put a solid dozen possibles uptown low on the list.

Yes, a rare git, as Eve would conclude the same and focus the search downtown.

If not a rare git, he considered, a ploy to shift attention away? But doubtful there, as he had no reason to think they were focusing on safe houses.

Ring me back, you shagging bastard, and we'll have ourselves a little chat.

He forced himself to put it aside — for

now — opted to read through the bullshit counteroffer first.

And on what planet, he thought as he scored through line after line, was the sky quite such a shade of rosy pink they'd think he'd give the lazy, inept, greedy execs — who'd mismanaged into the ground what had been a solid little company — golden parachutes to land so soft?

They'd take his offer — more than fair enough — as is, or end up mired in the muck.

He wrote a memo to that effect, copying his own legal team and Caro, then shot it off.

It lightened his mood, as work tended to do, so he read over Fitzwalter's detailed and sharp report, sent off another memo to those connected to the project.

He settled in with the specs, found himself largely satisfied. A few changes here and there, which he detailed with another memo to the chief engineer on that project.

Even as he sent it, Caro buzzed him.

"I've got him on hold, told him you were just finishing another call. Trace is going now."

"That's fine then. Keep it going, I'll bring the trace and the call up here."

He used his personal 'link to contact Eve

again. "He's rung back. We're tracing. I'm looping you in on the call and the trace."

"Hold it a minute, hold it."

"If I do that, he'll click off. I'm muting you," he said, and shifting to his desk 'link, blocked video.

"This is Roarke."

"Ah, the man at last. I've been wanting a word with you."

"Grafton for the street then. If a word's what you're wanting, come and see me. I'll put the kettle on the hob."

"There in your big black tower with all that security to protect you? Your life's behind walls and gates. Why don't you come out in the world, meet me man-to-man?"

"When and where?"

"As easy as that?"

On his screen insert, Roarke watched Eve obviously shouting orders, then all but flying down glides at Central.

"And why not? I'm not some unarmed woman walking in the park of an evening, or some poor cat for you to gut."

"How do you gut the gutless? You think your piles and pots of money keep you safe from me? You think your skinny slut of a cop wife can protect you?"

"I say again, when and where?"

"I'll let you know, you fecking wanker, and

the when and where will be your last. You've no right to the name you use that's mine. When you're done I'll take it all, then slice that bitch who married you from crotch to throat."

When Cobbe ended the transmission, Roarke was already at the door, rushing out.

"Sir, he's on Perry between —"

"I've got it."

"Should I alert Jenson?"

"I've got it," he repeated, and leaped into the elevator.

He didn't want a driver. He kept a vehicle in the garage for when he wanted to drive himself.

And now he surely did.

He leaped into the two-seater, peeled out of the slot. And with a roar of the engine, bulleted out into the street.

He hit vertical, cut the corner, and headed downtown airborne over uptown traffic.

Another corner with a speed that had pedestrians gawking overhead, and a glide-cart operator shaking both fists skyward in appreciation.

He touched down to gun it when he had enough clear, and wove at a screaming speed for a block and a half before he went up again.

He watched the street for openings, dived

down, soared up. Then whooshed over the downtown clogs of cars and people.

When he spotted Eve's car, the EDD van, two black-and-whites, he decided his best option was the flat roof of a triple-decker on Perry, set the car down between an old lounge chair and the wall.

In seconds he was through the door, thundering down the stairs.

When he burst out onto the street, Eve was only steps away and barking orders.

She stopped. "Jesus, how did you get here? Never mind. Get on the door-to-doors now! Carmichael, Shelby, sweep pedestrians, hit those sidewalk stalls. Somebody saw the son of a bitch."

She yanked out her comm, ordered more cops and cars for a perimeter.

"I'll get to you," she said to Roarke and jogged over to the van. "Subway."

Feeney nodded. "McNab, Callendar, take it. Stay together. I don't want either of you coming back with holes in you. What do you want from me?"

"What've we got within a five-block radius on the holes?"

Feeney consulted his map. "Got one and another right over the edge of that. We haven't scanned those yet."

"Do that. Do you need another e-man?"

"Be quicker with one."

She looked back at Roarke. "Since you're here, you go with Feeney. If you get a likely, let me know, and we're there. Don't let the civilian get out of the van," she told Feeney.

"What? You expect me to stun him?"

"Whatever it takes." She turned to Roarke, grabbed him by the lapels. "Stay in the van, or I swear to Christ, I'll stun you myself."

"And you would, no doubt." He grabbed her right back. "I'll give you your shot at him, Lieutenant. One shot, then it's for me."

He got into the back of the van, shut the doors in her face.

"She's worried about you," Feeney said as he eased into traffic. "She don't worry all that easy, so you gotta give her a break here."

"I'm giving her that, and could use one myself. I see your targets here. Let's see if we can drive this rat out of his fucking hole."

Feeney's basset-hound eyes lifted to the rearview mirror. "We'll get him, Roarke. I don't give my word unless I know damn well I can keep it, and I'm giving my word on it. We should've had him twenty couple years ago, me and Jack, but, fuck me, we'll get him now."

Roarke settled into the work, and the work settled him. "He's mad to kill me. Hot and mad to put me in the ground, and that's why he'll never manage it."

They swept, knocked on doors, reviewed footage from the subway.

They found a handful of people who'd seen him on foot — or thought they had — between Perry and West Twelfth.

He hadn't used the subway, not in that area in any case. One of the safe houses had a family of three — one barely old enough to walk — in residence.

Feeney spotted them going in, loaded with shopping bags.

The other showed no heat signals.

Eve sent cops to knock on neighboring doors, then sent detectives in soft clothes to scout the perimeter.

But her gut said Cobbe had gone back into his hole.

Because she had Abernathy in tow, Eve sent Roarke to Central with EDD.

"I hope you take this the way it's meant," Abernathy said as she drove back to Central. "You're a maniac at the wheel — the way it's meant's a compliment. We couldn't have missed him by much."

"We missed him, so by how much doesn't matter."

Abernathy consulted his notes, added more. "Why would he contact Roarke that way? Why risk it?"

"He needs to taunt and threaten. He thinks he's being cold-blooded, but what he is, is hotheaded."

Abernathy looked at her with a nod as they turned into Central's garage. "You're right on that. Roarke's his Achilles' heel. He knows how to be precise, focused, impersonal. He's none of those now. We might've taken him right on the street while he strolled along, stewing."

"We didn't," she said flatly.

He got out of the car with Eve while Peabody climbed out of the back.

"I understand your frustration, Lieutenant, all too well. There's been a time or two I knew I was close, when I believed we were within a hairsbreadth. But this is different. He could right himself," Abernathy continued as they walked to the elevator. "He may shake off this rage that's pushing him and right himself, be gone in a snap. But I don't think he will. I'm not at all sure he can. You heard him speaking to Roarke, you heard as I did that furious excitement, the depth of the hate."

"I heard him."

Eve got on the elevator. She wanted five minutes with Roarke — five minutes alone.

"I think . . ."

She sucked it up — and as Abernathy might have said, righted herself. He probably knew Cobbe better than anyone but Roarke. And maybe better yet.

"What?"

"I think he feels, believes, killing Roarke would be worth dying for. Until now, I would say self-preservation would be his number one, closely followed by the thrill of killing, and the wealth it brings him. But now? I think killing Roarke, and you as well, that's above all."

She studied Abernathy. "What about prison? Is it worth that?"

"You're right that for many prison's worse than death. He'd risk it, I think, yes. But he'd see himself dead first, going on a blaze, so to speak, as long as he takes Roarke with him."

"We agree on all of that."

"Dallas," Peabody interrupted. "Neighbors reporting the house is currently unoccupied. Nobody's been in or out in the last few days."

"Might still be using it, but likely outside the perimeter we set. Have the team use that perimeter for the shops — upscale menswear and all that. He had a reason to be in that sector.

"Blocked the video," she muttered, inside

her own head enough not to bother to push off when cops pushed on. "Didn't want Roarke to see where he was, be able to nail down where he was. Why do that? Because you're staying in that area, or doing business in that area. Restaurants, too. Bars. Keep it upscale. LCs," she continued as she did push off, on her level.

"Let's get his data to the top agencies in the city. He may want sex."

She turned into the bullpen. "Get that started, Peabody. Maybe you could assist there," she said to Abernathy.

She just needed to shake him off for five damn minutes.

"Of course, wherever I'm useful."

"You may have the best knowledge of the type of woman, food, drink, even damn footwear he goes for. We need to —"

She broke off as Roarke came in.

"Peabody, you and the inspector get —"

But Abernathy had already started forward, a hand outstretched to Roarke.

"Inspector Abernathy, Interpol. It's good to meet you. Can we talk?"

"I need to debrief Roarke," Eve began.

"Of course." Thoroughly pleasant, Abernathy nodded. "Shall we use your office?"

Not going to shake off. Well, Eve thought,

in his place neither would she.
"We'll use the lounge."

16

As they walked down, Roarke could all but hear the wheels turning in her head. How to handle this — or more specifically, the inspector. How to skim the line between cop and colleague, wife and shield.

He could have told her she had no need to worry. He'd dealt with Abernathys before. But he supposed it was, indeed, all different now.

And that meant he had a line to skim himself. He would do nothing, absolutely nothing, that would put his lieutenant in a squeeze.

Abernathy smiled, continuing the thoroughly pleasant demeanor — and Roarke imagined Eve saw, as clearly as he did, the cop calculation behind the facade.

Jamming him up, as Eve had put it, might not have been Abernathy's priority. But what cop could resist the attempt?

"I don't want to take too much of your

time," Abernathy began. "I certainly don't want to take you away from your work, especially at this point, Lieutenant."

"This is my work," Eve said flatly as she turned into the lounge. "The coffee sucks in here." She took a table, sat. "If you want something, I suggest you go with water or soft drink tubes."

"No need." The inspector sat, folded his hands on the table and looked at Roarke. "First, I want to express my sincere gratitude for all your help in this matter. The personal and detailed information you've offered regarding Cobbe is and will be extremely helpful in finally bringing him to justice."

"Our goals are the same," Roarke said.

"Of course. If I could, just to clarify . . ." He took out his notebook. "Working back from your sighting of Cobbe in Washington Square Park on the night of Ms. Modesto's death. You spoke of an encounter with Cobbe in a bar in the South of France. I wonder if you could be more specific on the time and place. Perhaps if you tell us what you were doing there it would help pinpoint that date and location."

Under the table, Roarke squeezed Eve's knee before she could object.

"It was some time ago," Roarke said eas-

ily. "As best I can recall, I think I was looking to acquire a small resort on the Côte
D'Azur. It may have been the spring, perhaps the summer of 2046 or '47. But that's
best guess."

"Of course," Abernathy replied. " '46, '46.
There was a bit of a scandal in May of that
year — you may have been there then, heard
the local reports. A jewel heist. Quite a
famous one."

He looked at Roarke, smiling, smiling,
with his rosy tie and pocket square and
upper-class accent.

"An American socialite, an heiress famed
for her jewels and her parties, and some ten
and a quarter million — USD — in dia-
monds, emeralds — a particular necklace
known as the Green Flash — stolen from
the vault on her estate in Cannes. The
Green Flash itself was — is — worth nearly
half that amount. It was never recovered."

"Is that so?" Roarke smiled back, just as
pleasantly. "I'm afraid I was focused on bro-
kering this deal — an important one to me
at the time. At that point in my life, I didn't
have much to do with rich American social-
ites. Or more accurately, they didn't have
much to do with me. What I recall of the
incident with Cobbe's in the file."

"Do you think Cobbe took time out of

murdering targets to steal necklaces?" Eve asked Abernathy.

"Oh no, he lacks the skill for such endeavors. Since he did, he worked as what you'd call an enforcer for Patrick Roarke back in his early days. You on the other hand," he began, turning to Roarke again.

"Then it doesn't apply," Eve interrupted. "And the exact date he tried to kill Roarke in a bar in the fricking South of France doesn't matter a damn, either."

Abernathy nodded, nodded. Pleasantly. "I simply try to pin down exact data, when possible."

"If you're screwing around with crap like this, it hasn't helped you nail Cobbe."

Abernathy's eyes hardened; his face tightened. And Eve pushed again.

"Don't fuck with me, Inspector. And don't fuck with him. Try it, and I'll find a way to have you booted back to London."

Roarke took Eve's hand with his right, held up his left. "A moment. She worries for me," he said to Abernathy even as Eve tried to jerk her hand free. "Before we go on, before I say anything else, before we waste time here with you hoping to score some points on the back end on matters far less important than Cobbe, let me ask you your opinion of the lieutenant's integrity and dedication to her badge."

Obviously struggling with what he might have called pique, Abernathy drew a breath. "There is no question of Lieutenant Dallas's integrity, her reputation, her dedication to justice."

"Good. But she did marry me," Roarke said with some cheer. "And that's a puzzlement, isn't it now, to a man such as yourself. You've speculated, I expect, that this relationship is a convenience for me."

Abernathy managed to look mildly appalled at the suggestion. "I wouldn't presume to comment on your personal relationship, on your marriage."

"Manners prevent you," Roarke agreed. "But you think what you think. Let me set you straight. She is often hugely inconvenient to me. And she is everything to me."

"Stop it."

When Eve jerked her hand again, Roarke merely brought it to his lips. "Everything to me. If giving you exact dates, reasons, confessing a thousand crimes would help you take Cobbe down, I would cite chapter and verse. Understand, believe, he would kill her to taunt me. Closing a jewel heist from fifteen years ago might add a sparkle to your file, Inspector, but it won't help you with Cobbe.

"Which do you want?"

Eyes on Roarke, Abernathy said nothing for a moment. Then, "Cobbe."

"And so again, our goals are the same. If I can tell you more than I've already said for the record, ask. Nothing is more important to me, at this time and place, than seeing him dead or put away. I don't much care which, and there's the inconvenience, as the lieutenant does care."

Abernathy huffed out a breath. "I believe I'll chance the tea. Can I get either of you something?"

"No," Eve said, still miffed.

When Abernathy rose to cross over to Vending, she hissed at Roarke. "Don't do that again. Hand kissing in front of Interpol."

"A point had to be made, and was. The French heist means little to him, but he had to try, didn't he? And he'd consider the possibility that tripping me up there might lead to other stumbles, which may — in some way — connect to Cobbe. As bagging Cobbe does mean quite a bit to him. And now he knows Cobbe is my priority, on a very personal level, as well."

"Maybe yes, maybe no. But keep your mouth off my knuckles on the job, or my knuckles are going to crack you in that mouth."

"I adore you."

"Shut up," she muttered, "just shut up about it."

"Only one choice of tea." Obviously perplexed, Abernathy carried the steaming go-cup back to the table. "It appears to be some anemic blend resembling horse urine. Ah well."

He settled again, sipped, winced. Looked at Roarke. "You've had no contact with Cobbe, no interaction, no business with him since that time in the bar in France until now?"

"No. I've kept tabs on him, as I'm well aware he'd like to see me dead, and he's skilled at killing. But we've managed to stay off the same road for some time."

Abernathy leaned forward. "Do you agree he believes Patrick Roarke is his father?"

"I'm sure he does believe it. I'm sure he needs to. Patrick Roarke was as hard and cruel a man as was ever born, and made my life a misery. But for Cobbe, he's a bloody star shining in the East. Make of that what you will."

"Would you stand as bait to lure him?"

"No," Eve said, fast and furious.

"Yes," Roarke said, cold and calm. "Yes," he repeated, turning to her. "You're a cop, not an eejit. My everything," he told Abernathy. "But while he's mad as a hatter, he's no fool, and unlikely to fall for it."

"I agree. But I wondered. You have family in the west of Ireland."

Everything in him went cold. Eve wondered if Abernathy felt the frosty sting of Scary Roarke. "They're not in this."

"Nor would I wish them to be, I promise you. Does he know of them?"

"He may, as you do. I've taken precautions there."

"As have we. You should know that."

Roarke eased back. "Then I'm grateful."

"I've kept you long enough." Abernathy rose, and left the tea on the table. "I feel we're close. I feel we can reach that goal I've strived for, for far too long. There are names and faces of the dead that live in me. You understand, Lieutenant."

"I do."

"If I've pushed where it's not welcome or helpful, it's for them." This time when he smiled at Roarke, it hit more friendly. "The Green Flash heist is legendary, for good reason."

"Is it now?"

"It is. It surely is. I'll be in your bullpen."

Eve said nothing until he'd cleared the room.

"You didn't have to say all that, give him all that. He pushed where he shouldn't have pushed."

"Oh, well now, it's hard to fault him. The heist was brilliant."

She sighed, scrubbed at her face with her hands. "Just tell me you're not draping me in pieces of some necklace stolen from some idiot American."

"Would I?" He kissed her hand again. "I sold it, as contracted, long ago. And bought the nice little resort in Cannes. We should go there sometime."

"I don't want to talk about it." She shifted in her chair, took a hard look at him. "Are you okay?"

"I am. Are you?"

"We nearly had him. I know it. So no, not okay. Let's go get some coffee," she decided. "I need to sort my brain out." She rose. "And I want to know how the hell you got downtown so damn fast."

"Ah, you remind me to have my vehicle picked up from that rooftop."

"Great, sure. Whatever." She cast her gaze at the ceiling. "Coffee."

She went straight to her office, shut the door, hit the AutoChef. "We couldn't have missed him by more than minutes. Close enough he might have seen us converge."

She paced her tiny office as she gulped down coffee. "Booked it out on foot. Fast walk a couple blocks, turn a corner, turn the next."

Roarke sat, gingerly, in the visitor's chair as she paced, as she thought out loud. And found it all oddly calming.

"He's not stupid. Sloppy now, yeah, sloppy, because he's obsessed and stepped into Crazy Town. If he spots us, he takes off, then he has to think. What does he think, because he's not stupid? He thinks: The bloody bastard had a trace on me, hooked to his cop bitch. That's not only true, it's basic logic."

She gulped more coffee. "Good."

"Good?"

"Yeah, because he thinks that — just that — he's got no reason to rabbit. No reason to switch locations again. Unless one of your sources weaseled to him —"

"Not the ones I used, no." Roarke raised his coffee and his eyebrows. "As neither am I stupid."

"Figured that, so. At this point, he'd have no reason to move. He thinks he's safe wherever he's holed up. But he's not. We'll find his hole."

She stared at her board, stared hard, then dropped into her desk chair. "Now explain."

"I drove very fast?"

She might've laughed, but she wasn't in the mood. "Not that. How he contacted you."

"Ah that. He worked his way up to Caro, using different 'links, different names. On the last he tried Grafton — like the street in Dublin. I was at the school, not that she'd have put him through without clearance in any case. He rang back, and she being Caro, started a trace. Then again, until I got back to the office. Then I contacted you, and you know the rest."

"One of two things," she decided. "Either he's tipped so far he just couldn't resist the contact, needed to say what he said to you, try to shake you, or it's about response time."

"Well, bugger me." Roarke leaned back despite the miserable chair. "I'm the git for not considering the latter."

"It's risky, damn risky, but it would be good data to have. How quick are we off the mark, how accurate, and how much manpower do we put on it?"

"And it's the pattern again, that I didn't consider." Distractions, Roarke admitted, anxiety. He had to put them aside. "He likes watching the cops work after a kill. He likes that edgy little risk. So he played me then, after all."

"Maybe. But you can bet your ass if he stuck close enough to see you walk out of the building, he got a hell of a surprise. And he's still trying to figure out how the hell you got in there."

She pressed her fingers to her eyes. "Do whatever and get that car off the roof."

"Right." He took out his 'link to take care of it.

Was he there? Eve wondered. Did he spot Abernathy? If so, would that change anything for him?

Doubtful, she decided. He wouldn't respect Abernathy, in fact, might be pleased, even amused to know Interpol joined with the local cops.

Local cops, she thought, and grabbed her comm.

"Nothing yet, Dallas," Feeney responded. "Give us time."

"He might have spotted the van. If he made contact hoping to get a response, mark response time and force, he could've spotted the van."

"Well, shit."

"Can you switch it out?"

She saw the sigh on his hangdog face before he let it out. "Yeah, yeah. Pain in my ass. But . . ." Then he puffed out his cheeks, considered. "We're getting mostly nobody home right now. It's a nice day, people are out and about, right? We'll come in, switch it out. We can do some more cruising, but we could have more luck after midnight, maybe after one."

She hated the wait, hated the hours in between, but . . . "That's a good point. You single out any solo occupancy. We run those and we could have a go before morning."

They banged it back and forth, and Roarke nodded when she clicked off.

"Best use of time and manpower. And no reason I can see why we wouldn't tag along with whoever Feeney puts on the late shift."

She could think of reasons not to have him tag along, but all of them were personal. "I'll clear it with Feeney. Are you heading home?"

"I've things I left undone in my hasty departure from the office."

"Your car's on a roof in the Village."

"I have others." He rose, stepped to her to rub a thumb between her eyebrows where a worry line had formed. "If he has the brass to be watching Central, he wouldn't know what vehicle I'd take out of it. But he knows yours now, so I've more reason for the worry."

"I made a promise to you. I'm not going

364

to break it."

"Then we're fine, aren't we, the both of us." He drew her in, and because she'd closed the door, she wrapped around him. Held on.

"I'll see you at home." He kissed the top of her head. "I expect we could use some downtime before what could be a long night."

She found it harder to watch him walk away than she'd imagined. She wished he'd go home, behind the gates, the walls, the security, where she knew he'd be safe.

Was this how he felt? she wondered. Every time she walked out of the house to do the job, did he feel this low, creeping anxiety?

While she'd acknowledged just how hard it was to be a cop's spouse, she hadn't really known until that minute.

She had to put it aside, had to lock it away, as she understood now he did on a regular basis.

She sat again, wrote her report, updated her book.

She got another cup of coffee, drank it with her boots on the desk, her eyes on the board, her mind in the investigation.

And got nothing.

It simply wasn't the usual, she admitted. Her target had no real ties to New York, no regular haunts, no family, no friends, no business dealings.

He'd come to New York to kill, and had stayed for a bonus round.

Well, she wasn't going to sit there until he gave it a try. She needed to get back in the field, back on the hunt.

As she got to her feet, her 'link signaled. Jenkinson.

"Dallas. What have you got?"

"A hit here at this fancy shop, Urbane. The fancy clerk guy said Cobbe was in this morning, right after they opened. Went by the name Patrick, and paid cash. Four thousand and change."

She was already heading for the bullpen. "Peabody, with me. Give me the address," she told Jenkinson. "I'm coming to you."

"Reineke's getting the full list of what he bought," Jenkinson began.

"I'm coming to you," Eve repeated.

"Do you want Abernathy?" Peabody trotted to catch up. "He just went in the break room."

"No." She hit the elevator as Jenkinson reeled off the address. "Sit tight," she told him, then clicked off. "We'll read Interpol in later. We've got a wit, sold him clothes this morning."

"That's a break, and a good call, Dallas."

"It's not a break until it gets us some-where." To satisfy a hunch, she used the frustrating ride on the crowded car to check a map. "The shop's six — no, seven blocks south from where we traced his call to Roarke. We're canvassing the wrong sector."

She nodded to herself. "That was smart. Yeah, yeah, that was deliberate. His hole's going to be closer to the shop than the position we tracked him to. Good to know."

She burst out of the elevator on the garage level. "We're going to keep uniforms out of the sector around the shop for now. If he thinks we're focused in another area, he may take advantage of the nice weather, do some more shopping, go out for something to eat."

Peabody climbed in the car. "I was think-ing he might head back uptown, try to keep an eye on your place."

"Yeah, that, too. But he's not going to try to take Roarke at home. He needs to bide his time, lure Roarke out, or wait until — he thinks — Roarke's guard's down."

"Roarke's guard's never down."

"That's right." And that single truth kept her sane and steady. "But he doesn't know Roarke. He knows the kid from the Dublin streets. He knows what he hears, not what is."

She blew out into traffic with Peabody's knuckles white on the chicken stick.

"And he sure as hell doesn't know me."

"Is Roarke okay?"

"Yeah. No. I don't know. He'll be better when we have this son of a bitch in a cage."

She bulled and bullied her way toward the address. She'd planned to double-park, then spotted a second-level spot, punched vertical.

Peabody gave a short, breathless squeal that ended on a grunt as Eve dropped the car down with a bone-rattle.

Eve jogged halfway down to the street before Peabody managed to open her door.

The display window of Urbane had several — always creepy to Eve's eye — fake people in snooty poses, in what she supposed were high-fashion clothes.

If some guy wanted to wear a jacket that looked like it had been skinned off a zebra, what did she know?

She pushed in where Reineke waited. Jenkinson stood across the shop at a display of ties. The air smelled like freshly peeled oranges.

"Clerk's in the back with a customer," Reineke told her. "He's cooperating. I've got an itemized list of what Cobbe bought this morning. Full description. Two T-shirts

— one black, one gray — like they call them noire and slate, but you get it. Two pairs of jeans — both black — and one hooded zip-up jacket, also black."

"That's it?" Eve said when Reineke looked up from his list.

"Yeah."

"Jenkinson said he shelled out four grand."

"Yeah."

"Well, that's insane."

"You think that's crazy?" Jenkinson pointed at the ties. "This one here's got pigs on it — little pink pigs you can't even see until you're right on it. And I can buy a freaking hundred ties at my stall for the price of this one."

Jenkinson shook his head. "I'll move him back out."

He strolled into the back.

"Anyway." Scratching his head, Reineke glanced around the shop. "The clerk's name's Bilbo, Trent Bilbo. Also assistant manager, employed here for six years. He was some flustered when we badged him, but it turns out his brother's had some run-ins, so he thought it was about that. He remembered Cobbe right off."

Bilbo came out, a skinny guy in tight black pants, tight black tee, and a vibrant purple jacket and tie. He had a sweep of black hair tinted purple at the tips.

And earnest brown eyes despite the heavy application of kohl.

"I'm so sorry. Mr. King is a longtime customer, and my colleague is out on break."

"It's fine. I'm Lieutenant Dallas."

"I know. I know. And Detective Peabody. I read the book. I saw the vid." He pressed both hands to his mouth as if holding back squeals.

If eyes could squeal, his did.

"I'm thrilled to meet you, even under the circumstances. It seems I waited on a criminal this morning."

"Tell us about that."

"Well, as I told Detectives Jenkinson and Reineke, he came in shortly after ten. I had just opened. Marcus wasn't due in until eleven, so I was alone in the shop. If I'd known he was a criminal, I don't know what I'd have done!"

His hands went back to his mouth.

If eyes could gasp, his did.

"What did you do?"

"I said good morning, asked if I could assist him. He had the most charming accent — Irish. He said he was from Dublin. In any case, he wanted to see the jacket on display."

"The zebra jacket?"

"Oh no, though that is so ultra mag, isn't it? The charcoal distressed leather bomber, the Yang, with the blackout zips and sapphire lining in silk. Gorgeous piece. Unfortunately, we didn't have his size. The one on display is too small — very broad shoulders he had. And the other we had in stock was too big."

As he spoke, Eve walked over to the display, studied the jacket.

"It's a shame because the two Leonardo tees — he dresses you. A genius. Those tees and the Granville urban jeans he did buy? The jacket would have been perfection with them."

"He paid in cash."

"Yes. He was very friendly, asked about the neighborhood, restaurants, bars, other shops. He said he had extended business in the city. We even chatted about the weather — just glorious! — while I wrapped his purchases."

"We got the list of the places Mr. Bilbo mentioned to him," Reineke put in.

"Okay. Did he say anything else, ask anything else?"

"Not really. I asked, as you do, if he was enjoying New York, and he said he was, and planned to enjoy it even more. Oh, I did tell him I'd be happy to see if I could get the Yang jacket in his size — and we could have our tailor come in and fit it to perfection. If he wanted to leave me a contact number. But he declined. He did say he might check back in a day or two, in case, but was reluctant to leave a contact."

"Which way did he go when he left?"

"Ah . . . To the right. Yes, to the right, as I saw him give the jacket another look, but he continued on his way."

"We appreciate your cooperation. If he does come back, it's very important you don't react, that you treat him exactly as you did today."

"Oh my." Bilbo pressed his hands to his mouth again.

If eyes could gulp, his did.

"Tell him you have the jacket coming in, but also put something in the back for him to see. Go back, contact me. Peabody, give Mr. Bilbo a card. Bring something out that suits him, something to keep his attention."

"I — I can do that. In fact, I did find the jacket in his size in our Chicago store, and it should be here first thing in the morning. I can put it in the back. I can do that. He was so charming. It's hard to believe he's done anything illegal."

"If he comes back in, just think of the

charm, go in the back, contact me."

Eve gave the two detectives a quick up and down. "You look like cops."

In response, Jenkinson grinned, fluttered his atomic tie at her.

"Even with that ocular nightmare. Get on soft clothes. He may be out in the area, and I don't want him spotting a couple of cops. Get a shopping bag, or a . . ." She pointed to what she thought of the manly version of a purse. "How much is that thing?" she asked Bilbo.

"The Joseph Karim City Bag? Eighty-nine hundred."

"Jesus. Forget that. Mock up a field bag. Bilbo, how much to put an empty box in a shopping bag?"

"Oh, no charge at all. I'd be happy to do that for you."

"Great. Thanks. Do that."

She studied Peabody. Despite the pink coat, pink cowgirl boots, the scarf bursting with pink-and-purple flowers, a trained eye would see cop.

"We look like cops. More, he knows what I look like. Give me the sissy scarf."

Frowning, Peabody unwound the scarf. "Not sissy," she muttered.

"And undo a couple of buttons."

"How come I always have to undo buttons?"

"Because you've got the tits."

Eve draped on the scarf while Jenkinson gazed at the ceiling and Reineke took an interest in a display of socks.

Bilbo just smiled. "It's a lovely scarf. Is it a Miranda Bester?"

"No. It's a Peabody."

"You made it yourself?" Hands to mouth again before he reached out to trail a finger over the material. "It's gorgeous. If I could suggest — if it's not overstepping — if you wanted to look less official, perhaps some kicky sunshades."

Peabody pulled a pair — oversize white frames, pink (of course) lenses.

"Perfect!" Bilbo exclaimed when she slid them on.

"I've probably got some in the car," Eve said.

Bilbo added a navy-and-red-striped ribbon to the handles of the shopping bag. "If I may say, that abso-mag Leonardo topper doesn't look at all cop-like, but you do have a — a kind of authoritative aura."

"Right."

He just beamed at Eve. "A newsboy cap — very on trend this spring — would add a flip of insouciance, unexpected in a police officer. Vanity, just a few doors down, has them on sale. If I could say, as an admirer, one doesn't expect to see Lieutenant Dallas in a newsboy cap and floral scarf."

Eve nodded. "You're all right, Bilbo."

He blushed as pink as Peabody's boots. "Oh my, thank you!"

"What do you do if he comes in?"

"I act normal, tell him I found the jacket, go into the back, and contact you."

"That's right. Thanks for your help."

Outside, she scanned the streets. "Soft clothes," she repeated. "And we split the list we got from Bilbo. Maybe we'll find a couple more Bilbos."

She hiked up to the car, dug out a pair of sunshades — sensible black frames — then detoured into Vanity as suggested.

She found it a huge leap from Urbane, about three times the size, pulsing with bouncy music, and full of high school and college types pawing the merchandise.

It smelled of cheap, teenage body spray.

Peabody snatched the black cap out of Eve's hands. "Not that one. Try this one."

Eve frowned at the purple cap with its tiny pink flowers. "Just no."

"It goes with the scarf — which looks good on you, by the way — and nobody spotting that cap is going to think cop."

So saying, Peabody grabbed some sort of hair tie with a pink-and-white butterfly out of a bin. "This is for my hair, since we'd look stupid if we both wore caps."

Eve accepted defeat. "Sometimes the job is embarrassing."

But she paid for the cap, put it on, paid for the tie, watched Peabody twist a section of her hair up so the butterfly fluttered just behind her crown.

"It's going to be more embarrassing if we take him down while we're wearing this stuff."

But, Eve thought, she'd suck that right up.

17

They hit bars, restaurants, shops, walked block after block.

They found where Cobbe bought his underwear — black boxers — where he added a light cashmere sweater — crewneck, steel gray — and two dress shirts.

He stopped into a market along the way, bought some basic provisions.

He would, eventually, return to at least one or two of those places. She had to depend on responsible citizens contacting her when he did.

She hated depending on civilians.

They made a last stop at a bar offering high-priced drinks with fancy names served by impossibly beautiful waitstaff.

They hit with the bartender, who nodded immediately when they flashed Cobbe's photo.

"He was in last night until closing. I guess he came in about midnight — I worked a double yesterday, so I was on the bar until closing. Gin Blossoms — that was his drink. I can look up the tab for you, but he paid cash, had four, and bought two glasses of champagne for Kaylee."

"Kaylee?"

"Kaylee Skye — our entertainment. She sings — old bluesy numbers — from ten to two. I say he came in about midnight because I know she was on her second break, and he hit on me a little. Friendly like, but definitely had the moves."

"Okay." Eve sized her up. The impossible beauty extended to bar staff. This one was tall, lanky, silvery blond with cheekbones that could cut glass.

"Then Kaylee came out, started her second set, and he forgot about hitting on me. Kaylee's a stunner, and she's got the pipes, right? Sexy, smoky, and she wears those sleek, sinuous sorts of gowns for her gigs, like you see in old vids? Can I get you a drink?"

"How's the coffee?"

The bartender smiled. "I'll say it's not our specialty."

"Got Pepsi?"

"Got Coke."

"I'll take it."

"The no-cal for me," Peabody said.

"Could we have your name?"

"Sure. Londa, Londa Stanski."

"So he focused on the talent," Eve continued. "Kaylee Skye."

"Big-time. Asked me what she drank, then sent her up a glass of the champagne she likes. It's primo, so he had the scratch. And you could hear the click, right?"

The bartender added a twist of lemon to the glasses, set them on bar coasters.

"She focused back?"

"She did, but that's not unusual for her. Part of the job's to get a little flirt on. Anyway, she came to the bar on her next break to thank him, and they got more of a flirt on. I'll say he had that dreamy accent, and a lot of style."

Londa took an order for a Zombie and a vodka martini.

"Did she leave with him?" Eve asked as the bartender skillfully mixed the drinks.

"Yeah. Now that's not usual for her, but they had that click — and she and the guy she was seeing for a while broke it off a few weeks ago, so she was loose. She's back on at nine tonight if you want to talk to her."

"I need her address."

For the first time, the bartender pulled back. "Look, I get you're cops, but I really don't like to do that, and she'll be back in a few hours anyway."

"Do you figure a couple of cops are in here showing his photo because they want to get a flirt on with him?"

"Well, no, but —"

"He killed a woman a couple nights ago. He's made a living doing that for a couple of decades. Give me her address."

"Oh my Jesus. She's only a couple blocks from here." She spewed out the address. "We're work pals, you know, Kaylee and me. Four years. Tell her to tag me, okay?"

"All right. If he comes in tonight, contact me." She nodded for Peabody to put a card on the bar. "Don't do anything to tip him off. Just serve him his drink, and contact me."

"You bet your ass. Have Kaylee tag me, please."

"I will."

"This is another break," Peabody said when they went out.

"Maybe. They'd have walked, just a couple blocks. Maybe she lets him come up, maybe not. How far would he push if it's maybe not? He's expecting sex, he bought her drinks, didn't he? Primo champagne. She led him on, didn't she? Either way, he probably got inside with her."

Eve paused outside the building. A nice

380

six-stack, fully residential, with good security, including cams.

"See if there's a super on-site who can give us the security feed. She's on the second floor. Meet me up there."

"On that."

Eve mastered in, entered the small lobby with its old, meticulously refinished wood floors. She ignored the elevators — a pair with doors painted with murals of New York's skyline — and took the stairs.

A clean building, she thought, on the arty side. Kaylee either made a damn good living with those pipes or had other income to afford the rent.

She paused outside apartment 2A, hit the buzzer. Tried again with no response.

Her gut went tight as she turned, tried 2B.

A woman's voice answered through the intercom. "Yes?"

"NYPSD." Eve held up her badge. "I'm looking for Kaylee Skye."

The door opened, and the voice became a woman in a black leotard, a swirly blue skirt, with red-streaked black hair worn in a tight bun over a striking face. "Why?"

"We need to ask her some questions."

"About?"

"Do you know Ms. Skye?"

"She lives right across the hall."

Apparently cop cooperation had hit its limit for the day.

Eve yanked out her PPC, brought up Cobbe's picture. "How about him?"

"Never seen him before."

"She has, and he's wanted for multiple murders. She was seen leaving her place of employment with him last night, and may have let him into her apartment. She would be unaware of his criminal record. Now, do you know where she is?"

"No." But the bitchy look and tone shifted. Some suspicion still, some knee-jerk dislike of cops — but concern, too. "She might still be sleeping, she works late. But I expected to see her before I left for my next class. My partner and I run a dance school."

"This man's dangerous," Eve began.

The elevator door opened, and Peabody came out.

"Got the feed — they came in together at two-twenty-three. No duress. He left at three-oh-one. He was disheveled," she added, casting a glance over at the dancer. "Dallas, his knuckles were scraped up."

The dancer leaped across the hall, began to bang on Kaylee's door. "Kaylee! Kaylee, it's Marta! Open the door. Wake up and open the damn door."

"The super cleared us to enter," Peabody said. "He's calling the lawyer, but he said to go in."

"Take her." Eve pushed past the dancer, used her master.

"NYPSD," she announced. "We're coming in."

She already knew it was too late for the warning, but stepped inside. A pretty, female living area, all quiet colors and plush fabrics. A pair of sky-high silver heels obviously kicked off, a long white and silver gown in a silky pool.

They'd started the dance here, she thought, excited, needy kisses, rushing hands, peeling out of the dress as they moved toward the bedroom.

Where something went wrong.

Too rough? Slow down? No, don't? Wait?

Any or all of that, she imagined.

Had she screamed, called for help? A place like this would be well soundproofed.

Because he hadn't slowed down, he hadn't waited. He'd used his fists to convince her. Maybe he hadn't meant to kill her. He hadn't used a knife.

He'd closed his hands over her throat and squeezed the life out of her so she lay, the bits of underwear she'd worn in tatters, her face — stunning even now — bruised, the bedding tangled from her struggles.

Eve could hear the dancer shouting at Peabody, so she turned and strode back to the doorway where her partner physically held the woman back.

"You need to stop. If you don't, we'll be forced to restrain you."

"Is Kaylee in there? Kaylee!"

"There's nothing you can do for her now."

The woman jerked back, then simply slid like water out of Peabody's hands to the floor.

"I've got her, Dallas. Come with me now. It's Marta, right? Come with me, Marta."

Trusting Peabody to deal with grief and shock, Eve shut the door.

And called it in.

By the time she'd finished, Peabody eased in the door. "I got her calmed down, and her partner's coming. Did he cut her?"

"No. Beaten — mostly facial — and strangled — manually. We need the field kits out of the car, and we'll need to inform the bartender, get a more formal statement."

"Okay, I'll get the kits, and tell the bartender. I can ask her to give a statement when we're done here."

"Good enough."

While she waited, she ran the victim.

Kaylee Skye, age thirty-one. Next of kin, a

mother, stepfather, and half sib in Dayton, Ohio; a father, stepmother, and half sib in Columbus, Ohio. And maternal grandparents, who'd established a trust fund, which explained how she could afford the rent.

Eve walked over, studied a tidy galley kitchen, the equally tidy bath — fresh, fluffy towels, a fat white candle.

A small alcove off the kitchen served as a kind of office — mini-comp, cream-colored desk and chair, with a royal blue cushion on the chair.

A lot of quiet blues and roses in the living area, with furniture arranged for conversation.

It didn't look as if Cobbe worried about conversation once he got her inside.

She'd wanted him — and why not? — this handsome, well-dressed guy with the lovely accent who'd laid on the charm.

Until he got her inside.

Then it was hurry up.

Maybe at first she found it exciting, all caught up in the moment, mouths and hands, and the thrill of being taken.

Then it got rough.

Eve looked around again, the female touches, the quiet colors, the pretty of it all.

"You weren't the type for the rough, were

you, Kaylee? You wanted some romance, some smooth moves, and he just wanted to bang, and bang hard."

She walked to the bedroom again, stood in the doorway. "You just wanted him to slow it down, take a little care. But he won't. He can't. It's who he is. And when you tell him to stop, to wait, he hits you. I'm betting nobody ever slammed a fist into your face before. It's a shock — that pain, that insult, that sudden fear. So you cry out, you struggle, and he hits you again."

Again and again, Eve thought. Again and again.

"Does he tell you to shut the fuck up, call you a whore, a bitch? Probably. He's tearing at your pretty bra and panties, and you're crying, you're begging. Maybe you manage a scream. So he closes his hands around your throat to shut you up while he rams into you, squeezing and squeezing the air, the life out of you while he pumps and pushes and grunts."

And when he's done, when he sees what he's done, he doesn't feel a thing. He just puts his pants on, and walks out.

"He got what he needed."

She took out her 'link, contacted Abernathy.

"He got another one."

"What? Lieutenant? Who? Where?"

She gave him the name, the address. "Your aide will get you here." Glancing back, she nodded as Peabody came in with field kits. "I have work to do."

They'd caught breaks, Eve thought when they left the crime scene to the sweepers and the victim to the morgue team. And still.

"I'm going to write this up at home," she told Peabody.

"I'll write it up. I'm closer to home than you are. I'll copy you. We couldn't have stopped this, Dallas. And there's nothing — Abernathy confirmed — there's nothing in his file that compares to this. He kills for profit, he cuts and guts. This isn't his pattern."

"He's not working now. This is a mission, even a kind of holiday. And he's not controlled like he is when he's working. And I'm saying the file's wrong, Abernathy's fucking wrong."

She felt the bubbling fury in her want to boil over, had to push it down again.

"There have been others. Unsolved or closed wrong that go back to him."

"I think you're right. It was easy for him, just another night."

"I can drop you back at Central or home,

wherever you want to work."

"I've got it. Quick subway ride. I'll see you later tonight. McNab's in the van — and I hear you and Roarke are, too. So I'm in."

"All right. I'll get the bartender's statement, then I'm working at home."

By the time she got back in her car, her mood hit bottom of the tank. She'd listened to the weeping dancer, the weeping bartender, the weeping parents.

Their grief rolled through her in waves.

She wanted home, she wanted Roarke, she wanted her cat. And she wanted the work. Because the work would lead her to this son of a bitch.

Then she remembered the school.

Too late, too much work, she thought. She'd go by another time. She wasn't in the damn mood.

And muttering curses, she changed her route.

Because, damn it, it was important. It mattered.

So she'd go by, ten minutes, do a quick walk-through, then she could tell Roarke she'd seen it. No point tagging him when she'd do a quick in and out.

Of course that meant finding a damn place to park, which added more time, then hiking to the school through the flood of people who apparently didn't want to go home.

And okay, it looked great — from the outside anyway. Dignified without being fussy and . . . what was the word? Staid? Weird word, but it wasn't that.

Good, solid security, as expected. She opted to buzz rather than master, to see who answered.

She hadn't expected Rochelle.

"Oh, I was so hoping you'd make it by!" Before Eve could react, Rochelle had her hand, pulling her right in.

"I didn't think you'd still be here."

"It's a big day, and I haven't been able to drag myself away. Wilson just left. I'm going to meet him for a celebratory dinner in an hour."

"I don't want to keep you."

"No, no, let me show you through. I've laughed and cried so many times today, I've lost count. So forgive me if I do both. The day students are gone now, and most of the live-ins are either in the kitchen or still unpacking, fussing with their rooms."

They went through classrooms, study areas, recreation areas — cheerful spaces, clean, bright.

Science areas, occupational areas, music

rooms, a theater.

"He didn't miss a trick, did he?" Eve mused.

"No, he didn't. I wish you could have seen the reaction of some of the kids today, of the parents and guardians. So many of them never had a place like this, an opportunity like this. I know not all will make it, but many will. So many will."

They went back, through the dining hall into the main kitchen. A small swarm of kids, three adults — staff — with the adults guiding the kids through making the meal.

It smelled amazing.

"We won't interrupt. Carlo, the head chef? He's a real find. He'll teach the students both the art and science of cooking. We'll educate them on nutrition, but also the fun of it."

"Cooking's fun?"

"According to Carlo. We also have the workshop kitchen for students who advance or have serious interests."

Upstairs, more classrooms, more areas for gathering, for study, for specific interests.

And in what Rochelle called the video and communication area, she saw a vid of the school on-screen with Nadine and Quilla watching.

"Sorry," Rochelle said. "We're interrupting. I didn't realize you were still here, Nadine."

"Nearly done." She gave Eve a long look with her sharp reporter's eyes. "Quilla, start on the edits we talked about. I'll be right back."

"Okay, but, I want to . . ." She rose, walked over to Eve, stuck out a hand.

Bemused, Eve shook it.

"I don't much like hugs, either — they're weird. I just want to say thank you."

"Okay. You're welcome. How's it going?"

"It's going freaking mag. Nadine's going to put a clip from my vid on *Now*."

"Do those edits," Nadine reminded her. "Then we'll discuss."

"I'm all over it."

"I'll leave you to talk." Rochelle stepped back. "Oh well, I'm sorry you don't much like hugs." And hugged Eve hard.

Since Eve had her back to her, she didn't see Quilla catch the moment on her camera.

"I'm going to go laugh and cry again before I meet Wilson for dinner."

"Tell Crack — ah, Wilson — the white girl said hey."

"I will. What a day. What an absolutely amazing day."

She went off, sniffling a little, and Nadine took Eve's arm to lead her out of Quilla's earshot.

"Tell me first, as a friend, how is Roarke, how are you?"

"We're fine. I can't say it's been an amazing day, but we're fine. We're handling it."

"I've done what research I can on Cobbe. There's probably nothing you don't know, but I'll send it to you. Now tell me if there's anything else I can do."

"We're handling it." She could see Quilla doing something — those edits — with the vid. She heard her recorded voice, the voices of other children, the energy of it all.

"We're close. I know we're close, and he doesn't know how close. I want to keep it that way."

"Nothing goes on the air unless you clear it. I say that as a professional who has always, and will always, cooperate with an investigation, but also as your friend. As Roarke's. You know that, Dallas."

"I do know that. Are you teaching her that?"

Nadine glanced back at Quilla. "You're damn right I am, but she's already got that. She's got integrity as well as enthusiasm, and considerable talent. I downplay that because she needs the discipline. I'm a little bit crazy about that kid."

"Looks mutual to me." Then Eve sighed.

"He killed another woman. Not professionally."

"Who? When? How?"

"You can break the murder — Kaylee Skye — but not the Cobbe connection. I don't want him to know we know. Not yet. Consensual sex that went south, turned to rape/murder. He strangled her."

Frowning, Nadine shook her head. "He uses sharps. You're sure it's him?"

"He wasn't working — you want to research? I'm betting he's killed like this before. Unsolveds. He goes for lookers, quick pickups. He may have killed some LCs along the way, but most likely civilians because it would be too easy to trace an LC back to him. He'd want to protect his aliases, so civilians, like Skye."

"I'll see what I can find out."

"So will I. I've got to go, get back to it." But she stood another moment. "This is a good place, isn't it? It feels like a good place."

"Rochelle wasn't the only one getting teary when she showed me around. So did Quilla, and she's a tough little nut. It's a good place, Dallas, and lives have already started to change in it."

"Okay. Good. I've got to go. I'll let you know when you can break the Cobbe connection."

"I'll be ready. Oh, and Dallas?" Nadine added as Eve walked away. "Lovely scarf."

"What?" Looking down at herself, Eve cursed, whipped it off. "It's Peabody's."

"Looks good on you."

Eve stuffed it in her pocket, kept walking. She had to be grateful she'd remembered to ditch the stupid hat.

She walked down and out, remembering the clean and bright, the smells of good food cooking, the light in Quilla's eyes when she'd shaken hands.

And aimed for home with her mood considerably higher.

Even as she kept alert for tails, she thought of the Marriage Rules.

"Text Roarke," she ordered her in-dash. "Heading home."

It felt good to say it, felt good to know the traffic she fought to get there would — most likely — be the worst she faced until morning.

"Accept text," she said when her in-dash signaled an incoming.

She heard Roarke's voice, another mood lifter. As am I. Turning toward the gates now.

"Respond: Open a bottle, pal. We're due."

His answer came seconds later. Consider it done.

Nice, she thought. Sometimes it was just nice to be married. Maybe especially nice with all the crap coming down on them right now to know they had each other.

The next signal came from her comm, and forced her to make a single wish.

Whatever it was didn't mean she'd have to turn the car around again.

She answered on her wrist unit. "Dallas."

"Santiago, with Carmichael and good news."

"I could use some."

"Yeah, we heard about the second murder. But we've ID'd his rental vehicle."

"How sure?"

"One hundred percent. I'm looking at the paperwork — including a copy of the driver's license he used to rent a '61 black Tuscan Regal all-terrain, fully loaded — right down to the license plate, Loo. He used the name Liam O'Patrick, with an Interstellar credit account under the same name. Both cleared the car rental agent's security scan. The agent who worked with him's gone for the day, but we have his address, and we're headed there next to talk to him."

"Get an APB out on the vehicle — use the license number with the caveat he may have switched it out. Orders: Track vehicle, but do not stop, do not approach."

"Carmichael's doing that now."

"Good work, Santiago. Both of you, good work. Get copies of any security feed they've got on him, send me everything. Let me know what the rental guy says."

"You got it."

Cop work, she thought, just good, solid, tenacious cop work. That's how it's done. And since there were more rules than marriage, she dictated a text to update Abernathy.

And finally turned through the gates.

18

When she walked inside, Summerset waited alone. Which meant Galahad had gone upstairs with Roarke. Since she wanted to be there herself, she dispensed with the greeting insult — there was always next time — and went straight to the point.

"Anything I should know?"

"There's lemon meringue pie for dessert."

"Not the best news I've had today, but it ranks." She tossed the topper over the newel post. "No weird attempts at communication, no attempted deliveries?"

"No. He won't come at Roarke here."

"No, but he might try for you."

Summerset smiled as she started up the steps. She had to admit it was the sort of smile that could set your hair on end.

"He'd be considerably disappointed."

"Watch your bony six anyway. You can always yank the stick out of your ass for an extra weapon."

And score! Who said she couldn't come up with an on-the-spot insult?

Considerably satisfied, she went straight to her office.

He'd opened a bottle, stood in the process of pouring a second glass of red that practically glowed in the crystal.

The cat stopped rubbing against Roarke's legs to trot over and rub against hers.

Then froze, sniffed. He cast one baleful look up at her out of his bicolored eyes before strutting away with his tail straight up in the air.

She knew the feline equivalent of the middle finger when she saw it.

Roarke angled his head as he looked down at the cat now sitting at his feet aiming lethal stares at Eve.

"And what's all this?"

"There was a cat. It sat on my lap while we interviewed the cat lady. He's pissed."

She aimed a lethal stare right back. "He'll just have to get over it if he remembers where his tuna comes from."

She jabbed a finger at Roarke. "And don't say Summerset."

He only shook his head. "You don't look nearly as tired as I expected after such a day," he said as he crossed over to brush his lips to hers, then offer the glass.

He, on the other hand, looked more tired than she'd expected, as he rarely looked tired at all.

"I got some good news."

"I could use some."

"There's lemon meringue pie for dessert."

His lips curved a little. "Pie is always good news."

"We've ID'd his transpo, make, model, color, tag number. We've got an all-points out on it."

"Well now, that's better news than pie."

She knew him. "You're thinking about the woman he killed last night."

"If he'd left New York as planned, she'd be alive." He took her hand before she could speak. "I know it's nothing I did that caused it. I know there's nothing I could've done to prevent it. And still, a woman's dead because he's here, hoping to end me."

"He doesn't get to end you. That's just it. She didn't deserve what he did to her. The murdered dead hardly ever do."

She laid a hand on his chest, on his heart.

"And if he'd left New York, yeah, she'd be alive. Somebody else would be dead, if not now, soon. And then another, another. Because we wouldn't stop him. But he's here, and we will stop him."

He leaned in to kiss her again. "I should've

stayed with you instead of going back to the office. You steady me at a time like this."

"I was just thinking we do that for each other. Let's eat something, including pie. And nothing for him until he stops sulking."

In response, Galahad shot up a leg and began to wash as if he couldn't care less.

She knew better.

"I'll see to that — it'll take my mind off the brooding. Update your board."

She set her wine aside to do just that.

"We got some other breaks beside his transpo — though that's a big one."

"Tell me," he said from the kitchen.

"Jenkinson and Reineke hit a shop he'd been in, with a cooperative clerk. Way overpriced men's stuff — which was what I figured he'd go for. Some place called Urbane."

"Yes, I know it."

She paused in the work. "You don't own it, do you?"

"I don't, just the building itself."

"Just the building itself," she muttered. "Anyway. He dropped four large on a couple T-shirts and whatever, and had his eye on a jacket. Not in his size, but the clerk said how he'd try to get it in, so he may return. If we don't take him down tonight, and he does, the clerk knows what to do. After that we split up the shops and bars, restaurants the clerk had suggested to him, nailed down a couple more places. Then the bar where he picked up his victim."

She finished the board as he came in with plates, and told herself she could update her book after dinner.

He needed some normal.

Maybe murder wasn't normal dinner talk for some, but it was for them.

Pasta primavera, she noted. It couldn't match good old spaghetti and meatballs, but it didn't suck, either. She retrieved her wine, sat as he opened the doors to the little terrace.

Spring flowed in.

She sampled a bite.

It definitely didn't suck.

"I went by the school."

Surprised, he lifted his wine. "Did you? As you didn't tag me, I didn't think you'd have time for it."

"Just a quick run-through because I wanted to see it. I was doing some brooding of my own, and that put a stop to it. Rochelle was still there, and, well, sparkling. She walked me through some of it — a lot of it. Everything's so . . . ."

She hunted for a word. "Possible," she

decided. "You can see and feel the possible everywhere. They were cooking in the kitchen. I didn't know you hired a chef on staff."

"I told you."

"I thought, you know, you'd have some cooks, not an actual chef guy."

"They should eat well, and hopefully some will do better than either of us and actually learn to cook a bit."

"The ones in there looked into it. Nadine was there."

"Was she?"

"Working with Quilla on a vid Quilla did."

"Ah yes, I saw a few minutes of the raw footage earlier. It's very good. Whatever innate talent she had, Nadine's already begun polishing."

"Hah. That's just the word I thought about it. Polishing. She's a smart kid. She sees the possible, Roarke, it's all over her. It felt good to see it, to know it. She won't be the only one who sees it, and uses it."

Just to check, she slid her gaze over. Galahad sprawled on her sleep chair, tail hanging down and twitching. His eyes slitted and staring.

"I met a boy there today," Roarke told her. "So young, playing a guitar as if he'd been born with one. Quilla won't be the only one, no, as he's another. He made me think of the boy who sang on Grafton Street, with his little dog. I wonder what became of him."

"You could find out."

"I don't remember his name, if I ever knew it. I put so much of that time behind me. Or thought I did. Not brooding," he assured her as they ate. "Considering. A school such as we've done here might be welcome there."

"That's big considering."

"Why go small?" Now he smiled and meant it. "Maybe the next time we go visit the family, we'll hop over to Dublin and have a look."

Reaching over, he squeezed her hand. "Now, tell me what you know."

So they did the normal, talked murder over pasta and wine.

"The shops, the market, the bar," Roarke mused. "He covered a number of blocks. I think you'd be right that his hole is in that area. Walkable to places he's frequented — and not where he led us today."

"He carried bags out, every time he bought something. Could've caught a cab, taken the subway, but it makes more sense to shop where you live, more or less. And he'd have no reason, yet, to assume we'd look in that area of the Lower West Side."

"I can refine the search results somewhat. If I dig any deeper, I'd have to go beyond those I trust to those who know him, fear him, or owe him, and that would, inevitably, lead to one of them, or more, getting back to him on it."

"Don't risk it," Eve said immediately. "We've got a good chance of finding him inside the next twenty-four. Let's leave it at that. We know where he shops, where he trolled for a woman, what he's driving. Hell, we know what he's likely wearing. And he wanted that jacket, so there's that. It adds up. Solid, incremental cop work adds up."

"As I've seen before. What does Abernathy say?"

"He was surprised Cobbe rented a vehicle. Not that he hasn't before, but he didn't expect that would pan out here. Good public transpo, he doesn't know the city. He figures the APB is a one in a million."

Roarke nodded. "Because he has a garage, either where he's holing up, or he's rented a space inside. You don't park that sort of car on the street, and you'd be lucky to find parking, regularly, convenient to where you're staying."

"Agreed, but he's going to drive it some-time. It's a tool when he manages, in his mind, to grab you up."

Those eyes, those wild Irish eyes, latched onto hers. "Or you."

"Or me. And it's something he needs if he has to rabbit fast. He's not stupid, so he's mapped out how to get out of the city if and when he needs to."

"We're same page again. What time do we start the hunt?"

"We're meeting at Central at oh-one hundred. He might troll for another woman, but I figure he's smart enough to lay low there tonight."

"Then I say it's coffee and pie while we finish up the work here."

He took his into his office.

Alone in hers, Eve wandered into her kitchen without giving the sulking cat a glance.

She came out with a handful of cat treats and walked back to her command center. In under thirty seconds as she scanned the paperwork from Santiago, Galahad leaped his pudge onto the counter. Still scanning, still holding the treats in her hand, she waited him out.

He padded over, gave her a butt on the shoulder with his head.

"You want something?"

He butted her again, added a rub.

"You know, there are going to be times on the job when I encounter another cat. If you recall, I was on the job when I found you."

She turned to him, shaking the treats in her hand.

"You're the one I brought home."

She set the treats on the counter. Instead of pouncing on them as she expected, he rubbed against her again.

Maybe with love, she thought, maybe to overlay the other cat scent. Probably both.

She gave him one long stroke, a scratch between the ears. "Plus, she meant nothing to me."

Apparently satisfied, Galahad pounced on the treats.

Equally satisfied all was forgiven, she went back to Santiago's report. She added it to her book, updated it.

She read Peabody's report, added that.

Sitting back with her pie, she studied the board. What was meringue anyway? Why was it so damn good?

She grabbed her signaling comm.

"Carmichael, what've you got?"

"Turns out the car-rental guy moonlights as a dancer — nice abs. We tracked him down. He remembers Cobbe — the high-dollar rental, the accent. He said Cobbe mentioned he was in New York on business

406

for a couple weeks, came off pleasant. The security check went through smooth. You can see from the paperwork, Cobbe gave them the hotel where he stayed for the Modesto murder as his New York address, and the address on his license, when we ran it, is actually a department store in Dublin, so phony-baloney, but it's good phony ID."

"Two weeks. So he's ready to put in some time. Okay, good work. Go home."

"Might stay for another dance. They've got bar food." She sobered. "We're closing in, Dallas. I tried to bet Santiago we'd have him within twenty-four, and he wouldn't take the bet. Detective I'll-Bet-On-Anything wouldn't take the bet because he thinks the same. Tell Roarke we're all over the mother-fucker."

"I will."

She got up, walked into his office, where he sat, jacket off, sleeves rolled up, hair tied back.

Work mode.

"I put Carmichael and Santiago off duty. Carmichael says to tell you we're closing in. Santiago won't bet on it because he believes it, too. And they're all over the mother-fucker."

"It's appreciated."

"Any luck refining?"

"Some. These are my top four, currently."

He brought a map on-screen, highlighted four locations. "This one is on the edge of what most would deem walkable from the locations he frequented, and it's not what we'll call a rental for shady characters. It's a small, converted warehouse, furnished and available to rent by the week or month. Its advantage to him would be it still has a covered loading dock."

"For the vehicle."

"Yes. And is advertised as offering full, state-of-the-art security, and an indoor lap pool in a fully outfitted fitness area. A quick inquiry tells me it was rented the morning after the Modesto murder for immediate occupancy — and for the month."

"Okay." She nodded. "A definite check-it-out."

"Another is, as you see, a bit outside the area, but again it suits. A gated home, with garage. It's owned by a rather nefarious Russian, whose name I imagine Abernathy would recognize."

"Friend of yours?"

"Not at all, not even back in the day. The other two are more convenient for his shopping route, but neither offer off-street for the vehicle. Still, both are well situated, and according to my information, offered at a price, or as a favor, to certain types."

"We check them all."

"I have three others, more distant." He highlighted them for her. "Unless he's after a strong walk, he'd likely use public transpo or the car for the shopping areas."

"Send the first four to me, to Feeney. We'll start there."

"Easily done," he said, and did so.

"Why don't we take a couple hours' downtime? It's going to be a long night. Longer if we hit."

He glanced up at her, then grabbed her hand. He tugged her into his lap before she evaded. "I don't think either of us would sleep before this."

"You're tired."

"I am that." He nuzzled her neck. "There are other ways to recharge body and soul." He skimmed his teeth along her jaw. "I've had a need for you all this day. A terrible need to just lose myself in you. Let me," he said before his mouth took hers like a man starving for it.

Where had this been with the fatigue and the stress? she wondered. Where had he hidden away this need that erupted from him and burned into her?

She shifted to wrap around him, to offer, to take, then jerked back.

"Jesus, I've got switchblades up my sleeves."

"Then have a care." He shot his hands under her shirt to take her breasts. "And don't stab me with them."

He made her breathless, already breathless. "I can deactivate them." Her head fell back as his mouth, his hands, roamed, possessed. "Take them off. I can —"

He just boosted her up onto his command center, dragged open her belt. "A terrible need," he said again, unbuttoning her trousers as she pushed up on her elbows.

"I get it, I get it, and it's contagious. I just need a minute to —"

His hands slid over her, his fingers into her.

"Never mind, never mind." The orgasm ripped straight up her center. "Jesus, never mind!"

He'd needed to see her, like this, hot and helpless with it. Writhing with it, flying with it.

And when she peaked, when she flung her hands back to grip the edge of the console, he dropped down to use his mouth on her.

The sounds she made, those cries and groans of mad pleasure, flashed like lightning in his blood. When he gripped those long legs, they trembled in his hands.

He nipped his teeth at her thigh, slid his tongue over her, into her, around her until she quaked, and quaked. And broke again.

She lay shivering, gasping for air, and he gripped her hips. Drove into all that wild, wet heat.

"Take more. Take me. Take all I am."

She opened heavy eyes, and through the desperate rush understood. All those memories, all those terrible moments churning through him. He needed the now, needed who he was, who they were together.

"Always." Even as sensation, rioting pleasure, swamped her, she pushed up to him, wrapped her arms around him. "You're mine. I'm yours. Always."

It tore through him, and that was love, keen as a blade.

When he let go, the love remained.

He pressed his lips to her throat. "I wouldn't be who I am without you."

She started to say otherwise, then settled. Understood the simple truth. "Neither would I, without you. Through everything, you were there. You never stepped back, never walked away."

She turned her head, brushed his lips with hers. "I'm here."

"I know it."

"Thank God I didn't slice something off

you during that."

"I'm grateful for it." He hiked up his pants, then with hers still dangling from her boots, lifted her. "What do you say to a shower?"

"That we could probably use one."

He carried her to the elevator. "Sex and a shower. Better than a restless attempt at a nap for recharging."

"I'm in no position to argue with that."

She dressed again, sweater, trousers, boots — all black. She reattached the stilettos — why take chances? — strapped on her weapon harness.

She noted Roarke had gone for black as well, but for whatever reason, his made him look like a sexy cat burglar.

Then again, he'd been just that once upon a time.

"You're authorized for a stunner," she reminded him.

"Quite right." So saying, he walked back to his closet, and curious, she followed him.

His clothes, the elegant forest of them, hung in perfect lines and groupings or lay folded, precisely, on shelves.

He went to the central cabinet, pressed some mechanism she couldn't see under the narrow lip. A mini control panel opened.

He tapped in a code, pressed his thumb to a pad. Then the entire side slid open to reveal a small, organized arsenal.

"What the fuck! Why didn't I know about this?"

"You never asked," he said simply as he crouched to choose a stunner and a harness.

"You're not licensed for all of that."

"On the contrary, I have a collector's license for all."

"But that's —" Why was she wasting her time? Priorities, she reminded herself. "Take the mini blaster and the combat knife."

He had to smile at her, this love of his life. "Am I so authorized, Lieutenant?"

"I'll clear it. We're potentially going to confront a dangerous contract killer who wants you dead. I want you fully armed."

As he removed the weapons, she crouched for a closer look. "You've got a long-range LX-25 repeater."

"And?"

"Nothing." She yearned a little. "It's nice."

"Would you like one?"

She turned her head, met him eye-to-eye. "If and when I do, I know where to find one."

He leaned forward, kissed her. Straightening, he hooked the knife in its sheath to his belt. Put on the harness, secured the stunner.

The mini he put in his jacket pocket.

"I need you to wear the coat — the magic coat I gave you for Christmas."

"Understood."

She stood another moment, scanning his face. "Okay, here's the deal. This is a police operation, and you're a civilian. It's also personal for you, which makes it personal for me. That's a complication, but that's how it is. It's important we take him alive."

"Also understood. And on that personal level? I want him alive as much as you. I want words with him, and I'll have them one way or the other. He has to be alive to hear them."

"All right then. But if you have the chance to give him a little pain? I've got your back on that."

Oh, aye, the love of his life. "I'd welcome the opportunity."

"Well, let's see what we can do about it. First, we need to find him. So let's get started."

"Eve. For all my life before you, and had fate been so cruel as to deem I'd never meet you, I'd have nothing, just nothing that could compare even to this single moment."

"Where we're standing in your closet

414

strapped with weapons?"

He laughed, cupped her face. "Yes."

"Let's go find this bastard, and make an even better moment."

They walked down. It didn't surprise her to find her long black coat, and Roarke's, waiting on the newel post. Roarke would have let Summerset know what they needed at some point.

Her DLE sat outside.

"You drive," she told him. "I'll let Feeney and Peabody know we're on our way in."

As she did, her 'link signaled.

"Nadine," she told Roarke. "Maybe she picked up something useful." She answered, "Dallas. Little busy here, Nadine."

"Too busy to hear Lorcan Cobbe's mother put her house in Dublin on the market today?"

"How did you get that?"

"Sources, Dallas." Nadine tossed her streaky blond hair, tapped a finger to her lips. "Sacred. But we'll say I have friends who have friends who cover the gossip and society beat in Ireland. Morna Cobbe lives high, so she's worth some clicks. It hasn't hit yet because the reporter wants more juice, but it's going on the list tomorrow. Well, today."

"Hold on." She muted the 'link. "Coincidence is bollocks."

"It is, yes."

"Okay. Top two reasons Morna Cobbe would suddenly sell her house?"

"The second would be she wants to move — downsize, upsize, different location. But that would be the bollocks of coincidence."

"Agreed."

"Number one? Her son's figured when he kills me, the heat turns up. Not only because he's all but taken out an ad blimp on his intentions, but because I have connections in Dublin that would squeeze him, and potentially his mother. So he's decided to get out, relocate himself and her to a cooler clime."

"And that's the winner. Nadine?"

"Yeah, yeah, still here."

"Find out what other properties — residential — went up for sale today in Dublin."

"Are you serious?"

"Because one of them's Cobbe's hole there, and it would be really nice to pin it down."

Nadine's foxy reporter's eyes lit. "It would, wouldn't it? I'll see what I can do. You're in the car," she realized. "Where are you going? Do you have a lead on Cobbe? What's the —"

"Cop work," Eve interrupted. "Sacred."

And clicked off.

When Roarke shot her a look, she shrugged. "When we get him, I'll tag her back."

"Fair enough. She's working late. And apparently her source in Dublin's working early."

"Let's hope Cobbe's sleeping the quiet sleep of assassins. Do they dream, you think? Of the last hit, the next? I don't think so. I think they go somewhere dark and still, and never have a single twinge. When ending a life means something — whatever it means, however it means it — your dreams aren't dark and still."

Because it brought her own dreams to mind, she shook it off. She programmed coffee for both of them, then spent the rest of the drive reviewing her notes, studying the map, planning the op.

When they got to Central, they rode the elevator up to Homicide. At least at that time of night the cars weren't generally jammed. The occasional cop with a mugger — or the victim of same — maybe an unlicensed LC or illegals dealer.

A man with a straggly stubble of beard, matted hair under a stained flop-cap, a torn T-shirt, and ragged pants — and an amazing smell — stepped on.

"Jesus, Rigby, you smell like a sewer."

" 'Cause that's where I've been. Caught me a couple of rats." He grinned. "Heading up to shower."

"You need the fume tube."

"Maybe, but I hate that shit."

When he got off again, she breathed out.

"You have the most interesting friends," Roarke noted.

"Undercover cop, works the underground mostly."

"As I said."

They stepped off on Homicide, walked to the bullpen.

She expected to find Feeney and McNab, probably Callendar, Peabody, and of course, Abernathy. Instead she found them, along with the rest of her detectives and a number of uniforms, standing around drinking cop coffee and shooting the shit.

"What is this? After-hours meeting?"

Baxter, in black nearly as elegant as Roarke's, turned. "Hey, LT, Roarke. Whatever hour, we're in this and on this."

"I haven't cleared —"

"We ain't looking for the OT," Jenkinson said, and scowled. "Somebody goes after one of us?" He jabbed a finger at Roarke. "He goes after all of us. And we fucking take the fucker down."

"So say we all," Carmichael added. "Santiago and I are up if we get a call somebody's dead. Otherwise, Feeney's got a second van for us."

"We're going to back you up," Trueheart told her.

She looked at Feeney. He wore black just as baggy and saggy as his usual shit brown. "Did you know about this?"

"I knew enough to have a van that can hold them."

"All right. Everybody suit up, nobody goes anywhere without vests. Roarke, give Peabody the map so she can get it on-screen, and I can figure out how to use this bunch of — Sir." She broke off, changed gears when Whitney walked in.

Not in a commander's suit and tie, but in operation black and carrying a protective vest.

"You remain in charge, Lieutenant. Consider me one of the team."

She had to rearrange her thoughts, and her strategy. She now had a small army of cops to — if they actually found the bastard — take down one man.

But she understood the sentiment, and the need. You came for one, you came for all.

"Feeney, van one, with the commander,

the inspector, his aide, Roarke and McNab, myself, Baxter, Trueheart. Callendar, van two with the rest. Santiago, you've got a half-ass talent for e-work, so you can assist Callendar should she require assistance. Officer Carmichael, van two for the rest of your uniforms."

She turned to the screen. "I ran priority on these locations, and we'll work them by top order. Location one," she began, and ran them through the op.

19

On the way through the garage to the vans, Abernathy touched Eve's arm.

"Lieutenant, if I may say, that was an inspiring display of loyalty and dedication. Those who serve under you are —"

"Cops," she said. "Damn good cops."

"They are indeed."

She climbed in the van, made room for the rest.

Feeney got behind the wheel, waited for Whitney to strap into the passenger seat. "You know if anything happens to you, your wife is going to kill me until I'm dead, then kill me again."

Whitney nodded, face somber. "Only after she kicks my lifeless body into a boneless husk."

"I'll have to take satisfaction in that." He offered Whitney his bag of candied almonds, started the engine.

Whitney crunched down, grinned. "Feels

like old times, Ryan."

"And we still have asses to kick." Feeney drove out of the garage. "Van two, fall in line."

"Falling in," Jenkinson told him. "Who's in for breakfast beers after we sniff this guy out and lock him up?"

He didn't get a dissent as they made their way on darkened streets, passed a few bright bars and sex clubs, then moved into an artier atmosphere with coffee bars and wine bars, trendy lofts and flats.

The converted warehouse sat quietly with a few lights glowing low against the privacy screens.

Eve ordered van two to wait half a block back.

"Scan it," she told McNab.

"Starting scan for heat signals, ground level. No filters or blocks in place, so we're . . . Whoa!"

"Whoa what?"

"We got a lot of movement, a lot of bodies — bodies in motion. Trying to separate for count, but that's gotta be at least eighteen or nineteen ground level. Ah, sitting, standing, lying down. They're . . . oh, okay."

Beside him, Roarke pinched the bridge of his nose and laughed. "I suspect you'll find more of the same on the other levels."

"The same of what?" Eve edged closer to the screen. Definitely got the picture. "Well, hell, it's a goddamn orgy."

"Sexcapades," McNab said with a grin.

"A bunch of people rented this place for a month to have sex?"

Roarke glanced at Eve. "I'd say some enterprising soul or group rented the place for a month to hold sex parties — for a fee. Explorations in Sexuality, or something akin to that.

"Likely," he added, "they have workshops and seminars. Perhaps door prizes."

Trueheart looked away from the screen, flushing, while Baxter leaned in.

"There's a threesome going on in the southwest corner, and that's a serious puppy pile right in the center of the area. I wonder what they charge."

"Sit back, horndog," Eve ordered. "Scan the rest. We need to clear it. And knock off the snickering comments, van two."

Since the scan indicated more than fifty people on various levels, in various groups, piles, and positions, Eve crossed it firmly off the list.

She grabbed her 'link when it signaled. "Nadine." After reading the text, she keyed in a response, then copied the data to Abernathy.

"I've just sent you Cobbe's probable hole in Dublin."

"What?"

"I got a tip shortly ago his mother's house goes on the market tomorrow — today," she corrected. "Figures he wants to move her somewhere . . . quieter after he's done with his mission. Which means, logically —"

"He'd put his own place up for sale."

She saw the light in Abernathy's eyes, recognized it as the gleam when a cop knew a sharp, distant corner had finally been turned.

"You've done a property search?"

"He used the Padriac O'Karre Foundation as the shell — that's *Roarke* when you unscramble it — and apparently he's been meticulous with the paperwork on it. Single-family home, just outside the city, listing price, when it lists tomorrow, is three and three-quarter million euros. A jewel at twice the price, according to the listing hype. You can read all about it yourself."

"And I shall, as soon as I relay this."

He got to it while they finished clearing the warehouse.

"Next location," Eve ordered.

"Alexi Godinov's pied-à-terre," Abernathy commented. "I'm just catching up with the synopses on each. Godinov runs a wide and dubious organization throughout Russia, Ukraine, and into the Baltic. Vodka and other spirits are his cover, though he does well in the distilling and distributing of same.

"Money laundering, false identification creation — excellent work, by the way — Internet scams, some smuggling. He steers clear of violent crime, and has a number of important connections to various government officials."

As he spoke, he referred to his PPC. "He often visits New York," Abernathy went on as Feeney drove. "Sometimes with his wife and children, sometimes with his mistress, occasionally with business partners. We're aware he makes the property available to some, for a fee, when it's not in use. But again, he generally steers clear of violence, and of someone like Cobbe."

"Steering clear of violence meaning he carefully puts a few degrees of separation between himself and any violence he may, indirectly, order."

Abernathy nodded at Roarke. "Just so. You're acquainted?"

"No, but I know his rep well enough."

Feeney pulled up just short of the gate.

"Some place," McNab said as he started the scan.

Security lights, decorative lights beamed and washed over the spread of lawn, the splashes of spring flowers and blooming trees. It outlined the classical lines of the three-story house with its attached garage.

"Electronic signals, main floor — two droids — no movement. Moving to second level. Two signals — human — horizontal. Sleeping. And two more — same deal, two rooms. Smaller. Kids."

Abernathy leaned closer to study the screen. "Very likely Godinov himself, as he has two children — eight and ten, boy and girl, respectively. I can check to see if he's traveled to New York."

"Do that. Scan the rest, McNab. Let's clear it."

"Moving on. Single signal, third floor, also horizontal."

"They have a nanny," Abernathy said, then shifted to a conversation on his 'link.

"Check the garage," Eve ordered. "And there's some sort of outbuilding there. Tool or garden shed, probably, but scan it."

"Godinov and his family, along with the nanny, arrived in New York just this afternoon. We're working on a warrant to enter and search the Dublin house. We'll get it, I promise you." Abernathy pocketed his 'link.

"Finish the scan anyway, then we cross it

off, move to the next."

She'd had a good feeling about this one — even though the comp had put the warehouse as top probability. She had to put that aside, focus in on the next.

"While the next two are lower probability, according to the run, they're more convenient to where he's shopped, to where he picked up the woman he killed. No garage for the vehicle he's rented, but there are rentals in the area for that, too."

"Let's see what we have here."

Abernathy pulled up the synopsis. "Ah, just outside the famous Meatpacking District. A three-and-a-half-story home, which includes the half basement area. And, yes, I see by the maps very convenient to his choice of shops — a bit of a distance from where he took that poor cat. Owned by the Amazonian Group, and listed as a business rental or event space."

Frowning, he glanced over at Roarke. "You have Reginald Privet as the owner."

"That's right. The Amazonian Group is a shell. It's his property."

"We don't have that information."

"I do."

"I need a moment." He pulled out his 'link again, shifted away.

"Who's Reginald Privet?" Eve asked Roarke.

"Someone you'd like to see in a cage, I imagine. He deals in weapons and sex, basic money laundering, gambling. Gambling's a personal issue for him, as he's unable to resist, often loses, and is, for the most part, a bit of a dick. His sister, Alicia, is smarter, a great deal meaner, and in actuality in charge. But she loves her feckless brother and gives him plenty of cover."

Eve glanced over at Abernathy, who continued to mutter on his 'link.

"Scan it."

"Starting scan, basement level. Got some blocks here," McNab announced. "Good ones."

Roarke moved over to work with him, and Feeney climbed back from the front to observe.

"Somebody doesn't want any sniffers. Keep working it. I'm going to take a better look at the alarms and security. See what we have to get through if this is the place."

Roarke passed Feeney his PPC. "I have it on there. But as these blocks weren't on the specs, I'd say they've done some updating without permits."

Eve followed her gut, tagged Reo.

The APA blocked video, groaned. "Oh,

come on, Dallas!"

"I need a warrant, and now. Now." She rattled off the address. "We believe Lorcan Cobbe is inside."

"Give me five. We've already got a judge on tap for your op. He just has to fill in the address."

"Get through the damn block," Eve ordered as Peabody made way for Whitney to crowd into the back. "Van two, stand by. Baxter, Trueheart, once they're through, take the rear. Santiago, Carmichael, the south; Jenkinson, Reineke, north. Officer Carmichael, mobilize your team. We cover every exit, doors, windows, rat holes. Feeney, Callendar, the second the warrants clear, start on the security. If we're wrong, we put everything back where it was, move on."

But they weren't wrong, she thought.

"We've got Privet," Abernathy announced. "That is to say, we turned him about three months ago — the gambling debts, trouble with a competitor. I've just spoken with the inspector in charge of that matter. He's never spoken of Amazonian, nor that we can find, tapped into its considerable resources to dig himself out of the hole he's in."

"The resources might not actually exist," Whitney put in.

"No, they do." Roarke paused in the work. "It's a good, hard shell, and funds are funneled in and out. Smuggling's its real purpose — people, goods, weapons, illegals. Ah, fuck me, it's not his, it's hers. Alicia's. She put his name on it."

Abernathy nodded. "He might not be aware of its existence. I'm assured he's babbled like a brook."

"He's weak," Roarke said. "She knows it, and love him or not, she's canny enough to keep him out of certain areas of the business. She might know Cobbe. He's her type, isn't he? Professionally, personally."

"Warrant's coming through," Eve said, just as McNab let out a hoot.

"Broke the block. Scanning."

"Wait!" But Roarke's warning came an instant too late.

As the scan penetrated, lights flashed on inside the house. Three quick pulses, before it all went dark.

"Fail-safe alert. Bugger it."

"We're go!" Eve shouted. "Go, go! Find him," she ordered McNab and pushed open the cargo doors of the van. "Move, move. I don't want a cockroach getting out of the building. Move! Get that security down. Get it down."

She held by the front entrance, weapon

drawn, as Peabody scrambled out to stand beside her.

"Second floor!" McNab shouted. "Single heat signal. On the move. Moving fast."

"Battering ram!" Eve ordered. "Callendar, scan this door for explosives. Roarke! Get out here and get us in or I'm breaking the door down."

Roarke jumped out of the van.

"Clear on boomers, Dallas, but the scan shows those doors are steel behind a wood veneer. We'd have to blow it."

"Give me a bloody minute," Roarke muttered as he worked. "A bloody minute."

"Still moving, LT," McNab called out. "On the main floor now."

"Keep on him."

"Five layers." Roarke set his teeth. "I'm through two."

Eve pulled the mini blaster out of his pocket, shifted, aimed at one of the windows.

It barely rattled, but alarms began to shriek, and the lights pulsed and pulsed again.

"Fucking fortress. Get me in."

"Three down, and there's four. Don't rush me."

"Moving fast, down to basement level, southwest corner."

"What the hell for?" Eve rolled heel to toe, heel to toe, ready to move. "Secure room? He's trapped anyway. He's trapped in there."

"And there's the last." Roarke shoved open the door and was in a step ahead of her.

Lights flashed, white, then black, white, then black. Alarms screamed.

"Clear it," she ordered Peabody and the uniforms with her. "Cover the front. Kill those damn alarms, Feeney!" She snapped other orders to the rest while she bolted for the southwest corner, and another secured steel door.

"Son of a bitching bitch!"

"I'll have it." Roarke pushed her aside. "I'll have it."

"Scan it first. I don't want to get blown up here."

Steel door on the basement level, she thought. Secure area? But why go down instead of out? Why —

"Smuggler?" she said to Roarke.

"Yes, bloody buggering hell. She'd have a way out. A way in, a way out."

"Dallas!" McNab yelled in her earpiece. "He's gone. He's just freaking gone. Poof. He's nowhere. I swear to Jesus, it's like he ran through a goddamn wall."

Roarke yanked open the doors.

The alarms died. The lights went off again, then came back and held steady.

Halfway down, she saw the next door fit into a wall that should have led nowhere.

"I'll have it," Roarke told her. "But I'll tell you it's the way out. The way of getting things in and out underground."

Steady as the steel of the door, he worked on the locks. "From this location, and considering its purpose? This likely leads to the docks, and with splits along the way that come up elsewhere. A warehouse, another building, a transpo station."

She pulled up her comm to organize the manhunt.

Whitney jogged down the steps as Roarke disengaged the locks.

He opened the door to a tunnel, pargeted and dry, and large enough to accommodate a compact truck. She heard the echo, distant, already distant, of an engine.

"He had his vehicle in there, or a vehicle. Fuck, fuck, fuck. I want a team of four uniforms to follow it, see where it goes. If it splits, two teams of three. In constant communication.

"We're going to shut this place down." She stared at Abernathy. "We're going to shut the bitch down who gave him this hole to hide in. You have your people pick her the fuck up. She's an accessory to murder. She's harbored a fugitive. You pick her the fuck up."

She yanked out her comm. "I need to shut down the bridges, the tunnels. He knows he has to get out, find another hole, bide his time."

"I'll handle that," Whitney told her. "The mayor's going to have some objections. I'll handle it."

"Yes, sir. He'll have had a go-bag ready, cash, ID. Passport," she considered. "This place would have elevators, but he didn't use them. Grabbing what he needed to take on the way down. He can pilot. Closest transpo station with global shuttles?"

"Southside. Near the docks," Roarke told her.

"Let's go."

"We're in this takedown, Dallas," Jenkinson told her.

"Then get in the van. Officer Carmichael."

"We'll secure the scene, Lieutenant, and begin the search."

"Affirmative. You find anything, I know about it."

When she got out to the vans, all of her detectives, the EDD team, and Whitney stood by them.

"Every-damn-body?"

"We're in this until he's down," Baxter told her.

"Southside Transpo. Move. Peabody, alert security at the center they have a fugitive heading their way. How fast does this thing move, Feeney?"

"She ain't built for speed, but I can coax some out of her."

So saying, he peeled out from the curb.

"He has to find a way in," Roarke told her. "He'd want to try at least to avoid the cams as much as possible. There's no overseas flights at this time of the morning, not commercial, so that would mean he'd need to wait for at least another hour. He'd try for their private area, as that runs twenty-four/seven."

"Private shuttle depot, Feeney."

"He'd need to bribe someone, and quickly, to get up," Roarke continued. "Or steal one. Or simply kill his way onto one."

"He's not that far ahead of us. If he gets one, they can track it."

"Off and on, but there are ways around that. He'd have to fly low. He won't be after filing a flight plan."

"Where would he go?"

"Ireland's his root, and where his mother is. But it would be brainless."

"Abernathy?"

"I'm already contacting my superior," he told her. "We'll have people at the Dublin centers. But I agree, he'd have to anticipate that. The problem —" He grabbed on where he could when Feeney swerved around a turn. "The problem is he could go anywhere if he hijacks a long-range shuttle."

"Then we better stop him here." Yanking out her comm, she began blasting out orders for patrols.

They knew what he looked like, knew his vehicle. All they had to do was find him and box him in.

"He's a master at evasion, Lieutenant," Abernathy said as he held on, worked his 'link. "I know you may feel we've bollocksed this for years, but the fact is, he excels at his work."

"He's going to be out of a job real soon."

"He's already scoped this out," Roarke added. "Routes to the closest private terminal, ways in, best access to a shuttle. In his place, I'd have taken an hour or two, under the guise I was in the market to purchase a shuttle, for myself or my company."

"Get a tour, get the layout, shit. Terminal security's on alert. He couldn't anticipate we'd be right on his ass."

With sirens screaming, they barreled

through the main terminal access, into the private. Eve was out of the doors before Feeney pulled to a complete stop.

As she ran toward the terminal entrance, security ran out.

"Handler, security. We're locked down tight. Cams are sweeping. You're the first vehicle to come through."

"How many private shuttles, copters, jumpers currently housed in this facility?"

"Fourteen shuttles, short- and long-range, three copters, about a dozen jumpers."

"I want men checking every single one, and alert your counterpart at the commercial area. If he can't get through here, he could try there. Rat hunt," she ordered her people, "two-by-twos. Commander, status on tunnels and bridges."

"Shut. We have officers working with dock security in case he tries jumping on a ship."

"We'd better notify any and all transpo terminals. Other shuttle depots, trains, buses." She glanced around as she spoke. "Where's Roarke?"

"He went in," Feeney told her.

"Son of a —"

She broke off because she heard it, she damn well heard it. The whooshing roar of a shuttle taking off.

"He's up. Motherfucker. Get tracking on

that shuttle."

She raced toward the entrance, and Baxter's voice sounded in her ear. "We've got a man down, Loo, hangar five. Unconscious, cut up pretty bad, but he's breathing, Trueheart's calling for a bus. We need a medic."

"You need medical in hangar five," she snapped at Handler. "One of your men is down. How the hell did he get through?"

"I'll find out." Grim-faced, steely-eyed, Handler called for medical. "You can bet your ass I'll find out." He tapped his own earpiece. "Unauthorized takeoff, runway three. Heading northeast. We've got him."

For how long? she wondered, as the terminal erupted in movement. And where the hell was Roarke?

"Make sure the injured is stable, then everybody get back here."

She turned to Whitney. "I'm going after him. I need clearance, sir. Roarke can get a shuttle faster than we can deal with the paperwork of requisitioning one. He can pilot. Inspector Abernathy, myself, Captain Feeney, Detective Peabody. This gives us manpower and e-skills."

"I'll clear it, and I'm going with you."

"Sir —"

"He doesn't get away from me a second time."

As he turned away to deal with clearance, she spotted Roarke coming out of a side door.

"We need a shuttle," she began. "We're going after him."

"Already done. Anticipating this possibility, I've arranged it. We're in hangar one."

Coming in on the tail end, Jenkinson caught the drift. "You're going after him, we're all going after him."

"Detective," Eve began.

"There's room enough," Roarke said smoothly. "One doesn't leave one's mates behind at such a time."

Jenkinson gave a sharp nod and a grin. Eve pulled at her hair. "I can't take my entire squad of detectives. Somebody has to cover the shift."

"I'll see it's covered." Whitney glanced back at her. "They've earned this."

She thought: For fuck's sake, but understood being outranked and outvoted. "Then we move. Get the lead out of your asses. Feeney, McNab, Callendar, for Christ's sake, get whatever portables you need out of the van to hangar one."

"Where are we going?" Baxter wondered as he came in. He had blood on his hands, on the sleeve of his jacket.

"Up," Eve said, and left it at that. "Hangar

one. Move. Status of the injured?" she asked Baxter as she moved her own ass.

"Medicals doing what they can. MTs already on scene. Looks like Cobbe gave him a couple gut slashes, went at the throat, but mostly got the shoulder. He'd lost a lot of blood by the time we got to him. How the hell did Cobbe get through?"

"We're going to find out."

In hangar one, she saw the shuttle — sleek, shiny, and to her eyes pretty damn small.

Baxter said, "Sweet! Got ourselves an LR-10." And jogged up the short stairs right into the cabin.

Shaking her head, she went up after him while the EDD team loaded on the portables. "No booze," she said immediately. "This isn't a damn joyride. We remain on duty and in pursuit. Commander, if you'd like to sit in the cockpit with the pilot."

"I'll leave that to you. I still have politics to deal with." Still working his 'link, he walked down the aisle to the back of the cabin.

"Peabody, get the commander some coffee. The rest can fend for themselves. You're not the flight attendant."

"Got it. On duty, in pursuit, but this is still pretty juiced. I'll take some of the relays from the ground team. They're going to start coming in fast."

Already in the cockpit, Roarke hit the fasten-seatbelt light.

"Strap it in! We're already ten minutes behind him and counting. Feeney, do you have anything that can track that shuttle if they lose him?"

Head bent, his ginger hair like exploded corkscrews, he showed his teeth. "Funny you should ask. We're working on it."

"Work fast." She walked into the cockpit — far from her favorite place. Sat, strapped in. "Jesus Christ, this is crazy."

"It's not," Roarke disagreed, and began to glide the shuttle out of the hangar. "We're faster than him. If we can calculate where he's going, we can not only have authorities at the ready, but we can beat him there. He boosted an LR-3 — and it was in for some maintenance."

"It's not safe?"

"Safe enough, but it needs work. We have a 10, and she's prime."

"You could've told me you were getting a shuttle."

"Things moved fast," he said as he taxied to the runway. "And they're about to move faster." He shot her a grin. "Wheels up," he said.

She set her teeth as the shuttle gained speed, and thought how much she hated this part as they left terra firma behind.

20

When they were in the air, and her stomach caught up with the rest of her, she swiveled to the cockpit's mini-AC, programmed coffee for both of them.

"Thanks."

"Yeah. We don't have passports, or the authority to pursue Cobbe to wherever the hell we pursue him."

"I could assist with the first part, though it would involve some less-than-official means. I'd suggest having Abernathy tug some lines."

"I figured to. I need to keep in contact with the trackers."

Roarke gestured to another earpiece. "They've lost him for now — but anticipating that, they've set up POS and bounce teams."

"What does that mean?"

Roarke spared her a glance. "Do you really want me to explain the technology?"

"No. What does that mean as far as I need to know?"

"They'll track him off and on — and if I can get a good enough signal from them, hold it long enough, I can set up what you'd call an echo, or bounce, that'll keep him on my internal tracker more often than not."

"Feeney said he's working on something that could track."

"That would be very helpful."

"I'll get the status." Before she got up, her comm signaled. The tunnel teams reported one split led directly to the shuttle terminal. They found Cobbe's vehicle at the end of it.

"Smugglers," Roarke reminded her when she clicked off. "Move what you want to move, in and out, using the tunnels. By water, by air, all underground. It would've been quite an expense to build those tunnels, but a very solid investment."

"Fuck it all." She got up to relay the information to the team.

"It's how he got there ahead of us by enough of a margin to access a shuttle, evaded security. Privet's going down," she said to Abernathy.

"Yes, and that will be very satisfying."

"We don't have passports or local authority, wherever local turns out to be."

"I'm working on that." He smiled a little. "It will be helpful, considerably, to know where we need that authority."

"You'll know when I know. Are you getting anywhere with the tracking?" she asked Feeney.

He, McNab, and Callendar sat at a table with e-guts, tools, furrowed brows. "We're jury-rigging a POS box with a bouncer. Don't ask."

"Wasn't going to. Roarke said he just needs a solid signal, and to hold it for — he didn't say."

"Yeah, yeah, we got it."

"Relaying with ground control," Callendar told her as she worked. "We'll hook with their spotters once we put this together." She glanced up at Eve. "Never been on a private. They are plushy-lushy. You think maybe we're going to Europe?"

"Can't say."

"Never been." The bloodred lettering on the black shirt under her black bibbed baggies read: ASS-KICKING GEEK.

"Been to Mexico and Jamaica for fun and Canada on a family trip that wasn't so much fun. But never been over the big water. Frosty. You gotta take the frosty when it lands on you. Got a green here, Cap."

"Good, good, keep it going."

They sat, working away, Feeney in his saggy shirt — that already had a coffee stain — Callendar in her ass-kicker, and McNab with his glittering earlobe.

The rest of the team, operational black — but she spotted Peabody's pink coat over a seat.

Is this what they meant by *motley crew*? she wondered.

"Okay if we hit the galley for some chow?" Baxter asked her.

She threw up her hands. "Who's going to stop you?"

"Dallas, our search team in Cobbe's hole found another hidden, secured area. Like a panic room. It has full comm capabilities, with unregistered equipment. They've verified it's been used in the past forty-eight hours," Peabody added, "and are working with EDD to decrypt."

"Who they got on it?" Feeney demanded.

"Detective Waver."

"Okay, good, but have them call in Yin. Waver's good, Yin's better."

"I'll relay it."

"Eat if you need to eat, then get some rack time," Eve advised. "Once we work out his most probable destination, I need everybody sharp. If you've got departmentally authorized boosters, fine. Otherwise, it's coffee."

Feeney gave a hoot. "We got it, we got the sweet son of a bitch. Tell Roarke we've got an in-flight tracker."

"You tell him. He'll understand you better. Take the second seat in the cockpit if you want it."

Feeney elbowed McNab. "Go. Sugar high, Callendar?"

"All day, every day, Cap."

"I'll get you a fizzy. How about you put those eyes and ears back together in case we need them?"

He rose, stretched, wandered back to the galley already crowded with cops raiding the AC and friggie.

She walked back to the cockpit and into e-speak. She tuned it out, paced up and down the aisle as she worked on various scenarios.

It all depended on where. Urban setting or rural? Populated or open? Would he have a hole or have to rabbit again?

Did he know how close they were on his tail?

She caught part of the cockpit conversation that sounded like regular English.

"If you can give me a ninety-second hold, I'll have a lock on him."

"We think we can give you a full two minutes, if he doesn't make a sharp change.

We're over the ocean, right? He's likely to keep cruising. Last echo he was at fifteen thousand, so he's flying low."

"And slow compared to us at forty-five thousand. We'll be on top of him within ten minutes, by my calculations."

"When you are, we hook with ground control's POS, boost the bounce, get the steady hold."

"He could change course, he could do that." She recognized Roarke's tone, the one where he spoke more to himself than the person next to him. "Tip south for Italy or Spain, Greece. Or do a fly right over western Europe, Poland, Russia. But as he's going now with these spot checks? Ireland's best bet."

"No place like home?"

"I suppose even he might think so."

Eve went back to Abernathy, sat. "He's going to contact his mother if he hasn't already. He may give her some sort of rendezvous. You need to have her picked up."

"We've no charges."

"Aiding and abetting. Come on, Abernathy, finesse it. If nothing else, put a shadow on her. She's selling her house. He's selling his. She'll know where to meet him. Box her in."

She walked back to the cockpit. Peabody walked in behind her.

"Brought you guys some eats. Got you a mocha latte, McNab."

"My best girl."

"We got egg san with ham and cheese," she told Eve. "You want?"

"No, I'm good." She pointed McNab back down when he started to get up. "Keep the chair. You're more use to him than I am in here."

"We should be over him inside two. I'm dropping altitude to get a better lock."

Eve felt the shuttle dive, simply closed her eyes. Nothing made sense about being thousands of feet over an ocean.

It was insanity. The human race was just bat-shit crazy.

"Holding at thirty thousand. Let's see what you've got, Ian."

"One sec. Captain, Callendar, we're going green."

"Gotcher back," Callendar told him. "Cap?"

"Right there. Count it down."

Roarke gave them the ninety seconds, the sixty, and at thirty, McNab tapped a series of keys on his portable. "Calling that echo in ten, nine, eight . . ."

"There he is," Roarke murmured. "Nicely

done, very nice indeed. Let's hold that. Just hold that."

He did something with the instruments that made things flash and beep — and Eve's stomach drop again.

"Go green!" McNab shouted.

Eve didn't know what she expected. Maybe an explosion. Because couldn't another bat-shit crazy person flying thousands of feet above the ocean just crash right into them?

Or those air pockets in the sky that made everything wobble and shake. They could shake something loose.

Or —

"Ten more seconds," Roarke muttered. "Give me ten more bloody seconds."

"We've got it. Lock it up, Roarke. Lock the bastard."

"I will, by Christ. Just . . ."

He twisted some dial, and for some reason, McNab hooted again.

So did Feeney and Callendar.

"Locked. He's locked," Roarke said.

She heard it — a slow, steady beep — and when Roarke tapped an instrument, she saw that blip — slow and steady.

"That's him?"

"That's him. And we've got a solid signal. This course, his longitude and latitude, it's likely Ireland. Add the rest in — his mother, his contacts — it's most likely."

"Do you think he'll actually try to land in Dublin?"

Roarke shook his head. "He'd know somewhere outside the city, a private strip, a smuggler's way. Now he's shifted course a time or two, but that's for evasion — and it's wasted speed and fuel. We'll get wherever he's going ahead of him. I just have to pin that down, and Ireland, Dublin's the best I have at this moment."

"Well, it's better than the whole freaking world. What's the flight time from here?"

"For us, to near around Dublin? A bit under two hours. If I go back up, less."

"Why less?"

He glanced back at her. "It's physics, darling Eve. The air's thinner, so we'll have more speed. I can cut our time to about ninety minutes. And in his slower shuttle, even pushing it, and at the lower altitude? He's about three hours or a bit more out."

"That's a big advantage."

She gave his shoulder a squeeze. "I'll let the others know."

When she turned, Peabody gave her a head-jerk signal, then walked back to the galley — cleared out now, as cops either chowed down or got some sleep.

"What?"

"EDD got into the comp, decrypted what was there. Cobbe used it to do searches on the Lannigans, the Brodys, on Tulla."

"Oh Christ." She flew down to the cockpit. "He's not going to Dublin."

"Odds are he —"

"He's going after your family. He's going to the farm."

He didn't ask how she knew, just increased altitude and speed. "Keep an eye on that signal, Ian. I've some people to contact."

"Give me an ETA," she snapped at Roarke.

"To Clare — fifty-five minutes."

"Plenty of time to get them away from the farm, to a safe location."

"I'll have it," he told her. "I need to arrange it now."

She felt the increased pressure as her ears popped, her stomach did that slow, sick roll. But she turned at the cockpit door, raised her voice.

"Listen up, Cobbe's heading for western Ireland, most specifically as close as he can manage to the Brody farm."

Feeney's sleepy eyes hardened. "Roarke's family?"

"Cobbe's behind us, a good two hours. We're having the family moved to another location. When that asshole gets there, he's going to find a bunch of New York City cops instead of a family of farmers."

"We have officers in that location," Abernathy said. "I'll have them mobilized."

"Low-key, and not yet. We're not going to scare him off. We're going to box him in. Peabody, get the locals. They can help transport Roarke's family, but they have to move fast. I don't want any obvious police presence at that farm when Cobbe tries to move in.

"Callendar, I need a map of the Tulla area — the farm's a couple miles outside the town — village — whatever. Things are different there. Get me a map on-screen."

Trueheart tentatively raised his hand while Callendar got to work. "Is there some sort of landing strip?"

"No. Roarke will figure that out. So will Cobbe."

She thought of the first time she'd landed there — in a jet-copter, in a field with cows. Lots of cows.

"Cobbe won't land too close, so that adds to our time. He'll need to ditch the shuttle, steal some sort of transpo or hoof it. He'll move as fast as he can. He can't risk us figuring out where he landed and putting it together. Right now he thinks he's got time."

"Got your map. I'm going to pull up a satellite image if you can give me where the farm is in relation to the town."

"East, about two miles. You've got narrow roads — like snake-skinny winding roads, bushes — hedges flanking them. Some woods. That's good cover for Cobbe. Low traffic, and fairly remote. They don't lock the damn doors," she murmured.

"Abernathy, any Interpol presence is backup, and remains out of sight. You can have the goddamn collar," she snapped when he started to object. "You can have the credit, the notch in your fucking belt, but I'm in charge of this. This is family, and I'm at the wheel, do you get me?"

"Yes. Very well. And the credit doesn't matter a tinker's damn to me."

"Good." She started to turn back to the screen and her gaze passed over Whitney. She'd simply forgotten him. "Commander —"

"Continue, Lieutenant. You have the wheel."

"Sir."

"Bringing up the satellite image. Give me a second," Callendar said. "I've got the area, I think. There's more than one farm-type place so —"

"There. That's it, bring it up some. The

454

house — three stories, about a dozen rooms. Front facing that narrow road. You've got multiple outbuildings. The barn, like a silo, stable."

"There's a difference between a barn and a stable?" Jenkinson asked.

"Apparently. Sheds, chicken place, pig place, lots of fields. Lots of cows. They're bigger than you think. Some sheep, those low stone walls, some trees. A couple of big trees, a little stream."

"It looks really pretty. Locals informed, Dallas," Peabody added. "And on their way to the Brody farm."

"Solid. If you go slightly west, there's another house, and slightly north another. The main house is occupied by Sinead Lannigan and her husband, Robbie — Robert. Their youngest son should be in Dublin, at college, like grad school or whatever. Older son, wife, kids I think three kids — in the house to the west. Her daughter, daughter's husband, a couple of kids in the one to the north. Her parents, a couple of brothers — Jesus, there are so many of them — scattered in the area. But he's going to hit the farm, that main house. That's the heart, and he'd know it."

"Nobody's going to touch them." Santiago

studied the screen. "He won't get near them."

"No, he won't." Calm now, cold and calm, she used the image and her memory of visits to lay it out. "Here's how we play it."

When she walked into the cockpit, she sat down. "I don't know how much you heard. We've got the locals moving your family into town. Abernathy's mobilizing Interpol as backup. I know you've got some security on the farm, and I'll need them to do what I say when I say it."

"They won't leave. The family."

"They'll have to."

He shot her a look. Grim, worried. "Haven't I just spent near to twenty minutes arguing with Sinead, my uncles all, countless cousins? They won't leave."

"We'll deal with that when we get there. What I'm telling you is he won't get through us to them, wherever they are. You're the big fate guy, right? Well, I'll buy into it right now. We've got a shuttle full of good, smart cops, and if that's not fate, fuck me."

He let out a breath. "I'm grateful for them."

"Right now, you're one of them, so suck that up. Where are you going to put this thing down?"

"The north pasture, nearest my cousin

Aidan's. They're clearing the cows out now, as I'll need to do a drop landing."

"Drop?" All the spit in her mouth dried up. "I don't like how that sounds."

He glanced at her. "You won't like it at all, but it'll be quick."

"I don't like *quick* and *drop* together in *landing.*"

"You'll strap in. Cobbe can do a glide, as he won't give two fecks about taking out livestock or anything else, though I think he'll try to be more subtle. If he's any sort of pilot, he'll cut his engines, glide for the quiet, and use the little forest to the south of the farm for cover. His shuttle's smaller, and he could manage it if he's any good."

"He's supposed to be. So, we look for him to come in from the south. Can you show me the most likely route?"

"Not now I can't, as we're about to start the descent. I'll show you when we're down."

"Landed. Don't say 'down.' "

He smiled a little, as she'd hoped. "Go on back and strap in."

"I'm fine here." With you, she thought, and grabbed the harness.

Roarke hit the intercom. "It's going to be a bit rough," he announced. "I'm sorry for that. We've got some rain, it's Ireland, after all, and we'll have a few bumps heading down. The landing's going to be a jolt, so you'll want to strap down any equipment and yourselves. I'm thankful for all of you. Pints are on me once we're done with this bastard."

Bumps, Eve thought. Heading down. Drop. Quick drop.

If she could get through all that, Cobbe would be a walk on the beach.

Then they hit the bumps.

"A few?" she said as her teeth rattled.

"Just clouds. Some bad-tempered clouds, a few crosswinds. Not to worry."

Some of the clouds — gray ones, spitting rain on the windshield — thinned enough for her to see land below.

Green, green, green, with the rich contrast of brown.

And rising up at a speed she considered entirely too fast.

She decided there was no point in looking.

She heard Callendar let out a wild laugh. "What a ride! Look at that! It really is green."

You could crash in green, Eve thought, just as effectively as you could on concrete, or in the ocean, or into the side of a mountain, or —

They dropped like a stone.

Her eyes flew open again. Always better to face death than hide from it, since it came anyway. Her ears slammed shut, then popped like a balloon as all that green rushed up.

She thought she heard her bones crack as they landed with a *thud,* bounce, *thud.*

"Welcome to Ireland," said Roarke.

She got off fast — her legs wobbled some, but she got off fast.

She recognized most of the group of men who stood in the field, hands on hips or in pockets.

"And there's our Eve." Sinead's husband strode straight to her, gave her a hard, welcoming hug. "And how's it all going then?"

"We're on the ground." In the soft, thin rain with cows watching on the other side of that low stone wall.

They could get over it, she imagined, anytime they damn well wanted.

"Robbie, it would make my job a lot easier, if you would take the family — everyone — into Tulla until we have Cobbe in custody."

He gave her an easy smile, and a pat on the shoulder. "We've sent the children off with the Garda, and some of the women with them to keep them behaving. As for the rest of us, well, it's our land, our home, you see. So here we stay. And it's Roarke himself."

Leaving her, he walked to embrace Roarke.

"Podock, security." The black man, built like a monument to fitness, offered a hand. "We have Trace at the main farm and Ando at Nan's house." He grinned a little. "She said we were to call her Nan if we were going to be in her kitchen."

Abernathy moved in. "Inspector Abernathy, Interpol. I expect four agents to arrive within minutes."

"You can station one in each outlying house, two in the main," Eve said. "Cobbe will most likely head in from the south, and we've got less than two hours to set this up. We'll stay in constant communication. If we're wrong about his direction, if he aims for one of the other houses, we'll converge. Since you already know the ground, Podock, you can direct the agents when they arrive."

She turned. "Aidan."

Roarke's cousin, a big man with a thatch of straw-colored hair under a battered cap, bent to kiss her cheek.

"Welcome back to the homeplace."

"Yeah, well. I need my team outfitted. I need them to look like farmers. I need them to look like they're doing whatever you would all be doing if this was a regular day."

"Oh, sure and that's easy enough."

"Is Sinead at the farm — the big house?"

"She is that, along with Mary Kate and Kevin and Rory, and Seamus. It wasn't easy to move Nan along, but we managed it. I got my Rosie to move as well, using the baby and the one on the way. But for the rest of us, we're staying."

"Let's just take a minute, all of you, because that's all I've got. I get this is your place, your home, but this man's a professional killer. We're the cops, and you're not. We're here to stop him, arrest him, and to protect you and your property. How are you going to defend yourself against a professional killer with hundreds of bodies, hundreds of dead? Do you have weapons?"

"Well now, we have these," Aidan said and bunched his fist. "And come to that, we've axes and picks and shovels, knives, oh, and that baseball bat young Ryan bought himself when we visited you in New York City last. We're Irish, you see. We've fought on and for the land for all time."

"Axes and shovels," she muttered. "We need to get to the main house. Baxter, True-

461

heart, you're with Aidan. Callendar, you're their geek."

"The grass is all spongy," Callendar commented.

"Well, we've had a bit of wet weather."

Grinning, she lifted her face to the rain. "I like it."

"It's this way. Those are fine boots," he said to Baxter. "They'll be mucked up in no time. We'll see what we have for you."

"Santiago, Carmichael, with McNab, second house. Jenkinson, Reineke, Peabody, Feeney, Roarke, with me. Abernathy, take your choice."

"I'll stick to the main."

"Commander?"

"The same. Commander Whitney." He held his hand out to Robbie. "This is beautiful land."

"It is all that. Is it your first time in Ireland then?"

"Yes."

"Ah, sure you must come back for holiday," he said as they walked on.

"They're treating it like a game," Eve said to Roarke.

Roarke shook his head. "They're not. It's not your way, but it's theirs. It's complicating things, Christ knows, but you can count on them."

"Feeney's got stars in his eyes."

"He's an Irishman at the heart of it, isn't he? You know he'll be steady as a rock when you need him."

They walked through the light rain as the walk gave her a chance to study her ground, to look for potential attack points, escape routes.

And all the while she heard one of the cousins talking to Feeney about where Feeney's people were from, if he had any cousins in Clare.

She ignored the cows when they crossed the next field — what choice did she have? But she kept an eye on them, just in case.

Smoke drifted into the sky — gray against gray — from the chimneys of the big stone house.

She spotted a couple of horses. "I need them to get the horses inside. Maybe he rides, or he'll try to. Or just kill them."

"I'll see to it," Robbie said over his shoulder. "Not to worry."

Not to worry? Was that the phrase of the damn day?

Chickens clucked in their chicken place; pigs snorted in their pig place.

And Sinead stepped out the back door.

She had her hair, that quiet gilded red, tied back and wore sturdy black trousers with a sweater as gray and soft as the smoke. Her eyes, sweetly green, smiled as she opened her arms to Eve, then to Roarke.

"I'm sorry," he began. "So sorry to bring this trouble to your door."

Her eyes stopped smiling, went to slitted sparks as she cuffed him on the side of his head.

Eve felt her own mouth drop open, but imagined it was nothing compared to the stunned look on Roarke's face.

"Never did I take you for such a lurk, and insulting with it. Are we your family?"

"Yes, but —"

"Yes is all. Don't let me hear such a foolish thing come out of your mouth again. Now." She cupped his face, kissed both his cheeks. "Come inside, out of the wet, and we'll see what's to be done about all of this. Your friend Brian's just arrived."

Eve gave Roarke a quick look. "Brian?"

"I asked him to come, got a jumper for him." With Eve, and the rest behind them, they stepped into the kitchen, where a fire simmered in the hearth and the air smelled of warm bread.

"Will you box my ears again if I ask you, out of love, to please take Mary Kate and go safe into town?"

"I won't, but Mary Kate might — box

your ears, that is. And no, though I know you mean it with love, I won't be driven from my own home."

"It's not being driven," Eve objected. "It's just a couple of hours. Just a few hours."

"The man who's coming here thinks of the man who murdered my sister, my twin, as his father. He would murder the child she gave that vicious man, the child who is mine now. And so, I ask you, would you leave and sit and wait? Do you think my man would, my boys would, my brothers?"

"I'm a cop."

"And we're not, but this is my home, and Roarke ours as he is yours. Now, I know some of your friends here, but not all. You're all welcome. I've got the kettle on, so we'll have some tea while you tell me what you need."

"We really don't have time for tea," Eve began.

"I could use a cup." Brian walked in. The Dublin publican and Roarke's oldest friend went straight to Eve. He lifted her right off her feet, planted a kiss on her mouth. "Ah, Lieutenant darling, how I've missed you."

"Thanks for coming," Roarke replied.

"Well, of course." He set Eve down. "So it's that bloody wanker Cobbe again, is it? He's always been trouble, but we'll end that now. And my God, would you look at all the cops!"

He grinned hugely at Roarke. "Times change, don't they, lad?"

"That they do."

"They look like cops, and that's the problem. I need them to look like farmers. Irish farmers," Eve added. "Who are out there doing farm stuff."

"Ah, I see, aye, I see that very well." Sinead beamed at them all. "We'll fix you right up. Mary Kate!" she called out. "Darling," she said to her husband, "there's some wellies and caps and such in the mudroom that should do."

He nodded, then kissed her. "You make me proud every day."

"Aw, go on then."

"Reineke, Jenkinson, once you look like farmers, take your positions. Constant contact," she added. "Feeney, there are too many windows in here. He may have field glasses. I don't want him spotting you working e's. There's that little room off the living area."

"You're wanting the side parlor. I'm happy to show you. Feeney, is it? I went to school with a Bridgit Feeney," Sinead said as she led him off.

21

"Teams," Eve reminded everyone as, a little bemused, she watched Whitney put on a brown cap. "Reineke with Robbie and his group, Jenkinson with Aidan and his. Abernathy, I want you with the commander in the barn. There's a loft, and you'll have a clear view of the south.

"You believe he'll try for the house, which is where you want him." Abernathy shrugged into a tan work coat. "I intend to stay close to the house."

"First, most of the family has Irish white or ruddy skin tones. Santiago is Latino, Reineke is mixed race, but their skin tone is light enough not to catch the eye right off. You, the commander, and Podock are very dark-skinned, and may have Cobbe taking a closer look. Which is why you and the commander are on watch in the barn, and Podock will be in the second house."

She watched him assess that, reluctantly.

"Second, while I know the commander can handle himself, I don't know if you can when it comes to hand-to-hand. Any of your agents who can't pass as one of the family also need to keep out of sight until we have him in the box. He'll want the house because he figures he'll find Roarke's aunt, maybe some kids inside. Easy targets. Possibly, he'll wander over to one of the men working outside as if he's asking for directions, but the house is more likely. Either way he kills close up."

"He'd kill who he can, then send me a vid of it," Roarke finished. "He may not have gotten me, but he'll have made me pay."

"That's Cobbe all over," Brian agreed.

"I have no argument with that. I agree with all that. I don't like being shuffled off to a bloody barn."

"We get him, he's all yours."

"Understood. Apologies. It's —"

"I'd feel exactly the same in your place," Eve told him.

"I'll take lookout in the barn with the commander." But his shoulders straightened. "And I can handle myself."

"Good to know. We have e-men at the three locations. Constant communication. They have scanners set up, looking for movement, but . . . people around here take walks."

"It's still raining." Jenkinson tugged on a pair of black boots.

"Sure we don't melt in a bit of soft weather," Mary Kate pointed out as she offered him a cap.

"There are a lot of places for him to run if we try to take him outside and he slips away. And there are other homes within running distance. I'm not risking him killing anyone else, so we take him inside — that's optimum. Should he approach anyone outside, stun his ass. Don't let him get close enough to use a sticker, and remember he's fast. Everybody goes home tonight, except Cobbe.

"How much time have we got?" she asked Roarke.

"We should move."

"Then let's move. Sinead, I need you and Mary Kate upstairs. You lock the door, and you stay inside."

"You don't look like me, or Mary Kate," Sinead pointed out. "If, as you said, he has field glasses, looks through the window, he'd know you're not either of us."

"I'm going to wear one of those things." Eve pointed at the aprons on pegs. "And a hat, and I'll keep my back to the windows."

"You won't look natural in a kitchen, as I've seen you in this one." Sinead smiled at her. "It's important you lure him in, and stop him. If you were in the mudroom there, there's no window, and I could do what I do here. You'd know, as you've people everywhere, if he's coming. He'll have to come in the front, won't he, or run into the men working outside. He comes in, I'll go up the back steps straightaway, and lock myself in as you ask."

"Damn it."

"If he tries to get in through the root cellar, it's the same thing. He'd be seen, and would know he'd be seen. He has to come in the front door. He may even knock and expect me to answer so he can kill me. But it'll be you who answers, and so he'll be done. If you don't bait the hook, you don't catch the fish."

"You're not to be bait," Roarke objected.

"If he gets away, somehow, he'll come back, won't he? When will we be safe?"

"She's right. I'm sorry."

Roarke looked at Eve. "I can know it and not like it."

"We might put the music on," Sinead added. "I often do when I'm working in the kitchen."

"It'll cover any noise, too. Do that."

"I know my way around a kitchen," Peabody began.

"He'll know your face, too. He knows your face by now." Eve paced as music began to play. "Put on an apron, keep away from the windows. Stick close to Sinead without being obvious about it. Make sure your weapon and harness are hidden. Take positions."

She drew Roarke toward the mudroom. "I won't let him touch her. I swear to God."

"We won't." He had his hair bundled under a cap and put on his borrowed work jacket. "Do I look like a farmer?"

"No, you just don't."

"Well, it'll have to do."

"We've got movement," Feeney announced. "Coming in from the southwest. Slow. Too big to be a dog or livestock."

"Positions, now. Commander?" She eased into the mudroom. "Do you see him?"

"Not yet."

"Movement stopped." He read off the coordinates for the rest of the e-team. "He's about a quarter mile from here, moving again."

"Got him, Cap," Callendar said.

"Same here. Definitely on foot."

"Getting his bearings," Eve said. "He doesn't know the area, wants to see the best

471

ways in and out. Just a guy taking a walk in the rain."

"He's passed the point it makes sense for him to veer off to this location," Santiago said. "We can start moving to the next house."

"Not yet. Wait it out."

"We see him. Black shirt, pants, boots. No jacket. He's getting pretty wet." Eve heard the quiet satisfaction in Whitney's voice. "Field glasses coming out. From his angle he should be able to see the east side of the main house, any activity outside in that area."

"Stay frosty. Roarke, don't let him see your face."

"He won't."

"Peabody, go out the front door, just a couple steps — for what, for what?"

"Shake the rug," Sinead suggested. "Go out and shake the rug."

"Yeah, fine, good. Just step out, back to the east, shake the rug, come back. He sees you, he sees the door's not locked. He's going to go for the front."

"Moving to the front." Peabody took the little kitchen rug from the back door, walked through the house, out, letting the door shut behind her.

She shook out the dirt, stepped back in.

"Moving faster now, but still at a walk."

"She got his attention. Easy prey. Unarmed woman, doing housework."

"Stopped."

"Scanning again," Whitney announced after Feeney. "He's taking a good look at the men out in the near field, the one crossing in front of the chicken coop."

He has to buy it, Eve thought. Too far away yet to pursue with a hundred percent chance of taking him down, even with stunners. He had to buy it, keep coming.

"Moving again."

"He likes what he sees," Whitney added. "Pocketing the field glasses, picking up his pace. Rounding the curve of the road. We're coming down."

"Don't come out yet. Sir, do not exit the barn at this time. We need him inside."

"Coming down, but remaining inside. Not my first day on the job, Lieutenant."

"I can see him from here." Jenkinson tried to look like a man at home in a cow pasture. "He's got a good visual on the house from his position. Just a guy stopping to admire the flowers out front. He should be able to see in the east-facing kitchen windows if he's angled right."

"Sinead, look busy. Relaxed, but busy.

When he makes the front door, upstairs. Quiet."

"Moving fast now, yeah, he's at the front gate."

"Go now, Sinead. Now."

"He's not at the door yet."

"Close enough. Peabody, stay in view of the windows, in case."

Eve crab-walked out of the mudroom, kept going until she got to the hall. Out of sight of the windows, she straightened, dashed, then got back into a crouch.

"Something distracted him. He's backing off."

"He can't see me, damn it."

"No, no, it's a car going by. He's waiting it out."

She took that opportunity to get to the door, and behind it.

"I'm at the door."

"He's rushing it now. Through the gate."

"Wait, wait, let him get inside. Move in on my go."

Feeney's voice dropped to a whisper. "At the door."

She watched the doorknob turn, slow, slow. Held up her left fist with her weapon in her right hand to signal the rest to hold positions.

Inside, she thought, come inside. All the way in.

The door opened a crack.

From the kitchen, music playing cheerfully. Peabody let out a quick laugh.

Good. Smart. Lure him in.

The crack widened; she waited.

He came in fast now. Eve moved faster, had her left arm around his neck, her stunner at his throat.

"Drop the knife."

Instead he pivoted, jabbed it. While it bounced off her coat, he shot an elbow back.

It hit her jaw, and she welcomed that bright pain.

She'd have welcomed a fight, relished one — recognized that dark need, and made herself suppress it. Instead, she gave him a light jolt so his body jerked in response.

Before the knife clattered to the floor, both Feeney and Peabody moved in, weapons drawn.

"On the ground!" She kicked his feet out from under him, dropped him to his knees. She heard the pound of feet as others rushed in, from the front, from the back.

"Cobbe's contained." Feeney alerted the rest of the team. "He's contained."

He fought her. For the sheer satisfaction she twisted her wrist, put the point of the stiletto in his eyeline.

"Keep it up, you could get a taste of your own."

Yanking his hands behind his back, she slapped on restraints, then patted him down. She took a folding knife from one pocket, a spring-action stiletto from the other. A jagged-edged combat knife from a sheath at the small of his back.

"Check the boots," Roarke suggested, and his voice had Cobbe's head swiveling.

"Getting to them. Somebody bag this fucking arsenal. Lorcan Cobbe," she continued as she took knives from the inside of each boot, "you're under arrest on multiple charges of murder, murder by contract, conspiracy to murder, possession of illegal weapons and transport of same, hijacking aircraft, and so on. These charges are brought by multiple jurisdictions globally, including the state of New York. You have the right to remain silent."

She recited the Revised Miranda as she continued to pat him down.

"You will be remanded into the custody of the International Police, represented here by Inspector Abernathy."

"Fuck the fucking lot of you."

Roarke stepped up to help Eve haul Cobbe to his feet. "Well now, it's looking like you're the one fucked, isn't it?"

"It's you without the balls to face me. It's you hiding behind a woman."

Roarke only smiled. "She's a hell of a woman."

When Cobbe spat in his face, Roarke didn't flinch, didn't blink. He simply kept his eyes locked on Cobbe's and swiped his sleeve over his mouth.

Eve felt fury rise in the room, from cops, from family. But it was nothing against what rose in her. Every cell in her body flamed.

She'd wanted a fight, she'd had that need.

And she knew the man she'd married.

She looked at him. "You want?"

Roarke's gaze snapped to hers, read her meaning. "Oh aye, more than I can say."

"Then you got."

"It's no wonder you're the love of my life. Not in here," he added. "I've too much respect for the homeplace to kick his sorry arse in the house."

"Out back. Let's move."

Abernathy all but leaped in front of her as she pulled Cobbe along. "What do you think you're doing? You can't let Roarke beat a prisoner. A man in restraints."

"What do you think I am? I'm taking them off."

"You certainly will not! This man is in my

custody."

Fierce, furious, she rounded on him. "I haven't turned him over yet, so back off. You back the hell off. This is family."

She turned to Whitney, not sure even his command could stop her. "This is family," she repeated.

Her detectives made way as she hauled Cobbe through the house, fell in behind her.

Brian stood at the back door, a wide grin on his face. He opened it, swept his arm in a flourish.

"Any other time I'd be making book on this bout. I'd still back you, mate," he said to Roarke. "I'll always put my money on you in a fight, fair or foul."

"Fair! With bloody cops ready to blast me when I get the best of him?"

Eve dragged Cobbe out into the thin rain, across the spongy green grass. "It's you and Roarke, Cobbe, because he earned this. Nobody uses a weapon unless you try to run. That's an order." She leaned closer, whispered, "He doesn't need us, you miserable fuck."

She used the stiletto to slice off the restraints. "Give them room," she ordered, and stepped back.

"You put a mark on my woman," Roarke said conversationally.

"I'll gut the slag throat to cunt before I'm done."

Cobbe charged — that was rage, Eve knew, hot and blind. Roarke had his own, but he knew how to contain it.

He did so now by shifting aside, graceful as a dancer, then booted Cobbe in the ass.

That brought on a roar from the onlookers.

The grass, slippery as soap in the rain, had Cobbe sliding, pitching forward. Humiliation joined rage. He jumped to his feet, charged again.

This time Roarke didn't shift aside, but met him straight on.

A fist to the face that had Cobbe's mouth dripping blood, his teeth coated with it. Another to the midsection, a follow-up to the jaw.

She'd sparred with Roarke enough to know his style, his moves. Cobbe had the more muscular build, a brawler's build, but his style was brute force.

He's playing with him, she realized when Cobbe landed a blow.

The blow rang like church bells on Sunday, and Roarke tasted blood.

He'd wanted to, needed to.

Tasting blood made a fight worth having, and this was a long time coming.

He heard the shouts around him, and they were a bit like music, that mix of West County and New York accents. Not Eve's voice, she stayed silent. But he heard her in his head.

Do what you need to do.

So he would, and he did.

"Our boy can take a punch." Robbie slapped a hand on Eve's shoulder. "And give one. Show the bleeding jackeen what a Clare man's made of!" he shouted. "Our boy's more Clare man than Dubliner, and make no mistake of it."

"Plenty of New York in him, too," Jenkinson claimed. "Fucking ring that fucker's bell! Sorry for the language," he said to Sinead.

She smiled. "Not a'tall."

Blood in his eyes now, and ribs singing, Roarke plowed a fist into Cobbe's throat, barely dodged a kick aimed at his balls.

That move incited boos and colorful objections from the crowd.

"Is that the way of it?" Dancing back, Roarke swiped at the blood on his face. "Fair or foul then."

He spun, knocked Cobbe back with a roundhouse kick.

There you go, Eve thought. There you are.

Cobbe flailed back into Brian and Santiago, who shoved him back into the make-shift ring where Roarke waited, crouched in a fighting stance.

He sprang up, blocked a blasting right cross with his forearm, answered it with a short-armed jab that had Cobbe's nose spurting blood.

A blow got by him, landed hard against his weeping ribs, but he didn't feel it. He was beyond that now. Elbow jab, backfist, cold, methodical. All he heard was Cobbe's labored breathing, the crunch of knuckle against bone.

When Cobbe tried to claw at his eyes, he swept Cobbe's legs out from under him. And went down with him.

He rolled once, ignoring Cobbe's attempts to short-jab his ribs.

And cold, methodical, battered Cobbe's face with three vicious blows.

He wanted a fourth, wanted forever as he stared into the bloodied face, the glazed eyes under him.

"We're a long way, you fecking bastard, a long way from the streets and alleys of Dublin when you made the misery of my life worse for the sport of it."

He swiped at his face again. "You're done now. And so am I."

When he stood, they cheered.

"Your prisoner needs some medical attention, Inspector," Eve commented.

"This isn't how things are done."

"It's how they're done here," Aidan countered. "I'll ring up Ailish — she's a medic and my wife's sister. She'll come tend to that worthless shite who meant to kill my mother this very day. Don't you tell us how things are done, English."

"Do that now, won't you, Aidan? And we'll get some whiskey and an ice pack for our Roarke. Will you have some tea, Inspector?"

He let out a sigh as he walked over to restrain a barely conscious Cobbe. "I wouldn't mind a whiskey, to tell you the truth. How the bloody hell do I explain the condition of the prisoner to my superiors?"

"In his attempt to escape capture and cause harm to civilians," said Whitney, eyes calm and sober as he stepped over to look down at Cobbe, "the prisoner assaulted Roarke, whom he vowed to kill. They engaged in a physical battle during which the expert consultant, civilian, attached to the NYPSD, contained the prisoner, who is now herewith remanded to your custody."

When Abernathy just stared at him, Whitney stared back. "Would you like to contradict the statement of the commander of the

New York City Police and Security Department, his lieutenant, his detectives, these civilian witnesses — all of whom assisted in your arrest of a contract killer who has eluded justice for more than twenty years?"

"No. Actually, that sounds about right to me. I need a secure area inside so he can get medical attention. I have to arrange for transport."

Whitney nodded. "A long time coming, Cobbe. Ryan," he said, "Ellen Solomen had a sister."

"Anja Greenspan. We'll notify her, Jack." He put a hand on Whitney's shoulder. "We'll close it up."

Eve waited until Roarke managed to break free of the men busy reliving the fight. Waited until he came to her.

"Thank you for that, for knowing I needed it."

"You'd have done the same for me."

"Have done."

"Yeah, I guess you have. Now you're all beat up, bloody, and wet. How are the ribs?"

"Hurt like a bastard."

"I bet. Let's go ice them down. What's a jackeen?" she asked as they walked to the house.

"It's a Dubliner — an insult to a Dubliner."

483

"Okay, well, apparently you're not a jackeen, but a Clare man. I can figure out what a Clare man is."

"That's a high compliment in these parts."

"They love you." She opened the door for him. "So do I."

Sinead waited with whiskey, ice packs, a first-aid kit. "Ailish will tend to that Cobbe, as he got the worst of it, but I can deal with you well enough. I've plenty of practice. And you as well," she said to Eve. "He caught you one there."

"It's nothing."

"Sit down, the pair of you. You don't care for the whiskey, Eve. I have some very nice wine."

"I'm on duty," she began. Then sat, then sighed. "Screw it, I'm really not. I'd like a glass of wine, thanks."

"Put this on that bruise then, and I'll get you some." Sinead passed Eve an ice pack, turned to Roarke. "Such a pretty face," she said, cupping his chin in her hand. "Even now, a pretty face. Your mother would be proud of you, my own, as I am."

She drew him to her, gently, kissed the top of his head. "Of both of you," she told Eve. "It takes a strong woman to stand back and let her man do what she wants to do herself. Don't think I didn't see it, and

484

understand it.

"Now." She walked over to get the wine. "Let's get our Eve a glass, and clean up that pretty face."

Just then Aidan opened the back door. "They said they need someplace, right and tight, to keep that bastard until they can fix him up and move him out."

"Take him to the root cellar. I won't have the likes of him in my kitchen."

Eve sipped the wine, sighed again. "It takes a strong woman to stand her ground when a bunch of cops try to move her aside. You're unshakable, Sinead. I see where Roarke gets it."

Smiling, Sinead wrung out a cloth from the bowl on the table. "Nothing you could say at this moment pleases me more."

Abernathy came in. "I beg your pardon."

"No, you're welcome. There's whiskey and glasses right there on the counter if you wouldn't mind pouring your own while I clean my boy up."

"Thank you, very much." He poured a generous three fingers. Downed half of it. "The prisoner's being secured in the root cellar. Your niece — cousin — I'm sorry, it's confusing. In any case, she's just arrived and will see to Cobbe's medical needs. We have my agents and your Detective Jenkinson, and Mr. Podock — who was very insistent — guarding him."

He sipped whiskey again, more slowly. "Lieutenant, I owe you."

"I did my job."

"You did, and with the fine officers of the NYPSD, including your civilian consultant, and madam, this family, have aided in Cobbe's capture. Within days of being assigned to the investigation of Galla Modesto's murder.

"With that in mind," he continued, "I'd like to offer you the first — limited — interview with the subject at this time."

"No shit?"

"Not in the least. It will, of course, be recorded, and I need your word there will be no physical contact."

Eve sat back. "Do you want a confession out of him?"

"It's not necessary, but as you know, it's the icing on the cake."

"My consultant comes into the interview with me."

"I don't see how that's —"

"You want a confession?" She jerked a thumb at Roarke. "He's the key."

Abernathy downed the last of the whiskey. "Bloody hell. We've gone this far. Once the medic clears him, you have thirty minutes."

Eve looked at Roarke, smiled ferociously. "That'll do it."

EPILOGUE

Outside the root cellar, Eve stood in the damp air.

"It's my lead," she told Roarke. "When I pass it to you, you run with it, but it's my lead."

"I've seen you work in the box often enough to know how it's done." He wore his own clothes again, and a black eye, a sunburst bruise on his jaw.

His ribs were killing him. And he found a dark satisfaction in the pain.

"I want to say I got what I needed out there, so if you'd rather Peabody or —"

"I'm not the hammer." Peabody, sans apron, shook her head. "You are. The way he fought you? He's probably better at it than that, but he couldn't control it. He won't control it down there, either."

"That's exactly right."

"I'm going back to the kitchen. You guys are going to miss out on all the food. Man, these people can put on a spread, and put it on fast. Go nail his sorry ass."

"Well then." Roarke rolled his shoulders. "Let's go nail his sorry ass."

They walked down into the dank. The light was dim, but strong enough to show Cobbe's face wasn't close to pretty.

Broken nose. Eve checked off the list. Split lip, two black eyes, and Roarke's sunburst looked like a guttering star in comparison with the black, blue, and purple over Cobbe's face.

The medic had dealt with it — reported three cracked ribs, now strapped for healing, had closed the numerous cuts.

Like Roarke's, his knuckles were scraped raw and swollen. But there, Eve saw with satisfaction, Roarke had him beat.

More blows landed.

"Record on. Dallas, Lieutenant Eve, and civilian consultant Roarke, representing the NYPSD, entering Interview with Cobbe, Lorcan, primarily but not exclusively on the matter of H-6981, H-6989, and H-32108."

Eve sat at a scarred wooden table in a scarred wooden chair in the windowless room that smelled of earth — and what might've been potatoes.

And felt right at home.

"Also present is Abernathy, Inspector

George, representing Interpol; Whitney, Commander Jack; and Feeney, Captain Ryan; also with the NYPSD. Podock, Marshall, licensed security, is also in attendance."

"Takes this many of you to hold me in a bloody cellar."

"You've been read your rights, first by me, and subsequently by the inspector. Do you understand your rights and obligations in this matter?"

"Cunt cop."

"I take that as a yes." Eve opened the file Peabody had put together.

"We have Jorge Tween — a recent client of yours — and his confession to hiring you to kill his wife, Galla Modesto, for a sum of one million euros, plus expenses of an additional fifteen thousand. We have security feed, and an eyewitness putting you on the scene of that murder. Do you have any statement?"

He smirked. "Bullshite."

"That's your full statement?"

He leaned forward. "Do you know why I haven't said *lawyer*?"

"No, I don't. Care to tell me?"

"Because I don't need one with this bullshite. Have you evidence — eyewitnesses — anything but some arsehole trying

490

to save his own skin that shows me sticking a knife in some bitch?"

"We have the arsehole's payment to you."

"More bullshite. I don't know that arse wipe. I came to New York to talk to Roarke. Nothing illegal about that."

Eve took a document from the file, laid it on the table. "Your account in Andorra, using one of your aliases, but your account, and the payment from Tween."

Cobbe shrugged. But his eyes flickered. "Not my name, not my account."

"If that were true, you wouldn't be upset to learn that account's been frozen, and the funds in it will be confiscated." She leaned over as if reading the numbers again. "Wow. That's what we call a tidy sum. But it is your account, as forensic accountants have documented. There's also the reversible jacket. Nice touch, by the way."

"Don't know what you're getting at."

"We have security feed of you in the black hoodie, and of course in the reverse red side. By the way, you left that back in New York, in Central Park, after you dropped the cat you'd slaughtered at my gates."

"Know nothing about some dead cat." But he smiled. "And it's not my jacket."

"I saw you, you moron." Infusing her face, her voice with disgust, she sat back. "I thought you were a professional. You're acting like the rankest of rank amateurs. You know we have you on Modesto. We've got you on Kaylee Skye — and don't bother saying you don't know who she is. You may not remember her name, but witnesses in the bar remember you. You left DNA behind in her apartment, for Christ's sake."

"You don't have my DNA." He sneered at her. "And by rights I don't have to give it to you."

"We've got your blood," she reminded him. "From the body of Kaylee Skye. From today, as Roarke spilled plenty of it for DNA. You were sloppy, sloppy with Skye because you didn't kill her for money. You killed her because you were pissed, maybe a little drunk."

"You're trying to set me up because I blackened your man's eye."

She tipped back now, laughed. "Jesus, Cobbe, you're sitting there with two shiners, a busted nose, the left side of your face swollen up like rotted meat, and you think I care that Roarke let you get a couple shots in? Two women are dead in my city, and you sliced them to pieces. You did the same to a damn cat, which is the low, petty, sick shit of a twisted child."

He smiled, wide enough to open the split

in his bottom lip. "So charge me with animal abuse. Just sending a message."

"It'll be in the charges. As will the attempted murder of Wayne Goddard, the security guard you stabbed when you stole the shuttle. He's still critical, so if he dies, that's one more murder on your tally. We found the shuttle — rough landing for you. And we recovered your go-bag. Lots of false ID and cash in there. Your tablet and PPC, which I just bet have some interesting data on them. Plus a whole bunch of sharps in a lead-lined case. I'm leaving all that to Interpol.

"Oh, and Sal Bellacore's been singing, another tie to Modesto. And our friends at Interpol have picked up the Privets, brother and sister. Imagine how pissed — and vindictive — Alicia's going to be when she finds out you flipped on her, gave us chapter and verse on her organization."

"That's a lie! I've said nothing, will say nothing."

"Really?" Eve studied her file again, smiling. "Things do get tangled up in translation, don't they? She's going down, so's her brother, so are you. I wonder what conclusion she'll come to, with a little help in that tangled translation."

His split lip dripped a thin line of blood.

Sweat popped to join it.

And now, Eve thought, over to you.

Reading her signal, Roarke spoke for the first time. "They've got your mother, Cobbe, and I'm sorry for that. A mother's a precious thing."

"You leave my mother out of it."

"I would if I could, but it's not up to me, is it? Then again, the old man didn't leave my mother out of it, but beat her, killed her, tossed her in the Liffey. Did he brag on it when he told you, all those years later?"

"Why wouldn't he? She was nothing but a whore, palming you off on him. I was his firstborn. I have the right to his name."

"I nearly tossed that name aside, but someone I respect told me to keep it and make my own out of it. You could've done the same for all I cared. For though you're not Patrick Roarke's son in blood, you're his in your cruelty, your bloodlust, and the rest."

"I am his blood!"

"If that were true, and it's bollocks, he'd be shamed of you now, wouldn't he? Getting nicked this way, and by a woman at that, going about your work sloppy, leaving such a trail a noseless hound could follow it. Taking no pride in that work, refusing to stand for it, stand up to the bloody cops and tell them to get fucked, as it took them twenty years and more than four hundred dead before they pulled you in.

"That's a run," Roarke continued, with some admiration. "That's a right glorious run. And here the one thing in this life you've done better than any, better even than the old man himself, and you take no pride in it. Refuting, you are, the way you made your fame and fortune, how you gave your mother a grand house, a grand life. So much more than I was ever able to do for my own, as I never knew her. There you bested me, didn't you, as I never saw the joy for me, the pride in me, shine in her eyes."

"She was naught but a muckshit."

Roarke said nothing a moment, and the ice in the room could've frozen fire.

"She was a Clare woman. But you? What are you but a sniveling coward? So feared of cops are you, you deny the only true legacy the man you call father left you. And there, you shame his name."

"I'm not feared of cops." Cobbe pounded his restrained wrists on the table. "I've run them in circles all my life. It's those who know me are feared. They give me what I want, pay me what I want, and speak of me in whispers lest I hear and take offense."

"So you say, a man I bloodied and beat to the ground, a man locked in a cellar with the turnips and potatoes. A man who won't stand up for who and what he is."

"I'm Patrick Roarke's son. You're but one of his by-blows."

"And yet you couldn't lift a lock or wallet without bungling it. It's why he sent me to the streets and alleys." Roarke wiggled his fingers. "I had the skill for it. You were best at slicing up little dogs."

"Practice. I'd've killed the boy as well if you hadn't set a cop who didn't know his place on me."

"Little dogs, little cats, they're a sick boy's kills, not a man's. Not a Roarke's."

The sneer came back to the bloodied lip, the fury returned to the blackened eyes.

"You never had the stomach for it, for the ease and power of sliding a blade into flesh — soft as pillows some of them. He saw it in me, my skill, and took pride in it."

"And his pride set you on that path of fame and fortune."

"As a father sets his son. His true son. And I feel his pride every time that blade slices through. Four hundred, you say. Oh, there's more, many more. Do you think I don't keep an accounting? Double it. That cheating cunt in the New York park, that was business, but the whore who sang like a nightingale? That was for the pleasure. I've built a fortune my father would envy, and can afford to kill for the pleasure of it when it suits me."

He sat back, his blackened eyes glinting. "He should've killed you that day, in the alley where you lolled around with a fucking book like a little lord. His fist in my face was worth the hope he would when I told him."

"He came close," Roarke murmured.

"I'll finish it for him. I took a vow, and I've waited a long time to keep it. I can wait longer yet. Do you think this worries me? These cops? I've money enough for all the lawyers I need. I've friends who'll do the job for me if needed. I'll get out, and I'll come for you, you and the whore you're fucking so the cops look the other way."

"You've no money a'tall, Cobbe," Roarke told him. "It's not just this one account they've frozen you out of, but all of them, as I found them, every one. It's not just your mother's house they'll lock away so the grand life you gave her from blood's at an end, but the one you kept for yourself as O'Karre, and put on the market this very day. If you have others, they'll find them as well now. Because you're done."

"I wouldn't count on those friends, either," Eve put in. "Or associates, as I doubt you have a friend in the world. Word's going to get out you helped take down the Privet empire, whining for a deal. Call me a liar." She shrugged. "Call me a whore, or whatever you want. I won't be the one thousands of miles off-planet in a concrete cage, wondering if Alicia Privet has any associates in the vicinity."

"She knows me."

"She knows she let you use the house you ran from, where we found her tunnels, and lots of interesting data on her unregistered equipment. Her knowing you? That's a shaky ledge you're standing on. From what I hear, she's not the forgiving sort."

Eve leaned forward again. "Think of this, and think of it often while you sit in that cage. You gave Roarke a black eye. He got justice for everyone you killed, and took your freedom. He won."

She looked at Abernathy. "Have you got enough?"

"Oh, yes, indeed."

"Okay then. Dallas and Roarke exiting interview."

"I'll come for you!" Cobbe shouted. "Be sure of it. I've killed better men than you."

"You've killed plenty of them," Feeney

498

said as Eve and Roarke started out. "But none better. Not one better." He sat, and Whitney with him. "Let's talk about the Solomen family."

They went up to the kitchen, where cops and family spilled from there into the dining room, with enough food to feed the army they were.

"You'll sit and eat now," Sinead told them.

"We have to get back as soon as the commander and Feeney finish downstairs. And I'd say Abernathy wants to get Cobbe out and in an actual cell as soon as he can."

"Then we'll pack food for those who don't have time to eat first."

"I want the air more than food at the moment," Roarke said. "But I . . . I said something to Cobbe that wasn't altogether true."

Sinead let out a *psst* sound. "And what of it? He deserves nothing from you than what you gave him outside."

"No, it's personal. I said to him I'd never seen joy for me or pride in me shine in my mother's eyes. But that's not altogether true, because I've seen it in yours."

"Oh, now look what you've done, making me cry."

He drew her to him, murmured in Irish. As tears spilled, she pressed her face to his shoulder, murmured back.

"Go on, go on out, get the air. We'll pack some food. Come and kiss me before you go. No, Sean, you leave them be for now."

The kids were back — Eve had already noted — and this one, the boy she remembered very well, stopped his charge toward them, deflated.

"I'm just after asking if they —"

"You're after sitting down until you're excused, Sean Lannigan."

When Roarke winked at him, opened the back door, Eve turned to the boy. "Got him cold, full confession. Details later."

He grinned at her, ran back to the dining room.

"That was kind of you," Roarke commented.

"Kid's got an interest in law and order, why not feed it?"

"Jesus, let's not make a cop out of him." He took her hand. "A bit of a walk would do me. Everything's going stiff as plank boards on me."

She thought, but didn't say, how his Irish rose up whenever he was here, or around his family.

"I can't stay."

"Oh, I know. We'll likely leave within the hour, and be home again by . . ." He checked the time. "By half-two anyway."

"It makes no sense, and I don't want to hear about the screwy time deal and the rotation of the Earth. You did good down there with Cobbe. You don't want to hear it, but you did cop good."

"I don't, and say it again, you'll hear all about the rotation of the Earth." But he kissed her fingers. "I told you I didn't need it, to be down there. I thought I'd gotten all I needed, my way, out here."

He walked her beyond the thriving kitchen garden as thin spots of blue pushed free of gray clouds, as the light went pearly with the soft glow of sun pushing behind the stacks of them.

"I was wrong there as well, because I did need it. It was your way, down there, the cop way, and I needed to be part of that. Thrashing the bastard, well, that was fine, and it helped close something in me I forgot was there until he showed up again."

He walked her out toward the fields, toward the hills that rose beyond them, into the green and the green under the gray and the spots of hopeful blue.

She hoped like hell he didn't intend to walk where the cows were.

"Up here, outside, that was a payment, long due — between him and me. But down

501

there? That was justice. There was a time, before you, when the payment would've been enough. But justice, it's come around in me, it's justice matters more — and it sets the payment."

He paused at the big tree, one rioting with pink blossoms — and she knew why. They'd planted it for his mother. And he'd stood there looking out when she'd come to him, when he'd needed her.

"You earned the payment. And you played a major part in getting that justice. He was telling the truth about doubling his kills. It's going to take a long time to identify them, and they'll never find all of them. So, even for those whose names we'll never know, you helped bring them justice."

"I was telling the truth when I said the old man would be shamed of him being afraid to stand up for what he was."

" 'Feared,' you said — you got so Irish. Anyway, it rang true, and that's why it got him to own it."

"If she can — Alicia Privet — she'll find a way to have him killed in prison. And he knows it."

"That's not our problem."

"I want him to live, and live long." As they stood, he draped an arm over her shoulder, looked toward the hills. "There's another that's come from you. Once I'd have wished him dead and done. But I've come to see it's the justice of a long life that's true.

"Ah, look there, would you? We've a rainbow."

She looked out over the fields, toward the rise of hills, and saw the shimmering arc of it against the bluing sky.

"Isn't there something about a bag of money in a rainbow?"

"A pot of gold at the end of it." Laughing, he turned her into his arms. "And I've better than that right here."

He held her there, his ribs throbbing, his eye aching, and felt as content as he ever had in his life.

ABOUT THE AUTHOR

J. D. Robb is the pseudonym for #1 *New York Times* bestselling author Nora Roberts. She is the author of more than 200 novels, including the futuristic suspense In Death series. There are more than 500 million copies of her books in print.